Clan of the Dung-Sniffers

"Wounds of the body heal swiftly
in comparison to those of the mind."

In the center of the Marble Tower, in the center of the City, there hangs the Radiance, a mystical object of prayer and devotion.

When the Radiance suddenly vanishes, eight young men: a nobleman's son and his servant; a Bedouin mystic; a cobbler and his cousin; a City guard; a cross-dresser; and Glane, the boy who wants to fly, are suspected of its theft.

Yes, they took it ... but only because it needed repair! And, since *they* broke it, they must repair it.

But the situation is not as simple as that — and there are many, many reasons why the perpetrators is WANTED!

To elude capture, this octet of unlikely conspirators forms a secret clan, *the Clan of the Dung-Sniffers*, and vows to repair and replace the Radiance before the authorities can catch them.

But their plans are derailed by bees and feathers and blackmail ... and they are sent headlong into a brewing rebellion that might potentially dissolve their first great achievement — friendship.

In a beehive of mistaken interpretations and murderous intrigue, and while under the constant threat of termination, the *Clan of the Dung-Sniffers* must strive to overcome their prejudices and personal fears while attempting to piece together the fractured Radiance, and the shattered fragments of their lives.

Clan of the Dung-Sniffers

by
Lee Danielle Hubbard

EDGE SCIENCE FICTION AND FANTASY PUBLISHING
AN IMPRINT OF HADES PUBLICATIONS, INC.
CALGARY

Edge Science Fiction and Fantasy Publishing
An Imprint of Hades Publications Inc.
P.O. Box 1714, Calgary, Alberta, T2P 2L7, Canada

Editing by Matt Hughes
Interior design by Brian Hades
Cover Illustration by Jeff Johnson

EDGE Science Fiction and Fantasy Publishing and Hades Publications, Inc.
acknowledges the ongoing support of the Canada Council for the Arts and the
Alberta Foundation for the Arts for our publishing programme.

Library and Archives Canada Cataloguing in Publication

Hubbard, Lee Danielle, 1986-
        Clan of the dung-sniffers / Lee Danielle Hubbard -- 1st ed.

ISBN-13: 978-1-894063-05-0
ISBN-10: 1-894063-05-8

        I. Title.

PS8615.U218C53 2008   C813'.6   C2008-900052-8

FIRST EDITION
(n-20080226)
Printed in Canada
www.edgewebsite.com

DEDICATION

To Matthew

Clan of the
Dung-Sniffers

Prologue

My brother Leque has told me how the City looks from the highroads, like an island of sandstone and glass. The heat off the acid sea ripples the City walls, turning them to silk and mirrors. Around the walls the sea glows garnet-red. Journey farther, my brother says, days and nights, and the sea turns violet, indigo, beige and steel gray. It always glows. It always burns and shimmers. Don't touch the acid, my brother tells me, unless you want to see it eat your skin, and feel the layers peel back like a grit-fried onion.

I have never stepped outside the City myself. The highroads stretch forever. If you want to see the rest of the world, anywhere else, you have to walk for days. I would rather not. My sandals don't fit, and what would the purpose be? Silk traders make the trek from settlement to settlement, and spice traders, and Bedouin in flowing, clove-scented robes. They set up their stalls in the marketplace. If ever I wanted to know of the world, I could ask the Bedouin as well as my brother.

"They come for the Marble Tower," says Leque. "That's why they come to the City. It's the first thing you see from the highroads. And it's strange," he says, my brother, "that the Tower is made of dark marble, when everything else is sandstone."

Leque always notices where laboring jobs may be found, which job pays the best, and where to buy the cheapest wine. He does not notice smells or sounds or the color of stone. Only the Tower can hold his attention.

I hate the Marble Tower. I'll tell you why.

1

In the dry season of the
Year of the Mandarin Turtle

At ground level, Glane and I were tallied by the green-robed monk at the reception desk. They liked to keep track of numbers at the Marble Tower, one sheet for arriving visitors and another for departing. They liked to make sure that the numbers correlated. It was meant to discourage rag-tags and beggars from spending their nights in the upper rooms. Glane and I looked like rag-tags. Besides all that, it gave the monks something to do.

I turned to Glane at the top of the first flight of stairs. He worried me. Last week he was stung by a bee and began to grow feathers. None of us knew what to do, how to stop the plumage. Not even Kem knew how, or the Bedouin Yaryk who pretended to know all things.

"Are you all right?" I asked Glane.

He mopped a hand across the damp of his forehead. He pushed the dark hair from his eyes. "Ksar," he whispered, "I want to fly."

"We have to check the door," I said.

He pouted.

I tried to ignore him. The camel blanket itched on my head. Everyone told me that blanket was a bad idea. "Come on," I said.

The Marble Tower soared above every spire of the City, and so we climbed more stairs, through the labyrinth of rooms where pools of acid, multi-colored, bubbled beside the steps. Over the pools grew almond, peach and pistachio trees, their branches bedecked in wish papers, scribbled and hanging on golden threads. As we climbed, we passed other early-risers, here to make their morning prayers. Many stared as we hurried past: Glane muttering to himself, and me with my cloak of curtains, rose petals painted around my eyes, a beard dyed blue and curled.

In the evenings the monks would gather the wish papers. They would pray and chant and invoke all kinds of powers. Supposedly the wishes would then come true. More likely they gathered the papers and burned them.

Glane and I no longer came to make wishes.

Halfway up the Tower we turned off the main stairwell and went down a corridor of twisting gray marble. Yellow veins pulsed through the walls. We climbed more stairs, ramps, another passage. We came at last to a door that was locked.

Glane rattled the handle. His pout became a scowl when the door would not open. He scratched his neck. "Is there time to go to the balcony?" he said. "For just a while? I want to see the balcony, Ksar."

"A short while," I said. "The others are waiting for us."

We climbed to the top of the world, the balcony at the tip of the Tower, where a handful of other men stood around and gazed down at the view. The haze of the City stretched far, far below. We went to our customary bench and sat down. It was too hot to sit for long. If the City were not made of stone it would have incinerated by now.

Glane wore a jacket pulled over his toga. He pushed up a sleeve and picked at the inside of his elbow.

"Stop it," I said. "You look like a dog pulling worms. I thought Kem got them all out last night?"

"Not all." He dug his nails down into his skin. They emerged with a wet blue feather. "They grew back," he said. "There are more in the other arm. Want to see?"

"Not especially."

Glane leaned forward and dropped his feather over the railing. It unfurled, hovered for a moment over the void, and then it was gone, waving down to the City, one gust of hot air at a time until it was lost in the haze. He sat back on the bench and dug again into his skin. I tried to ignore him. He pulled out a second feather, a third. He sniffed the blue barbs. On a cord around his waist, Glane wore a pouch where he kept a family of miniature cobras. He fed them his feathers, one at a time. Some of the feathers he dropped through the railing instead, down toward the City.

Glane had been stung on the shoulder by a bee. Within an hour the mark swelled to the size of his fist. His eyes turned from green to hard gold. He began to grow feathers the following day.

Glane was gone a long time before I realized it, when I turned and found him no longer beside me. Two blue feathers, copper-tipped, lay on the bench. They fluttered in the breeze. Conversations buzzed around the balcony. I stood — a head taller than anyone there — and straightened my toga. Curtains separated the balcony from the Tower's interior. They hung there beaded like the beards of the nobles as they ride through the streets in their hidden beds, carried on the shoulders of their slaves. Not slaves, says Leque, but servants. He worked as a litter-bearer once, several years ago in the rainy seasons, tramping from civilization to civilization, the acid sea forever beside him. He worked for the pay, not the scenery. It was hard to find men who would work through the mold and slog of the rainy season. My brother would always be one of them.

I parted the curtains and ran down the almond-lined stairs, down and down. I dashed across the marble reception room. The green-robed monk slashed a tally mark across his sheet. I skidded through the doors and out into the street.

"Glane?" There was no use calling through the City chaos. Caravans streamed past in droves. Donkeys brayed. Street vendors swarmed in the alleys, calling their wares. Perhaps Glane had at last jumped. I would find no more than a smear of red cloth on the stone.

But he had not jumped yet. I found him on his face by the side of the road. The camel-drawn carts churned through the dust; a breath closer and the beasts' hooves would have spurned him into the gutter. He lay with his eyes pressed into a grate, half hidden in the lee of the curb.

"Glane, what are you doing?"

He rolled and squinted up at me. "I wonder what's down there," he said.

"The sewers."

"But what's in the sewers?"

"Sewage."

"Where's the proof?"

"The name is a fair indication," I said.

"But not proof."

"I call you Glane. Isn't that proof enough that's your name?"

"No." He blinked at me through the rags of his hair.

I must have been a silhouette against the twinned light of the suns behind. Some say that there used to be three, and that the sea was once water. The third sun fell. It burned the sea. Everything drowned and seared to acid.

"Come on." I hauled Glane up by the arm. "They're probably waiting for us."

He stooped, reached beneath the strap of his sandal and drew out a feather. "It beat us down," he said. "Why do we bother with all those stairs, Ksar? There are so many faster ways to go."

"Not a good idea." I pulled his arm to make him walk.

Merchant's Alley was stirring into life when we reached Skiy's shop. Skiy's shop was a cobbler's shop, with tables under red and white awnings set out in the street. In the front room, Skiy himself sat behind his workbench. A tallow wand smoldered between his lips. He held a sandal half-finished in his hands. A scroll hung tacked to the opposite wall. He was reading. He was always reading. I always wondered if his customers noticed.

"Hello," said Skiy. He scratched a bald patch behind his ear. He said: "Kem and Gyanin are in the back."

As if I couldn't tell for myself. Their voices carried through the curtain.

"Three sacks of narcotics," came Gyanin's voice. He always mumbled. Perhaps his beard was to blame.

"Ah," said the voice of Kem. "How the City would suffer without your protection."

"So true," said Gyanin. "There are few who appreciate the work of us guards. You should see the illegal imports! We confiscate wagonloads daily."

Who but Gyanin could talk with such zeal about so thrilling a topic? Yes, thank you Skiy, I think I've noticed they're here.

Glane pushed a pile of shoes aside and sat down on a table. He took a handful of dead insects from his pocket and began to feed his cobras, each serpent the size of his finger and half as exciting. They ate. They wiggled. That was all they did. From a smaller pouch, hanging on a thong around his neck, he extracted an enormous dead worm.

"What in Stone is that?"

"A glass worm," said Glane. The worm was twice the size of the snakes. He dropped it down into his pouch. A litany of hissing and squelching followed.

"A glass worm?" Gyanin appeared in the doorway. Incense drifted from his beard. He wore his uniform, the shield of his office glued to his arm. He peered at Glane's lap. "Glass worms are illegal," he snapped. "Where did you find it?"

"Maybe a store."

"They are illegal parasites," said Gyanin.

Gyanin and Skiy had been friends since childhood. Every day after duty found Gyanin here, lurking in the depths of the cobbler's shop, as if he had no rooms of his own to return to, or as if he'd forgotten the way.

"They chew their way into the hearts of glass weeds," said Gyanin, referring again to the worms. "They deplete the plants of their minerals. Without the fibers of the glass weed, how do you expect the fishermen to fish? How do you expect them to fix their nets? The City's economy could flounder, Glane, because of your worm." Gyanin's breath smelled of lavender. It always did.

"So?" said Glane.

Gyanin pointed at the pouch on Glane's chest. "Do you have more worms? Are you keeping them there?"

Glane shoved the pouch inside his clothes, up against his skin. "What pouch?"

Kem emerged from the back room, smoothing the folds of his toga. "Ah, Ksar, Glane, I'm so glad you've come!"

As if we had a choice. And as if he hadn't seen us yesterday. We could not escape these meetings.

Kem worked at the hospital. He was Skiy's third cousin, and the two of them were all but identical. Skiy the cobbler was thicker-set, perhaps, and his hair more white and sparse, but other then that they could have been twins.

Kem hurried over to Glane. "How are you doing?"

"I have feathers," said Glane. "I'm not good."

Gyanin rocked on his feet. "He has a pouch of glass worms," he pronounced, solemn as a pillar of lard.

"They're dead," said Glane.

"They're illegal," said Gyanin. "I hereby confiscate that pouch."

"No," said Glane.

"Glane," said Kem, "once the worms are removed, I am sure that Gyanin will return the pouch. Now please give it to him."

Glane pulled the pouch off over his head. He did so because Kem told him to. He threw the pouch into Gyanin's hands, still scowling. Duty complete, Gyanin retreated to the back room. There he would sit and say nothing. I envied his capacity for silence.

Kem rounded on Glane again. "Any changes in your arms?"

"More feathers," said Glane.

"Does it hurt?" A pause as he lifted Glane's arm. I could not quite see what he did. "Does it hurt when I do this?"

"Yes," said Glane.

I tried to block out the conversation. Kem always helped. When he was not helping, he was trying to coerce people into joining one of his many social action groups. Kem was a member of every brotherhood, organization and clan I could name, with the exception of the Tower monks, and he possessed a reputation for doing everything and existing everywhere at the same time.

Kem finished his examination of Glane and turned on me. My time had come. "What happened to your beard?" he demanded.

"I dyed it."

"And the yellow skin?"

"I can wash it off."

"Do you know how harmful these toxins are? You—"

The door saved me. It swung open with a scream of hinges to admit my brother Leque, late as always. He and I shared that attribute: we could not be expected to keep track of things like time.

"I found a new job," Leque announced, by way of greeting. "The Stone Masons' Guild has hired me for the building of a new housing complex, over by the east gates." He waved his arm in a vague westerly direction. Muscles rippled on his shoulders, thick as copulating snakes. "Is Blade here yet?"

"Not yet," said Kem.

It was Blade's father, Y'az Zeth Ven, for whom Leque once worked as a litter-bearer. There he met Blade (known to everyone outside our little group as Xavier Ven), the fourteen-year-old heir to the greatest family in the City. Leque could tell stories about lands beyond the City walls. Xavier knew nothing but wanted to learn. He fastened to my brother like a sand-fly leech to its host. My brother loved him. He carried him around every street of the City. He showed him every building he had helped construct. My brother talked of Xavier Ven at every meal.

Until it changed. Xavier met Yaryk. Compared to Yaryk and his Bedouin sagas, Leque and his little stories could no longer satisfy. I think my brother tried to hang on, but I don't think Xavier even noticed his trying. Leque stopped working as a litter-bearer. He found other work. Xavier dropped the name Xavier and took up Blade, as a secret-code when he whiled the hours with us. Sometimes we forgot who he actually was.

"The wages from the Stone Masons' Guild aren't the best I've seen," said Leque. He singled out Kem and came over to talk. "But I have the mornings off," he said. "They only want me in the afternoons. The work is hard, but it's steady." He rattled the sleeve of his toga. The pocket there jingled faintly.

"Too bad *you* aren't steady," I muttered.

"I'm better than you," said Leque. "How old are you now? Thirty? Thirty-one? Still living under your big brother's roof? You could look for a job for yourself some day." He turned back to Kem. "Ksar squanders his allowance on piercings and tattoos. He—"

Again, salvation arrived by the door. Yaryk made his entrance in a swirl of gray-black robes. He ushered Blade in before him, small and pale in comparison. Yaryk was late. If not late he would have been early, first to arrive. He did it on purpose, for maximum impact.

"Hello!" called Blade. He smiled. His face was thin, though I was sure he was well fed on sugar, grease and all manner of delicacies.

These meetings were always the same. Only Glane's feathers changed the note of the day.

The noble-boy Blade shrugged off his cloak — ermine skin, shining — and Leque bounded to hang it on the peg by the door.

"Good morning, Leque," said Blade. "Oh!" He caught my brother's sleeve. "Do you know what one of my servants did last night?" Blade talked of his servants as if we all had our own. He told us their stories, and recommendations of adventures we should try, and dangers in need of conquering. As if he had ever stepped outside the City walls, ever done more than stand on his palace balcony, the wind in the beads of his silver-blonde hair, and stared down away toward the acid sea, the fumes rising up and the roads twisting far into the brink of forever. In fact he had never done more.

Yaryk pushed a table in front of the door. He turned the sign in the window from "OPEN," to "CLOSED." "We're all here," he said, as if we couldn't notice for ourselves. "Let us begin."

We filed into Skiy's back storeroom. The storeroom was dim and smelled of smoke and butchered animals. We sat down on our cushions, Glane and I with our backs to the curtain-door, able to escape as soon as the opportunity arose. In front of each cushion lay a stick of incense. Yaryk always brought incense for Stone knows what reason. At the beginning of every meeting each of us lit his stick of incense to show he was present. Today Kem leaned over and lit Glane's for him. Perhaps he feared the feathers might catch on fire. The sickly sweet reek of camel dung filled the room. I did not support Yaryk's use of perfumes.

"We will now begin," said Yaryk. He could hardly be seen through the smog. "Was the door locked, Ksar?"

"It will always be locked," I said, and coughed. "We did discover, however, that feathers travel faster than we can." I treated them all to an invisible sneer. Sometimes I wanted to kill them, I really did — all these solemn men, sitting around in the dark and discussing nothing.

"How are your arms, Glane?" came Yaryk's voice again.

"Not good," said Glane.

"More feathers?"

"Maybe."

Silence followed. We weren't usually this focused, but Glane's condition frightened us.

"I blame the bee," said Glane.

"But haven't there always been bees in the City?" Blade chimed when he spoke, because of the beads in his hair. "There's a nest in our stables. They've never caused problems before. Right, Skiy?"

"It's true," said Skiy. We always went to Skiy for information. His readings told him every statistic, from the year's export figures to the exact date that the butterflies stampeded, more than a hundred years ago. He would tell you the truth because he did not have the imagination to lie.

"I know it was the bee!" said Glane. "Look at this!" He ripped back the sleeve of his jacket. We all bent close through the fog. Blue veins radiated from the welt on his shoulder. The red point where the stinger had entered now glistened a bloated red, like the entrails that hung in the backs of butchers' shops.

"You should have that examined at the hospital," said Kem.

"What do they know about feathers?" said Glane.

"It's true we've never been faced with pinion growth before," said Kem, who valued his hospital job second only to his life, "but new conditions appear every day for treatment. How else can we learn their care?"

"I'll only go if Ksar comes."

"Fine." I shrugged. "I'll come."

"Why don't we all go?" said Blade. He bounced on his cushion. "I've never been to the public hospital before. I want to see it."

"You won't say that in retrospect." Glane bit his collar.

"What's wrong with the hospital?" said Kem, indignant.

"Dead people live there."

"The purpose of the hospital is to prevent them from dying," said Kem. "I remind you that the City would be filled with much more death if it were not for the hospital."

"The house of the dead," said Glane.

"The house of departure from this world, perhaps," said Kem, "but what's wrong with being on the doorway between worlds?"

"If there's a world that rains gold coins," said Leque, "I'll go." He laughed.

"Why do you have such praise for money?" said Yaryk. "Money may be wasted, and then it's gone, as you yourself have so frequently proven. Power is the real thing."

"I read a book about a tree of power," said Skiy the insatiable cobbler. "People would climb up into its branches to pick its golden fruit, and if they could find their way down to earth again their wishes were fulfilled. They became the fathers of kings and warlords."

"Why would you want to sire kings?" laughed Yaryk. "Why not be one?"

"How could you climb into a tree?" said Glane. "The branches would break."

"This was at the beginning of the world," said Skiy. "Trees were stronger then."

"And had golden fruit?" Glane took another bite of his jacket. "Is golden fruit edible?"

"I don't know. It doesn't matter, Glane." Skiy coughed up a wad of tallow and wiped his mouth. "It's a legend," he said. "It's not meant to be believed."

"Then why was it written?"

"Entertainment," said Yaryk. "The power of a story well-told is phenomenal."

I wondered if Yaryk considered his own stories phenomenal. He recited them enough.

"You should tell your stories to the stars," said Glane. "Maybe they would stay still long enough to listen."

"The stars have no need of my stories," said Yaryk. "They come from the stars to begin with."

"And they write them down, do they?" said Glane. He was more belligerent today than usual. "I didn't realize they had hands."

"Bodily features are immaterial," said Yaryk.

"They seem pretty material to me." Glane poked the swollen mound of his shoulder. He watched the pus, reddened, run down his arm. "That hurts," he said.

"You really should come to the hospital," — Kem sat forward — "before the infection spreads."

"Do you have cures for double eyelids too?"

No one answered. What could you say to a question like that?

"I have the day off work tomorrow," said Kem. "Why don't we meet at my house for breakfast. We can visit the hospital after we've eaten."

"If Ksar comes," said Glane.

"I'll come."

"I can pay the physician," said Blade. He produced a silk pouch and waved it.

"No, no," said Kem. "The hospital acts from charity. But if you wish your money to go to a worthy cause, the Fellowship of the White Horse could use some help."

"What do they spend their money on?" said Glane. "Soap to keep the horses clean?"

2

In the early morning, when frost still glittered the ground, Yaryk awoke before the suns. Only one had risen by the time he entered the Bedouin district. The district was un-official, but its boundaries were recognized by all; anywhere within a stone's throw of the gates belonged to the Bedouin after nightfall. Yaryk breathed deep as he walked. The scent of fleas and sweat mixed with cloves in the air. He smiled.

Nestled against the wall, one camp stirred. Behind their colossal wagon, men in fur robes squatted around a fire. The wagon's sides leaned inwards, covered in fabric and hides like a tent on wheels. Camels slept in their harnesses. The men looked up as Yaryk approached. He recognized them as fur smugglers. They were not true Bedouin. They had no pride. They were more like outcasts. They were men who had cast themselves out, away from their hard-stone homes and their families. They paid no taxes on their imports. Guards — such as Gyanin — never questioned what they carried in their reeking carts. For centuries their crimes had gone ignored.

One man held out a pan of boiling fat. "Stop for a meal, my friend?"

"I would be honored," said Yaryk.

The smugglers shuffled over. Yaryk accepted the pan, and took his seat beside their leader.

"Where are you from, my friends?"

"The Fortress Meadows," they told him.

"Is the hunting still bountiful there?"

"As ever," said the leader. He picked a flea from his shoulder and ate it. "Have you traveled to the Meadows?"

"Many years ago," said Yaryk. "And where is your next destination?"

"Back to the Errata."

"Ah." Yaryk looked up from the pan. "The road passes close to the Citadel, does it not?"

"Close."

"Will you stop to barter?"

"At the Citadel? No." The smuggler inserted a bone between his two front teeth. He toyed with the bone as he spoke: "Why do you ask? Are you from those parts?"

"I am."

"A Bedouin from the Citadel..." The smuggler sucked his teeth. "Were you a member of the Guild?"

"I was," said Yaryk.

"Were you driven away?"

"Yes."

"And now you intend to return?"

"Perhaps. When my affairs here have reached their conclusion."

After a pause the smuggler said, "I would not go to the Citadel if I were you. From what I hear, your people are still scorned."

"Ah," said Yaryk. "That saves me the inquiry. I'm a news-seeker. I was about to put the question to you." He set down the pan. "There's another matter I would like to know. Tell me: do you know of Tallos, Ryas, or Almir? Do you know if they are still alive?"

"Tallos... Alm..." The smuggler rolled the words over his tongue and spat into the fire. "The old Guild leaders? No, I don't know what's become of them. I go to the Citadel to trade, not to entwine myself in politics. You would be wise to adopt the same tactic if you return there."

"'Those who do not see the rain clouds may still be caught when the squall arrives,'" Yaryk quoted. "'It is best to be involved in matters of import, so that their dangers may be fully understood.'"

"Proverbs?" The smuggler laughed. A blue hexagon tattooed his tongue. "Thank you for your advice, storyteller."

"Yes," said Yaryk. "Accept my thanks for your food and company." He rose and strode away, into the glare of the second sun rising.

Under blankets of embroidered ermine, Blade lay in bed and thought back to his father's Release. It came to him when he was bored, or saddened, or had woken up early and lay there waiting for Yaryk to arrive at the palace, and for the servants to come and dress him for another day. He was waiting now. He thought of the Ceremony, in the crypt behind the palace where all the patriarchs of the Ven family went up in steam — and down in the record books, with the names of their associates penned beside them.

During the Ceremony, Blade had stood on the steps around the vat. It contained blue acid, undulating, sunk into the floor. His grandfather, Y'az Xvazen, had said that the City was too crowded for burials.

"What are burials?" said Blade.

His grandfather laughed and did not reply.

The crypt was lined with plaques of his ancestors — dedications each the size of his palm, carved into the gold and quartz and amethyst. Some were carved into wood — sycamore, alder and aspen. These last were the most expensive.

To Blade, the eldest son, went the privilege of holding his father's plaque. The inscription was carved into polished pewter. If he tilted it wrong, it caught the light from the acid and glared hard blue in his eyes. "Zeth Ven," said the text. It branded the backs of his eyes.

They wrapped the body in silk and carried it swaddled to the edge of the pool — the four servants who had always borne his father's litter on excursions to the Fountain Gardens, or the Marble Tower with its throbbing stairs. Nothing of his father could be seen beneath the silk, only the shape of the body. The head appeared so small at one end, the feet at the other, with the great tumescence of his stomach between. His arms were folded. They scarcely touched each other over that mound.

The servants reached the pool's edge and stopped and waited. The chanting vibrated into Blade's spine and the soles of his feet. Every noble in the City stood around the acid pool and chanted: there stood the entirety of the Ven family, the business associates of his father, and traveling lords from across the seas. Blade did not chant. He did not know the words. His voice would quail and break if he tried. They would hear and laugh — all the men in their silken beards — and so he kept silent.

The servants raised his father over the pool, held him by the shoulders, vertical, then lowered him slowly down into the vat. The steam devoured his ankles. It rose to his knees, up to his waist. Y'az Zeth's legs disappeared. The steam stank of burning peppermint.

Blade cried. The smell and the burning in his eyes made him cry. His cousins sniffed around him. Blade turned his head away from the plaque. He did not want to tarnish it. His tears ran down his neck and into his collar. His grandfather had warned against harming the plaque. He had told him how many gold coins the plaque had cost — to pay the miners, the transporters, the engravers and finally the men who applied the lacquer.

Blade's grandfather sat on a raised chair, away on the other side of the vat. The blue light of the acid shone on his face, lighting it up from below. His cheekbones jutted in hard, bright lines beneath the caves of his eyes.

Blade did not understand the world. He would lie awake at nights, drumming his eyes across the ceiling, and pondering all the things he did not understand. He lay there now, in the morning's calm. He waited for Yaryk. Why did the ceiling tiles look like flowers, four petals and tipped in gold? What flowers were they meant to be? How did one fix glass squares to the ceiling without the glass falling to shards on the floor? Blade imagined his bedroom knee-deep in down, in order to save their breaking. Why, he wondered, when his father died, had the family assets not passed to him? Blade was the eldest son. He wondered but could not explain. He was not sure, (as he was never sure), about his father's true thoughts on anything. And so he said nothing. But surely it made no sense that his grandfather should rule the family again. Why had his father ever been the head of the family when his grandfather — Y'az Xzaven — still lived?

"I'm almost fourteen," Blade had told his grandfather, the day after his father's Release. "Don't worry. I'm almost fourteen, and then I'll be old enough to become the Y'az, and you can retire again. Right, Grandfather?"

Y'az Xzaven laughed. He said, "Xavier," his cheeks less bright than the night before, "you'll have to gain more than years before I trust you to handle our family's name."

Blade, to his family, was always and only Xavier. Only out in the City, away from the palace, did anyone name him Blade. It was his secret identity.

Xavier said, "I *am* the heir though, aren't I?"

"Indeed," said his grandfather, "but I will not allow you to inherit anything until you prove you understand what it is you're inheriting."

"I don't understand."

"You might begin by attending my business councils."

"I suppose that sounds interesting, Grandfather."

"I am glad it does." His grandfather picked his teeth with an ivory barb, fine as a needle.

Blade trailed his grandfather for a week, into every gaudy room and reception hall around the City, where they talked with other nobles, merchants, and sundry dignitaries of whose existence Blade had been blissfully unaware. It didn't matter to him who they were, these beaded men, for all of them acted the same. They ignored him throughout the meetings, but often gifted him with sweets at the end. The sweets were good, all wrapped in paper and pearlescent ribbon. They would add to his stomach at least.

Beyond the sweets, the business councils bored Blade. He attended for a week, and then stopped.

Blade rolled over in his blankets. He lay on his side, watching the edge of the window. The curtains were drawn but the light filtered through the muslin. "The twin suns," he muttered, and smiled. He imagined the City below, spread out like a stone mosaic. The door of each house stood small and bright.

"Hurry up," he whispered. "I want to go, Yaryk. I want to go to Kem's house and eat honey cakes and apples. He makes the best honey cakes in the City, don't you agree?" Blade smiled to himself and rolled the other way beneath his blankets.

Every morning began with Yaryk's arrival. Blade never rose or dressed until Yaryk had come; he never ventured into the City without the Bedouin, nor told the palace servants where they went. It must be secret, and Blade could keep secrets. The palace servants had no inkling that Kem and the others even existed.

Yaryk would return him to the palace before noon. If his grandfather wanted him, Blade could be at his disposal the rest of the day. Traveling by litter was enjoyable enough, with the beaded curtains and the bowing crowds, but nothing compared to walking with Yaryk, who could point out every perfume shop and every stand that sold amulets. He could say where every stone was mined.

"Far south," said Yaryk, "half a season's journey from here. There are many pockets of civilization beyond the City walls, Blade. Some are larger than the City, some smaller."

"Have you been to them all?"

Yaryk laughed.

"Will you take me to see them all?" said Blade.

"Perhaps, when this business is over." Yaryk concealed his hands in the sleeves of his robe. "I will take you to the Borough Ring, or the Metropolis, or wherever you wish."

"I want to go everywhere," said Blade.

Outside the chamber, up the stairs, footsteps padded against the stone. Yaryk was coming. Blade stretched. He yawned and smiled.

Servants emerged from their alcoves. They slid their arms beneath Blade's back and lifted him from his blanket cocoon. They placed a goblet of coconut milk in his hands. He stood in the middle of the floor, sipping warm milk while the servants worked silently around him, draping and winding the folds of his toga. Golden thread embroidered the green. He had never seen this toga before, nor ever worn the same toga twice in his life. The eunuchs presented him a toga each morning and carried it away each night.

Blade sat in an armchair beside the bed, a mirror in front of him, and regarded his reflection. His hair fell straight to his shoulders, no wisps, no imperfections, every bead in place. The servants brushed away the blue beads of yesterday, and threaded green glass in their place. Blade fidgeted. He wanted Yaryk to enter. He wanted the day to begin.

At last the door opened. Yaryk swept his robes around him and bowed. "Good morning, Xavier."

Not even his personal attendants called him Blade. He waved in their direction and they retreated back into the wall.

"It's a wonderful day, Yaryk, isn't it?" Blade sprung from his chair. "I've never been to the public hospital before. What is it like? No, don't tell me. I want to be surprised."

Yaryk sat down on the bed. He turned toward the window where daylight streamed in through the curtains. "It is a beautiful morning," he said.

Blade sat down beside him. "Is it a good traveling day?"

"Yes. As is every day."

"Yaryk, why did Leque stop working for my father?"

"He feared your father would discover," said Yaryk, "what had happened and what he had done." Yaryk's eyes, blacker than Bedouin basalt, reflected no light from the window.

"You mean at the Tower?" Blade swung his feet above the floor. "That had nothing to do with my father though, did it? Why would he care if Leque worked here or not?"

"Leque's reasoning is not always as strong as it should be," said Yaryk. "But come." He stood. "We wouldn't want to miss Kem's breakfast."

They left the chamber and descended the spiral stairs. Blade traced his hands through the pile of the red carpet on the walls. A man with a dish of incense bowed as they passed. Another serving boy staggered beneath an armload of drapery. He lowered his eyes. Blade smiled. He hurried to catch up with Yaryk.

"Yaryk, do you not trust Leque?" He brushed the green beads from his eyes. "Before I met you, Leque..."

"As far as loyalty is concerned," said Yaryk, "I'm sure that Leque can be trusted to any extreme. Where he lacks is in deductive faculties, and the ability to make responsible decisions."

They emerged into the palace courtyard, scented as always with jasmine and golden orchids. Across the yard a causeway opened, sloping downwards and running away east toward the City core. Yaryk led the way. He turned down the first side road.

"Yaryk," said Blade, "I was thinking about my father before you came."

"Yes?" said the Bedouin.

"Do you know why he died?"

"He was *your* father, not mine," said Yaryk, "but I would surmise it to be his weight that killed him."

"His weight?" Blade paused. He hurried to catch up. "What do you mean, 'his weight'? The more weight you have, the better it is. Isn't that true?"

"Not always, Blade. I believe that is a philosophy unique to the nobles. Too much weight can be harmful."

"My grandfather says that he died in his sleep."

Yaryk nodded. He wore his hood pulled over his face. He always wore it this way, making his features invisible within its folds.

"How does weight kill?" said Blade.

"You have nothing to fear in that respect," said Yaryk. "Don't trouble yourself."

Blade frowned. He waved silver dust-flies out of his face. "I wish I weighed more," he said. "I wish I had a stomach like my father had. He let me sit on his lap sometimes and he'd feed me sugared kumquats and brandy milk. If I drank more brandy milk, do you think I could look like him?"

"You would need a lot of milk," said Yaryk.

"Do you think Kem will give us milk?" said Blade.

"We shall see." They rounded a corner, out from the last shade of the palaces, into the full suns and the swirling flies of the public streets. It would be another day in the City.

3

I awoke to the sound of Leque leaving the house; the front door rattled like a dying camel every time it closed. I sat up in bed. He had left a plate of naan and a jar of cashew oil on the floor for breakfast. I stepped in the jar of oil, but once I had cleaned the sticky-wet nut residue out from between my toes, the remainder tasted none the worse for the excitement.

I ate, and then proceeded on to the arduous task of dressing. First a toga, plain. Add to that a strip of green leather, formerly a camel harness, slung over one shoulder and twisted around my waist, and I was looking a little more interesting. I inserted a fishing lure into the hole in my left ear, a broken spoon into my right, dipped my beard in a bottle of red ink, and while that dried I entertained myself by shoving Leque's pillowcase onto my head. The case was small and I had to rip it in several places, but at last I had the victory. Now for the final touch. I was running late — no time for anything elaborate. I thrust my fist into a canister of orange paint and knuckled myself in the eye. Considering the time restraints, the effect was acceptable.

I arrived at Kem's house unescorted and perfectly on time. Glane was not there.

We waited a while. Leque straggled in late and we waited some more.

"Glane said he was spending the night with his family," said Kem. "Perhaps someone should go fetch him."

I watched the pendulum of the clock, ceiling-high, swing back and forth until my eyes watered. I rubbed them and got orange paint on the back of my hand. "I'll go," I said.

No one objected, and so I left. The streets had begun to stir into life. The surrounding houses, cut into the sandstone, opened and disgorged their occupants into the chaos of another day. I avoided the crowds, which was not difficult because everyone avoided me. I wanted to find Glane first, before Kem found him. Kem could stifle. He nurtured and nurtured until you could hardly breathe. Didn't he remember that Glane was *my* best friend, not another of his nameless patients? Shouldn't *I* be the one responsible for Glane's decisions?

I turned off the main road, down a side alley heaped with refuse. All the doors were identical — low, arched, with shields of hide stretched over the frames. A yellow glass wind chime hung outside Glane's door. I knocked.

A man in a burlap toga opened the door. Apart from the beard and the strands of white at the temples, Glane and his father could have been replicas.

"Ksar?" said the man.

I said, "Yes."

He peered at me. He held a glass beaker in his hand and another hung from a chord around his neck. Glane's father was an alchemist. He could recognize iron oxide at the blink of an eye, or manganese, or sodium compounds, but he never could identify me.

"Is Glane here?" I said.

"No." His father looked past me, up and down the alley in either direction. "No, he's not here." His upper lip twitched. He squinted at me, bright in the morning sun. "Is he missing?" he said. "Where did you last see him? Did he say he was coming here?"

"I think so."

"You don't think he would leave the City, do you?" said his father.

"Stone, I hope not!" I hadn't considered that. "Why the Stone would he leave? I don't think he'd leave now."

"Why not now?"

"Because he's sick," I muttered.

"Sick?"

"Er..." How to explain without frightening him? I wished I hadn't brought it up. Maybe I had to frighten him though, because that was the only way to be honest, and weren't the rest of us frightened already? "Glane has feathers," I said.

"Ah." His father leaned back against the doorframe. "Yes, I know about that."

"You do?" I said, and, "So, yes, he's sick. Actually, I was looking for him because Kem thinks we should take him to the hospital."

"Oh, that's not necessary." His father swilled the contents of the beaker. "It will run its course, I'm sure."

I blinked. I could not think what to say. "What are you making?" I said.

"Gold," he said. "We have very little."

"Good luck."

A tousled brown head appeared at the door. The boy yawned and rubbed his eyes at me. "Ksar?"

"Good morning, Sfin." I doffed my pillowcase. It would either be Sfin, or another of Glane's younger brothers. They all looked the same. The boy made no objection to my greeting, so it must have been Sfin the genuine, the second-oldest of the household and the one who actually looked after his brothers — not a duty observed by their father and definitely not by Glane. I couldn't tell you how many brothers there were — I would've said about eight million, but I might have been wrong.

"I want to talk to you." Sfin tugged my sleeve.

"I have to go," I said. "I have to look after my millipede farm." I didn't like children.

"No, come inside," he said. "Please, Ksar? Just for a second?"

Glane's father stepped out of the way and Sfin dragged me into the house. The interior consisted of one room, just a low-roofed rectangle cut into the stone. Two smaller chambers opened at the back, one room for the father and one for his eight million sons. Between the two doors sat the alchemy workbench, hedged off in netting. The air hummed, like a swarm of insects far away. I thought of bees and shivered, but there were always strange sounds around the workbench — invisible crickets, sheets of bubbling metal — and so I ignored the humming as best I could.

I'd been to Glane's house many times to play crystal wars, or to sit together and stare at the walls and discuss new methods of eating live armadillos, and keeping them alive the whole way through. We'd never put those plans into practice. The house looked odd without Glane. I should be able to see him in the corner there, chewing his collar, or there in the middle of the floor with his cobras in his lap. And where were the brothers? Locked in the bedroom, maybe? Now and then a spurt of laughter burst out from behind the doors.

A table occupied the center of the floor. It had once stood at chest-height, but the legs had been butchered gradually over the years, and it now stood no more than a breath above the floor. Sfin led me over to the table and sat down. Glane's father stole along the wall and disappeared behind the alchemy netting.

"Glane is gone?" said Sfin.

I shrugged. "He was here yesterday. He must not be far away."

"Do you think he's all right?" said Sfin. It was uncanny: the same hair, the same tiny nose, ears that stuck out and caught in the light, like a chinchilla about to be fried. His eyes were the same dripping jade. "Do you think he's all right?" he repeated.

"All right?" I said. "You mean with the feathers?"

"No, not the feathers." Sfin glanced toward his father's bench. He leaned toward me over the table. "I think the feathers are bad. He shouldn't be growing them."

"No," I said, "I don't think so either."

"But that's not what I mean," said Sfin. "I mean, do you think he's all right otherwise, generally?"

"Generally? You mean generally healthy?"

Sfin's forehead wrinkled like rice paper in an acid vat. "No, I mean ... do you think he's happy? No, not happy. I mean, do you think his head is all right? Is he sane?"

I laughed. "No."

"Oh."

"I think Glane is crazy," I said, "like me."

"You're not crazy, Ksar."

"Ah, no, of course not." I shuffled where I sat. "Can I leave now?" I said. "Your floor is not comfortable. What happened to the carpet?"

"We sold it."

I stood up. "Why would you sell your carpet?"

"We traded with the baker. He gave us a bag of flour."

"So..." I looked around again, the bare walls, the cooking niche in one corner with only a coil of onions on the floor, a jar of dried figs and a bag of flour, small enough to hide down my shirt. "You don't have very much food," I said.

"I know," said Sfin.

"Why?"

"We don't have any money," he said. "Wait a minute. I have something for you." Sfin left me by the door. He ran across the room and into one of the bedrooms, disappeared for a moment and reappeared with a glass jar under one arm. He handed me the jar. "For Glane," he said. "It's a birthday present. He's turning twenty-one."

I looked at what he'd given me. "A jar," I said. "Wow."

"They're mice." Sfin puffed out his chest, so his ribs showed under his shirt. "I caught them myself. They're for his cobras. Tell him they're from the garbage heap, not from around the workbench. They shouldn't be poisonous."

"Er, thanks," I said. "I'll tell him."

Sfin let me get as far as the doorstep, out of sight of the netting now, before tugging my sleeve again. "Ksar?"

"Yes?"

"You're taking Glane to the hospital?"

"Yes."

"Because of the feathers? Are they really that bad?"

"Yes," I said. "I suppose."

"My father doesn't think he should go. Maybe you shouldn't take him to the hospital. Why don't you bring him here instead?"

"I'll see," I said.

He looked as if he might have something else to say, but I slammed the door in his face. Too many twitchy people. I couldn't take it. Why in Stone should I keep Glane away from the hospital?

Half way back along the alley, a copper-blue feather shimmered in the shade.

I picked it up. "Glane?" I said.

No response.

"Glane?" There was no one around. Unless you lived down these alleys, why would you come here? The sky was so blue it hurt, like a wash of cobalt dye. A faint breeze ruffled my toga. I was cold. My face still dripped with sweat.

And then I saw him. Glane. He lay half-buried under dirt-copper and cyanide feathers, sprawled at the side of the road. He had wedged himself into the wall, into a niche in the crumbled sandstone. I knew it was Glane only because of the color of the feathers. He no longer looked like Glane. He blinked at me. His eyes had expanded to fill half his face — over, around and through the bridge of his nose. The pupils gaped like tunnels into his skull. He opened his mouth. It was no mouth at all, but a hole in his face, hard-rimmed and beak-like. We stared at each other. Thank Stone I had found him, and not some stranger.

"Glane, you look like a bird."

He gaped at me.

"Get up," I said. It wasn't healthy, how shrill my voice had become. "We're meeting at Kem's," I said. "Why didn't you come?"

Glane shook his head.

"Come on." I reached to take his arm and haul him to his feet. He no longer had either — not arms nor feet. I sweated so much my palms felt like water. "Can you stand?" I said.

He shrugged. He still had shoulders, sort of.

"Or why don't we take you home," I said, "to your house. It's closer. Just over there."

Glane shook his head.

"Why not?"

His voice rattled. I could not understand him. He seemed to be speaking through layers of phlegm.

I said, "But—"

"No!" Glane gargled. He coughed up a wad of feathers: down and pinions, dripping in slime. They had caught in the back of his throat and raked his tongue, leaving it raw and red-striped.

I sat down against the wall. What should I say? What do you say when your friend is half bird? Half something? Glane himself had nothing to say. Nothing at all. If this really was Glane.

"Do you still have your cobras?" I asked at last.

"I let them go."

"Sfin gave me something for the cobras," I said. "Dead mice, I think." I uncorked the bottle and squinted inside. "Yes, three of them. Dead. Very dead."

"The snakes couldn't eat them anyway," said Glane. "Mice are too big. They'd have choked."

"Ah," I said.

"I feed them ants," said Glane, "and roaches. And worms when I have them. When are the others coming, Ksar?"

"Not until I go get them."

"Ksar?"

"Yes?"

"Do you like birds?"

"Why do you ask?"

"Because I think I'm turning into one."

"Sure," I said. "I like birds."

"Blue ones?"

"Especially blue ones. And copper," I added, looking at him, "with gold eyes."

"When I was seven, I saw a parrot drown in a pool of acid," said Glane. "All it's feathers burned off before its head went under. It started breathing smoke. The squawking was horrible. I stuck a stick in to save it. I forgot birds don't have hands. It couldn't grab on. The stick caught fire. When I leaned out over the pool, to bring the stick within reach of the parrot, I hit it in the head and its eye fell out."

"You're not that kind of bird," I told him.

"I wish I was," he said.

"You're insane."

"So are you," said Glane.

"You're worse."

"No, actually," he said. "At least I don't paint my skin green and drill my ears full of holes, and look like a different person every day."

He had a point. I wasn't going to admit it.

"You used to have pierced ears too," I said. "It's your fault you let the holes grow over."

"Ksar!"

I jumped and looked around. Yaryk's robes filled the alleyway, wall to wall.

"Ksar, why haven't you come back? What are you doing here, sitting in the dirt?"

"Glane—"

"Where is Glane?"

"Here."

Yaryk's expression could not be seen behind his beard, and behind his turban, behind the strings of beads and braided rope that hung before his face. He stood still for several moments. I could guess what he was thinking: all those feathers. At last he bent. He shrugged off the outer of his robes and handed it to me.

"Wrap him in this," said Yaryk. "We'll take him to Kem's house before he's noticed. Come on, Ksar. We can't let him be seen."

I fumbled through the mass of feathers to find Glane's arms. I pulled him from his wedge-hole in the wall. He was all but intangible under his down, featureless except for his face and the vague protrusions that had once been his limbs. Once? Only yesterday. It was only yesterday we had climbed the Marble Tower, sat on the top of the world, and Glane pulled out one feather. He had only had one. He had had to dig. When I ran down the Tower and found him lying on the street, staring into the sewers, he had still been a man, hadn't he? He had still been human. Only yesterday. And now?

We draped the robe around Glane's shoulders, then a second robe over his head, and Yaryk cradled my friend in his arms like a baby. I stamped the scattered feathers into the dust and kicked them into the wall, out of sight, before hurrying after. We went swiftly back the way I had come, through the labyrinth of streets. The breeze died down. The air was motionless. It was so dry it drank from my skin. Glane lay muffled under feathers and burlap. I wanted to cry, but I didn't know how without smearing orange paint all down my face.

We arrived at Kem's house. Once more in the oval back room, shrouded in incense, Yaryk spoke: "Listen to me, everyone." We always listened to Yaryk, but now he told us to anyway. "We must determine the cause of Glane's ailment," he said. We had reached this revelation days ago.

Kem leaned in. He examined the thing that had once been Glane's face. He seemed unfazed by the eyes, or the drooling hole of Glane's mouth. Not even the lack of limbs deterred him. "We must take him to the hospital," said Kem.

"Have him poked and prodded by public physicians?" Yaryk sneered. "Men who are trained in no more than amputations and bandaging? No. I say the City must not know what has happened. Pandemonium would spread to the stars."

"If there's danger, shouldn't we warn people?" Blade's voice was high. "Shouldn't they be told to keep away from bees?"

"No," said Yaryk. "The average bee is harmless. I have been stung often enough in my time here, and I am as featherless as anyone."

"It hurt," said Glane.

"What hurt?" said Yaryk the Bedouin.

"The feathers, when they grew last night. I could feel them under my skin." His voice sounded distant, as if he was at the end of a long, wet tunnel. "They felt like worms," he said, "burrowing out. They tickled. No, they itched. It itched all over, until I went numb." He sniffled. The sound was hollow. "My legs went numb and then they went away. I don't think I have them anymore. Ksar, do I still have legs?"

"No," I said. "I don't think so."

"Where were you when you were stung?" said Yaryk.
"At home," said Glane. "It hurt."

Kem began to speak, but there was too much incense in my lungs and I coughed and I could not hear him. I crawled from the room. I stood on Kem's doorstep and purged the smoke from my lungs. The streets wound away in either direction. My breath jolted down my throat. It was hard to breathe. I could not stop sweating.

The sandstone appeared gray-brown in the shadows, white in the full morning sun. The sky shone crisp as the edge of fire. Pearl halos ringed the suns. A bee landed on my shoe.

I forgot to cough.

I kicked. It wobbled through the air and hovered. I pushed the door open. I staggered inside. I slammed the door behind me and coughed again.

"Ksar!" Kem's voice called from the inner room. "Are you all right, Ksar?"

The bee had followed me.

"Ksar?" called Kem.

I did not answer.

Kem appeared through the curtain of the smoking room. "What is it, Ksar?"

I pointed.

The murmured voices in the other room stopped. Yaryk's head appeared through the curtain. Incense wreathed his beard. "Are we not in the middle of dire council? What is the interruption?"

"Bee," I said. I pointed. It crawled over the carpet toward me, one woolen cord at a time, up one side of the bristle, down the other, up the next. Its eyes sparkled, multi-faceted. They bulged from its head, under its feelers as it came, wings like crystalloid star paper, dragging, one leg bent, twisted, broken in landing.

Glane began to scream: "Don't let it get you!" he shouted. "Ksar, don't let it get you!"

I backed away. I hit a bookshelf and stopped. I could not move my eyes from the bee. I stared at its kaleidoscope eyes.

Glane burst out from the incense. "Where?" He smashed into my chest. "Where is it, Ksar? Let me kill it! Let me kill it! Where is it, Ksar?"

I pointed. Glane pounced. He screamed like a dying kestrel. He ground and stamped. Feathers flew. The bee smeared into the carpet.

Kem dragged Glane away and pushed him to the floor. My friend was gibbering now, trying to force the words out through the nothing in his head. What was this thing? This spitting, slavering thing on the carpet — this wasn't Glane. It couldn't be Glane.

Kem looked at me and grimaced. Perhaps he had meant it as a smile. It did not reassure. The others piled out of the smoking room, fanning themselves. Gyanin alone was not present. Not even Glane's trouble had been enough to drag him from his post as guard.

Glane scrabbled out of Kem's hold. "Go away!" The words came screeching. He sounded like a lemur and a dying monkey. "Go away, go away, you're all afraid!"

Blade clung to Yaryk's robe, one hand across his mouth. I could not tell if he was crying yet, or still on the verge of tears. No one spoke.

Kem motioned for the door. "Leave." He was begging, not ordering. They shuffled out. Even Yaryk left.

Kem did not make me leave. I knelt in the carpet and trembled. I forgot my cough. Glane's arms were the length of my hand; they bent like wings. He tried to wrap them around me. Flight muscles rippled on his back. When had Glane ever asked for wings? Yesterday perhaps he had. Yesterday he had wanted to fly. It was the worst embrace I had ever received.

"I don't want to be a bird, Ksar." Glane clung to me, fast as a leech. "I don't want to eat insects and dead dogs. I had to let my cobras go, Ksar. I had to let them go. I would have eaten them otherwise."

I patted his back. "Eating snakes is disgusting," I said. "Don't do it." My fingers crawled at the touch of his feathers. "What do we do now?" I asked Kem.

Kem chewed his lip. "I don't care what Yaryk says," he said at last. "Glane is going to the hospital. We have a lot of rare medicines there. I'll appeal to the head physician. I'm sure we can establish a long-term care program. Is that all right with you, Glane? We can put you into special treatment. No one will pry. Only the people you invite."

Glane nodded.

We went outside. The others sat on the doorstep. They turned when we came out, Glane muffled again in the sacking.

"We're going to the hospital," said Kem.

Not even Yaryk objected. He stared at the sky with a distant air. "The wind is from the south," he told Blade. "We call that a 'cinnamon wind.'"

My brother Leque took Glane in his arms. Leque carried things to prove his strength. I wanted to tell him that carrying Glane, as he was today, would not prove anything, not after the way he had shriveled overnight, his bones hollowed out to husks. I did not say anything. I did not want to hear myself speak.

Between us and the hospital stood two hundred doors identical to Kem's, leading into rooms identical to Kem's, where the other workers whiled away their lives. We hurried. The hospital's hub loomed before us in a great, smooth dome. Other buildings groped out from the central dome, like the legs of a tangled spider. Kem led us into the hub, into the bulk of the reception hall. Passageways branched in every direction. Placards labeled the doors: *ACID-RELATED INJURIES, EMERGENCY, APPOINTMENTS, OTHER.* He herded us to the far end of the hall, dodging the clustered patients, the physicians lounging on benches, bragging no doubt of the atrocities they had handled that morning, the epidemics that, thanks to them, would not be ravishing the City tomorrow. But there was no one with feathers, blue or otherwise, and so we kept Glane out of sight.

One of the men behind the reception desk looked up from his paperwork and smiled. His hair was a finger's breadth in length, slicked back along his temples like a helmet. One ear was naked; a beaded earring hung from the other, the beads swinging all the way to his shoulder. "Hello." A practiced smile graced his face. He looked like a portrait in marble. He looked at me and blanched. "You're not a cult, are you?"

I was about to say 'yes' and gaggle my tongue ring at him to see what he would do.

Kem pushed forward, indignant. "Of course not, Maelin. It's me."

"Ah, Kem." The man relaxed. "Follow me." He looked again like a statue. He bowed his way out past the backs of his fellow receptionists.

We trailed after Maelin, down a side passage and into a windowless room. An empty washbasin and a bed filled the floor.

"Have you come about the patient we discussed earlier?" said Maelin. "The one with feathers?"

"Yes," said Kem.

Yaryk glared. "Who else have you told?"

"No one." Kem waved a hand. "Please, let me deal with this."

"Which of you is growing feathers?" said Maelin.

"Glane." Leque laid his burden on the bed. He unwrapped the sacking.

Maelin stared. "That's more than I imagined." His face paled, becoming as white as alabaster.

Glane scrabbled at the sacking. He tried to pull it back over his face.

"He can't stay in the lower levels." Maelin toyed with the end of his beads. "Wait here a moment," he told us. "I'll see if the preparations have been made for the room in the South Wing."

Maelin hurried away. We stared at the floor between each other's feet.

"Kem," said Yaryk, "how many people have you told about Glane?"

"I assure you: only Maelin. He is entirely trustworthy, I guarantee. He has prepared a room for us and concocted a variety of possible medications. He's agreed to give Glane constant attention. He will not seed the City with rumors."

"What can a medical assistant know of possible treatments?" Yaryk sneered. "Is he trained in magic? Familiar with the transmogrification tendencies of exotic birds?"

"I'm not a bird," said Glane.

"By the Stars you're getting close," said Yaryk.

The door opened and Maelin peered in. "The room is ready. If you'll just ... er ... conceal him before following me."

Leque rolled the cloak around Glane, and once more designating himself as the carrier we hurried after Maelin. The receptionist's sandals flapped silently over the carpets. His toga reached precisely to his knees, exactly half way to his elbows. He held a board under one arm, with a sheaf of papers clipped to its side. Up all the ramps and corridors of the hospital, I tried to distract myself from Glane by wondering what he recorded on that paper. I did not ask. Perhaps he recorded how many patients died in a week. Perhaps I did not want to know.

Maelin led us down a passage with green carpet. We stopped at a door near the end. Maelin opened the door and ushered us into a square room. In one corner stood a bed with a rail around it, to prevent patients from rolling out in their sleep, perhaps, or for tying them down. Above the bed swung what looked like a perch.

"That is not a perch," said Maelin. He watched my face. He did not like my orange eyes; I could tell. "We use it to hang clothes to dry."

"Why would you hang clothes there?" I said. "They would drip down your throat all night."

He did not reply, but regarded me as if I were a rodent.

A window graced the far wall. Blade ran and pressed his hands to the sill. Perhaps in a nobleman's palace they do not have such things as windows. He leaned out as far as he dared, farther than I would have done. "Look!" he cried. "Look, Yaryk, is that the ocean?"

Yaryk shaded his eyes. "That? The red glimmer on the horizon? I doubt it, Blade. We're in the heart of the City here, facing south. It is likely no more than a haze."

Blade jumped up and down where he stood.

"I'll take you to the sea some day," said Yaryk.

How many times had Yaryk made that promise? A hundred? No, more like a thousand. It elicited the same response every time. Blade clapped his hands.

"Yes, I want to go! I want to see fishermen, Yaryk. Do you think we'll see fishermen, too?"

"I have no doubt," said Yaryk.

Blade turned and saw us watching him. He coughed an apology. His hair shone pyrite-bright.

"...large and airy," Maelin was saying to anyone who would listen. Only Kem gave his full attention. "Suitable for any final form: human or otherwise. This apartment is also sufficient..." The speech sounded memorized. Maelin's calm was ludicrous. It had to be forced.

Glane crawled across the floor. Feathers trailed behind him. He climbed over the railing, onto the bed, and burrowed under the coverlet; he became a shivering mound at the headboard. Pigeons trafficked past the window. We waited by the door but Glane said nothing.

"Does anyone wish to remain," said Maelin, "while I administer the first medication?"

"My grandfather will be wondering where I am," said Blade. He slipped away and Yaryk followed.

"Customers are waiting," said Skiy. He looked up from his scroll. All this time he'd been reading. "I must tell Gyanin what has happened."

Leque edged into the hallway.

Kem turned to me. "What about you, Ksar?"

Under my paint and dye, I writhed. I hated the smell of the hospital, the stink of disinfectant and burning.

"I'll stay," I muttered.

"No, you can't." Leque pulled my sleeve. "You have an appointment to get your ear pierced, remember?"

"But Glane—"

"It will be the same whether you're here or not."

I paused for a moment in the doorway, waiting for Glane's voice, but he did not speak. I followed my brother out into the hallway. I shouted back over my shoulder: "I'll come tomorrow, Glane! I promise I'll see you tomorrow."

When he still said nothing, I decided to be offended and hurried after my brother.

"Leque, I don't actually have an appointment you know."

"I know," said Leque. We had a myriad of ramps to descend before street level. "I don't like this," he said. "Why, out of all the millions of people in the City, did this happen to Glane?"

I pushed the edge of the pillowcase away from my eyes. "Glane is strange."

"I'm going to apply to be a litter-bearer again this rainy season," said Leque. "The first rain can't be far away. I need to get away from the City." His voice dropped. "If I were you, Ksar, I'd leave as well. We should all leave the City, especially Glane; somehow he's given himself away." Leque paused. "We can't all leave together; it would be too suspicious. Too conspicuous. If the two of us go together though, it should be safe. We're brothers. People expect us to travel together. But the rest of them?" Leque ground his teeth. The muscles twitched up and down his neck. "It will be difficult for the rest of them to get away unnoticed."

My cold sweat began again. If Leque had enough interest to stay on one topic this long, it must be serious.

"Do you really think Glane's feathers have to do with ... you know?" We emerged onto the tile floor of the reception hall, ducking our heads against the stares that followed me and my fluorescent beard. We scuttled out into the comparative safety of the streets. "Do you think it has anything to do with that?" I said.

"I don't know," said Leque, "but it seems suspicious. Ksar, think of how difficult it must have been to load a common honeybee with poison potent enough to do this. I have no idea how it was done. But you wouldn't go through all that work and then let the bee fly free across the City, to sting whomever it pleased. You'd use it as a weapon. A weapon to punish a criminal. Or criminals. You'd do it carefully."

"You think someone injected the bee and *made* it sting Glane?" I hated Leque's paranoia. I hated it now because he had good reason.

"Injected it, fed the poison to it, something like that," said my brother. "And then there was the bee that almost got you this morning. Think about it, Ksar: when Glane was stung, it didn't go after one of his brothers, it didn't

sting his father — it stung him. And the bee this morning didn't go for Kem's neighbors; it came for us."

"You don't think Glane was crazy?" I said. "I mean the
way he killed that bee?"

"Glane is the craziest person in the world," said Leque.
"I think that's why he was targeted first, because he's crazy.
He could complain of growing feathers for a long time
before anyone would take him seriously. They're going
to come for the rest of us soon. Perhaps for the next most
crazy. That will probably be you. I bet they'll save Blade
'til last, maybe spare him altogether. It would be all over
the City if one of the nobles turned into a bird. I'd be on
my guard if I were you."

I slouched closer to Leque. "You're my brother," I
whispered, "remember? You have to protect me."

"Not against killer insects." He laughed, nervously. "I'll
remind you to feed yourself three times a day and make
sure you don't get your testicles tattooed. That's what I
protect you against — not this. The only protection I can
offer is what I've already said: leave the City, and don't
tell anyone about what we did."

"I wasn't going to," I said. "I never have."

4

In the rainy season of the
Year of the Spotted Pebble

Outside, the deluge pounded the Marble Tower.

Glane leaned over a pool of coral acid. An almond tree stood above the pool. He struggled with the thread of his wish paper. "It's not working, Ksar," he said, and pouted up at me. "You do it. You're taller."

I don't know what Glane wished for. He came to the Tower every day to make a wish. I leaned out over him and wound the string around the almond tree's twigs until it caught and held. I stepped back. Glane's wish disappeared among all the others, ready for the monks to come and gather in the evening.

I tried to count all the trees in the Tower once, but lost count at somewhere over five hundred. They grew along the public walkways and out of the strangest places. Some had soil around their trunks, or pots of gelatinous crystal. Others seemed to grow from the stone itself. If you asked a monk about the trees he would only scratch his beard, or rub his shaved head, and say that he was not sure how the foliage functioned, but that yes, he was sure the trees were sacred, and yes, he was sure your wishes would be fulfilled.

The wish-hanging done, Glane and I continued to the top balcony: up, up, onto the peak of the world. The rain lulled. We watched the clouds shuffle across the sky, and the twin suns blink in and out behind the rag doll wisps.

The rain returned. We ducked back inside. The press of people in the Tower was stifling now. I craned over the heads in search of Leque. His hair was lighter than most; I could often find him. He stood out like opal in a sea of black and ocher. He said he'd be here some time today, because Y'az Zeth Ven had planned a day's outing and all the litter-bearers would be needed to haul his bulk up these stairs.

I didn't see Leque. It didn't matter anyway. He wouldn't acknowledge me if he was with his employer.

Glane tugged my sleeve. "Let's go exploring, Ksar." The more people pressed around him, the more Glane's mind seemed to overheat.

"Where?" I said.

"Around the Tower. Please?"

"We'll get lost," I said.

"Please?" said Glane.

I shrugged. "Go ahead."

We edged our way out of the crush, down a maze of twisting corridors, each one emptier than the last as we left the main thoroughfares behind. Yellow veins pulsed through the marble. There were no more windows. We were now in the pith and core of the Tower, the rest of the City far away.

We came to a room like a vertical tunnel. The floor dropped away into gloom. A platform with a railing around it ringed the wall. In the middle of the room, suspended from the ceiling, a crystal casket swung, the size and the shape of a body. The crystal reflected the walls. It hovered. It watched us. We watched it back. Scarlet feathers plumed the glass, twice the length of my arm, interspersed with yellow tendrils. Each tendril ended in a pinpoint of silver. The plume was so close I could have reached over the railing and touched it. I knew Glane's palms itched to do so.

A handful of other admirers loitered around the railing. A noble boy and his servant stood close to us, talking quietly. Only after Glane and I had circled the platform did I realize the servant was Leque. The boy must be Xavier Ven, about whom Leque had told me everything. I knew he preferred sweet lemon over orange. I knew what time he woke up every morning. He only ordered his servants when he thought another noble was watching. Glane and I hung back against the wall.

The other bystanders were: a Bedouin; a City guard in full uniform; a cobbler with half his hair burned away (his trade was obvious from the sandal soles hung from his belt); and another man who could have been the cobbler's brother. The latter two were talking.

"This is the Radiance," said the cobbler.

"But what is it?" asked his younger replica.

"A monument in honor of the fallen sun." The cobbler coughed. "You're familiar with the legend, aren't you, Kem?"

"Yes, of course."

"The crystal represents the sun," said the cobbler, "elongated to illustrate the motion of falling, speeding earthward. The crest represents the trail of destruction in its wake."

"It is beautiful," said Kem. "Skiy?"

"Yes?"

"Would it not be wonderful to hang such an ornament in the hospital? We could hang it from the dome of the reception hall, as a beacon of reassurance to the patients."

"You would be hard-pressed to find a duplicate of the Radiance." Skiy laughed. "It was blown by master glass smiths over a millennium ago. There is nothing to rival it, not anywhere in the world. Even the crest is sacred; the plumes of the scarlet roc are said to bear magical powers for those who know how to harness them. The yellow strands are the tongues of lance sharks. They can only be fished off the City's eastern coast in the lowest of the dry season, and even then they are the fiercest, most enduring, and most cunning of fish. And those," he said, pointing to the silver tips, "are pearls of the acid oyster. The Radiance is adorned with more than ten thousand. Many divers lost their lives in this undertaking."

The Bedouin sidled over. His robes billowed out as he walked, making him twice the size of a regular man. "You hold amazing stores of knowledge, cobbler. Where have you learned this?"

"Reading," said Skiy.

"He knows everything," said the guard, who had stood like a statue until this point. He now glared up at the Bedouin. "I know your face. You're the man who tried to smuggle narcotics through the gates yesterday."

"I've told you once, and I'll tell you again, I carry incense." The Bedouin produced a stick from his sleeve and waved it beneath the guard's nose. "Incense."

Leque's young noble lost interest in my brother. He bounced around the railing toward the conversation. "Are you from outside the City?" He looked up at the Bedouin. "Can you tell me what's out there?"

"Everything."

"Scarlet rocs?" said Xavier.

"Many years ago, yes, but they are gone now."

"Why?"

"Extinction."

"Like acid trolls?"

"Yes," said the Bedouin. "You seem to know about the outside world already, my young friend."

Xavier blushed. Behind him, my brother Leque bristled at the sudden familiarity.

From my perspective the exchange was becoming dull. I fidgeted with my wig and wondered when the rain would stop. I couldn't leave in the rain, because my face paint would run. Beside me, Glane fed his cobras dead roaches.

"I wish scarlet rocs hadn't gone extinct," said the noble boy. "The feathers are so beautiful." He leaned over the railing until his sandals left the floor, and the bar pressed into his stomach. He reached out with a trembling, twelve-year-old hand. His fingers caressed the plume. He wound his fingers into the tendrils.

Leque jumped forward. Panic swarmed over his face, like flies on a mashed banana. He seized Xavier around the waist and hauled him back. The boy's fingers were still entwined in the tendrils. The tendrils still clung to the plume. Leque pulled Xavier to safety, and the Radiance swayed. It screamed like a banshee, one long scream. The crest tore. It broke from the crystal casket. Xavier sprawled backwards on the marble platform. The crest tumbled over him. It covered his chest and face. He sat up, spitting feathers. Scarlet-red dander clung to his hair. Blood encircled one finger where the tendrils had gouged his skin. His mouth turned down as if he were about to cry.

Everyone else in the room stood still. We stared and said nothing.

The Radiance groaned on its gossamer line, swinging there bald above the abyss.

Xavier peered up at Leque who stood over him. "I didn't mean to," he whispered. "My finger's bleeding."

"Not your fault," muttered Leque. He snapped around. He waved his fist in Skiy's face. "It's your fault, cobbler! What were you thinking, planting crazy ideas in his head?"

"The cobbler provoked nothing," said the Bedouin. "The boy is entirely to blame."

"*You* are to blame," said Leque, wheeling on the black-clad nomad. "Scarlet rocs? Acid trolls? Is this really the time for stories?"

"There is always time for stories."

"You're to blame, servant," said the City guard. "You should have been alert. We of the—"

"Please," said Kem, the shoemaker's companion, "your arguments are doing no good. We must restore the crest to the Radiance before a monk comes and discovers the accident."

"Restore the crest?" The Bedouin's mouth twisted up on one side. "How do you propose we do that?"

"Someone must climb the railing," said Kem, "and lean out over the drop."

I was stupid enough to speak. "You can climb, can't you Leque?" Some vague memory of my brother climbing to the roof of our childhood house came to mind, and then of my father lying on his back and counting the new cracks in the ceiling.

"Wait," said Kem, "before we do anything..." He ran around the circle of the platform to the door, grabbed the handle and wrenched. The door did not move. He strained, and the door slammed shut. It slammed like thunderclouds.

The walls amplified the sound. It crashed and crashed. We all bent double, hands over our ears. My thumb caught in one of my earrings. Finally the noise subsided.

"Do you want some help?" said Glane.

The earring would not let go. I said, "No." Essence of cockroach covered his hands.

"Kem!" Skiy shouted. "Kem, we could have had hours to decide our action. Not now. I imagine the whole City heard that."

"I'm sorry." Kem looked from one face to another. "I am so truly sorry."

We shook ourselves out of our shock. Now we panicked in earnest. We introduced ourselves in a jumble of names: Yaryk the Bedouin; Gyanin the guard; yes, Xavier Ven, and I wondered what punishment Leque would receive when Y'az Zeth found out about this.

When we had finished confusing each other, Gyanin and Skiy stood with their backs to the railing and Leque climbed onto their shoulders. Glane and Yaryk took hold of Leque's ankles to steady him. I passed the drooping crest to my brother. It was lighter than a dream and twice as menacing. I slunk back to the wall, massaging my ear. Kem wrapped Xavier's finger in a strip of cloth.

Leque leaned forward and touched the Radiance's cord, so thin it was almost invisible to the rest of us. He pushed the crest into place. It slipped. It slid back into his hands. He pushed it again and it quivered.

"It doesn't want to stay," he grunted. "I think it's broken. Here." He reached to remove it again, before it could fall. "I'll just..."

The door flew open. A monk charged in red-faced, his feet a blur. He stopped, gaped, and charged again. "What! What! What!?"

He ran to Gyanin, the City guard, and kicked his legs out from under him. Gyanin moaned. He sank to his knees. Skiy bent under Leque's full weight. The monk hollered. He drove in, fat arms flailing like luck chimes caught in the wind. He struck Leque's legs. Leque refused to fall. The monk climbed onto the railing itself and redoubled his attack. Leque stared down at the floor below — far, far below. The walls tapered out like an up-side-down funnel. You could not tell how far. My brother's eyes bulged.

"Stop it," he cried, unable to kick, unable to strike. He clung to the Radiance with one hand, the crest with the other. "Stop it," he begged. "I'll come down. I wasn't even... Please!"

"Defiler! Defiler!" The monk's face flamed as red as a pomegranate.

Gyanin hauled himself to his feet.

"Help!" I'd never seen Leque so desperate. I was too shocked to move. He would fall any second. "Ksar!" he shouted. "Someone! Help!"

Gyanin lunged. He lifted the monk and threw the man over the railing. It happened so fast the monk did not even scream as he fell. His body crunched when he hit the floor.

We helped Leque back to safety. He leaned on the railing and retched. Then all was silent.

"This isn't good," I said.

Everyone nodded.

"I committed murder," said Gyanin. He ran for the door. "I murdered him! I have to tell them. I have to..."

"No." Skiy pulled him back. "Tell anyone, and you'll be locked away. You'll lose your job. I won't let that happen. We're all responsible."

"Speak for yourself." I stared at Glane. We'd spoken in unison. "Glane and I didn't do anything."

"You cowards." Leque wheeled on us. "You were both here, the same as the rest of us, and so you're as guilty as the rest of us. Except Xavier." His face pleaded, suddenly pale. "Xavier's twelve years old. We must let him go."

"Let him go?" said Yaryk, the billowing Bedouin. "He instigated it. He is guiltier than the rest of us combined."

"There is no 'guiltier' or 'less guilty,'" said Kem.

"Except for you," said Yaryk, "who slammed the door and brought the monk. You have done more than I have."

"No," said Skiy, "listen. You have to listen. We have only a few minutes before someone else comes. For the moment, no one knows we were ever here. The only one who saw us is dead." We all looked across at the railing. "Now," said Skiy, "the problem is that we can't put the crest back because it's broken." He took it from Leque and turned it over in his hands. "If we take it to my shop, I'm sure I can repair it. The support rods that attach it to the body of the Radiance have snapped — that's all. They're thousands of years old. The damage is understandable. It has most likely been broken for years, unnoticed by the monks."

"Yes, repair it." Kem rubbed his hands. His nails were perfectly manicured. "Good. Let's go."

Yaryk removed an outer layer of his robes. He draped the robe over the feathers and placed the feathers in Skiy's waiting arms. Yellow tendrils snaked out through the burlap and whisked the floor.

"It's too big," said Leque.

Xavier sniffled.

"Here." Yaryk took the plume and wrapped his robe tight around it and tied it in place — a huge, bulging parcel.

"That will damage it further, you fool!" said Skiy.

"Don't call me a fool." From somewhere under his robe, Yaryk produced a rope and strangled the bundle still more, while the rest of us watched in horror. "See?" he said. "It fits beneath my cloak now. We can go. We can go and repair it. You don't need to stare at me as if I were a murderer."

"I'm a murderer," said Gyanin. He wandered back and forth across the platform. "I killed the monk. I..."

We straggled out of the room, Glane and I last.

"Ksar, what's going on?"

"I don't know."

"I think my father could fix it," said Glane.

"No!" Leque dropped back and hissed at us. We all halted outside the door of the Radiance room. "Don't tell your father," said Leque. "Do you understand, Glane? We can't tell anybody. Nobody, you understand?"

"We must form a pact of silence," said Yaryk.

Skiy unlocked the door of his shop and we filed in.

"Into the back," he told us. "Through the curtain. Kem, you show them."

Skiy pulled the drapes across the front windows of his shop. Kem and Gyanin led us into the storeroom. We cleared away the worst of the books and the piled parchment, old tools and rolls of twine, until there was space enough to sit.

Skiy unwrapped the crest. We all bent toward it in the gloom.

"Is it damaged?" said Kem.

"No more than before," said Skiy. He lifted a toolbox from a shelf and opened it.

We watched him work, hands buried in the feathers, before Yaryk claimed our attention.

"On the open roads," said the Bedouin, "we burn incense at meetings of weight. Each man lights a stick to show he is present in will." He produced eight sticks and handed them around the circle. He produced a flint from somewhere inside his sleeve and each of us lit our sweet-smelling wand. "If you wish," said Yaryk, "I would be happy to relate a story to pass the time."

"Please!" Xavier bounced where he sat.

"Very well." The Bedouin folded his hands. Silver-black dust embedded his nails. "Millennia past," he said, "when the stars were new and burning, not the cold lights that adorn the sky now, there lived a merchant and a wandering minstrel..."

I turned to Glane. He was chewing his lip and feeding his cobras. He saw me watching and shrugged. "It's a good story," he said.

"Exciting as mold," I muttered. It didn't make sense. Since when could you throw fishing nets into the sky and come down with newborn stars? The last time I'd tried that had left me in a tangled mess on the doorstep.

"Done," said Skiy.

"Good," said Leque. "Good, I'll take it back to the Tower. Who wants to come with me?" He looked around at Xavier. "I think you should come, Master, and I'll take you home before your father worries."

"But I need to hear the story."

"I'll come," said Kem.

There were no more volunteers. Leque and Kem rewrapped the Radiance. Kem wrapped it carefully; Leque tried to hurry. He wanted it done. My brother Leque was not a patient man. He wanted to finish this crime, return Xavier and keep his job.

They left. We waited, fidgeting, and Yaryk talked. The room stank. I would fall asleep soon unless something happened.

At the end of the story, Xavier clapped. "That was amazing!" he said. "Do you know other stories?"

"As many as there are stars in the sky," said Yaryk.

"Will you come to my palace and tell me another one?" Xavier's silks appeared garishly out of place here, with the rolls of untanned leather on the shelves behind him, and a flock of sandals strung like charms from the ceiling. "I'm sure my father wouldn't mind. Oh, and Yaryk?"

"Yes?"

"Why was the minstrel called 'Blade'? Isn't that a strange name?"

"On the open roads, men name themselves whatever they please. Blade, Ebon, Zephyr. They name themselves with names of freedom."

"I want to be Blade," said the noble boy. "From now on, whenever I'm out of the palace, I'm going to be Blade."

"A fine name," said Yaryk.

"Before you came to the City, what did you do?" said Blade. "Have you always been a storyteller?"

"I mapped the stars. I tell prophecies to those who can offer me a reward in return."

"Reward?"

"Payment," said Skiy. The cobbler coughed, long and loud, drowning out Yaryk's speech.

I took my crystal wars set from my pocket and dumped it on the floor between Glane and me. We shuffled back as far as possible, and I encircled the playing field in a length of string. Before beginning, we had to fabricate an alternate set of rules, ones that would work in the darkness. We had barely finished arguing when the squeal of the shop's front door interrupted us.

Everyone froze. We waited.

"Hello?" The curtain parted. Kem peered in. He squatted in the doorway. "It was locked," he said.

"Locked?" Skiy coughed again.

"Locked. The door to the Radiance room. We couldn't get in." Kem hung his head. "I'm ashamed to have brought this upon you all."

Leque stepped over Kem and dropped the bundled plume on the floor. "Xavier," he said, "your father's searching the Tower for you. We have to go now, before they discover you're gone."

The white-haired boy said nothing.

"Master Xavier?"

"I'm not Xavier," he said. "I'm Blade now."

Leque glared at Yaryk. He swallowed his anger and said, "Are you ready to go, Blade? You're father's looking for you."

Blade climbed to his feet. He wore silk slippers. He followed Leque out. "Goodbye!" He waved in the doorway. "Goodbye everyone!"

"Tomorrow morning!" Kem called after them. "Don't forget, tomorrow morning! We have to reach a solution."

Glane and I packed up our game and left.

The next day, no solution arrived. No real solution at least. Not one that I liked.

"We'll go to the Tower every day," said Kem. "Different people will go each day. Eventually the door will be open, and then we'll replace the plume. I'll give you directions to my house," he finished. "Tomorrow we'll meet there. We can alternate houses. Does anyone else have a back room? A place suitable for meetings?"

Leque said that we did, and Kem recorded the information on a piece of paper. This done, the meeting adjourned.

Glane and I left.

"The incense smells like dung," I said.

"So do you," said Glane.

"I'm going to choke on it," I said. "Then I'll die and I won't need to worry."

"Don't die." Glane pouted. "If you die I'll have to go to your Release and those things are so boring."

We stopped. A poster was tacked to the front of a tailor's shop. "Tower monks offer substantial reward," it read. "Wanted: the vandals who defiled the Radiance. The search will continue until the miscreants are discovered and brought to justice. Not until the crest is returned will the vigil be lifted."

"So if the crest *is* returned..." I trailed off. It didn't seem likely. I lifted my toga and urinated on the poster. The ink ran and cried in the yellow deluge.

"I want to try that," said Glane. "Let's find another one."

We didn't have to go far.

5

In the dry season of the
Year of the Mandarin Turtle

When I woke the next morning, after Glane's intern-
ment in the hospital, I woke to the sound of conversation
from beyond the curtained door of the sleeping chamber.
In the outer room I found Leque and Skiy in the doorway,
hissing and waving in each other's faces.

"I went to the gates to look for him," Skiy was saying,
"but the other guards hadn't seen him. He didn't come for
his shift yesterday. That's unheard of."

"Maybe—"

"No, I'm not done," said Skiy. "I went to his apartment
to look for him. I knocked but he didn't answer. I peered
in the window. He was sitting on his bed, polishing his
shield as always. I knocked on the window to get his
attention. I'm sure he saw me. He looked at me as if he
didn't know who I was. Then he slid off the bed out of
sight. He left a feather on the pillow. And Glane's pouch."
He held it out to Leque: the little pouch Glane wore around
his neck, the one where he kept his glass worms before
Gyanin took them.

"Don't give it to me." Leque backed away. "Find a trash
heap on the other side of the City. I don't want it."

"What's going on?" I gouged the sleep from my eyes
with my palm.

"Gyanin's been stung," said Skiy. "The welts were all
over his arms. He was stung ten times at least." He dropped
Glane's pouch at my feet.

I gaped.

"Close your mouth," said Leque. "It's not a pretty sight."

"I took him to the hospital," said Skiy. "He has a room next to Glane's."

Leque: "And all of this happened this morning?"

"Yes." Skiy coughed up a lungful of tallow and turned to me. "Glane wants to see you, Ksar."

I wanted to ask if Glane could still talk, or if he'd started using the perch above his bed, but I didn't know how to ask, and my eyes stung, and I didn't really want to know the answers. What was happening to us? Glane, and now Gyanin? When would they come for me? Or Leque?

I turned to my brother. "Can we go visit him?"

"I'm not stopping you."

"But won't you come?"

"Do you need me to hold your hand when you walk ten blocks, Ksar?" Leque pushed past me into our bedroom. I heard him rummaging in the linen basket at the foot of his bed. He called, "You know your way to the hospital as well as I do."

"But the bees."

"What about them? They're insects. They'll be just as deadly whether I'm there or not. If they come for you, they come for you. I don't want to listen to you scream and watch you flap your arms." He reappeared, knotting the rope belt over his tunic. "I should be back by dinner," he said. "If you're not here, I'll come looking for you."

"Where are you going?"

"To work."

"But you only work in the afternoons," I said, confused, "don't you? I thought the Stone Mason's..." Nothing made sense anymore.

He bent and fastened the strap of his sandal. "I have a new job," he said.

"What is it?"

"City guard. It pays better."

"But that's Gyanin's job!"

"And how well do you think a bird can guard the City?" he snapped. He looked up from his sandals, saw my mouth open, and glared. "By Stone, Ksar, close that hole in your face. Gyanin can't work, and someone has to fill his shifts.

It might as well be me." He slammed the door behind him, leaving Skiy and me to stare at each other's feet.

At last the cobbler rubbed his ear and coughed. "You'd better get dressed before we go to the hospital," he said.

I nodded. I could just imagine Glane, perched above his bed, a ring of medical attendants all trying to coax him down, "Come and have another mouthful of medicine. Come on, it's not that bad." I hurried into the bedroom. I dropped Glane's pouch on the floor, kicked it under a bed. I grabbed Leque's toga and threw it around me.

We navigated our way through the streets. Skiy didn't want to talk, not even of books, and so we were silent.

Maelin met us at the reception desk. He stood there identical to yesterday, down to the hanging earring. "You're here to see your friends?" he said.

"Yes," said Skiy.

He led us up the stairs and ramp-ways and running corridors, faster this time, as if he thought we should know our own way.

At the door to Glane's room, Skiy stopped. He chewed the black tallow out from under his nails. "Where's Kem?" he asked.

"Ministering in the children's ward," said Maelin.

"I have to talk to him." Skiy hurried away.

Maelin took a ring of keys from his belt, opened the door, and ushered me in. Glane sat at the writing desk against the wall, his back to me and his head down. The door closed behind me. It was time to say something.

"You have hair again," I said.

Glane jumped. He flapped and fell off his chair. I bent to help him. He skidded backwards under the desk and stared up with eyes that swirled from gold to turquoise every time he blinked. His hair stuck out from his head like a fan, interspersed with feathers. At least he had hair again, and fingers again, small as an infant's, clinging to the legs of the chair. "Who are you?" he demanded.

"Skiy told me you wanted—"

"Who are you?"

"Ksar—"

"You're not Ksar. You can't be. You're too boring."

I am rarely accused of being boring. It took me a long moment to think of a response. "I'm as boring as a singing pear," I said.

"You sound like Ksar."

"I am." Why did he have to be so suspicious? I wanted to throttle him. "I didn't have time to dress properly," I said, "that's all."

"I thought you had orange skin."

"Sometimes I do. But this is its real color." He knew that. He'd known me before the face paints.

Glane looked skeptical, but at last he came out from under the desk. "I never knew your hair was black," he said. His upper lip overshadowed his lower, hard as a beak. "It's very short. I never realized how short your hair was."

"You look a lot better," I told him.

"It's the medication. It makes my head leak, though." He waved at the basket beside him, overflowing with tissues.

"When will you be able to go home?"

"When I leave." He shrugged. "Birds aren't told."

"Oh." At least he wasn't pouting. But now that he wasn't, I wished he would. I wanted some proof that his face could move again. "Why did you want to see me?"

"I want my cobras back."

"You're sure you won't eat them?"

"I hope I won't." He sniffled.

"Where did you let them go?" Pigeons danced past the window. I wondered if pigeons would eat his snakes.

"Somewhere close to my house." He blew his nose on a handful of tissues. The tissue was already soaked. "Why are you still here?"

"Why shouldn't I be?"

"You should be looking for my cobras now."

"Er, all right." I headed for the door.

"Wait," said Glane.

"What?"

"Thank you for coming."

"Sure."

Pause.

"Wait," said Glane.

"What?"

"Do you want to bring your crystal wars set this evening?"

"Sure," I said, and waited to see if he would give me any more orders, but he only returned to blowing his nose, and so I left.

I stood in the hallway, listening to my heartbeats. Should I visit Gyanin? I was here and so I may as well. On the other hand, Gyanin and I had never exchanged more than a sentence or two in the years we'd known each other. A conversation with Gyanin might be comparable to talking with a broom. I decided against it. I did not want to talk to anyone. I did not ask for directions to the reception hall. I could find it myself.

I was tramping down a blue-carpeted passageway, dodging the trolleys of many a medical attendant, when I ran into Glane's father. He jumped backwards and clutched his chest.

"By Stone!" he said, "Ksar?" He stood on his toes to look into my face. "Time, Ksar, you're hardly recognizable."

This seemed to be the theme of the day: not being recognized. I decided not to be offended.

"Er," he said. "Were you visiting Glane?"

I said, "Yes."

"Where is his room?"

"Upstairs in the South Wing," I said, "somewhere."

"Can you show me?"

"No."

"I'm his father, Ksar." He drew himself up. He was shorter than Glane. His hair smelled of metal shavings, as if he'd been chewing on nails all day. "I expressly requested that you and your friends not commit Glane to the hospital, and what do you do? You do not even consult me. You don't even tell me his whereabouts. Am I not allowed to see my own son?"

"I didn't mean it like that."

"Oh? How did you intend it?"

"I'm trying to get out of here," I said, "but I'm lost. I don't know my way back to his room. Besides, I'm hungry. I have to go. Find a receptionist named Maelin. He knows about Glane. Ask him."

"Thank you," said his father, curtly. "You are always misguided, Ksar. If you used your head, you would treat me differently."

"Maybe." We parted ways. I bumbled off toward street level and the anticipation of something deep-fried for breakfast. I did not want to think about bees. I did not want to think about feathers, or sniveling Glane. It was only the medication, I told myself. He would not have been rude to me if not for the medication.

"Master Xavier?"

Blade sat in the alcove of the window. He held a plate of sugared kumquats on his lap. At the servant's voice, he turned.

"Your grandfather requests an audience."

"Now?"

"Yes. Immediately."

The servant held out a damp cloth. Blade wiped the sugar from his fingers. He set the kumquats on the floor beside him, slid from his seat and followed the servant up the twisting stairs of the palace spire. When other nobles ascended their spires, they needed to be carried. Their bulk would not allow them to climb. Blade could still run on his own. If he ate enough kumquats, he assured himself, he would lose the ability.

Outside the door to his grandfather's room, he stopped and adjusted his stance: shoulders back, stomach out. He thrust his stomach as far as it would go. It was almost visible, almost.

The door opened. Y'az Xzaven's attendants all wore blue bands on their arms. They bowed Blade into the sitting room. Three of the four walls were no more than gauze, a lacy division between themselves and the City. Y'az Xzaven reclined on a couch. Across the room reclined another noble: Y'az Tyfel, whom Blade had known all his life. Y'az Tyfel wore ivory robes. His beard formed two white braids down his chest. They smoked tea pipes and sipped fruit juice cordials, Tyfel and his grandfather. The smell of hibiscus and citrus filled the room.

"Xavier!" Y'az Xzaven waved him in. He rarely requested an audience.

"What is it, Grandfather?" Blade licked his lips. They tasted of kumquats.

Y'az Xzaven frowned. He poured tealeaf powder from the bowl of his pipe and said nothing.

"Do you want me to tell him?" said Tyfel.

"No, no." His grandfather toyed with the ring on his smallest finger. It bore an insignia shaped like a star. He looked up. His jaw set. "Xavier, a strange man came to the stables this morning."

Blade waited. He twisted his hands in his sleeves.

"He told me something about you, Xavier. I was happier before I knew." He paused. "When I go," he said, "when I die, I'm afraid I will not pass the family inheritance into your hands."

"What?" Blade forgot his pretended belly. "Why not?" he said. His voice squeaked.

"Because of a story that has recently been attached to you. Your involvement with theft, some years ago. I believe you know what I am referring to."

Blade did not understand immediately, but judging by his grandfather's glare he was supposed to know. He hung his head. He remembered the cylindrical room in the Marble Tower, the blossoming red feathers. He remembered the feel of a yellow tendril wrapping his hand and remembered how it came away, and the ring of blood that it left behind.

"It wasn't theft," said Blade. He would have laughed, if Tyfel and his grandfather had not looked so grave. How could they call it a theft? He had not hurt the feathers on purpose. If not for that day in the Tower, he would never have met Yaryk. He never would have made those friends. How could he regret it? "It wasn't a theft," he said again. "The Radiance's plume just—"

"Will you also tell me it was not a murder?"

"It wasn't! Gyanin—"

Y'az Xzaven held up a hand. "There was a body, and a missing artifact; the wanted posters covered the City. Now

I find my own house is involved? I don't want to know what happened, Xavier, and especially not your role in the affair. I am happier believing you an ignorant child, the one who did not know what he was doing, though I doubt this to have been the case. I don't want your image to sink any lower in my eyes."

Blade stared at the quivering gauze. He lowered his eyes. He could not keep the trill from his voice. "Who told you?" he said. "Who came to the stables? Was he also involved?"

"How should I know?"

"He didn't say?" said Blade.

"And admit himself a criminal? By Stone, Xavier, have you learned nothing from council meetings?" His grandfather snorted. "Now I see the company you've kept since your father died: thieves and murderers!"

"You're being hard on the boy." Y'az Tyfel tipped juice in his beard.

"You are a great disappointment, Xavier."

"I'm sorry." The smell of tealeaves nauseated Blade. He could not raise his eyes. "Grandfather?" he whispered, "who's going to inherit?"

"Your cousin Nazev."

"He's only ten!"

"He will be of age by the time I die." Y'az Xzaven blew smoke in the air, coiling and orange as a cloud of rust. "You should leave the City."

"Grandfather?"

"Travel."

First he was punished, and now rewarded? Blade stood in a daze. Swallows beat themselves against the gauze. "You're sending me away?" he faltered.

"I'm not 'sending you away,'" said his grandfather. "I'm encouraging your departure. Your friend also encouraged it, with less tact than I employ, and with certain threats as to what would happen if you did not leave."

"But where should I go?"

"Wherever you wish beyond the City walls. I will arrange for one of your servants to accompany you. I will give you sufficient money to speed you on your way."

"Grandfather—"

"Where is your gratitude!" Y'az Xzaven leaned forward. His jowls twitched. "You haven't been publicly disinherited. The populace has not been told. You are allowed to leave with an escort. An escort! This is great generosity in the face of your crime!"

"Grandfather—"

"This is childish, Xavier. In the name of Time, boy, this is for your own good. I will not lie to you. I don't know what would happen if you stayed in the City, if news of your involvement spread. Shame would descend. Shame for all of us. The end of the Ven family. Shame to all nobles, to have one of our numbers implicated in such a crime. The people would hate you. Elsewhere, in other cities, the nobles are losing their hold. Do you want that to happen to us? Foolishness, Xavier! Any man with wits would have left long ago, not loitered for three years and done nothing."

Y'az Tyfel leaned forward in turn. "Enough, Xzaven." He smiled at Blade. "You have no life sentence, Xavier. Matters will calm themselves. It will be safe to return before long. You may take my word."

"Can Yaryk come?" Blade sniffled. "Instead of a servant?"

Y'az Xzaven flashed his five-point ring. "Yes. Fine. By all means, rid the City of the wandering rogue. I don't doubt he's a criminal the same as you."

I returned home to find the front door locked. I never locked the door. I always hoped someone would infiltrate the house and steal Leque's clothes. Then he'd have to wear mine and that would be something to see. I unlocked the door and went in.

"Hello? Are you here, Leque?"

The curtain between the front room and bedroom twitched.

"Leque? Are you sure you're not here?"

"Ksar?"

"Who are you?" I shouted.

The curtain parted and one blue eye, red-rimmed, peered through the hanging cloth.

"Blade?" I said. "What are you doing in my house?"

He stuck his head through the curtain and blinked at me. His hair was tangled and his ermine cloak askew. "Is Leque here?"

"Obviously not, or I wouldn't be yelling for him."

"You look weird," said Blade.

"Everyone's telling me that. I'm not dressed properly, that's all."

Blade wormed up beside me, grabbed the front of my toga and pulled me into the bedroom. He wrestled the curtain closed behind us. It smelled like camel dung. Sure enough, in the oily, windowless light, the smoke of an incense wand trickled up from the floor. It rose to the ceiling and congregated there in a noisome pall.

"What are you doing here?" I fanned the smoke away from my face. "I can't sleep in a room that smells like this." I moved to open the curtain, but Blade jumped in front of me and blocked my way.

"My grandfather told me to leave the City." He wiped his nose with the back of his hand. "Someone's going to hurt me if I don't leave."

"Why are they going to hurt you?"

"I don't know, but my grandfather said that they are. He said I should leave the City for my own good." His lip quivered as if he might cry again, though it was hard to be sure in the gloom. "I want Yaryk to come with me, but I can't find him and I don't know where to look because he doesn't really have a house, he just wanders. But I need to leave now, and I don't know where to go, so I need to go with Leque. Do you know where Leque is? I need to find Leque."

There were red stripes down his cheeks, and I remembered how much I hated talking to people younger than me. I tended to treat them like rodents. "Leque works all day," I told him. "Of course he's not home. He's at the City gates right now, pretending to guard."

"I can't go to the gates! People will see me!"

"And people didn't see you coming here?"

Blade had nothing to say to that.

"Go wait in the other room," I told him.

"Why?"

"I'm going to take off these clothes and put on other clothes," I said. When he didn't react immediately, I said, "Please don't watch."

Blade stared at me for another second, then slunk out, sticking to the wall like shoe-tallow to Skiy's lungs, and I was left in peace to apply my lampshades and fishing hooks.

Evening came, but Leque did not. I wasn't worried — he never came home when he said he would — but I was annoyed. I couldn't prepare food. I'd never mastered the skill, so without my brother I tended to go hungry. I stood in the front room and stared out the window. The suns hung close today, pendulous as testicles. I remembered my promise to Glane.

In the bedroom, Blade lay spread-eagled on the floor between the beds.

"And I thought *I* was crazy," I said.

"This is the most hidden place in your house."

"Maybe," I said. "I would have thought *under* a bed would be better. Anyway, I'm going to the hospital now. You can come if you want, or you can stay here; it doesn't matter."

Blade's eyes protruded in the gloom. "You're leaving? What if they come looking for me?"

"I don't know who 'they' are," I said, putting on my sandals, "so I'm really not qualified to answer that question."

"You need to stay and protect me," he insisted.

"I'm as useful as a cucumber when it comes to protection." Strange, I thought. These were exactly the arguments I'd put to Leque. But Leque was obligated by family ties to protect me, whereas I had no responsibility for Blade. And Leque was actually capable of protecting people, whereas I was not. I had no idea what Blade was talking about, so I left and slammed the door behind me, locked it three times and secured the bolt.

The City was always quiet in the evenings, when the suns dipped down toward the horizon, painting the sky in greens, yellows and pinks, all running and streaking their way into crimson. A cool breeze blew, but the residual heat off the sandstone warmed the air. Soon the suns would be gone all together and lacewing frost would glaze the City for the night. During the dry season the cold of night could be deadly. Beggars turned up every morning, frozen like icicles. If you wanted to be out after dark, you had to run to keep warm. If you were lucky you'd only lose your ears and maybe some fingers. I wanted to make it home before frost. My visit to Glane would have to be brief. Either that, or I would have to spend the night in his room.

The hospital glowed like candlelight through the cracks of a skull. Inside the skull, the reception hall was more subdued than on my previous visits: a few emergencies on stretchers; Bedouin camps around the circle of the wall, the smoke from their fires channeled up through ventilation grates in the roof, into the sky beyond. I decided to brave the labyrinth unaided. I set off to find Glane's chamber without so much as a pause to catch my bearings.

After no more than a hundred wrong turns I reached the corridor in the South Wing. A fence had been stretched across the top of the stairs. It was only knee-high but I stopped. On the other side, the corridor twisted sharply to the right. Nothing was visible beyond the fence. Voices muttered, and that was all. I stood and glared at the barrier.

Maelin appeared from around the bend. He stopped. "This hallway is restricted," he said.

"Glane invited me."

"I'm sorry," he said, "this is a very bad time."

Skiy appeared beside him. The cobbler's face was pale as salt. "Oh," he said, "it's Ksar." The skin around his eyes was swollen, pink and moist as an under-cooked sausage.

I stepped over the fence. "What's going on?"

Skiy turned away. His shoulders jumped. "Gyanin is dead."

6

I told Skiy I hadn't heard him.

"Gyanin is dead," he said again.

I stepped forward. I gaped, I could tell. If Leque had been there, he would have told me to close my mouth. Down the hallway, Kem stood amid a cluster of hospital-workers, all with their heads bowed. In the middle of the cluster lay a stretcher on wheels. Yellow-green feathers littered the floor, a lurid pink here and there among them.

A hospital attendant, possibly Maelin, stuck out an arm and I stopped. I could see above the heads of the cluster. The thing on the stretcher could not be Gyanin. It could not be him. It was no more than a mass of plumage, a sprawling wreck. Appendages hung over the sides of the cot and onto the floor. At one end was something that might once have been a head. It lay at an angle so I could not see the face. I didn't want to look closer but I did all the same. I gaped at the cot. The head dripped moisture, as if this creature had baptized itself, or attempted to drink, or fallen head-first into the wash basin and not stood up.

The cluster around the stretcher argued. "No," said one worker, "we can't leave the body here overnight. Have you seen the state of the room? We must begin the steriliza-tion process immediately if it's going to be fit for a new patient in the morning."

Another worker jabbed his finger at the stretcher. "How do we get this down to the morgue without public notice? Hardly a sight to reassure the patients."

"It is better to move it now than in the morning," said Kem, who stood with his back to me. "The hospital is quiet now. Cover the stretcher in a blanket. We..."

I edged around the cluster with my fingers in my ears. I did not want to hear what they said. I hurried to Glane's door and knocked.

Someone behind me, who may have been Maelin, said, "It's locked. Here." A hand reached under my armpit, stuck a key in the keyhole and turned.

I didn't say, "Thank you." I went in and closed the door behind me.

Glane sat on the bed, blowing his face. I can't say nose, because his nose seemed to have disappeared again since my visit that morning. The basket of used tissues had been replaced by a barrel. I hated this room. Green-orange matting glazed the floor. I prodded the weave with my toe.

"You look worse," I said.

"You look like Ksar," he said. "That's bad enough." His voice rippled. The pitch rose and fell, gargled. I had to strain to understand.

I sat down on the bed and took our crystal wars sets from my pocket. I marked the ring of combat with a length of string and dumped my crystals in the middle. I handed Glane his bag of pieces and he did the same. I set the white pebble on the mattress beside us. When my turn came, I would aim the white pebble, drop it, and hope to knock Glane's crystal men out of the ring. Of course on his turn he would do the opposite and aim at my men. Whoever lost all their men first was the loser. Glane and I played crystal wars often.

"Ksar?"

"Yes?"

"What's going on out there?"

"I don't know. Nothing." I didn't want to think about Skiy or the thing on the stretcher. Over the City, frost would be settling soon. "Did your father come and see you?" I asked.

"Yes," said Glane. The combat ring reflected upside-down in his eyes. The crystals cast glowing shadows on the blanket. "I told him about the Radiance."

"What?"

"The Radiance. I told him we broke the crest and the monk fell over the railing."

"Leque's going to kill you." I mouthed at him, looking for words. "We're not supposed to talk about it."

Glane was silent.

"Why did you tell him? Did he ask you?"

"No."

"Then why?"

"I'm going to die!" Glane pounded his wing on the pillow. "I'm full of chemicals. That's the only reason I'm still alive. Maybe Gyanin didn't take his properly!"

Or maybe he killed himself, I thought. "Who says Gyanin's dead?" I snapped.

"You didn't say it, but you should have. I heard Skiy when he came. He cried so loud you could have heard him from the Tower. He wouldn't stop crying. Do you know I'm locked in here to die?"

"Feathers won't kill you," I said. "Think of all the birds in the City. They survive with feathers. But you shouldn't have told your father about it."

"He's my father and I'm going to die!" screamed Glane. "You don't care." He lunged. His wings dug into my neck. "We've all been starving — my family — but you didn't notice that, did you? We haven't had gold now for over a year! You don't care! You're not telling me anything! Why won't you tell me anything?"

Feathers swam in my brain. They were blue. "Glane—" I couldn't speak. He strangled my breath.

Glane sniffed and rattled. Mucus ran down the sides of his beak in glistening streams. "You don't tell me anything! Why don't you tell me what's going on? I don't know what's going on. Do you think that's funny? Are you trying to laugh? Are you trying..."

I was trying to breathe.

He pushed me into the rail of the bed, so hard that the barrier snapped. My head hit the floor and the world swam black, then purple, then clear and bright. The feathers retreated from my neck. I scrambled for the door. I turned the handle. It was locked and it did not turn.

"Hello!" I coughed, shouted, pounded. "Hello? Let me out!" No answer. The party had dispersed. My throat burned. I sank to the floor and sat with my back against the wall.

When I dared to look up, Glane was sitting on the bed, blowing his nonexistent nose as if nothing had happened. He blinked. The action engulfed his face. "Well?" he said, innocent. "Are you ready to play?"

We played crystal wars while the mucus streamed down Glane's face. His eyes vibrated. He scratched them to make them stop, and they leaked red tears. No sound of rescue could be heard from outside. I let him win. We played a second game. I let him win again. I was afraid to do otherwise. The side of my head throbbed.

The doorknob turned. Kem came in with a metal box. "Ksar?" He blinked at me. "What are you doing here?"

I swung off the bed and ran for the door. "I'm leaving," I said. "Goodbye."

"Wait! Ksar!" Kem dropped his box. It crashed on the floor. He ran after me. "Ksar, where are you going? You don't have to leave." He caught my sleeve and whirled me around. "Glane's lucky to have you as a friend," he said. "Staying all night and playing crystal wars. How is he doing?"

"He tried to kill me!" I pulled away. "I couldn't get out of the room!"

"He tried to kill you?" Kem's skin was a perfect olive. "Ksar, are you all right?"

"He tried to strangle me." I batted him away. I would not let him pat my shoulder. "Strangle me, do you understand? I'm not hurt. He didn't kill me, but he tried!"

Kem shook his head. "We must adjust his medication. If he tried to harm even you, his closest..."

"I'm not his friend," I shouted. I could still feel Glane's claws eating into my jugular. Human beings should not have claws. "He's turning into a bird. I hate birds. I hate him and I'm leaving."

"Ksar! Stop!" Kem ran after me as far as the top of the stairs, before he remembered the open door of Glane's room and ran back.

I could hear his footsteps disappearing as I crashed down the stairs. I didn't know where I was going. I didn't know how the hospital worked — all carpeted halls, here and there a torch, not many. I ran for as long as I could, until everything launched into acrobatics, and I stopped and leaned against a wall and wrestled the oxygen back into my lungs. I didn't want Glane's medication to be adjusted. He'd already complained. I didn't want to make it worse. I didn't want him to be punished. I didn't want Kem and all the hospital angry, viewing Glane as a social danger, chaining him to his bed and feeding him through a chink in the door while the feathers spread, erupted, devoured the room, spilled through the window, burst through the glass, cut off the circulation to his arms and hands, numbed his fingers, claws, whatever they were, until they dropped off and he ate them. I didn't want to know about the metal box, the one Kem carried. I didn't want to know what pills and needles it might contain. All I wished was that Glane had never existed.

I didn't cry. My mind was full of Glane and there was no room for anything else. I didn't have the energy for tears. I didn't want to think about Gyanin, and the twisted thing on the stretcher that had once been him. I didn't want to think about Glane but I could not stop. Didn't he remember our friendship from over the years? I had helped him with his cobras; I had dragged him back from the edge of his flying experiments. Now the old Glane was dead. Bury it, I thought. Bury the squawking remains before they hurt me more. I didn't want to see him, not ever again. Never. It was too hard. I wanted to vomit.

I wandered until I found the reception hall. It was almost morning. The Bedouin camps stirred into life; hospital workers trickled in for the day; and the world outside faded into dawn.

I wove my way home. I prayed Leque would be there with breakfast waiting.

Leque was not home. Curtains still covered the window. The door was still locked, and, by all the signs when I pounded, barricaded from the inside.

"Blade!" I pounded harder. The door rattled. Something buzzed in the eaves. "Blade, what in—"

Bees. They streamed from the eaves. They poured from around the door, out from the hinges, out from under the mat at my feet. They crawled from everywhere, drunken-wobbling, buzzing in circles and pirouettes around my head.

I flailed and screamed. They dove in my mouth. I swallowed them whole. Their wings and legs and poison stingers scored my throat and burrowed deep into my stomach. They swarmed my wig. I tore it off and threw it on the ground. The bees buried themselves in its scarlet curls.

"Kill!" I screamed, but no sound came out. I jumped on the wig with both feet. I stamped and kicked. My feet were on fire. They burned. Wings, intestines, twitching legs, all spilled across the stone. The wig was alive. It spat its organs, burning.

I grabbed the wig. I flung it in the air. It sailed over the roof, still buzzing.

I turned back to the door. It was hard to find the handle through the murk. A face disappeared from the window. Curtains swished. It was Blade.

My feet swelled. I knew they were swelling. My skin would burst. I would spill my guts like the bees. I swelled all over. I slumped to my knees and fell against the door.

"For the love of anything!" The words came out slurred. My tongue was too big for my mouth. My lips were bloated. It was hard to breathe. My throat closed off. "Please! Blade! I'm dying!"

The door opened. Hands grabbed the back of my toga and dragged me in. The door slammed on my foot in a shower of pain. "Cut it off!" I wanted to scream. "Cut off my foot! Someone!"

"You are the greatest fool I have ever seen." That was Yaryk's voice, close to my ear. "There's always a reason for barricaded doors, Ksar, son of Qual. You fool! If you had succeeded in breaking in, all three of us would have been killed."

I muttered through swollen lips: "I'm dying." The world distended, red. I thought I saw trees through the scarlet haze. Nothing made sense. Buzzing. I heard Blade crying.

"I want Leque," I said.

"He's not here," said Yaryk. "He hasn't been here since yesterday morning."

I tried to speak but my tongue expanded to the roof of my mouth. It lolled down my chin. The words could not get out.

"Is he dying?" said Blade's voice.

"He's eating the floor." Yaryk dripped disgust. "He'll suffocate unless we turn him over."

They rolled me on my back. Yaryk's beard brushed my cheek, like the tendrils of an electric jellyfish. I whimpered and Blade whimpered back. More trees danced around me. Two lines of trees.

"Are they still there?" Yaryk demanded.

"What?"

"The bees. Are they gone?"

I shook my head against the floor.

"Wait here," Yaryk's voice told Blade. Light spilled over me as the door opened, and then darkness again as it shut. "It's safe now," said Yaryk. "Have you got everything?"

"Yes," said Blade.

"The blankets?"

"Yes."

"Bring more," said Yaryk. "The ones from Leque's bed as well. It is cold on the open roads."

"Yes, Yaryk."

"And wipe your eyes," said Yaryk.

They talked. Their voices smeared around and through me. Maybe Yaryk explained something, or maybe he only accused people of stupidity — again and again. He wasn't talking to me, whatever he said, and I could hear nothing but my breath as it moaned in my throat. Oozing volcanoes in my throat. I'm dying, I thought. Here we go, I'm dying. Off to the trees in the sky. I can see them — red, orange, black-veined and cutting my face. I wanted to wave a hand and fend them away — these trees of death. I could not move. Why were there trees?

Yaryk did not forget me for long. He seized me around the waist. His shoulder bit into my stomach. I jolted as he walked. He carried and dragged me. Light burned into my eyes. Oh Stone, it burned.

It went black. It was black a long time, and then gray. The floor was hard. I smelled tallow. I smelled leather, dirt and tack nails. The odors of incense and books wreathed the air. I smelled my columbine perfume. It reeked out of place and choked me.

I tried to say, "Skiy." It came out as nothing. I would scream if I could. "I smell you, Skiy!"

"We're leaving the City," said Yaryk's voice, faint through the buzz in my throat.

Another voice spoke, and Yaryk laughed in reply. Footsteps retreated, a door, and then silence.

I waited in the leaves. Lines of saplings. Where had they come from? I waited to be lifted off the floor. Maybe they would tell me the color of my feathers. Maybe they could bring me a pillow, couldn't they? No. They couldn't. I tried to wonder who would next become a bird — Kem, or Skiy or someone else — but then the trees came in with a vengeance. I blinked and it all went black and pitched away and I could not catch it.

7

The smell of Skiy's shop disappeared a long time before the dream began.

Saplings with leaves of yellow and red stood in lines, one to either side of me. The wind raised the feathers on my back and bent the saplings double so they swept the ground. The ground was gray marble. Pistachios and peaches hung from their twigs. The fruit was unripe. It blew in the wind and rolled off onto the stone.

Liquid shone to either side of the trees, a substance that reflected a bloody sky. It reflected the leaves upside-down. Three suns hung low, two of them faded to gray. The third sun bled. Steam rose up from the sea. It stank of boiling salt.

I stood. Feathers weighed my back. They clung to my shoulders. I raised my hand to my face and found that I had no hand. I had claws like Glane's. I felt Glane standing behind me. I did not turn. I knew he was not really there. It was part of the dream. He was back in the hospital, wasn't he? Something stood behind me. I did not dare turn. I knelt, hard marble. I was afraid to look up. I was afraid to look around.

"Why did you run away?" said Glane's voice. He sniffed and coughed behind me. "You abandoned me there and the door was locked. I couldn't leave, Ksar."

"You're out now," I said.

Glane's voice: "I flew. I broke the glass in the window and flew with the pigeons, down the aisles of the wind and here I am."

"Am I dead?" I asked. "Is this what happens?"

"No."

"Am I a bird?"

"Yes," said Glane, "like me." His voice slurred. I knew he was pouting behind me, if birds can pout. I still could not turn.

"I was given the choice of death," he said. "I could have hit the cobblestones and died like the parrot. I could have let my eyes fall out and roll to the acid. But then I remembered, Ksar, that here at the beginning of ruination there is no acid. Not yet. I came to see you instead." Claws touched my shoulder. They could have been my own. "You won't even look at me," said the voice of Glane. "Why won't you look at me?"

The wind increased. It pulled at my feathers and churned them into my face. I bent my head. I could not shield myself against the quills. The marble ground reflected red from the sky. The third sun would fall. The wind pushed me. I pitched forward and lay on my face. I had no hands to catch my fall.

I lay for hours. Skiy's voice spoke above me. "Look, Ksar," he said.

"No."

"Get up and look," said Skiy. "It's safe now. Glane is gone."

I sat up and turned. The pistachio saplings were ripped raw, naked of leaves. The wind scorched my face. No Skiy. I turned in a circle. A tree with yellow bark stood beside me, a thousand times taller than the saplings. It had not been there before. A ladder leaned against its trunk.

"I read a book about a tree of power," said the voice of Skiy, beside me now. "People climbed its branches to pick its fruit. If they found their way down, they became the fathers of kings and warlords."

"Why would you want to sire kings?" Yaryk's laughter floated in the air. "Why not be one?"

Kem's voice lilted from somewhere. I could not understand what he said. Leque and Blade drifted in on the wind. They were too far away. The branches of the tree braided up to the sky.

"Where is the fruit?"

"You have to climb," said Skiy.

I crawled to the ladder. My feathers were black. I gripped the ladder with my claws. I watched them uncoil, wrap, clench as I climbed. At the top of the ladder the branches wove themselves into a platform. I lay down on my back. The tree smelled of linseed oil, sharp and old. I did not understand the smell. Clusters of fruit hung motionless, out of my reach. The branches ran circles around me, into the distance, broad as the roads of the City. Footprints marked the limbs.

"Who was here?" I asked, but Skiy said nothing. "Skiy?" I said. He did not answer.

I chose a branch and began to crawl. The golden fruit glowed out of reach. The branch spiraled. I could not reach the fruit, glowing like apples, pomegranates, pears and nectarines, golden globes at the top of the world. The branches twined like stairways, merged and crossed in a dizzying mesh. The footprints led me on. A hundred men had come this way; and none had returned. One set of tracks had only four toes. I dug in my claws and I climbed. The other branches dropped away. I climbed toward a lone pinnacle. Below, the rest of the tree seemed to writhe like a nest of straw. My feathers now stank of linseed.

At last I reached the top of the branch. Skeletons covered the platform. I sat in my linseed-feathers and stared at the bodies. Wake up, I told myself. That was all I could think. I closed my eyes and pictured the kebab stand at the end of my road. I pictured the owner, a man with one arm, cutting the meat as the silver flies licked his ears. It made no difference. I opened my eyes; I was still in the tree. The skulls of the skeletons grinned in my face. Twigs as fine as fiber wove up from the branch and held the bones fixed — a band around the neck, another through the cage of the ribs, around the ankles. The golden fruit glowed in their mouths, pear-shaped to fit so perfectly in the human hand. I did not touch them. Crowns draped the skeletal necks. Rings shone like mist on their fingers. Here was the signet of nobility, there the badge of an emperor, and there a commoner with fishing nets snagged on his arms.

Overhead, the red sun dipped lower. It bled in torrents.
Feathers rained down. They burned the ocean. Far below,
the gray steam rose and the surface roiled. Great monsters
breached the surface, all tails and bulbous heads. Their fins
struck out and flailed like wish chimes caught in the wind.
They died on the surface, black-burnt and thrashing. They
bellowed. I covered my ears, but my claws dug into my
head and I cried. I cried for an explanation. I cried for Leque
to save me.

Snakes as long as the Marble Tower knotted on the
surface, intertwined and lay still. Turtles the diameter of
the City walls made reeking islands. Their shells split open.
White meat spilled and cooked. Fish erupted. Their scales
fell away. The acid ate into their bones.

Below, small in the midst of death, stood the two lines
of saplings. My eyes stung. The saplings' stone ridge
seemed to rise through the air, out of the sea toward me.
The platform tilted and the skeletons danced, crazy-jerked
in their bindings. I dug in my claws and clung there,
vertical. Where was Leque? Come and peel me out of this
dream, Leque, please, like you helped me down from the
wall behind our house when I was seven, like you doused
my hair when I set it on fire, like you always came when
I needed you most.

The sun went down in blood feathers beside me. The
light diminished. It reeked of sickness. The other two suns
glared pewter through the pall of steam.

The world groaned. The saplings rose vertically beside
me. The marble walk folded in like the walls of a tower.
The marble pressed in on the tree, absorbed the branches,
pressed them into stairs and passageways. The twigs and
fibers disappeared into the marble. They pulsed in yellow
bands. I knew those veins from the Tower.

The skeletons chattered. They lolled their heads as if
drunk. The acid hissed and stank below. It was coming to
devour me, here in the Marble Tower at the beginning of
the world. The world should have ended here.

"Skiy!" I shouted. "Where are you, Skiy?" Did he know
this was how it began? Did he know the Marble Tower rose

up from the sea? Did he know about the Tree of Power? Your precious Tree of Power, Skiy. Just let me out. Neck of a zebra! Where was my brother?

My claws tore free of the bark. I fell and fell. I was going to die. The City I knew did not even exist. The smell of burnt turtles filled my nose. Stone closed in around me. The world was black. I smelled the acid. I smelled the sweat and feathers, the rubber of the burning meat, the linseed stench I could not escape. My wings beat the air and I fell.

8

All the smells disappeared except the stink of burnt sweat. I rolled my head. I was lying on stone. I could not get away from the smell. I moaned. Something caught in my mouth. Oh Stone, I thought, I'm a skeleton with golden fruit in my mouth.

It tasted more like wet rag. I twitched my hand to move it away, whatever it was, but my arm was too heavy. At least I no longer had feathers.

"Ksar?" Kem's voice came from nowhere. It came at me hard and sudden. Smoke filled my head. Exhaustion riddled his voice. He sounded like an empty corridor in the hospital. I wondered if his voice was disembodied, like Skiy's and Glane's in my dream. I wanted to cry. I never wanted to hear Glane again, or feel that crushing terror, as I had on the aisle of saplings.

"Ksar?" Kem again. Something squeezed my hand. Don't leave, I thought. Please don't leave. I'm not another dying patient. I'm Ksar, remember? I've been so frightened. Of course he remembered my name. Kem remembered everything. I envied his calm.

I twitched my fingers.

Kem's hand squeezed harder. "Ksar, wake up."

I moved my tongue. The swelling had decreased, but my mouth was still hard and dry. It tasted of rotted fruit and fishmongers' hands. "Get the thing off my face," I croaked. "I can't breathe."

Kem removed the rag. He was haggard in the gloom. He looked down at me. "Is that better?"

I nodded. I lay on my spine in the back room of Skiy's shop. I recognized the shelves, bending in around me,

overflowing with tools, rolls of leather and books. Somewhere on one of those shelves hid the crest of the Radiance. I couldn't remember which shelf it was. It was here
we met and sniffed dung in the darkness. The room looked
strange in the light. The light flowed in blinding from the
doorway to the rest of the shop. The room seemed lonely
and over-large with only Kem and I here — not Leque, or
Glane, or anyone else.

"Is it too bright?" said Kem. "Skiy insisted on airing the
room, though I thought..."

I lolled my head on the stone. No, it was fine.

It hurt to speak, but I could not stand the confusion.
"Why don't I have feathers?"

"I don't know," said Kem.

"What happened to me after the bees?"

"You passed out."

"I know I passed out. What happened?"

"Yaryk and Blade brought you here," said Kem, "to
Skiy's shop." His brows drew together like a thin black
walkway over his nose. "Can you see? Your eyes have
undergone considerable swelling."

"Of course I can see," I snapped. "I know where I am."

Kem sat back on his heels. He chewed the inside of his
mouth and gazed out to the rest of the shop.

"Where's Leque?" I said.

"Sorry?" said Kem.

"Where's Leque? Where are Yaryk and Blade?" My feet
burned in a quiet, disgruntled fashion.

"They've left the City." He glanced away, then back at
my face. I was no longer interesting now that I was out
of danger.

"Really left?" I said.

Kem nodded.

"Did Yaryk say when they're coming back?"

"I think he plans not to return."

"What about Leque?"

"I don't know about Leque. No one knows where he
is." Kem's eyelids drooped. I was not sure he could see
me. He repeated my questions before responding. When
had he lost all this sleep?

"Where's Gyanin?" I asked.

"Gyanin? Gyanin is dead. I thought you—"

"I know, but where is he?"

"We've taken him to the sea," said Kem. "The Ceremony of Release was two days ago."

"What?"

"The day before yesterday. We would have waited for you, but the body was beginning to smell. We had to Release him."

"Where's Skiy?" I asked, after a pause during which I could not remember his name. "He hasn't disappeared too, has he?"

"Skiy? Disappeared? No, he's out in the front of the shop, dealing with a customer. He hasn't disappeared."

I couldn't think of another question. Kem helped me sit up.

"We've adjusted Glane's medication," he said. "His behavior has stabilized, even if his outward appearance has not."

I held my jaw tight and said nothing. All I could see were blue feathers and mucus rivulets. I didn't want to know what Kem meant — about his "outward appearance." I didn't want to know about Glane.

Kem brought me a bowl of mashed mangos and another of camel fodder soup. He helped me drip the slime in my mouth. I had to swallow on my own, though, unaided, and that was the most difficult part, to force the food past the bags of pebbles in my throat.

After I'd eaten, Kem hauled me into a chair with wheels. "I borrowed it from the hospital," he explained, as if I had asked.

He wheeled me out of the incense den. I could not walk. My feet were still twice their normal size. Sitting on them helped. It rendered them numb so I could not feel the burning.

Out in the front of the shop Skiy was not, in fact, helping a customer. Neither was he reading. He sat on the floor behind his workbench, cluttered with half-finished shoes. A tallow wand smoked in the corner of his mouth. He stared at the opposite wall. Now and then his eyes twitched.

Kem wheeled me past without a word, out the front door. We stopped beneath the striped awning. Kem wedged me between two display tables.

"You won't roll away," he told me. He sat down on the ground beside my chair.

"What's wrong with Skiy?" I asked.

"He has suffered from depression since Gyanin's death. We must be sympathetic. He has lost a best friend."

I saw the bait but I did not take it. I sat with my arms in my lap. If I closed my eyes, I thought I would tip over backwards, as if I were on the platform of branches at the end of the world. I tried not to think of the tree. It was only a dream, I told myself, but the only alternative for thought was the real world. Everything had fallen apart. Kem alone was untouched. Everyone else was insane or gone. Except that Kem had to look after us now, Glane and Skiy and myself. All of our lives had been ruined.

"Ksar," said Kem, "do you want to talk?"

I shook my head.

"Not about Glane? He asked to see you."

I turned away and ignored him. I could not talk of Glane. I had known Glane for years. Or perhaps I had only known *of* him for years. I thought I'd known who he was, what he would do, how he always behaved. How stupidly he always acted. I'd known he was stupid, but I hadn't known he was dangerous. Perhaps I didn't know him at all, had been wrong all this time. I didn't want to talk.

People passed on the street and stared. People always stared at me. But why now? I had no wig, not even a pillowcase or a lamp on my head.

"Am I ugly, Kem?"

He looked at me and pursed his lips. "Your appearance is as to be expected from one recovering from severe facial injury. Not to fear; the scars will become less pronounced with time."

"Everyone's looking at me."

"You don't like it?" Kem yawned and stood up. "Don't worry." He stepped around me into the shop. He was gone for several minutes. Everyone stared at me. I couldn't even see myself to join in the fun. One boy screamed and darted

behind his father's legs. He peered back at me with eyes
the size of camel hooves. My discomfort was almost
worthwhile if I could elicit such a desperate response.
Except that it wasn't.

Kem returned. He handed me a mirror. He sat down
on the edge of a table. I looked in the glass. My face was
a war zone of welts. I looked like a butcher's shop. I smiled.
The reflection did not smile back.

"Oh. Very funny." I passed the mirror back to Kem.
"What are you doing here?" I asked him.

"Doing here? What do you mean?"

"Why aren't you at the hospital?"

"I filed for a leave, due to unexpected circumstances.
I'm staying here to look after you and Skiy. Now that you
have regained consciousness, however, I shall probably
return to work."

"Why do you care?" I said. "You didn't even know me
five years ago."

"Of course I care about you, Ksar."

He cared about everyone. I hated him for it. He had not
even answered my question. Kem dropped his chin to his
chest and dozed. I let him sleep. I would have to wake him
up eventually, before my bladder exploded. For now he
could sleep.

9

"Yaryk, is it true that acid trolls used to roam on the highroads?"

"It is," said Yaryk. He walked ahead. Blade crawled behind, over the roadway-hammock of skins. Pillars of glass jutted out of the acid. The long skin bridges swayed between them, spotted like leopards and leaping deer. "It was a long time ago that the trolls roamed free," said Yaryk. He glanced over his shoulder as he spoke. He betrayed no fear of losing his balance, falling and burning below. "When humans were still a minority in the world," he said, "the trolls roamed free. We grew and expanded, however, and drove the trolls to inhabit the reefs and their numbers dwindled."

"I thought they lived *in* the acid," said Blade.

"For a short period of time, a few hours, they could tolerate the acid. But they could not live there." Yaryk reached the end of the bridge and stepped back onto stone. They had walked stone paths since leaving the City. "The reefs are a dangerous habitat. The land shifts every season. You cannot make a map of the reefs."

Blade scrambled after him, onto the solid ground. Yaryk handed Blade a flask of water and he drank. He wanted to pour it over his face, let it soothe the burning peel of his skin, but he'd been warned against waste. They could not risk traveling without water, Yaryk said, and wells on the highroads were few and far between. It was expensive to barter for water, and folly to admit your oversight.

"What happened to the acid trolls, Yaryk? Are they still in the reefs?"

"No." Yaryk laughed. "Mankind has pressed them to extinction. After the fall of the sun, we thought for a time we were doomed. But the years passed and we realized that although the sea level had risen and the life-giving water was gone, we could still travel. We trafficked again, not by ship but by foot, as you and I do now. We multiplied again and the troll race diminished. We encroached on their lairs, burned and smoked them out, and carved their teeth and hearts into hunting trophies."

"My grandfather has a troll heart," said Blade, "as a family heirloom. It would have been given to me when I came into my inheritance." He swallowed. It was hard to swallow, his mouth was so dry. "I don't know what I would have done with it, anyway."

"After the troll itself has died," said Yaryk, "the heart continues to pulse for thousands of years, though there is no longer blood to circulate. If you are wounded, holding a troll's heart to your injury can postpone your death until aid arrives."

"Is that why they're so valuable?"

"In part. The respect is more important though. Anyone who possesses the heart of an acid troll commands great respect."

The heat rose in sheets from the road, wave after wave. It rippled on the surface of the acid. During the night its warmth was appreciated, but now, during the day, it burned like animal fat in a fire. The heat was unbearable. It stank. Blade's robe fanned around him. He wore an old robe of Yaryk's. It was too long and it tripped his feet.

"Yaryk, can we slow down?" he said. "Please? I'm tired."

"The people of the open road do not use that word," said Yaryk, "*tired*. Bedouin do not tire easily." He slowed to let Blade keep pace.

No sign of civilization could be seen in any direction. The hide bridges stretched behind, strung out as far as Blade could see. Ahead was the ridge of stone they walked, dark as a line of soot to the horizon. It seemed to hover over the sea, or dip beneath it in places. That was only illusion. *Mirage*, Yaryk called it. Yaryk had warned him of mirages. Keep to the middle of the road, he said, not the sides. With enough exhaustion, you may not see the embankment until you reach the bottom. By then it would be too late.

Here and there a pillar twisted up from the sea. Ropes hung from some of the columns, burnt at the ends like dead worms. Blade wondered who had strung those bridges — had the courage to climb out and tie those ropes — and why the paths had now fallen away. Where had they led? How long ago? Yesterday he had seen a bird atop one of the pillars. He thought about Glane and shivered.

"Is that a scarlet roc?" he asked Yaryk.

Yaryk had laughed and said, "No."

They had come six days from the City now. Blade estimated six. On the first day they passed other travelers — fishermen, messengers, Bedouin. But now Yaryk led them down smaller roads, all deserted. Now and then they passed an old man with a wheelbarrow, or a huddle of naked worshippers around a cairn. Yaryk ignored them all.

He draped an arm around Blade's shoulders and pointed to the stone at their feet. "Do you see those marks, Blade, like craters? Do you know what causes them?"

Blade shook his head.

"The highroads are treacherous in the rainy season." Yaryk's elbow dug into Blade's shoulder. "When the clouds come, they bring with them ash and sparks, sand and even gravel. The gravel gouges the road, falling from so great a height."

"We're going to stop before the rainy season, aren't we?"

"Indeed yes." Yaryk withdrew his arm. "With the rain, in places the sea level rises to eclipse the road. We would not want to be trapped here then."

"Why don't the roads dissolve?" Blade was thirsty again. He would not tell Yaryk. He had already drunk more than his share of the water, yet Yaryk never complained. When *did* the Bedouin drink? When would he show fatigue? Blade struggled to match his pace.

"These roads are not stone," said Yaryk, "but glass. Glass does not dissolve in acid. The fish, too, use glass. Their scales are made of it."

"What about fishing nets?" Blade peeled his tongue from the roof of his mouth.

"The fishermen weave their nets from the roots of the glass weed. Yet even the most resilient lines will fray after a week's use, for nothing can deny the sea forever."

For six days, Blade had been listening to Yaryk. He tried to ignore the sun's burn, the sand that whipped and filled his eyes, the blisters that flowered on his feet where his shoes rubbed thin. He tried not to notice as the straps of his pack dug into his shoulders. He knew he had the lighter load — nothing but blankets — while Yaryk carried food, water, and whatever other valuables he owned. Blade tried to ignore the constant throb in his spine and the way it burned at the end of the day.

"Look." Yaryk pointed. "Crossroads ahead."

Blade squinted. All he could see was the glare.

"If we had kept to the main roads, it would have been days yet before we reached this point," said Yaryk. "Come. We have made good time, and now perhaps we will gather some news for our travels."

Blade was too tired to ask. He dragged his feet as Yaryk walked faster. He all but ran to keep up. The road turned and turned, like a snake. Ahead, even Blade could see the crossroads now, where a score of paths converged. They formed a plateau the size of a market square in the City. Carts and messenger chariots milled about in the open, camel trains and men with all their possessions heaped on their backs. Blade clung to Yaryk's sleeve, afraid to lose him in the press.

On the far side of the crossroads, one cart towered over the others. The vehicle was enormous, shapeless, thatched in furs from which tusks protruded, or the faces of great cats and other animals Blade did not recognize, all stretched to fit the frame, their mouths and eyes open and empty. A group of men leaned against the cart. They ate red watermelon. The fruit smelled out of place, here in the middle of sweat and acid. Blade peered around for the vendor. He had not had fruit in days. Yaryk elbowed his way to the cluster of men. They wore hide skirts. The suns had burned their skin ocher, almost purple from the hours of exposure.

"Greetings," said Yaryk.

One of the men looked up. He spat the black seeds at Yaryk's feet. "Ah," he said. "I remember you. From the City, no? You've come a long way."

"I have," said Yaryk. "You're on your way to the Errata?"

"We are," said the smuggler. He spat at Blade. "Your son, is it? A slave boy, maybe? Where are you going?"

"The Citadel."

"Hah! I thought we agreed that would not be wise."

"My affairs in the City have changed," said Yaryk. "Perhaps I do not intend to stay in the Citadel for long. Or perhaps I do. I will see."

The smuggler peeled himself from the side of the cart. "You may travel with us until we turn for the Errata."

"I am honored." Yaryk bowed.

The smuggler pushed his watermelon rind into Blade's hands. "You had best accustom yourself to the smell of hides, boy."

10

I stood on the spiraled stairs, blocking the flow of traffic, and regarded the pool of acid at my feet. My own face stared back. Most of the scabs had peeled away now, leaving only white marks like crystal pieces under my skin. Pistachio trees shimmered behind me. I imagined them reflected in an ocean of water, sometime before the third sun fell, and imagined the saplings standing in lines.

Wish papers waved from every side. How many years had it been since I hung a wish? Or maybe I never had. I had always left the wishing to Glane. If I could hang one now, it would say that I wanted Leque home.

As it was, I didn't have a home; Kem and Skiy passed me back and forth. I didn't know which house to dread more. Kem's was clean and close to the hospital. It smelled of disinfectant and needles. I had never minded the smell in the past, but now I hated it. I hated the thought of the hospital. It stank like rotten eggs in my mind. Skiy's shop, on the other hand, stank of grease and nails. The clutter ebbed and flowed like the tide. It waxed and waned. I dreamed of death, of being eaten by bins of nails and strangled in shoelaces. Skiy sat and stared at blank walls. He inhaled more incense than a tanning factory.

Some days I escaped to the Marble Tower. Perhaps one day I would hang my wishes for Leque. Perhaps I never would.

"A beautiful shade of chartreuse, is it not, my son?" said a voice.

A monk stood on the step below me with his hands in the sleeves of his habit. His head, shaved, reached only my elbow. His beard stuck out from his chin in wiry braids.

"The pool," he said, by way of explanation, "is it not a beautiful hue?"

"Beautiful," I said. I squinted at the acid, looking for the beauty.

"It would seem, my son," said the monk, "that you have a great appreciation for enlightenment."

I changed my mind. If I could hang a wish right now, it would be for all the monks in the Tower to select a balcony and jump.

"I have seen you at the Tower many times," said my new acquaintance. "You bask in the atmosphere of wisdom, do you not?"

"Yes," I said. "I love basking."

"Your friend has not accompanied you of late," said the monk.

I leaned my head against a branch and said nothing.

"I see you are troubled. Does the absence of your companion trouble you? Do you suffer an illness? Some other misfortune?"

I smiled to myself. How would Leque enjoy this? Here I stood conversing with a monk. The monks of the Tower had noticed our visits all along.

"Illness is no cause for depression, my son." His robe was so green I could not look at it directly. "Wounds of the body heal swiftly in comparison to those of the mind."

"I don't like wounds," I said.

"Perhaps you wish to tell me of your troubles," said the monk, "but are yet ill at ease in my presence. I understand your sentiments. I will soften the barrier between us, therefore, with talk. Allow me, my son, to relate to you the history of the Marble Tower." When I made no objection — no reaction at all, in fact — he went on, "The story of the Marble Tower begins more than two thousand years ago, in the Year of the Goldfinch. And yes, my son, that is the self-same year that the third sun fell from the sky. You are familiar with the legend of the third sun, are you not?"

I nodded. The turtles had cooked when it fell.

"It is no mere chance that these events coincide," said the monk "—the death of the sun and the birth of the

Tower — for the instant the sun struck the ocean floor, the Tower rose fully-formed from the depths. Indeed, each spiraled stair and each corridor rose as you see them today."

I remembered the branches of the yellow tree, the way they twisted and climbed. The veins in the marble pulsed like sap. Was there golden fruit then, buried in the stone? Or skeletons entombed beyond rescue?

"How did it rise fully-formed, you ask?" said the monk, though I had not asked him anything. "That, my son, is the greatest mystery of the Tower, and one that every brother here strives through meditation to solve." He raised his brows. "It was through meditation, many years ago, that we discovered the connection between the Tower and the fall of the sun. In honor of that link, we once displayed here a monument symbolic of the third sun. It was made of glass, with a crest of scarlet feathers in representation—"

"Of the path of destruction," I said. How had they made it so accurate? Had someone else seen the fish go up in steam? "And the glass," I said, "represented the sun, tapered to show its speed." Skiy would be proud if he could hear me now.

"This is true," said the monk. He stood below me, smiling behind his beard. "Were you a great admirer of the Radiance, my son?"

I nodded. It was strange. I had only seen the Radiance once in my life, and yet here I was, years later, its crystal shadow hanging over me like a swarm of flies. Who knew where Skiy had buried the crest in his shop? What a jest that would be, if Skiy had thrown the crest out with the trash — he could have done it years ago — to lie in the gutter for the rats to explore.

"They say," said the monk, "that many things died with the fall of the sun. Before that time, when water still filled the seas, the oceans hosted life of all kinds: fish, whales—"

"Snakes and turtles," I said. "They were hideous."

"What was hideous, my son?"

"The snakes and turtles," I said, "that lived in the sea. They smoked on the surface. They smelled like fried rubber."

The monk swayed on the step where he stood. He tilted his head and looked up at me. "How do you know this, my son?"

"I don't know." I shrugged. "I dreamed it."

"You experienced a vision?"

"I hope not," I said. "I dreamed I was a bird."

"Is that all?"

I said, "No."

"Tell me," said the monk.

I stared down past my feet to the pool. I stood at an angle where I could no longer see my face. I told him the dream. If the monks had sent the bees, I was already dead. What did it matter what I told him now?

"The third sun looked like feathers," I told him.

The monk was silent. He frowned and buried his hands still deeper in the sleeves of his habit. He would judge me insane, no doubt, and no longer worth the energy of conversation.

"Anyway," I said, "I'm off to buy a nose ring."

"No," said the monk. "That is a powerful vision, my son."

I shrugged. "It wasn't very pleasant."

"Visions of enlightenment are rarely enjoyable to the beholder." The acid pool twinkled between us. "Tell me, my son: in the vision, was there any appearance of the Marble Tower?"

"It came at the end," I said. "A marble strip rose out of the water. It folded around the tree. I was sitting in the tree and everything went dark after that."

The monk removed his hands from his sleeves. "I am the Father Paramount," he said, "head of the order here. I would be honored if you would join our Brotherhood."

"What did you say?" The wish papers fluttered in my face.

"A vision of such intensity is worthy of a place in the Tower Brethren," said the Father Paramount.

"I don't want to be a monk."

"Ahh, but my son! The potential you show. You could be a great aid to our understanding of the Tower's beginning. Or in our understanding of power in the heart of man, for you have sat in the branches of the Tree of Power and seen the skeletons and the fruit with your own eyes."

"Dream," I said. "It was only a dream."

"Still it was your own eyes."

"No, I borrowed someone else's."

He tilted his head the other way. His beard stuck out straight from his face.

"I was a bird," I insisted. "I wasn't me."

"All the monks here have experienced visions of enlightenment," said the Paramount. "Such is the requirement of entrance. But few have beheld images of such power as the ones you describe. Your aid to the Brotherhood would be beyond measure. In the area of restoring the Radiance, would you perhaps be interested in offering your aid?"

I said, "No."

"We have searched the City for the culprits," said the Paramount, "as I am sure you are aware. As yet they have not been found. With your wisdom, however, I am sure we could unearth their identities."

"I need to go."

"Will you not come tomorrow for the Conference of Entrance? Will you not aid us in bringing these vandals to justice?" His eyes shone bright as pebbles, small as the end of my finger. "A Brother was killed by their crime. Do you not wish to aid in this noble cause?"

"Not especially." I wanted to tell him it was the monk's own fault he'd been killed, that Gyanin had not meant to push him over, that even if he had, it was only to save my brother Leque. Leque had been trying to replace the crest, and it had only fallen because Blade had touched it, and how could you expect Blade to know any better? He'd only been twelve. And even if Gyanin had been wrong to push the monk, Gyanin was dead, so hadn't he already been punished?

Glane was as good as dead; Yaryk and Blade and my brother were gone; Skiy was depressed; I was myself. What more did they want?

I pushed past the monk down the stairs. "I don't want to help," I said. "Sorry."

❖ ❖ ❖

Kem was not home. He had left a note on the floor. It said, "Ksar, help yourself to the food in the back room. Kem."

I searched for the food. The stench of camel-dung incense buffeted from the back room. Someone lay in the dark there, snoring. It smelled like dung.

"Hello?" I rapped the wall with my knuckles. "Skiy?" The snoring faltered. Bees didn't snore, did they? My palms prickled with sweat.

"Is that you, Skiy?"

A candle flickered up from the corner. Red feathers leapt into my face. Yellow tendrils whipped out like jumping ants. I screamed.

"Shut up." Skiy's face appeared through the plume. "Is anyone out there, Ksar?"

"No," I said. "Why are you hiding?"

Skiy raised an amphora to his mouth. Wine sloshed down his chin. He dropped the amphora and the blood of red grapes soaked into his lap. "Where have you been all day?"

"At the Marble Tower."

"The Marble Tower! Why the flaming aardvark were you there?"

I shrugged. "Where else should I be?"

"You were talking to monks at the Tower," he shuddered, "and here I am, holding the crest of the Radiance in my arms!"

"Why are you holding it?" I asked.

"I don't know. I don't need to." He pushed the feathers off his lap. Underneath he held a book. Soles and sandal straps protruded from its covers like so many page-markers. He wore his apron, smeared as always in tar and grease. Something brighter and redder splashed the front.

"What's on your apron?"

"Blood," said Skiy.

"Er, you don't mean *blood*, do you?"

"When does Kem get home?"

Incense filled the air. It made me dizzy. "Why is there blood on your apron, Skiy?"

"I don't want to explain." He opened his book with a red-smeared hand. He held the book upside-down. He turned the pages. "I'll explain it when Kem gets here. I don't want to say it twice. Now where's the wine?" He hiccupped.

"You spilled it."

"No," he said, "*you* spilled it." He snored before he hit the ground.

11

Blade sat in the dust at the side of the road. He listened as Yaryk and the smuggler talked.

"Here we turn for the Errata," said the smuggler. "I'd like to take you as far as the Citadel." He laughed, a gargle and click in his throat. "But we've already been there this season." A shape with six sides, blue as lapis, tattooed the man's tongue.

"You say it's only a day's walk from here?" said Yaryk. The smuggler spat in Blade's direction. "Maybe more with him. Two days at the most. And friend? Don't expect a welcome. The nobles are still afraid of your people there."

"With reason," said Yaryk. "Less than a decade ago, the Citadel was under our control. The nobles hold a fragile influence."

"They worry about losing it again," said the smuggler, "though it seems unlikely to me. You'll see what I mean."

"What *do* you mean?" said Yaryk. "Tell me plainly."

"They allow few Bedouin inside the gates. You should tell them you're a traveling merchant, or say you've only come for supplies. They won't let you enter if you tell them you intend to stay."

"I am not yet sure of my intentions." Yaryk's eyes were invisible beneath his hood. "I want to see what has become of the Citadel without the Guild to govern it. That much at least I have decided. I doubt it will be worth living in."

"Don't tell them where you stood in the Bedouin Guild," said the smuggler. "You had some influence, didn't you? I recognize your face." He picked a flea from the collar of his robe and licked his fingers.

Blade looked away. They spoke of wind conditions on the roads, and hunting prospects, and life at the Errata. When the fire zephyr came from the west, said the smuggler, they sprayed their cart with the spores of the glass weed to ward against flying sparks. Blade scanned the horizon for signs of fire.

He had spent ten days on the road now: ten days of travel with Yaryk, ten days without feathered pillows, baths, or sugared kumquats. Ten days with no walls to protect him from the running sand, or the suns that burned his skin and peeled it away, the suns that reflected off the acid before him. He closed his eyes but could not escape the glare. He turned away. The smugglers, all but their leader, worked around the cart. They nailed fresh skins down over the old. The cart was forever expanding, burgeoning out. The men ignored Blade. They always ignored him.

Everyone ignored Blade. Sometimes Yaryk remembered him and would walk beside him and talk, but more often he strode ahead at the front of the procession beside the leader, or sat with the leader on the driver's seat, taking his turn at prodding the camels. They spoke to each other in gestures and rattles, grunts in the backs of their throats. They spoke in the language of the road. Blade could not understand what they said.

Yaryk's shadow fell over him. "Ready to go?"

Blade stood. There was no use dusting off his robe; it would only gather filth again. His feet were numb and he fell over.

Yaryk hauled him up. "We are breaking company with the hides." He smiled. "What do you say to that, Blade?"

Blade smiled in return. He was tired and his lips felt heavy. "I like it," he said.

Yaryk waved his arm in the direction of the side road. "They go to the Errata. We will not go with them."

The smugglers, their skin-nailing complete, sat back on the steps of the cart as it heaved into motion. Others walked along beside. Yaryk watched until it dwindled in the distance. Blade stood beside him. He shifted his weight from one foot to the other, though both of them throbbed.

"Yaryk?" he said, "what's the Errata?"

"In size," said Yaryk, "it rivals the City." He folded his arms across his chest. The wind caught the tassels of his turban and flailed them over his face. "The Errata provides an escape for criminals and outlaws. I won't take you there, Blade. Not unless you want it."

"Thank you," said Blade.

"The Citadel may be little better," said Yaryk. "Shoulder your pack; it's time we moved on."

They had parted ways with the smugglers in the morning when the suns were still low. The suns now dipped again, low in Blade's eyes. The Citadel wall loomed ahead.

"No sleeping on the highroads tonight." Yaryk laughed. A wall of white sandstone towered before them. "Behold the Citadel."

They stepped to the side of the road, out of traffic's way. Blade leaned back until his neck throbbed. The wall smeared and leaked up into the sky. Carts trundled past, as did men on camels, and men with fishing nets in bundles on their backs. Blade could feel their glares. I must be dirty, he thought. I haven't washed in days. He didn't want to think of his filth. He could smell himself and it made him blush. He would rather sleep. He wanted to sleep right now.

"Come," said Yaryk. "I hear that Bedouin are no longer welcome here, but we shall see if we can enter."

"Why don't they like you, Yaryk?"

"I will explain it later," said Yaryk.

They crouched in the lee of the gates, twice the height of the City walls. The gates were open, guards arrayed in a line beneath the arch. The suns reflected bright off their armor. Metal bands like the stripes of tigers glowed on their chests. Yaryk and Blade joined the queue to enter.

Yaryk draped his arm over Blade's shoulder. "If they ask," he whispered, "tell them I am your father. We have come to the Citadel only to trade for medicine. We will leave tomorrow."

"Why do we need medicine?"

"For your skin condition," said Yaryk.

Blade nodded and grinned. "All right," he said. His cheeks felt tight as the skin of a drum. His face itched like fire at night.

"Don't let them see your eyes," said Yaryk. "Blue eyes are rare among Bedouin."

They reached the gates, right under the arch. A guard blocked their path, his face shadowed by the brim of his helmet. A red-orange stone adorned the top. He pointed at Yaryk. "Are you Bedouin?"

"We are," said Yaryk. "We do not plan to stay in the Citadel long."

"How long?"

"One night only."

"Why have you come?"

"My son," said Yaryk, "has a rare skin condition. I hoped that in such a metropolis as the Citadel, medication might be found."

The guard took Blade by the chin and tilted up his head. Blade shut his eyes.

"Ugly. Very ugly." He released Blade's chin and motioned to the guard beside him. "Take them to an apothecary, the closest you can find, and be sure they do not trade in narcotics."

The second guard took Yaryk by the arm. Another seized Blade. The guards steered them out of the crush around the gates and onto an open road, three times as broad as any street of the City. Customers milled around the store fronts. Many of the fronts were made of wood, not stone. People turned and watched the guards as they passed. After several blocks, Yaryk's guard released his arm. He walked behind Yaryk with the point of his spear at Yaryk's spine.

In front of a fruit stand stood a man in a conical hat. "Jail them all!" he shouted.

"Jail the Bedouin!" another man joined. The cry erupted. "Take them away! Don't let them stay here! Jail them!"

Blade stared. All he could do was stare. Were they shouting at him? At Yaryk? These men in peaked hats and buttoned jackets. Why did they hate him?

A vegetable cart ran into Yaryk. The driver laughed. Yaryk stumbled into Blade. "At the next alley," he whispered, "run."

The spears prodded their backs.

Yaryk walked into a cart of jewelry. Bracelets cascaded. He tripped on his robe. He pretended to trip, reached out a hand and pulled Blade sideways. "Run!" Yaryk lifted his robe. He ran. Blade stumbled after him. The blisters burst and squabbled inside his shoes. Yaryk churned through the scattered jewelry. The vendor shouted and swore. Blade seized Yaryk's sleeve. They ran down an alleyway. The air stank. Rotted vegetables strewed the cobbles.

Metal-shod footfalls sounded behind them. "Bedouin!" the guards shouted. "Bedouin filth!"

Yaryk swerved between buildings, so close on either side Blade's hands struck the walls. They ran between houses. So many houses, everywhere. Blank walls. The alleyway split and split again. Yaryk turned with each split. Pain stabbed Blade's chest. They had to stop! He could not breathe and he could not speak. The ground faded black and red as he blinked.

A door swung open. It caught Yaryk's robe. He jerked backwards into Blade. Behind the door a voice cursed.

Blade's fingers numbed on Yaryk's sleeve. They swerved down another alleyway. Yaryk stopped. Blade ran into his back and fell down. The alleyway reeked of dried figs and fermented beans. Blade half sat, half fell against the wall. Yaryk squatted beside him and fished the water flask from his belt. He pushed it into Blade's hands.

"Finish it," he said.

Yaryk pushed the last of the water into Blade's hands. "Finish it," he said. The boy looked as though he would die if he did not drink soon. He could not let Xavier die, at least not until his purpose had been fulfilled.

The alley ended in a wall. Wooden planks surrounded them. Yaryk surveyed the wood with narrowed eyes. Where had this timber come from? Where were the trees to supply this wood?

A pile of rags lay against the wall.

"Wait here." Yaryk patted Blade's arm. He strode over to the rags. A head emerged and blinked at him with crusted eyes.

Yaryk produced a bag of almonds from his sleeve. He handed the nuts to the man. "Tell me, do you know the affairs of the Citadel?"

"Wha' d'you mean?" The man looked from almonds to Yaryk and back. Yellow pus ran down his cheeks.

"I mean who rules here. No, let me do that for you." Yaryk reached out, untied the cinch on the bag, and pushed it back into the man's hand. "Do the people have rights, or is it only the nobles now?"

The beggar sucked one almond. He swallowed it whole. "I'm one of the people, aren't I? Do I look like I have a say?"

"And no Bedouin live here?"

"Looks like *you're* here." The man gargled. "No," he said. "There might be some who used to be Bedouin, but you're the only one I've seen who's idiot enough to dress as one."

"What of the Glebe?" said Yaryk.

"Glebe?" The beggar blinked. He rubbed the crusts around his eyes. "Only the nobles go to the Glebe."

"Why? What have they done to it?"

"I don't know. Do you think I've been there? Stone, does it look like they'd let me in sight of the Glebe?"

Yaryk wanted to spit — this broken, crushed, pathetic specimen. He said, "And the old Bedouin leaders — Ryas, Tallos, Almir — are they still in prison?"

The rags laughed. "Tallos is."

"And the others?"

"Dead."

"Where is Tallos?"

"The Gaol."

"What? A common plebeian penitentiary?" Yaryk swept his robes around himself and stood. He motioned to Blade. "Come."

Blade struggled up. He held the empty flask as if it were a jewel. "What's the Gaol, Yaryk?"

"It's a prison."

"And the Glebe?"

"It used to be a gathering place of the Bedouin," said Yaryk. "Now I don't know. We shall see. And no more questions. I must find the street from here." He retraced their steps down the alley, down another, and wound along side roads and dirt trenches. "These roads were never here," he muttered. "What have they done?" He held out an arm and stopped Blade before they crossed a road. If he looked at the boy he would strike him. He could not tolerate those shallow blue eyes, all questions, no comprehension. He did not want to hurt Blade but he would if he must.

"We will go to a sheltered place," said Yaryk. "To get there, we must cross many streets. Stay close to me."

Blade nodded.

They reached an empty storefront. It had taken them an hour, running and ducking in doorways. Glass fragments littered the roadway.

Yaryk turned to Blade. "Be careful," he said. "Wait here. Stand back from the glass. It is sharp enough to bite through shoes." He knocked on the door, but no answer came. He stepped through the glass fragments to the empty window and straddled the sill. He brought the other leg over and tore his robe free from the snag of the frame. He stood inside. It was colder and darker than the street. The walls had a close, dank feel. He leaned out again into the glare. He held his hands cupped low as a stepping block.

"Come here," he told Blade. "Go around to the left; the glass is less."

Blade scrambled over the sill. He stood in the gloom and rubbed his eyes. The boy's face was so burned it looked like the scales of a fish. It peeled in ribbons and flaked down his collar.

An array of shelves had been cut into one stone wall. At least there was no wood here. Something had happened to the Glebe. An open field could not produce wood, not in the quantities he saw here now. Nor could a field produce

exports worthy of so much trade. The nobles had done
something, while he, Yaryk, had been mired in the petty
politics of the City. He ran his hand along a shelf. A small
ivory box brushed his fingers. He lifted the box and brought
it to his nose.

"What is it?" said Blade.

"Incense." Yaryk pushed aside a table with charred and
splintered legs. He knelt in the ash and traced his hands
along the floor. He laid his head to the boards. When he
pounded them, they echoed hollow.

"Blade," said Yaryk, "go to the wall."

The floor was burnt black. The soot dusted Yaryk's
hands. He dug his fingers into the wood. It splintered.
Blood smeared under his nails. The slivers bit into his skin.
A metal panel emerged from the floor. Yaryk turned a dial.
The floor creaked.

"Stay there," he told Blade.

The panel pulled back. An aperture, wide enough for
a man to enter, opened at his knees. Blackness yawned.
A ladder twisted down, the rungs all frayed and broken.
Yaryk swung himself over the lip and began the descent.
The ladder groaned. The walls of the shaft had once been
wood — a sign of prestige — but now the boards had been
burned away and the stone showed through underneath.
The smell of old fire clotted the air. Every sound reverberated, like the fall of a stone in a well.

"Blade!" Yaryk shouted. It sounded like a hundred
voices, all calling and fading at once: "Blade, bring me a
light! There should be lanterns on the shelves."

Blade's footsteps padded over the floor. "What size?"
said his voice.

"Small," said Yaryk. He liked the way the boy obeyed
him.

Blade lowered the lantern on a length of curtain. Yaryk
struck a match from his pocket and lit the wick. It sput-
tered and caught. He replaced the glass hood. He did not
want to risk another fire.

The tunnel wound vertically and then horizontally.
Yaryk crawled on hands and knees. The roof grazed his

back. The boards smeared black on his hands and robe. As he went, he disturbed plumes of ash that filled the air with powder and stung his eyes. He ran his tongue around his mouth; the ash was dry and sour.

The walls dropped away and his hands touched sand. Yaryk straightened and dusted his robe. He stood in the hall of the Bedouin Guild. He set the lantern at his feet and folded his arms. He stood in what had *once* been the hall of the Bedouin Guild, the chief council chamber of the Citadel, the seat of power that had governed the lives of the people. Decisions made here became law. This space had been the rallying point of the world's Bedouin — Bedouin everywhere. And now, what had it become? This yawning cavern?

Yaryk had spent so long in Blade's company the boy's voice now played in his head: "I thought the Bedouin wandered, Yaryk. I didn't know they stopped anywhere."

"Ah," said Yaryk, as he had when they sat together at the side of the road, stars overhead, Blade with all the blankets but one, so that Yaryk would wake before dawn in convulsions of cold. Oh, he cursed Blade then, but the next night again he surrendered his coverings. The boy must reach the Citadel alive, as trusting of Yaryk as possible. "Ah," said Yaryk, "Yes, we wander, but sometimes we meet to take council. We used to meet here in the Citadel."

"You don't anymore?"

"No," said Yaryk. "Matters changed some years ago."

Blade shuffled deeper beneath the blankets. Only his eyes could be seen, and wisps of hair bleached white as the stars. "What happened, Yaryk?"

"A long tale." He sighed. "Perhaps it *must* be long to be understood."

"Please tell it," said Blade.

"When the third sun fell," said Yaryk, lying there under his single blanket, "the sea level rose and acidified. Many civilizations perished and their peoples scattered. Most of the highroads dissolved. Of all the people in the world, the Bedouin suffered the greatest loss of life."

"Why?"

"We lived on the highroads."

"How many were killed?"

"I cannot say," said Yaryk. "Thousands. But those that remained, grieving the tragedy, sought to find unity amongst themselves. They came to the Citadel, which was at the time uninhabited. There were many uninhabited islands then, for there seemed to be so many to choose from. The Bedouin chose the Citadel and the Glebe."

"What is the Glebe?"

"It was once a field."

"And now?"

"Now we shall see," said Yaryk. "I will take you there before we leave these parts." He watched his breath, frozen in plumes against the black of the sky. "When the Bedouin rallied at the Citadel, they decided they would still be wanderers, nomadic, but that some number of them would always remain at the Citadel with stores of supplies and aid. In this manner, if any tribe was struck with great hardship, they had only to seek out the Citadel and there they would find assistance. The governing body was known as the Guild."

"Is the Guild still there?" said Blade.

"Until three years ago, yes." Yaryk imagined his hands folded on his chest. He would pause here, give time for Blade's curiosity to build, before he continued at last: "The seed for the Guild's overthrow was planted a thousand years ago, when they held their first gathering." He paused again. "Some wished to give up the nomadic life. They rooted themselves in the Citadel and ceased to travel. As the years went by, they lost their Bedouin identity and became the people of the Citadel, just as there are people of the City. They became a faction apart from the travelers and merchants."

"What happened to the Guild?" said Blade.

"The people decided the Citadel was theirs, and they no longer wished to serve as hosts to the Guild. This was a grave injustice on the part of the people; moreover, it was treasonous. The Guild had been generous to allow any to remain in the Citadel permanently."

He would answer Blade's questions like that. Blade would ask, and he would answer, calmly and sorrowfully, as if telling a tale of long ago, not a recounting of his own past.

Yaryk held up the lantern. It spread a puddle of light around his feet. "The Bedouin population was slow to replenish," he whispered, as if Blade stood beside him, "after the fall of the third sun. But when at last we regained our strength, and became too numerous to confine ourselves to the Glebe, our first meeting grounds, the heart of the Guild moved here, within the Citadel walls. They established the high council where we stand today."

"Why is the room burnt?" said Blade.

"The people burned us out."

Yaryk had been here when it burned. He remembered the torches, the buckets of oil thrown down the tunnel, the smoke, billowing black as a living thing. It stifled the council. They had only been sitting, conversing, committing no atrocities. Yaryk had been there with the other Bedouin. That night they had climbed through flames, up the tunnel while the walls licked death. Slats of wood fell around them. Yaryk tasted the flames, the shouts, the smoke of the choking fire. So many had died. They had died here, where he stood in the dark. Perhaps the skeletons remained, entombed in the ash of the floor, burned where they fell. He did not want to look. Oh, but how they had burned! Fifty men could not climb a ladder at once, all robed and turbaned. So much hair had burned. He smelled it still. He could almost taste it, hot and bitter as salt-fried lemon. The people had grumbled for years and the Bedouin ignored them. When the hall burned down, everything ended.

Not even in Yaryk's imagination did he tell Blade these details: that the Guild oppressed the people, and the people complained for years and the Guild did nothing. He would not tell Blade how the people had protested in the last few years, and the measures the Bedouin had taken to subdue those riots.

Yaryk felt his way along the wall to a sconce. Its metal grid was twisted and melted. The torch itself was no longer there. He shuffled the perimeter of the hall — all the sconces empty — then steered for the center. There was no sound but the shuffle of his feet through the ash, fine as peacock down. Here in the middle of the hall a ring of benches had once been set. The high council sat here, while the rest of the Guild ringed the darkness beyond. Yaryk leaned back and gazed up at the dome of the cavern. Metallic residue glittered on the ceiling, catching the light of the lantern and sparkling it back like stars. The high heavens, they called it. The heavens followed them here, even under the earth. Yaryk told stories of the heavens to the newcomers and snared them in. If he told his tales well enough, and usually he did, the newcomers stayed a while, and helped in the governance of the people. It was Yaryk's function in the Guild to bring in new members, and he performed his duty with alacrity. It was not the awkward attempts of Kem and his brotherhoods in the City; if Yaryk found men of competence, he made them join. He persuaded until they thought they had reached the decision themselves. There were tasks they must perform for the Guild, once they were members, and if they did not perform properly he persuaded them to leave.

This — the Guild — had been the true brotherhood. Back in the City, crouched in a cobbler's storeroom, was only pretend. That had been acting as children, mocking the rituals of their elders and betters. Here, the Bedouin had been the betters.

But now the Guild and its rituals were dead, and the Glebe usurped. They had always had the Glebe, the open grasses to the northwest, where tents upon tents stood rooted, and the fires of camel dung rose through the stars. But now that the nobles held sway, Time only knew what had happened to the Glebe.

Yaryk retraced his steps to the base of the ladder. The lantern guttered, the candle a puddle of wax. He left it in the hall, a spectral light as he climbed in the dark.

Blade slept in the corner of the shop. Yaryk closed the panel behind him. The tunnel mouth disappeared. He climbed over the windowsill, wrapped his robes tightly around himself and hurried away. He knew the way back.

12

Kem opened the curtain and fanned the incense away from his face. He looked harassed, eyebrows drawn to a bridge across his nose. In the gloom it was hard to be sure. "So you're back," he said. "Did you enjoy yourself at the Tower?" Kem did not know about sarcasm.

"No," I said.

He squatted beside me. "Why not?"

"I met the Father Paramount," I said, "the head of the monks, I think."

"Yes?" said Kem.

"He wants me to join the brotherhood."

"What?" He rubbed a hand across his eyes.

"The brotherhood," I said. "He wants me to become a monk."

"Oh." Kem tilted his head. He said, "Why?"

I shrugged. "He wore an ugly robe."

Kem settled to a more comfortable position on the floor. He thought for a moment, then said, "It would be the perfect opportunity, Ksar, to access the Radiance room."

"No." I couldn't see myself in the same green habit every day. The same Ksar, day after day with the same monk's beard. "I don't want to be a monk."

"True, it could be dangerous." Kem rubbed his chin. "Why are you sitting here in the dark?" He waved his hand as if the dark were a tangible entity he could brush away. "Do you know how damaging this smoke could be to your lungs?"

"I didn't light it," I said. "Skiy did." I found the candle, struck a match, and pointed to Skiy. He slept silently now, with his arm draped over the crest.

"Oh." Kem stood for a moment, stiff as a pillar of quartz, then he shook himself and lifted the crest from his cousin's face. "Was he stung?"

I said, "No, he's drunk."

"The fumes cannot be conducive to his recovery," said Kem. "Help me move him to the bedroom."

Skiy was short but with shoulders as broad as any stonemason's. We dragged him into the bedroom. I lifted his knees and Kem wrapped his arms around his cousin's waist, but we could not elevate him as high as the sleeping cot. We laid him on the floor and I stuffed a pillow beneath his head.

This done, I sojourned to the rain barrel at the end of the street, brought back a bucket of water, and watched as Kem sprinkled it over Skiy's face.

"Don't you have any medicine?" I said.

"Self-inflicted ailments are difficult to cure. Inebriation, Ksar, is a sad disorder."

He poured the water without restraint over Skiy's head. Skiy snorted. He rolled over, convulsed like a poisoned rat, and spat a wad of phlegm the size of my fist on the carpet. He sat up.

"Ah." Skiy crossed his eyes at Kem. "You're here," he said. "Good."

Kem put a hand on his shoulder. "Why don't you come into the living room and lie down on the couch? It might be more comfortable."

Skiy shuddered. "Windows." He tore off his apron and shoved it under Kem's bed. "Do you want to know about the blood?" His hands shook like saplings.

"Blood?" said Kem. "You're not bleeding, Skiy. You've been drinking. It's only wine."

"It's blood," said Skiy. "I killed a monk." An artery twitched in his neck.

"You're not a murderer, are you?" Kem stroked Skiy's hand. "You didn't *murder* a monk, did you? Skiy, tell me what happened."

"I was in my shop," said Skiy, "working to complete an order. A monk came in."

"And that was it?" I said. "You just killed him?" If that was it, I would have to forget Skiy the same as forgetting Glane. I would have to forget the whole world soon enough.

"That wasn't it," said Skiy. "At first I didn't realize how dangerous it was, to have a monk in my shop. I'm sure I've served monks before. I didn't think about it. The monk was a customer. Customers are always welcome. I asked him what he'd come for and how I could help him.

"'Leather,' he replied. 'I am looking for hide of cattle.' He spoke with a Clebean accent. I can't imitate it. 'Can hide of cattle be purchased here?' he said.

"'That's not the primary purpose of my establishment,'" I told him, 'but if you tell me what you wish to use it for, I'm sure I can find something suited to your needs.'

"'The business is private,' said the monk. 'I will see the varieties you have. I will see if you have hide of cattle that pleases me.'

"'Follow me then,'" I said. I led him into the back storeroom, which, as you know, is where I keep the raw supplies. I showed him the leather rolls, dyed and plain, tanned and raw. I forgot..." Skiy coughed. "I forgot about the crest. I forgot I had hidden it behind the rolls." He kneaded his temples. "The monk selected his leather. I helped him pull out the roll so the quantity could be measured and cut, and there was the crest of the Radiance. It lay on the shelf right there. Right in front of us. He hadn't seen it. I started to sweat. I stood in front of the Radiance, hoping to block his view, but I knew I would have to move to cut the leather, and then he would see it."

"So you killed him?" I asked.

"Quiet," said Kem.

"I didn't mean to." Skiy kneaded his face. "I was holding my knife — to cut the leather, you know. I stepped forward. He saw the crest and froze. Then he started to yell. He yelled in Clebean. I couldn't understand what he said. He lunged at me. I wouldn't have killed him if he hadn't attacked."

Skiy looked at Kem, his eyes pleading. He did not look at me for forgiveness. "Kem, he would have killed me if I hadn't stabbed him. It was self-defense. Even if he wouldn't have killed me, he would have gone back to the Tower and told about the crest. That would have killed us all." Skiy rocked where he sat. "I shouldn't have killed him," he said. "I could have knocked him out, tied him up—"

"And what could we have done with a prisoner?" Kem rubbed Skiy's fingers. "We couldn't let him go."

"But now I'm a murderer" — Skiy hacked — "like Gyanin. Gyanin is dead."

"Skiy, anyone would have—"

"You wouldn't." Skiy's voice became low and hollow. "You wouldn't kill anyone, Kem. You should have been there instead of me. You would have let him go. We deserve to be arrested. That's what we deserve. I should have done what you would have done. I shouldn't have killed him."

"But you did," said Kem, quietly. "We are criminals already. We've lived as criminals for years. We may as well continue as criminals. Skiy?" he said. "Skiy, please don't. Oh Stone, Skiy." He knelt and held his cousin. Skiy shook in his arms. Kem rocked Skiy back and forth. "Skiy, you had to defend yourself. You acted in the moment. Skiy!"

I blushed. My eyes itched. I feared I would join in the tears if I stayed. I would smear the stenciled clematis leaves under my eyes. I slunk away to the far end of the living room. I could go no farther, bar leaving the house. If I left the house I would not want to come back, and then Kem would worry and they would need to come find me and that would only make everything worse. I barricaded myself behind Kem's couch and wondered why everyone else in the world had more compassion than I did. Leque would never hold me if I cried; I cried too often as a child. Everyone was falling apart. They left the City, turned into birds. They died, killed, cried and drank. Everyone I knew smoked incense. Maybe I *should* go to the Marble Tower.

I should sit beside acid pools for the rest of my life and pretend to meditate.

Skiy's sobs rose to a crescendo. I stuffed my wig in my ears; I could not escape the pound of my blood. My thoughts rattled in the darkness. They wandered my skull with their arms outstretched, walked into each other and grunted apologies, shouted their curses. They had no direction and I could not lead them.

Kem touched my arm. Tears soaked the shoulder of his toga. "Are you all right?" he asked.

I hated his compassion. Sometimes I wanted to kill him. I would never kill anyone. I wished I had never known him, Kem with his dripping eyes. "Don't kill," I said, more as a reminder to myself.

"No," said Kem. "No more killing."

"Good."

"How do you feel about becoming a monk?"

"Right now I'm wedged behind a couch and I think I'm stuck," I said. "I don't feel good about anything."

Kem leaned away from the couch. He mumbled an apology. "Sorry," he said more clearly. "I have to be forceful here, Ksar. Please be a monk. We must replace the crest to the Radiance. Think of the opportunity this has opened. As a monk and a resident of the Marble Tower, you will be able to gain access to the Radiance room. Once the crest is returned, you have my permission to leave the Brotherhood. Please, Ksar? We need this to end." He glanced over his shoulder to the bedroom. Skiy's sobs had fallen silent.

"Is he dead?" I asked.

"No one is going to die," said Kem. "Skiy is asleep. Now, please answer my question."

Answering questions. Kem was all about answering questions. I had to get away from this hospital apartment, away from Skiy and his shop, and the way they both reeked of incense.

"Fine," I said. "I'll become a monk. Do you want me to go today?" I uncoiled from behind the couch. "Do you want me to go right now?"

Kem would not let me just leave. Neither did he expect me to go by myself. Before we departed, he had to make breakfast for Skiy. I lay on the couch and stared up at the ceiling, listening to the frying of eggs. Kem peeled vegetables. I heard more than one of them drop to the floor.

I packed my possessions into a pillowcase. They did not fill it. There seemed little purpose in wigs and curtains. When would I be given the opportunity to wear them? I packed only my favorite accessories, the ones I could not be parted from: a handful of earrings and a tie-dyed carpet, three fishhooks and a lure of blue glass. I packed one toga of Leque's. Out of all my possessions, his clothes were the least descript. If I needed normality, I could wear his things. The toga smelled of dust and camel kebabs. I folded it into the pillowcase. Then we were ready to go.

"I can carry that," said Kem.

We said our farewells to Skiy, who said nothing in return. We walked together through the early-morning streets. I had spent all night in the backroom with Skiy.

At the base of the Marble Tower, Kem handed my pillowcase back to me. "Come and see us tomorrow," he said. "Tell me how you're doing."

"Sure," I said.

Kem stood in the street and watched me until I had passed through the glass doors and into the Tower, whereupon the reflection became too much and he could no longer see me. I watched him walk away.

Once he was gone, I turned to the reception desk. A monk sat behind the desk. Strings and strings of numbers covered the paper before him. He seemed to be adding the columns, moving his lips as he worked. He and I stood alone in the reception room. It was always uncrowded in the mornings.

"I need to talk to the Father Paramount."

"Are you here for your Conference of Entrance?" He did not look up from the columns.

"Er, maybe. How do you know?"

"He told me." The monk set down his quill. "He told me you would come today."

"Where is he?"

"You can find him in the dining hall," said the monk. "Do you know your way?"

I said, "No."

He relinquished his desk to the hands of an identical counter-part and led me himself, up winding hallways and spiral stairs, away from the acid pools and trees, down other passageways locked against the public, where torchlight reflected hard-gold in the veins of the wall. We stopped outside a door. I smelled food: cayenne, cinnamon, coconut, oregano. The monk pushed open the door into a room of tables. They were set haphazardly around the hall. Some sank into the floor, while others stood out from the walls. A counter stretched along one wall. Beyond the counter, monks bustled to and fro with pots and spatulas.

The Father Paramount sat at a circular table with twenty other monks around him. He rose and smiled. "Welcome, my son. Please, sit with us."

I ambled over and sat down.

Dishes were spread across the table, empty except for the odd heap of chicken bones or crust of pastry.

"Fear not, my son," said the Paramount, noting my despair. "One of our brethren attends to your nourishment as we speak." He nodded. "After brother Eln's disappearance, I have worried for your safety."

"I'm safe," I said, because I didn't know what else to say. The monks did not look at each other. They did not talk. I thought about Skiy with blood on his apron and I wondered how it would feel to kill one of these men, and see the contrast of red on these so-green robes.

After an eternity my food arrived. I selected a morsel that may have been a scallop. Everyone around the table leaned in and watched.

"We may now begin," said the Paramount.

He spoke like Yaryk at our dung-sniffing meetings of long ago. Long ago? Two weeks ago. It was no more than two weeks since Glane and I had sat with our backs to the

door, ready to charge for freedom. I had no idea where
freedom now lay.

"Let this be your Conference of Entrance," said the
Paramount. "Ksar, my son, here we uncover our naked
souls."

I choked on a mouthful of broccoli.

"The nudity is purely emotional, you understand," said
the Father Paramount, "not physical. Here each man shall
answer with honesty all questions addressed to him. All
shall be known and all laid bare." He caught the horror
in my eyes and smiled, then turned to the monk on his
right. "Brother Iander," he said, "tell us of the death of your
father."

"In the year of the Elucidated Jewel," said Brother
Iander, a short monk with hands that twitched on the table
before him, "my father left our house at suns' down and
that was the last time that we saw him alive. In the morning,
a hog farmer found him cold outside a drink hall. His beard
was hard with frost and dried blood. He held a dagger in
his hand, or so my uncle told me. I never saw him myself,
as I was quite young at the time." The speech sounded
memorized. How often did they hold these meetings? Did
they spill the same secrets every time? I would tell them
a tapir had trampled my father and all would be satisfied.

My plan, however, shattered against the Paramount's
next question. "Brother Iander," he said, fingers stippled
in his beard, "what emotions did you experience after the
loss of your father?"

"I don't believe I was consciously angry..." The little
monk faltered and began again. "No, I directed my anger
at my uncle, not the murderer. He would not allow me to
see my father until after purification measures had been
taken. They washed and scented the body and wrapped
it in fresh white linen." The monk's voice grew bitter. "My
father never wore clean linen in his life. He never wore
fragrances. They forced him to betray his identity. He no
longer seemed to be my father."

"Does this still anger you, my son?"

"No, Father."

"Why not, my son?"

"I now understand why they cleansed him." Brother Iander prodded the olive pits on his plate. He spoke into his beard. "After his death, they rendered my father the man he should have been. The man, perhaps, that he could have been had times been more forgiving."

"More forgiving toward the whole of your family?"

"Yes."

"Were you pressed for food? Money? Shelter?"

"Yes, Father. We had shelter — the back of my uncle's house — but no more. My father was a proud man. He often lied and told my uncle he had found employment and now possessed money to spend on my brother and I. He denied we were starving and insisted we did not need the scraps from his brother's table."

"This was all untrue?"

"Yes, untrue. We starved. I do not know how my father spent his hours away from home, but he had no employment. Or if he did, he spent his earnings on himself. My brother and I suffered from hunger."

I swallowed another scallop.

"What has become of your brother now, my son?" asked the Paramount.

"The last I spoke with him he was begging on the streets. I believe he has leprosy, Father."

The questions blundered on like moths, lunging and burning against the glass of a lamp. I nodded into my food. This was only the first monk in the circle. There were still fifteen, maybe twenty more before my turn came. This was not like the gatherings we had had as dung-sniffers. There we assumed that all secrets were told, all thoughts known and all angers vented. No one forced you to speak. No one *made* you tell anything. I never did. My conversations were always pointed:

"Where have you been, Ksar?"

"The tattoo stand."

"What did you do there?"

"Pierced my tongue."

"Did it hurt?"

"No, Blade, not really."

Apart from that, no one wanted my opinion. I preferred it that way. On most points I had no opinions to offer, and when I did, experience had taught me it was often best to keep them to myself. Now, however, I would have to invent some thoughts or die in the attempt.

A hand touched my shoulder. I opened my eyes. "Do you wish me to repeat the query, my son?" said the Father Paramount.

I said nothing. The bone of a thread-like fish had wedged in my teeth. He accepted my silence as an invitation to speak. "Why is it, my son," said the Paramount, "that your appearance changes so frequently, and to such extent?"

"I don't know," I said.

"You must know." The Paramount's voice cooed like honey, as did his smile. His hand on my shoulder weighed as much as a melon. "Why the peculiar choice of attire, my son?"

"It amuses me," I said.

"And?"

"And people stare."

"Yes?"

"At first my brother didn't like it." What else could I say about lamps and fishing weights?

"Ahhh. You crave a place in his heart, do you not? You crave to purchase his notice."

I blinked. "I can't buy anything from Leque," I said. "I only have the money he gives me. He left the City last week. I don't know where he is now."

"You misunderstand, my son." The Paramount removed his hand from my shoulder. "You wish your brother to notice you, do you not?"

"He notices me."

"Is this because of your attire?"

I considered it. "I don't think so," I said. "We lived together. It would have been hard to ignore me."

"Did you live with your brother because of your choice of attire?"

"Er, not as far as I know."

"It was not your attire that convinced him you needed his care?"

"Not as far as I know. We've always lived together."

"When did you begin?"

"Begin what?" If I had ever wanted to kill Kem and the rest of them, it was nothing compared to how I now longed to be rid of these monks. I willed them to strangle themselves with their beards.

"Dressing in your current style," said the Paramount. "When did this begin, my son?"

"I don't know," I said. "Twenty-seven, maybe? After I met Glane."

The Paramount leaned forward, fingers so stippled and knotted in his beard I could not imagine how he hoped to free them. "Who is Glane, my son?"

I shut my mouth and decided to sulk.

"How did you and Glane meet?"

"No," I said. They didn't need to know about Glane. They didn't need to know how he'd tried to jump, the first time I met him years ago. I didn't want to think about Glane.

"Ah." The Father Paramount sat back. He twitched his fingers and gave up trying to disentwine them from his beard. Perhaps he hoped his predicament would go unnoticed. "You shun this barrier," he said, "but I shall attempt to pass it. Tell me, who is Glane?"

"He used to be my friend."

"He is no longer your friend?"

"No," I said. "I think he's dead."

"Did he die of an illness?"

"Yes." If chemicals, saliva, mucus and feathers counted as such. I shut my eyes and wished that Glane had never existed.

"How did you meet?"

I said, "No."

"You *will* tell us, my son." I could not help but wonder, as I sat and felt the scallops and vegetables settle like rocks in my stomach, why the other monks just sat there, listening, why none of them saved me. Couldn't they see that I suffered? I didn't want to answer these questions. "We are here for your Conference of Entrance," said the Father Paramount. "If you will not speak candidly, we cannot accept you as a brother of the Marble Tower. Now please," he said, and his voice again smiled, "how did you meet your friend Glane?"

"Glane's family owns an apothecary shop," I lied at last. "I contracted a rare scalp disease. I went there for treatment. That's how we met."

"That also explains your odd choice of attire, does it not, my son?" The Paramount smiled. "Am I right in surmising the ailment has not abated, and you choose your extravagant apparel in order to conceal this fact?"

"Yes," I said. The scallops squirmed in my stomach. "You are absolutely correct."

The Father Paramount pushed back his chair and stood, hands still in his beard. "Let us welcome Brother Ksar into the fraternity of the Marble Tower."

Three monks applauded. Most of my new brethren nodded in their beards.

"Brother Iander will show you to your quarters," said the Paramount.

Brother Iander tipped over his chair. "Follow me," he said. He caught his foot on one leg and stumbled. How long until I saw the Radiance?

13

Yaryk entered the first clothing store he passed. He patted his turban and ran his hand along the maze of fabric. It would have to go. He could not spare the time to lament. He would be a sad storyteller, bereft of turban. It was best not to think of the loss.

A striped tunic hung on the rack beside him. Yaryk fingered the seams and grimaced. The clothes of the people surrounded him.

A man ran up from the back of the shop, a round cap glued to his head. "Out!" He glared at Yaryk. "Out of my shop, Bedouin! You frighten my customers!"

"Five years ago you would have been honored." Yaryk rattled the coins in his pocket. "I will make my purchase in the back, if you prefer, where passersby will not see me, and then I will leave."

"Yes, yes." The man bobbed at the sound of the coins. "How do you like these colors? Burgundy, yes? Or blues? Grays perhaps? Beige?"

"It does not matter." Yaryk drew one of the tunics to his nose and sniffed. It smelt of fabric, low-grade dye and nothing. "This one." He pushed it into the man's face. "How many silver coins?"

"Three?" said the man.

"Two, you thief." Yaryk tossed the money at the shopkeeper's hands. One coin missed its mark, landed on the corrugated floor and rolled. "Show me to a room where I can change," said Yaryk.

The man showed him into the back. Yaryk changed quickly. He did not allow himself time to regret. He took the knife from his belt and cut his beard around his chin.

He had never worn it so short, not since his adolescence in his father's tribe. There were so many brothers and uncles — easier to remember the stars than all those relatives. He spread his robe on the floor and placed his beard in the center, twined in stone beads and leather lashes. He un-wound his turban. His hair reached his knees. He cut it off, lopped it off down to his scalp, and laid it beside his beard. He spread the turban on top of the hair and rolled his robe around it all. The bundle was enormous. He could not fit it under his arm. He took a scarf from the chest beside him — some discarded thing from the front of the shop — and tied the scarf tight around the bundle. He pulled out a second scarf, and then a third, and wound them also. The tunic he'd bought hung sleeveless on his back. The jacket overtop was too short; his wrists protruded. Yaryk threw another coin at the shopkeeper and left.

The streets of the Citadel had shifted in the years since he had seen them last. Shops had changed hands. Walls had crumbled, risen again, and far in the distance the spires of the nobles' palaces multiplied like thorns.

Only the Gaol remained unchanged, the largest prison in the Citadel. Yaryk seethed to think of Tallos there now, a leader of the Guild in a common prison. Yaryk strode down the streets he knew. The Gaol hulked in the blister-sun, a mound of white stone and age-charred wood. Red mortar, applied in some forgotten era, secured the wood and stone in place.

A guard stood sentry. He stood by the hole in the mortar that served as a doorway.

"I've come to see Tallos," said Yaryk, "the Bedouin."

"Have you come from Y'az Gyrt?"

"I have," said Yaryk.

"You're early," said the guard.

"I know." He didn't. Who was Y'az Gyrt? He did not ask.

"Go on." The guard nodded over his shoulder.

Yaryk went inside. Three lines of cages stretched the length of the hall. A man huddled in each cage. The only light was what trickled through the door behind. It smelled of human refuse and breath.

Another sentry materialized. "Y'az Gyrt?"

"Yes," said Yaryk.

"You're early," said the guard, but shrugged. He led Yaryk down the aisle of cages. "There you are." The guard pointed. He left Yaryk alone with the hundred prisoners. Every one of them watched him.

In the cage before him, a man sat on the floor with his back to the world. A heap of blankets spilled out from one corner and a mound of excrement stank in another.

"Tallos," said Yaryk.

The man turned. His cheeks were concave. His hair, thin, grew only in patches. Underneath, his skin flaked off in mottled strips. His eyes streamed red.

"Who are you?" He squinted. "You're not Gyrt's servant. I don't know your voice."

"I'm Yaryk."

"Who?"

"Yaryk." He spoke softly. "Do you not remember the High Council?" He wanted to spit at this thing in the cage. How could this creature be the same man who had once held sway in the Citadel? How?

"Yaryk." Tallos whined like a rusted zither. "I remember you," he said. "You were the one who told stories, yes?"

"That is true," said Yaryk.

"You said you talked to the stars. I remember that. Do your stories still come from the stars?"

Yaryk said nothing. He sneered at the old man, sitting there blind in his excrement. Insult me, he thought. Fine, I will not answer.

"Yaryk? Yaryk, are you still there?"

"Yes."

Sinew and tendon stood out in Tallos' neck, rank as a nest of snakes. He turned his head this way and that. "Have you been in the Citadel all this time? Yaryk," he said, "are you there?"

"I have just returned." How could he allow himself to live in such shame? Would it not be better to end your life than to spend it here, in this state? "I left with the others," said Yaryk, "when they forced us to leave."

"Some stayed," said Tallos.

"Who? What do you mean?"

"Neath stayed, with Jarb and Bry his brothers."

"That was foolish," said Yaryk. "Do they visit you?"

Tallos laughed. His face contorted and his shoulders shook. "Oh, Neath often visits. More often than he intends, perhaps. For extended periods of time he comes. A whole season once. Tavern fights, petty theft. Look around. You might find him now."

"I see," said Yaryk. "We've become petty criminals, have we?"

"Neath has. I don't know about Jarb. One-legged criminals are easy to catch. Can't you see it? Climbing through a jeweler's window with a cane?" He laughed again. "He would catch on the sill and be done. But why have you come back, Yaryk? Life on the highroads must be desperate indeed if you think you can find better work here. Ah, the highroads. I hardly remember them now. Tell me of the highroads, Yaryk."

"They are the same as always," said Yaryk, "with the ghibli and the zephyr forever in combat."

"You still talk in proverbs."

"Maybe I do," said Yaryk, "for all the fortune it has brought me. In the City, I too have become a criminal."

Tallos laughed again. "Yes, you should talk with Neath. You have much in common now. But what kind of crime would Yaryk commit? Surely you wouldn't waste yourself on petty theft?"

"No. I was caught in the stupidity of others. I don't wish to discuss it."

"Very well," said Tallos. "I'm sure if you told me you would offer me nothing but lies. I know your stories, Yaryk, and your arts of persuasion. Very good. Very useful at times."

"On a later visit perhaps I will tell you." Yaryk clenched his jaw. "What has happened to Ryas and Almir?"

"Dead."

"They died in prison?"

"Executed," said Tallos. He waved a hand. "Sit down, Yaryk. I know by your voice you're standing over me."

Yaryk sat reluctantly. He did not want to bring himself to the level of the prisoner, closer to the excrement and festering rags in the corner. He squatted, fingertips braced on the floor.

"Yes," said Tallos. "Almir and Ryas are dead. The people — those squabbling hordes — imprisoned us three." He choked another silent laugh. "It's served me well, leading the Guild."

"Yes," said Yaryk, "I see."

"Not all the Bedouin left as you did," said Tallos.

"They forced us to leave," said Yaryk. "They herded us out to the gates, and those who refused were shot. The rabble combed the Citadel and rounded us up in the night. They knew where we lived, and where we ate and gathered. I do not see how Neath could have stayed, or anyone else."

"Many came back," said Tallos. "A week after the meeting hall burned, Liop — you remember Liop, don't you? — he rallied the Bedouin at the Glebe. In the night he attacked. They stormed the Citadel wall and surrounded the nobles' palaces. Many people were killed. Many Bedouin were also killed, and the others were driven away."

"Was Liop killed?"

Tallos waved his hands like the claws of a bird. "Yes, yes, most likely. The Bedouin assaulted the High Penitentiary, where Almir, Ryas, and I were rotting. Liop planned our rescue, for all the good that would do for the Bedouin. We would have no Council to govern, and no authority to wield. What does it matter? The armies of the nobles caught them and beat them to death with hickory switches.

"The next day, the nobles' guards took Almir to the roof of the Penitentiary and hanged him. They did it as a warning to any Bedouin still within the Citadel walls. Another rebellion would lead to more death. At the next sign of an uprising, they told the crowds, Ryas would die."

"The nobles did this?" said Yaryk. "The *people* began the rebellion, not the nobles. How did the nobles usurp power so quickly?"

Tallos laughed. "They didn't usurp it. The people gave it to them. They held an election the day after they destroyed the Guild. They were mimicking us, that was all. They brought down our system and sought to replace it with one of their own. Several nobles ran in the election." He rubbed his eye. He smeared red pus on the back of his hand. "There has been no show of democracy since."

"Bribery," said Yaryk.

"I suspect," said Tallos. "What does it matter?"

"And Ryas is also dead?" said Yaryk.

"Last year they moved us from the High Penitentiary to here," said Tallos. "They did not expect us to live long anyway."

"They have no mercy," said Yaryk. "The Gaol is for short-term residence. That was all we used it for. Not even criminals should spend their whole lives here."

"We tried to run," said Tallos. "The guards shot at our feet. They crippled me. I still have the marks on my heels. The wounds went black for weeks before healing over. They hit Ryas in the back. The arrow came out his stomach. He lived for nine days. They put me in a cell beside him. The ants came long before he died. After that the guards blinded me so I would not try another escape."

"I am sorry," said Yaryk.

"Now you should leave," said Tallos. "I heard you talking to the guards. They think you're Gyrt's servant. It would not be wise to be found here when the real emissary arrives."

Yaryk stood. He held his old robe bundled under his arm. "Who is Y'az Gyrt? A noble?"

"Yes."

"Why does he send you his servants?"

"He is only half noble," said Tallos. "He came to the Citadel last season. He was still a Bedouin then."

Yaryk laughed. He kicked his foot on the excrement floor. "A Bedouin noble? I doubt that, Tallos."

"He bought his way into the nobility. The man was incredibly rich. He stumbled on a vein of gold on the highroads perhaps, or a platinum mine. When he came to the Citadel he showered all the nobles with gifts, and now he is one of them. I believe they distrust him, though. If he didn't continue to pay them, they would not allow him to stay."

"Why does he send you his servants?"

"I too am a storyteller, Yaryk."

Yaryk's lip twitched at the comparison. A storyteller, yes, perhaps. But like him? That he doubted.

"They come for the stories," said Tallos, "and relay them back to Gyrt for entertainment."

"Buffoon," said Yaryk.

"They bring me bread," said Tallos, "and ointment sometimes."

Yaryk clenched his jaw. "I am leaving."

"Will you come back?" Tallos rose to his knees. He struck his temple on the cage and sat back. "Will you visit again?"

"Yes," said Yaryk. There was nothing more to be gained from this place. He left down the aisle of cages. The prisoners screamed at him as he passed.

Blade woke to find himself not in a satin bed, gauze-lined, but in fact on a wooden floor, burnt and hard. A man sat beside him, braiding a black rope.

"Yaryk?"

"Yes." He did not look up from the rope of his hair.

"What are you doing?" Blade pulled himself up on his elbows.

"It is not safe to be a Bedouin here." Yaryk looked small and shrunken without his robes: just a thin dark man in a tunic. Muscles twitched on his arms as he worked. Under the muscles his bones stood out like rods. Blade had never seen Yaryk so thin.

"Why are you braiding your hair?"

"I don't want to lose it." Yaryk looked up from his work and met Blade's eyes. "I must cut your hair next."

"I'm not a Bedouin. I don't understand."

"You've traveled with one, all the way from the City." Yaryk's face was now visible, his beard lopped off and trimmed. The Bedouin's nose hooked as long as the bill of a heron. He grimaced and sneered as he worked. His lips formed yellow lines below his nose. "Take off the robe I gave you," he said. "Put this on instead." He held out a russet brown jacket, the same style as the one he wore: straight buttons down the front, close sleeves. Blade pulled it on. It was too big.

Yaryk took a knife from his belt. "Turn around."

Blade stepped away. He had never feared Yaryk 'til now. This short-haired man was unfamiliar.

"By the Stars," said Yaryk, "don't behave like a frightened sheep. I have no desire to cut your throat."

Blade shuffled a step toward Yaryk. He stood still. Yaryk took a lock of his hair and pulled it taut. The dagger sawed back and forth. The sound of it reverberated into Blade's skull. He winced at the sound, so close to his ear.

"Your beads tell everyone you're a noble," said Yaryk. "That may be equally unsafe here. No one wears the star of the Xzaven house. Or here, the four-petalled orchid." The dagger sawed. The beads fell. They ran pattering over the floor. Blade reached out. He tried to catch them but they slipped between his fingers like dandelion spores and rolled, bounded, disappeared into the cracks of the floor.

"Here." Yaryk handed him his hair. It sat in his hands like a pile of flax. It was so pale it was almost white.

Blade pointed at the tangled mass. "What's that?"

"You have lice."

He held the hair in his lap. Black specks crawled in and out of the clots, and out from the centers of beads. "What are we going to do?" he whispered. "When can we go back to the City?"

Yaryk smiled, his teeth as off-white as Blade's hair. He lifted Blade under his arms and hauled him to his feet. "Not for some time." He steered him to the window and helped him over the sill. "We're going to see a friend of mine now. He might be suspicious. You will tell him that you are my son. You are my adopted son. All right, Blade? You were once a refugee, orphaned. I took you under my care." Yaryk followed him over the sill. "Do you understand me, Blade?"

"Is your friend a Bedouin?" Blade rubbed his eyes in the light.

"He was," said Yaryk. "Now we shall see."

Why did it matter so much, thought Blade, whether or not men were Bedouin, or nobles, or something else entirely. Why did it matter? Was he, Blade, still a noble? Was he really a noble at all anymore? He could not say. He had been once. He had once been Xavier Ven, heir to the richest family in the City. Now, who knew?

They walked for a long time. Blade could not think what to say. Hunger. It ate at his stomach like a sour root. He had never been hungry at home. They dodged around men on foot, men with wheelbarrows, litters and camels in tassels. He didn't have the energy to talk. He stared at the litters. He closed his eyes and felt the sway of the silk walls, the embroidered cushions propped under his head. He smelled sweet jasmine. A boy with a lute walked along beside. He drowned all the sounds of the world.

Yaryk caught Blade's shoulder. "Don't fall asleep." Stone and wood spires wheeled around them. The smell of dust hung thick in the air.

The traffic thinned. Yaryk turned down an alleyway, stopping in front of a door carved out of the stone. A curtainless window yawned beside the door. The smell of sesame cakes wafted out from the dark. Yaryk knocked. They waited. The smell of the cakes ate holes in Blade's stomach. He had not eaten cakes since the City. He had eaten nothing but nuts and dried fruit from Yaryk's pack, and salted meat from the smugglers, hard and refreshing as leather.

The door swung open. A boy, the same age as Blade, glared up at them. His face was brown, his hair a black mop above his eyes. "Who are you?" He waved a cooking pan in Yaryk's face. "Go away."

"Bry?"

The boy squinted up, his eyes as black as cobalt. "How d'you know my name?"

"I remember you," said Yaryk. "I've come to talk to your brothers."

"You can't. They're busy."

"Bry!" called a voice from inside the house. The voice was a man's, out of breath and nasal. "Who is it, Bry? Ask them what they want."

"He wants to see you!" the boy shouted back.

"Who?"

"I don't know." Bry's teeth shone a shocking white. Blade leaned against the wall and watched them flash.

"Bring him into the kitchen," said the voice.

Bry stood back and let them in. The room inside was all but featureless. A mat of straw fibers carpeted the floor. It snagged Blade's feet as he walked. The smell of sesame strengthened, wafting up from a flight of steps. Heat radiated up the stairwell and firelight flickered the walls.

A man with a cane hobbled up the steps. "Please accept my apologies for last night's commotion," he said, not looking up. He produced a rag from his belt and wiped his hands. "If there is anything I can do—"

"Neath's brawls do not concern me."

The man looked up. His mouth fell open. "Yaryk?"

Yaryk bowed. Without his robes, the motion was scant. "I am relieved to see that you at least remember me, Jarb."

Jarb's face was pale, a few black wisps on his chin in place of a beard. He dropped his rag, took Yaryk's hand and shook it. "Yaryk, gone for years! Where have you been wandering?"

"I have wandered every road," said Yaryk.

"What is the world like these days?"

"As vast and beautiful as the stories of our ancestors." Yaryk shook his head. "I mapped the stars and traveled to the Fortress Meadows. I lived in the City a while. I have now returned."

"I would not have returned if I were you," said Jarb. "Why would you choose the Citadel over freedom?" He gestured to the bare room, and the close stone walls.

"You never left," said Yaryk. "Why didn't you leave?"

"I'm a cripple, Yaryk. The nomad life would be hard. The people let me stay. They said I was harmless." He grinned. His teeth were chipped. "Neath and Bry could have left. They pleaded to stay and look after me. The people let them. We were watched all the time for a while."

Bry glowered. He disappeared into the kitchen. Blade wanted to follow, into the smell of sweet sesame. He had not eaten since coming here, to the Citadel or whatever it was called. Yaryk carried the pack of supplies. Blade's hunger did not matter; Yaryk had the power to feed or ignore him.

Jarb turned to Blade. "And who are you?" he said. His voice was kind

"Blade," said Blade.

"I befriended his father during my travels," said Yaryk, "before he passed away last season. I have now taken Blade under my protection."

Jarb extended a hand. He smiled his chip-toothed smile. "Please," he said, "come into the kitchen. It's warmer there."

Bry sat in a corner, a short-stemmed pipe in his mouth. He set the pipe down and blew white smoke from his nose. There were no chairs and no cushions. They sat on the floor by the fire pit. Jarb lifted the sesame cakes from the grate with a pair of tongs and handed them around. He produced a stick of incense from his pocket and lit it in the embers.

"When did you arrive here, Yaryk?"

"This morning. We evaded the escort from the gates."

Blade nodded. "We ran," he said. He liked this man, Jarb.

"Where will you stay tonight?" said Jarb.

"We can sleep in a doorway if no lodgings present themselves," said Yaryk. "We carry blankets innumerable from the City."

"Please, stay here." Jarb waved a hand. "We have only this room for sleeping, I'm afraid, but it's warmer and safer than the streets."

"Except when Neath is out of prison?"

Jarb sighed. "Yes, Neath is at the Gaol, now as always. He was free for less than a day before last night's brawl."

"Are you and he the only members of the High Council left?"

"There are others who were once part of the Guild," said Jarb. "They adopted trades and the nobles allowed them to return. Merhzh and Gwall are among them. Do you remember them?"

Yaryk shook his head. "They weren't in the High Council?"

"No," said Jarb. "Of the High Council there are only the two of us, and Liop, and you."

"Liop?" Yaryk glanced up from the fire. "Tallos lied to me then. He told me Liop was killed."

"You've talked to Tallos?"

"Yes, by the Stars. This morning."

"I doubt Tallos knows about Liop. But yes, he has been here since the uprising. Did Tallos tell you of that? Of Liop's attempt at a counter-rebellion?"

"Yes," said Yaryk. He didn't need more details. It had happened years ago, and there was nothing he could do to change the outcome now. "Do you know where Liop can be found?"

"Yes," said Jarb. "He keeps himself hidden, but I know where he is. Do you want to talk with him?"

"Yes, tomorrow."

"Time has not improved him any." Jarb laughed. "Bitter old men and defeat do not breed well together."

"Hah, no," said Yaryk. He scratched his beard. "In return for your hospitality, I have no money to offer, but I would gladly relate a story in token of my thanks."

"Oh, yes please!" said Blade.

Bry sneered in the corner.

From a basket against the wall, Jarb produced a bottle of wine. He set it on the floor between them.

"Ah," said Yaryk, eyeing the bottle. "One more question: what do you know of Y'az Gyrt?"

"Very little." Jarb removed the cork from the bottle. "From what I hear, he cares about prestige, money and little else. If you're thinking of talking to the Y'az, I advise you to change your mind. He's a faction all his own. You will do no more than expose yourself as a Bedouin."

14

I sat on the edge of my new bed and shivered. The robe reached barely to my knees. I watched Brother Iander. "What are you doing?" I asked.

"This room is too cluttered to contain your things," he said. He stuffed Leque's toga and the one tunic I had brought back into my pillowcase, and slung it over his shoulder. Apart from beds and the pulsing walls the sleeping quarters were empty.

"Those are my clothes," I said. "Shouldn't you ask me before taking them away?"

"You won't need them," he said.

The thought dawned on me that perhaps Brother Iander did not like me. I had already decided I did not like him.

"Wait here," he told me. "On my return I will introduce you to your first task as a brother of the Marble Tower."

"When can I have my clothes back?"

"Possibly never."

"What are you doing with them?"

He did not answer. He left and closed the door behind him. I stared at the back of the door.

I had not seen the Father Paramount again since my entrance into the Brotherhood. I had not done anything since entering the Brotherhood, but wander the back passageways of the Tower, proving to myself again and again that the hospital was not the only labyrinthine torture-house in the City. Now and then a righteous brother would ambush me and tell me to sit and meditate. Were those my only missions here? To eat nameless foods and clear my mind of all thoughts? If Kem's house had been dull, this was far worse. Brother Iander frequently hovered around me. He irked me like dander, caught in my bloodstream. He produced the same irritation.

The door opened. The dander returned. "Follow me," he said.

I followed. Several passageways later, he opened a door and ushered me into a small room, the floor of which was covered in scraps of paper. Wish papers rose to the ceiling. Golden threads danced in the gloom. I thought of old Glane, struggling with strings and knots. I'd always helped him hang his wishes.

"We sort the papers here," said Brother Iander. He dropped to his knees beside the colossal heap. "All we have to do," he said, "is read them." He gathered a handful. "Put the ones that you've read into one of those baskets." He pointed. "If they're interesting, put them in the white basket. If not, the black one."

"What qualifies as interesting?"

He blinked at me. "Anything about defacing the Radiance or killing monks. Brother Eln has not merely disappeared; he's been murdered, stabbed to death. We found his body this morning." Brother Iander gulped. His eyes stuck out from his head. "He was found in the back of a cobbler's shop!"

"Oh." I picked up a handful of papers, turned the first one over and read: "Let this piece of squid be removed from my teeth, and I will be happy." I looked at it hard and wondered if I'd misread the wish. "What if it's interesting in other ways?"

"Why? What does it say?"

I read the note aloud.

"That's not important."

"But isn't it interesting?"

"No."

None of the wishes were interesting. Not, at least, in Brother Iander's judgment.

"How about this one?" My side ached from laughter. "'Let me find my ear!'"

"Evidently someone is in search of their ear," he said, coldly. "If you were faced with such a dilemma, I doubt that you would find it amusing. Though this one," he said, after a pause, "I must admit is rather bizarre."

"What does it say?"

"'I found my brother's cobras, but they won't let me in to see him. I hope he stops growing feathers and comes home soon.'"

My laughter gargled off. "That's not funny." I grabbed the wish from his hands. There it was, scrawled in a child's writing. Sfin's writing? Did Sfin know how to write? "What happens to the ones in the black basket?" I asked.

"We burn them."

"Hah! I knew it!" I stared at the wish again. So Glane was still growing feathers. He wasn't dead. Not yet at least. Why were his brothers not permitted to see him? Perhaps I would not be permitted either. Kem could drag me along, but then I'd get down on my knees, say I was one of his younger brothers, and they wouldn't let me in.

I turned to Brother Iander. "Can I take this wish?"

"Why?" He blinked at me. He always blinked. "Why would you want someone else's wish?"

15

Yaryk stepped into the alley and closed the door behind him. One horizon leaked gray. He wove his way through the silent streets, into the higher levels where the ground was tiled, not dirt or stone.

By the time both suns had risen, Yaryk was still searching. The nobles' palaces grew thick as blisters here, but none could be the residence of a Bedouin lord. The great placards over their gates read, "Feln," "Zlav," "Drens," "Kli'elm." No "Gyrt."

Mid-morning, he stumbled into a public square where a fountain, shaped like a swan, drooled into a marble bowl. Beyond the fountain loomed a palace different from all the others he had passed. It sprawled horizontally, without a spire. Its arched doorway yawned across the square. A million windows caught the morning light. This, perhaps, was the palace of a Bedouin, if true Bedouin could live in palaces.

The square was deserted. Yaryk stood beside the fountain, folded his arms, and waited. He watched the curtains, one by one, pull back from the one hundred windows. He crossed the square and rapped on the door. There was no wind and no answer. He knocked again.

A panel slid back at eye level, revealing a nose and pouting lips. "What's your business?"

"I've come to speak with Y'az Gyrt."

"You can't." The panel shut.

Yaryk stood beneath the arch of the doorway. He tapped his heel in time with his thoughts.

The panel slid open again and a different set of nostrils appeared. "The Y'az demands to know your business."

"I've come to speak with him."

"He doesn't want to speak with you," said the nose, "but if you tell me your business, I will relay it to him."

"I'm a Bedouin," said Yaryk. "Tell your Y'az he must share his position with his fellow Bedouin. It is our right."

The panel shut. What cowards. What unspeakable cowards these servants were.

The panel reopened and the nose said: "Have you come for money?"

"Money?" Yaryk laughed. "Your master is Y'az Gyrt, is he not? Does a Bedouin lord truly equate money to power?"

"Yes."

"Power," said Yaryk. "Power! Influence! A place in the Citadel! That is what I have come for. Power and money are different. Different things! I must speak with Gyrt about the state of the Citadel."

"You can't," said the servant. The panel shut.

Yaryk ground his heel down into the stone, while overhead the suns moved crazily across the sky. The door opened. Guards bristled out. They pointed their spears at Yaryk's chest. Yaryk spat at their feet and strode away.

Blade kept behind Yaryk as they walked, following Jarb into the bowels of the Citadel. The walls crowded in and the alleyways narrowed, dead-ended and doubled back. Cracks laced the cobbles. Sudden chasms cut the sides of the roads.

"Sewers," said Bry. "Are you thirsty?"

Blade did not see the connection.

They stopped at the end of a dirt-paved alleyway, so narrow Blade could stand with his arms outstretched and touch both walls at once. The backs of buildings leaned in from every side — storerooms, dwelling complexes — none with windows facing this alley. They stood before an edifice of crumbled brick. The mortar had been chiseled away at one point, an arm's length over their heads, to form a hole just wide enough for a man to crawl through. Blade edged closer to Yaryk.

Jarb threw a stone at the wall. "Liop," he called. A hot, dry wind whistled down the alley.

"Go away." The voice echoed around them.

"Yaryk's here," said Jarb. "He wants to see you."

"Yaryk?" said the voice. "What is Yaryk doing here?"

"Let us up and we'll tell you."

Blade did not want to go up that wall, into that hole. He wanted to remain where he was, in the alley, where at least there was light and solid ground beneath his feet. He wanted to sit. The soles of his sandals had worn away to near-nothing — shreds of leather, held to his feet by a cake of blood. The breeze rustled Blade's hair. It whipped in his face, lighter than feathers now that he had lost his beads.

A rope ladder uncoiled from the wall.

Jarb hobbled to the base of the rope. "He's letting us up." He grimaced. "Here, Bry." He handed his cane to his brother and started to climb, laboriously slow with only one leg.

Hands reached out from the hole and hauled him in. "Come up, little Yaryk," said the voice.

Yaryk climbed quickly. He brushed the hands away when they reached to help.

Blade swallowed. He stepped to the base of the ladder. Before he could touch its fiber, the line danced away. He stepped back and rubbed his hands on his shirt. They clung with sweat.

Bry tugged his sleeve. "Come here." He dragged Blade down the length of the alleyway, where the sun pelted orange on the stone. "Forget it," said Bry. "You don't want to go in there. Trust me. I've been up there once and that's enough." Bry lit his pipe. He kept his matches behind his ear. "It smells like old man," he said. "He doesn't come down to piss."

Blade glanced behind them. Arms wrapped in burlap drew in the ladder.

"Are you worried about your father?" Bry laughed with his diamond teeth. "Liop will let them out eventually. He'll talk riddles for an hour. Then he'll tell them to rebel. Jarb won't agree and he'll make them leave." Bry spat. "That's the way it usually goes."

"Oh," said Blade.

"Liop wants to kill everyone in the Citadel." Bry sat down by the side of the road. He splayed his legs and rested his elbows on his knees. "He wants to kill all the nobles and all the common people at least, and after you do that, there's not gonna be many other people left. If I were Jarb I'd do it. Once I killed the nobles, I'd kill Liop too and keep the power myself." Bry leaned against the wall. He folded his arms behind his head. "What about you, blue-eye? Do you like the nobles?"

Blade scratched his head and said nothing. The sun made him squint.

"I heard you crying last night," said Bry.

"No you didn't," said Blade.

Bry laughed. "Our kitchen is the size of a rat's nest. I could have heard you fart from across the room. Why were you crying?" He chewed his pipe. "Do you wish Yaryk hadn't made himself your father?"

"No," said Blade. He had cried for too many reasons. He wanted to eat sugared dates. He wanted a bath of warm milk and jasmine. He did not want to talk.

"I bet you never wanted to come here, did you?" Bry's hair shone orange in the light. "It was all Yaryk's idea to bring you along. I bet he brings you everywhere with him, for his own enjoyment."

"Fine," said Blade.

"Fine what?"

"Fine if you think that."

Bry rolled the pipe around his mouth. "I know what Yaryk keeps you for."

"What?"

"Your hands." Bry held up his own. They were paler at the fingertips, and the hollows of his palms. He ran his hands down his chest, caressing himself from cheek to groin. "Does he do this, little blue-eye?" Bry moaned. He caught Blade staring and laughed.

"No!" said Blade.

"Not like this? He didn't touch you like this? Touch you with those great strong hands? He didn't uncover your sweaty little secrets?"

"No, he didn't!"

"You didn't uncover his?" said Bry. "Maybe he gave you money and you lay on top of him and licked him all over." Bry spat out his pipe and licked his lips. He rolled his eyes. "'Oh Yaryk, Yaryk!' 'Oh Blade, touch me there Blade, touch me again!'"

Blade stepped backwards, into the wall of a shack and sat down. The dust billowed up around him. His stomach crawled. He scrambled to his feet, his throat thick with salt.

"You don't want me to know about it?" Bry slid across the dirt between them. "Don't worry, I won't tell. I'll keep your secrets. Maybe you don't like old men anymore. Is that it? How about someone younger?" He ran his tongue in and out through his lips. "What do you think of my teeth? Come here, Blade." He held out his arms. He laughed so hard his chest shook. Who knew where his pipe had gone? "Let me hold you, blue-eye. Don't shy away like that! It's all right to be interested. There's no one to see us. We can hide behind the shack." He grabbed Blade's tunic. His sesame breath washed into Blade's face. He raised one finger, traced the almond fingertip over Blade's nose, wove circles down his chest, his stomach, and lower. He twisted his face into a laughing mask.

"Stop it!" Blade kicked. He no longer cared if he showed his fear. He kicked as hard as he could, like a cock in a fight in the market. He climbed to his feet. "Go away!" He dug his knee into the soft between Bry's legs.

Bry's smile disappeared. His mouth contorted. "Son of an ass." He crumpled to his knees. "I was only joking. You spoiled, blue-eyed, ass!" He struck Blade in the back of his leg. Blade fell and Bry rolled on top of him, teeth bared, tears glittering in his eyes. "You want to fight now, do you? I'll give you a fight!" He struck Blade's temple, straddled his chest, and dug his knees into Blade's ribs. Bry's weight crushed into Blade's stomach. He could hardly breathe. He could not free his arms.

Bry tore at Blade's hair. He wrenched his head forward and slammed it down. "You have beads in your hair," he hissed. "You little noble boy." He spat. "I thought you were. You can't fight, can you?" His fist swung back, crashed into Blade's nose, and the blood splashed into Blade's mouth. It tasted of metal and mucus and so much salt.

Blade spluttered. He opened his eyes and saw nothing but Bry, black against the suns. The Bedouin boy bent in for another strike and the suns blinded Blade. Blade tried to scream; he could not draw breath.

Bry's fist came down for his mouth. Blade bit. He tasted more blood and metal. He wrenched his hands free. He jerked his knee and caught Bry in the crotch for a second time, and then he was free, too terrified to remember how to stand. He crawled away, out of reach. He dragged himself up and ran.

Blade ran as well as he could in bare feet, with his blood flying up from his nose and into his eyes. He was not pursued. He collapsed against a wall. He pounded the stone with his fists. He screamed and cried at once. He tried to make each sob louder than the last. He had come out on a main thoroughfare now. Everyone stared as they passed.

He tried to remember how to curse. He wanted to curse Yaryk for bringing him here, and curse his grandfather for sending him away, and curse that stranger — whoever that stranger had been — who'd come to his grandfather and told of the Radiance. Curse the Radiance too. But he didn't know how and so he knelt there, pressed into the stone, and let his nose pour a fetid fountain down his neck.

"Xavier?"

Yes, thought Blade, why not curse myself as well? He could curse himself for visiting the Tower, and reaching out and touching red feathers.

The voice came again, in front of him now: "Xavier Ven?"

Blade opened his eyes. They were full of his hair. He pushed the hair away and looked up, into a white-bearded face. He knew that face. "Y'az Tyfel?"

"You *are* Xavier, aren't you?" The Y'az's forehead wrinkled. He dabbed his hands with a clean white cloth. "You certainly have come a long way from the City."

"Take me back!" Blade wiped his nose with the back of his hand. It came away red with blood. "Please, please, take me back!"

Tyfel snapped his fingers. A retinue of servants appeared behind him. Blade sobbed again. He had not seen servants in days.

"Do you want him in the litter, Y'az?"

"No, carry him."

One of the men lifted Blade. Blade let himself sag and go limp. His arm throbbed. The blood ran down his nose and down the back of the servant's toga. The world spun. The streets swayed below him. Y'az Tyfel's voice drifted in through a fog. The servants helped Tyfel up into his litter. Blade nodded to sleep as they walked.

Liop's home reeked. It smelled of burnt wax, herbs, and human habitation. Candles lined the walls, gasping for air.

"The City didn't want you?" Liop leaned toward Yaryk. Burlap smothered his head and arms. A beard wisped out from the folds like strands of spider web. "What did you do, Yaryk, that they drove you out?"

"I was not driven out," said Yaryk. "I chose to leave."

"You're not a criminal then?"

"I am a criminal."

"Yes, I wonder what you did?"

Yaryk folded his hands in his lap. His wrists felt exposed without sleeves.

"Here in the Citadel," said Liop, "do you know who the criminals are?" He answered before Yaryk could speak: "Everyone," he said. "Everyone is a criminal."

Jarb shifted on the floor beside him.

"I'm the only one in the Citadel who is *not* a criminal," said Liop. "Why, you ask? I'll tell you why. They destroyed the Bedouin Guild — the people. We decided thousands of years ago to orbit the Citadel. We have always met here! We have always ruled fairly, but the people destroyed us. Once I cared for them but now I disown them." Liop spat. "They perpetrated treason, not a revolution."

"A revolution is simply an uprising that succeeds," said Jarb. "It doesn't matter if the cause is worthy or not."

"We should not accept it!" Liop's head jerked back and forth as he spoke. "They are all criminals."

"They petitioned with their complaints," said Jarb. "We ignored them."

"They had no right to complain! We provided the link to the outside world!" Liop's voice rose and fell as he spoke. He sat forward with his back stooped, elbows on his cross-legged knees. "The nobles," he hissed, "are criminals for robbing the people. They distorted the elections with bribery. It must have been bribery. They have debased us, the Bedouin, as if we ourselves were criminals. And what do we do in response? We hide in our holes like vermin, and talk!"

"I find no fault in conversation," said Jarb. "Isn't it better to plan ahead than charge blindly into action?"

Liop's eyes flickered. "You admit we must act."

"None of the actions you propose are wise," said Jarb. "I know your counsels, and I know that none would succeed. How many Bedouin are left in the Citadel, Liop? Fifty perhaps at the most? And of those fifty, how many own a robe or turban? I tell you, precious few. They have all become locksmiths and jewelers now."

"Criminals. We are sitting idle."

"Why should we fight for change?" said Jarb. "We three may be the only ones in the Citadel who want it."

"Yes, you may speak your philosophies of hopelessness, Jarb son of Jathen," said Liop, "but I know you're afraid to fight. That is all it is. I've heard your views before. You are afraid for yourself. I would call you a coward." His voice remained even, like an old man to a foolish child. "You don't want to lose both legs, is that it?" The burlap-covered head jerked back to Yaryk. "What do you say? You are the one who wanted to talk to me. Why don't you say anything?"

"'*The man who breaks silence last shall receive the greatest reception,*'" said Yaryk. "That saying came back to me during my travels."

"You've had it longer than that," said Liop. "Story-tellers are full of sayings. What good do they bring you, words and clever quoting?"

Yaryk waited for Liop to finish. "And what do you propose?" he asked, calm as a sheet of glass. "Do you propose immediate rebellion?"

"Yes."

"Against whom?" said Yaryk.

"The nobles! They rule the Citadel! When we were the Guild, we left the nobles in peace. We allowed them to run their businesses, bathe in riches and scented oil, and go to and fro as they liked. And now? The guards stop Bedouin at the gates and beat them if they try to enter."

"Assaulting the nobles is ridiculous," said Jarb. "They live in guarded palaces while we are beyond scattered; we don't even know each other's names. We have no leader. Half of our people now deny their heritage."

"Bite your tongue," said Liop. "I know what you think. And you, Yaryk?"

"Open onslaught is not feasible." Yaryk seethed. Liop directed the questions to him as an afterthought, as if he, Yaryk, were another child, not a man who had wandered the highroads for years, dabbled in City politics, advised the nobles of the City and given them prophecies.

"What do you think?" said Liop. "Assassination?"

Yaryk ran a hand through his beard. He hated its length, so short against his chin. "I am not an assassin myself," he said, and smiled. "Such a thing may be possible, but my knowledge of killing is limited." The last killing he had seen had been the death of a monk — a far cry from assassination.

Liop leaned forward, about to speak. A stone flew between them. It struck the opposite wall.

"Jarb!" cried a voice from below.

Yaryk leaned out past the ladder. Bry, the boy with teeth like chisels, stood in the sun at the base of the wall. His chest heaved. He waved his arms.

"Let me up!" he shouted. "They took Blade!"

Liop threw down the end of the ladder. It ran down the stone to Bry's feet. The boy climbed quickly, hand over hand with his hair in his eyes.

Jarb dragged him over the lip. "Who took Blade?"

"Nobles!" Bry waved his arms. "It was hot in the alley, so we went for a walk. I was going to show him the knife shop, just over there, Jarb." He waved again. "We were walking along the road when some nobles came along with servants. They had guards with them, lots of them. We got to the side of the road." He broke off and wheezed. What shape were this boy's lungs in? Yaryk felt himself sneer. "One of the guards saw Blade. 'That's the boy who broke into the Citadel!' he shouted. The other guards turned. 'Take them both!' they yelled. They meant me as well. They charged us. I would have fought them off, but there were too many. We had to run. They threw spears. One hit Blade. I tried to go back, but there were too many guards. I had to keep running." Bry looked at Yaryk. "He was still alive, I think. I heard him screaming. He's with the nobles. They took him away."

Yaryk rose to a crouch. They'd taken Blade. They thought they could do that, did they? Kidnap a boy for entering the Citadel? Punish him for being a Bedouin? So this was how his people were treated? But to do it to Blade, who would have no comprehension ... Yaryk shuffled for the door, then stopped. "Liop, where would they take him?"

"Oh, they have many prisons." Liop waved one burlap arm. "How can I say which one? All the prisons are at their disposal now. They may not lock him up at all. Perhaps they'll beat him and throw him out the gates. Or no, now that my thought dwells on it, I've heard of this happening before. In similar cases, the Bedouin is kept in a private cell of the noble's palace — a week or maybe more — for interrogation. They still fear us."

Yaryk clenched his fists. Blade had been a source of annoyance on the highroads, but this? The boy did not deserve this. Yaryk sat back and smiled. He did not let the others see. He had wanted a catalyst and here it was.

Jarb was speaking to his brother. "Do you know which noble house it was?"

"How could I?" said the boy. "I didn't ask."

"Yaryk," said Liop, "what will you do?"

"They have taken my son," said Yaryk. "What would any father do?" He swung to the top of the ladder. "How many Bedouin remain in the Citadel, Jarb? Fifty? I want to address them."

Blade lay on a bed in a dim-lit room. He lay on silken sheets. He smiled at the ceiling. Palace walls surrounded him. A guard stood outside the door. The air smelled of honeydew melon.

A servant appeared above him with a towel draped over his arms. "Are you well enough to bathe now, Master?"

Blade smiled and nodded. The eunuch helped him sit. Blade's nose was plugged with gauze and the clothes he'd worn from the City still clung to his body. He leaned on the servant's arm as they crossed the carpet, into the adjoining room. Cinnamon steam filled the air. A pool of rose water lapped the walls. A towel and clean clothes draped a stool at the water's edge. The servant moved to help Blade undress but he cringed away.

"Can I help you, Master?"

"No." Blade blushed. "I'm fine."

"Do you wish me to leave?"

Blade twitched his arm. "I'll call if I need you."

"Very good." The eunuch left the room.

Blade stood and inhaled the steam. He wanted to drink its fragrance. Alone now, he peeled his robes away. He could feel Bry's fingers down his stomach, down his chest to his waist, down ... Blade slid beneath the water. The heat of it seared his skin. His hands were sun-burnt red as garnet. Rose petals and scented oils glazed the surface. He did not want to see himself beneath the water. He wanted to dive and wash away this filth. He wanted home. He no longer cared about the family name. He wanted only the City; he wanted his room and his ermine bed. He would live with Leque if no other options appeared. He would risk the bees. He did not care about anything else.

Blade sank beneath the petaled surface and ran his hands through the butchered locks of his hair. Roses closed over his head and the soap stung his eyes. He held his breath until his ears throbbed. The weight of sand, sweat, fleas and blood fell away. He dragged his hands through his hair again. It was so short where Yaryk had cut it, so long on the other side where it still reached his shoulder. He raked his fingers to the knotted ends. They came away with strands, invisible-sharp as fishing twine, caught around his thumbs.

The flower petals sank around him. He could not hide beneath them. They lay along the bottom, slippery as skin on the tiles. He could see himself now. Every ripple of the surface warped his body. He looked so skeletal, his hands and feet so peeling-red. He still remained white where his robes had covered him. The line of his collar-bone jutted out like a shelf. He counted his ribs. What other noble could see his own bones?

Blade dragged himself out of the water. He wrapped a towel around his shoulders, stood at the pool's edge and dripped the water away. It ran in rivulets down his legs. It soaked the carpet from red to burgundy.

Blade dressed himself slowly: loose-fitting trousers, embroidered only at the hem with a tracery of men on horseback; a velvet tunic; a gold-linked belt; a cloak to match the tunic; and finally, in a jewelry box beside the rest, a pair of ivory earrings.

Blade called the servant. The eunuch appeared and slipped the earrings into his ears. He produced a barber's knife. Blade closed his eyes. The blade ran straight along the back of his head and the knotted hair fell away. Blade touched a finger to his lip where Bry had struck him.

"The swelling will ease soon enough," said the eunuch.

He would never fight again, Blade swore. No more sun. No more walking in sandals.

The eunuch led him down carpeted hallways to a private dining room, where Y'az Tyfel sat at a table, smoking his pipe and reading a scroll.

He looked up. "Xavier Ven." He smiled. "You look more like yourself. My, my. My, my indeed. How did you come to the Citadel?"

"Yaryk brought me." Blade sat down. He was hungry. The hunger made him faint. He had eaten nothing since the sesame cakes of the night before. There was food close by; he smelled it.

"Where is this 'Yaryk?'" said Tyfel.

"I don't know."

"It doesn't surprise me he would bring you here." Tyfel puffed on his pipe. "This is the old Bedouin capital of the world."

Blade said nothing. He had nothing to say.

"Do you miss the City?" said Tyfel.

"Yes."

The old man's forehead puckered. He rubbed a hand through his beard. "I tried to discuss this with your grandfather. You understand, Xavier, he's concerned for your safety." He rocked in his chair, thinking. Blade envied his stomach. Y'az Tyfel embodied wealth and rich dining. Blade wondered if he could rise to his feet unaided.

"Will you take me back to the City?" said Blade.

"I do not know how wise it would be." Tyfel frowned as he rocked.

"Please?" said Blade.

Behind the curtain wall, a bell chimed. A train of servants appeared with steaming dishes.

"Ah," said the Y'az. His frown vanished. "Our long-awaited meal!"

Blade swallowed the salt in his throat. He wiped his eyes and ate.

16

I was reading the wishes again, alone this time.

Brother Iander came in. He looked down at me and folded his arms. "Someone at the bottom of the Tower wants to see you," he said.

I found my way to the reception room with only three or four wrong turns. Beside the double glass doors, Kem stood with his back to the wall, smiling at everyone who passed. His arms were filled with brochures, which he distributed at a horrifying speed. I was about to turn and retrace my steps, but it was too late; he had seen me.

"Ah, Ksar!" He hurried over, trimmed and polished as ever, his hair a finger's breadth from his scalp, his toga scented faintly with vanilla. But creases I had never noticed before bent the skin around his eyes. "Ksar, you look well," he said. "I'm glad to see your skin free of chemicals for once. Do you plan to give them up at last?"

"I hope not," I said. "The monks took them away. When I get them back, I'll wear them again."

Kem motioned me closer, as far from the tally-monk's desk as possible. "How are you doing as a monk, Ksar?"

"It's boring."

"What do you do?"

"I haven't seen the Radiance," I snapped. What else could he have come about? "Why don't *you* invent a vision and join the Brotherhood? You'll discover all there is to know about enlightenment in a day."

"Invent a holy vision?" Kem retracted his hand from my arm. "Ksar, that's unethical."

"The food is the only good thing here," I said. I was going to add, "Though anything is better than the gruel you made, or the dried meat that Skiy always ate," but I restrained myself.

"What do you do?" said Kem. "Do you clean the Tower? Do you pray?"

"I read wishes. It's good that *you* came and not Skiy. They're trying to find out who killed the monk."

"Yes," said Kem, "we thought it would be wiser if I came. Skiy is doing much better, though. I introduced him to the Board, and he has established himself as the official hospital cobbler, in which position he fashions the shoes for all those patients too poor to buy their own. For his services, he receives a share of the publicly-donated money."

"He must be rich," I said.

"Many fine deeds," said Kem, "hold no monetary reward." He adjusted the brochures under his arm and lowered his voice. "Are any of the wishes pertinent? Do they mention the monk Skiy killed?"

I shook my head.

"Nothing points to his guilt?"

"No," I said. I dug a Sfin wish out of my pocket. "This is the most exciting thing I've read. It has nothing to do with Skiy."

Kem looked at the note. He raised one brow but said nothing.

I shook it in his face. "You don't understand. This scrap of paper is the most exciting thing I've seen since you brought me here." I pushed it into his hand. "It's not exciting at all."

Kem unfolded the paper. "'I found my brother's cobras, but they won't let me in to see him. I hope he stops growing feathers soon and comes home.'" Kem sighed. "Glane is in a grotesque state," he said. "That's why we haven't allowed his brothers to see him. His father visits regularly. Glane still asks about you, Ksar. He asks for you every day."

I snatched the wish back from Kem's hand. "I don't need your commentary. I was showing you how boring it is, that's all."

"And I'm telling you that you've abandoned Glane. He's like a child, Ksar; he can't survive without you as his friend."

"He's not my friend." I stuffed the note back in my robe. "Even if I wanted to visit him, I wouldn't be able to. Monks aren't allowed to leave the Tower. You can thank Skiy for that."

"You could write him a letter."

"Glane, or Skiy?" I scratched my ear. "I don't think Glane can read."

Kem eyed me, forehead creased. He was going to call me selfish soon, or call me childish. I knew he would. I hated Kem for always being right, and for never intentionally offending.

"Why are you so bitter?" He put a hand on my shoulder. I shook it off. "You interrupted me from valuable reading." I turned away.

"Here." He thrust a stack of pamphlets into my arms. "Save the Fellowship of the White Horse!" read the sheet on top. "Could you do me a favor, Ksar, and distribute these among the monks?"

I left Kem in the reception room and climbed the Tower stairs. I dropped the pamphlets into the first acid pool I passed, and watched the pages curl and melt. I pictured a copper-blue bird on a perch overlooking a bed. I pictured a man, half-feathers, smashed against a window trying to reach the pigeons. Perhaps if Kem stopped telling me to, one day I would visit Glane. I could not see him now. It would be too much like giving in. Everyone had given in to Kem already. When I thought of that bird, that thing, my throat ached. I could not face the strangling room.

17

"I don't believe," said Y'az Tyfel, "that it would be wise to return to the City." Over the rim of his glass he watched Blade, as they sat together on the canopied balcony. Tyfel called this palace the embassy lodgings. Visiting nobles resided here. He came here often, once a year at least for social obligations, none of which interested Blade. He came also for political reasons, none of which Blade understood.

"I also come to enjoy the Glebe," said Tyfel.

"What's the Glebe?"

"Ah, the trading power of the Citadel. Have you noticed all the wood here? Yes? Very expensive. It can only be afforded because of the exports we grow in the Glebe." Tyfel drew on his tealeaf pipe. "The Glebe is worth seeing, and no mistake. Something to see for yourself." He rocked on his cushions. "Would you like to accompany me this afternoon?"

"Yes," said Blade. "Please." He stopped himself from clapping his hands.

Blade sat beside Y'az Tyfel on the balcony overlooking the road. He watched the servants pack refreshments onto the backs of the camels, decked in tassels of red and gold. Two litters waited in the street.

He turned to the Y'az. "Why can't we go back?"

"Because your grandfather sent you away. He is the most powerful man in the City, Xavier. I do not think it would be wise to flout his commandments, however overwrought we may think them to be."

"But if my grandfather is so powerful," said Blade, "why can't he protect me?"

"Ah, but the stranger did not threaten to hurt you alone." Tyfel tapped the side of his pipe, dislodging a dust of leaves. "He threatened to slander you in front of the people. That is a significant threat. If it came to be known that you, the heir to the Ven family, were involved in questionable activities, it would reflect badly upon your entire family, your grandfather not least. He is a proud man, Xavier. For him, it is better to lose a child than public face."

"But..." Blade coughed, trying to deepen his voice. "What will happen to me when *you* go back to the City? Will I have to stay here?"

"I won't depart for some time," said Y'az Tyfel. "I have come to enjoy the many pleasures of the Citadel, the Glebe not least among them. I will be here several weeks at least, perhaps all rainy season." He inhaled, and spoke again as the smoke trickled out from his lips. "Travel during the rainy season is frightful. The filth of it all." He waved a hand. "But not to worry. We'll find someone to shepherd you until your grandfather relents."

"But..." They could not stay in the Citadel, not for long; rebellion was coming. Wasn't that what Bry had said? Liop wanted everyone killed.

Tyfel looked at him. "Yes? But what?"

If he told of the rebellion, he betrayed Yaryk. Yaryk was not truly a criminal, was he? Blade did not understand. He did not comprehend the Bedouin at all. "Nothing," he said. "Never mind." He concentrated on the camels. Their lips sagged into smiles in the street below.

A servant appeared on the balcony and bowed. "The litters are ready, Y'az."

"Thank you. We'll be down shortly."

Blade watched the old man roll to his feet, dwarfed as they were beneath the folds of his stomach. Why couldn't he, Blade, have the same? Why did he have to be thin? He'd eaten all he could at breakfast, but it sat in his stomach like a burning rock and did nothing.

They descended the steps from the balcony, down to the courtyard and the roadway beyond. Blade had his own litter now, though he noticed his bearers were smaller than those who bore Tyfel: behemoths of men, all chests and arms, with calves like the trunks of trees.

Blade drew the curtains closed. The air inside the litter was hot and close. Clasps pinned the curtains down at the corners, but Blade did not trust them and held the fabric tight with his hands. He did not want to see the world. He did not want to remember the dirt beyond the litter walls, or the uncontrollable sand, or the animal hides of the smugglers.

The babble of the Citadel faded around him. Blade peered between the curtains. They had passed from the Citadel gates and plodded now down a pathway of colored flagstones. Trees flowered to either side. Beyond the trees the acid sea danced. It shimmered a gentle, translucent coral. Blade craned to look from the litter. Below the surface, creatures with waving tentacles, no longer than his finger, drifted in the current, or swam in schools, hundreds together. They somersaulted and twisted like a single body. Now and then one broke the surface in a spectrum of glowing drops.

Other creatures danced beside the path: jellyfish refracting the light, eels as long as his arm, bright with metallic veins. Blade remembered Leque's stories. Here was the acid sea as Leque had described it — a separate world, untouchable and filled with beauty. As you walked the roads of the world, Leque said, the acid sea always accompanied you, different and shifting each day of your travel. If you returned the same way a hundred times, each time it would change.

The litters stopped before a white wall and a gate of gold bars. When the guard who stood beside the gate saw Y'az Tyfel, he saluted. He opened the gate and the litters passed through. Kiwi vines stretched away in rows. Beneath the vines, workers crouched in the shade, weeding the unwanted grass into baskets. Other men stood on ladders, pruning the boughs.

Blade jumped down from his litter and clapped his hands. He could not restrain himself. The scent of fresh-

cut leaves swept over him, mingled with other fragrances,
fainter — flowers and fruits whose appearances he could
only imagine.

"Tyfel!" Blade skipped on the grass. "Can you smell it,
Tyfel? Doesn't the air smell wonderful?"

The Y'az extricated himself from his litter with the help
of two servants. His face flushed with exertion but he
straightened and smiled. "Yes, yes, very pretty. And to think
that the Bedouin once used this place to pasture their
animals! They built campfires here. Campfires! The crudity.
Right here where we stand!"

"Can I walk under the vines?" said Blade. "Please?"

"The sitting area is more easily reached by the path."

The servants folded the litters and a single man carried
both, one under each arm, while the others shared out the
cushions between them. Y'az Tyfel led the procession,
waddling like a newly-hatched gosling. Sweat ran down
through his beard. The servants sauntered behind, camels
in toe. Blade drifted up and down their ranks. He paused
to admire a flower, ran ahead to be the first around the turn
of the path, then doubled back to let the others catch up.

The sitting area, a sward of grass, opened against the
surrounding wall. The sun canopies of other nobles and
their retinues spattered the lawn. One of the serving men
tethered the camels to a ring in the wall before unfolding
the red and gold cloths from the animals' packs. The litter-
bearers worked together, setting out cushions, erecting
poles, and securing the fire-bright cloths to the tops of the
staves. They arranged the cushions underneath the canopy,
into a nest for Blade and another for the Y'az. Tyfel settled
himself on his silken throne. A eunuch stood behind him
and fanned his face with a palm frond fan. The other
servants wandered off among the kiwis.

Tyfel opened a basket of refreshments. Blade watched
for a while, too hot to join in. When the Y'az had finished
eating he lay back, clasped his hands on his stomach and
began to snore.

Blade waited for another servant to appear. "Will you
come with me?" he said. "I want to explore."

"Of course." The man nodded. He assisted Blade from his nest of perfume.

They ducked out from under the canopy. After a hundred paces, the kiwi vines gave way to flowering bushes, mist-bedecked and dripping in yellow. Pollen filled the air. Great white bees, banded in yellow and black, drifted among the flowers. Blade hurried on. He almost ran.

They came to the kingdom of orange trees. He stepped off the path, under the shade of the branches. Nearby, a line of men stood on ladders, gathering the fruit into baskets strapped to their chests. Blade watched them work. He wondered how much each basket weighed. He watched the muscles underneath the men's skin. Blade bent and picked up an orange. It felt synthetic between his hands, cool and smooth as a marble sphere. It smelled of kumquats and sugar.

"Excuse me." Blade held out the orange to the nearest worker. "You dropped one."

The man froze. Slowly, he turned on the rung of his ladder. He unstrapped the basket from his chest and lowered it to the ground. He stared at Blade.

"I..." Blade backed away. "You dropped an orange. That's all. Here you go."

The man's face was clean-shaved, smeared over with sweat and dirt. He wore his hair, a pale brown, tied in a knot at the nape of his neck. He pointed to Tyfel's servant, standing silent behind Blade. "Is he with you?"

Blade stared. "Leque?"

"Whose servant is that?"

"Y'az Tyfel's. But—"

Leque pointed at the litter-bearer. "Don't tell your master about this," he said. "Don't tell him anything." He climbed down the ladder and looked over his shoulders this way and that as if the wind-fallen oranges might rise and attack.

Blade leapt forward. He wrapped his arms around Leque. "I'm so happy to see you." He did not care how childish he appeared, or how many workers watched. "I couldn't find you, so I left with Yaryk." He started to laugh. It was hard to go on. He was crying as well. "I wanted to leave the City with *you*. Honestly I did, but I couldn't find you."

Leque pushed him away and held him at arm's length. "Your nose is swollen. What happened to you? Wait." He rolled Blade's sleeve up to the shoulder and dug his fingers into the soft skin of his inner elbow.

"Ow! What are you doing?"

"Good. You don't have feathers."

"Should I?".

"Stone, no! I was afraid you might... like Glane and Gyanin. I had to see. That was why we ran away, wasn't it? So we wouldn't get like Glane."

Blade had almost forgotten the feathers, but he remembered now and he nodded. "I don't want to be like Glane."

"Is he still alive?" said Leque.

"As far as I know..."

"And Gyanin?"

"As far as I know..."

"Anyone else?" The skin around Leque's eyes was a shade of gray, deep and burrowing into his skull.

Blade swallowed. "I think Ksar's dead."

"Dead?"

"He was stung by a million bees." Blade hung his head. He did not want to meet Leque's eyes.

Leque seized Blade's shoulder and shook him. "Don't," he said. "Don't cry. So you left the City with Yaryk, did you? Fine. What else?"

Blade could not stop crying. The third time in two days. He could not help himself. "I've lost Yaryk. I don't know where he is." He wanted to cling to Leque, because Leque was so solid and strong, but he'd already done that, and to do it again would make him appear even more of a child. "Y'az Tyfel found me. All the nobles here hate the Bedouin. I don't know why. I can't ask about Yaryk. I wish he'd never brought me here."

"I never liked him," said Leque.

"I didn't know that."

"I decided just now. Why did he bring you to the Citadel? It's a good place to find work, but not a good place for you, Blade. No, I never liked Yaryk." He folded his arms.

"I always liked him." Blade sniffled. He wiped his nose on his sleeve.

"Stop it," said Leque. "You're going to stain your clothes."

Blade stopped. "What should I do? I can't go back to the City."

"None of us can. The others were fools to stay."

"No," said Blade. "I mean I really," — hiccup — "can't go back, not until my grandfather lets me."

"Y'az Xzaven?" Leque's arms folded tighter. "Is Y'az Xzaven trying to kill us, Blade? Did *he* send the bees?"

"No. I don't know. He sent me away." Blade hiccupped louder. "I'm not the heir anymore."

"I'm sorry," said Leque. His shoulders relaxed. "Why don't you stay here," he said, "in the Citadel? If Y'az Tyfel..."

"I miss the City, Leque. Don't you miss the City?"

Leque shrugged. He bent to sort through the basket of oranges. He threw the rotten fruit into a bin at the foot of the tree. "Not yet," he said. "And the work here is better. You could work here as well." His mouth grinned. "They're always looking for more hands."

Blade looked at his hands. "Really?" He did not know what to say.

"It's almost the rainy season," said Leque. "When the clouds come, picking will be twice as busy."

Y'az Tyfel's servant tapped Blade on the shoulder. "Excuse me, Master." He bowed an apology. "I believe we should return to the sitting area. The Y'az will worry."

Blade reached out and seized Leque's wrist. "Leque?" he said.

"Xavier?"

That halted him. It was years since Leque had called him that, not since he worked for his father. "Leque?"

"Yes?"

"You work here all the time?"

"During the days, yes."

"What do you do at night?"

"I work as a guard for Y'az Gyrt." He swelled his chest.

"If I come here tomorrow," said Blade, "or the day after that, you'll still be working here?"

"Probably." Leque shook his wrist free and returned to the oranges. "Gyrt pays well. If he promotes me I will stop working here." He glanced at Blade's face. "I'll warn you before I do anything." The dark rings showed around his eyes. "And Ksar is dead?"

"I... I... think so."

Leque bent again. He focused on the fruit in his basket.

"Do you miss me?" Blade whispered.

"Of course." Leque did not look up.

Blade watched his hands. "Good-bye," he said at last.

"Good-bye."

Blade stood in the grass. The foliage dripped. Tyfel's serving man touched his sleeve and they walked away. At the end of the aisle of trees, Blade turned and looked over his shoulder. Leque stood beneath the oranges with his legs apart. He held the ladder in both hands. He raised it over his head and smashed it down. He lifted it again, smashed it down again with the force of a falling star. A rung split apart. It struck Leque's hand. Blade saw him jump.

Three men rappelled down from their trees. They pulled the ladder from Leque. "What are you doing?" They shook him. "Stop it!" They shouted in his face. "Stop it!" They pulled the ladder away.

"Come." The servant tapped Blade's shoulder again. "The Y'az will be worried."

Yaryk, Liop and Jarb sat with their backs against the Citadel wall. Gravel stretched before them and beyond that the sea, pale gray, fading to rust in the late afternoon. Bry squatted at the shoreline. He heaved glass globules into the sea and watched the steam as they struck the surface.

"Be careful, Bry!" Jarb shouted. "If it splashes back it will burn!"

Bry turned, his expression swallowed in the sun behind. He was no more than a black silhouette, crouched against the flame-orange sky.

Yaryk turned to Jarb. "Did you talk to them all?"

"Every Bedouin in the Citadel, yes. Or every man who was once a Bedouin. Many were slow to admit it."

"You told them the meeting place?"

"Yes." Jarb laughed. "They may not come, Yaryk."

"They'll come," said Liop.

Yaryk watched Bry. The boy moved his arms in staccato jerks. He was so restless, the energy radiated sulfur-hot. He should have left the Citadel and wandered years ago.

Feet crunched over gravel. Yaryk turned and shielded his eyes. Four figures made their way across the beach.

"Arn, Kurren!" Jarb pulled himself up, ready to greet with an outstretched hand. "Morren, Gwall, you have come. How wonderful to see you. Welcome."

Bedouin trickled along the beach, strung out in a line like goats on the highroads, one animal tied to the tail of the next. Jarb greeted each man. Yaryk bowed and committed their names to his memory: Iln; Morren the locksmith; Mehrzh in the yellow toga. And these men called themselves Bedouin? A yellow toga? Liop sat and said nothing. Yaryk folded his arms. Fifty men in tunics and togas, like any other men of the Citadel, ranged themselves along the sand. Few had beards. None wore turbans. They talked of their blacksmith shops, guanaco farms, and fruit stands with lowered voices.

A mound of boulders stood against the wall, memorial to some dead fisherman. Yaryk climbed to the summit. "Bedouin!" he shouted, "Bedouin, listen to me!"

The babble continued.

"Bedouin!" Liop raised a burlapped arm. "You *were* once Bedouin, were you not?"

Discussions dwindled. Gwall the blacksmith waved his fist. "Bedouin!" he shouted. He turned to Jarb. He whispered something, but Yaryk on his perch could not hear the words.

Yaryk spread his arms. "How many of you were once members of the Bedouin Guild?"

"Yes," some murmured. Others said, "No." In the dusk he could not tell who said which.

"Do you see how far we've fallen?" said Yaryk. "If we want to keep our homes in the Citadel, we are forced to give up our heritage. We are wanderers, yes, but even *we* deserve a place to return to."

"They burnt my door last week!" shouted Morren the locksmith.

"See?" Yaryk waved his arms. "They persecute us still."

"There's a man who's been coming to my shop for years," said Gwall, "for wheel shafts and harnesses. Last month I told him I had once been a Bedouin. He has not returned since. They do not want to deal with Bedouin."

"'Once been'?" said Yaryk. "My friends, our identities do not change with age or status. Bedouin are always Bedouin, whether we travel or not. Do you know how difficult it was for me to enter the Citadel? All I wished was to purchase medication for my son, yet when I arrived at the gates the guards would not allow me in without an escort."

"No!" shouted Gwall. The others joined in. "No!" they shouted, black silhouettes against the sunset.

"We broke free of the escort!" Yaryk shouted, "but yesterday the nobles saw him — my son. They have taken him away."

"Those sons of yaks!" shouted Gwall.

"They are leeches on the Citadel." Someone raised a fist. "They have blocked us off from the rest of the world."

"The nobles don't frequent the public shops," said Morren. "They weed out the best craftsmen and pay them to close their shops and come work in the palaces, and have no further dealings with the populace. They rob us of resources."

"And you would never be one of those craftsmen, would you?" Liop spoke for the first time. He stood, small as a cricket against the sandstone wall. "You could be the most skilled of any worker, and still they would not hire *you*."

"They hate us," said Morren.

"Yes, they hate us all."

Someone pointed at Yaryk. "They stole his son!"

"They rob us of our lives," said Liop. "Do you know how many Bedouin try to enter the Citadel each year, only to be taken prisoner, tortured, and killed?"

Yaryk folded his arms. He doubted torture, even here. The men on the shoreline cheered. That was a dangerous lie to tell, Liop. A dangerous lie. It was simple to enrage fifty men. Simple to make them act. It was not so simple to make them act properly.

"And now Yaryk's son?" said Liop. He did not shout but his voice carried. "The boy was no more than twelve! The nobles have taken a mere child. Stars only know what lies in wait. I say that we do not abandon this boy to his suffering!"

Cheers.

"Yaryk, we will liberate your son!"

Yaryk looked down at the mass of faces and open mouths. They appeared as more than fifty now, as the suns went down, one blue, one red. Each man cast a double shadow. Bry yelled in that crowd, his voice cracking high above the others: "Kill the nobles!" he shouted. "Kill them! Kill!"

Jarb stood back. He looked up at Yaryk and their eyes met. It did not matter that Yaryk stood on raised ground; all the attention was Liop's. The Citadel wall burned red behind him. He spoke again, and Yaryk forced himself to listen:

"Assassination!" Liop waved his arms. "Assassination by night! We will enter the palace—"

"No!" Jarb pushed his way through the press. "No assassination, please! You'll gain nothing but death. If not your own, then Tallos' in prison."

"The nobles will not foresee it," said Liop.

"No," said Jarb. "I cannot support this."

Liop turned. He spoke to Morren the locksmith, too quietly for Yaryk to hear. Yaryk climbed down from the pile of stones.

18

In the dry season of the
Year of the Zephyr

Sometimes when my brother Leque was at work and there was nothing to do I would go to the Marble Tower and enjoy the vista. You could see the whole City from the top of the Tower: so much sandstone and so many little doors. On clear days you could see the people, moving about like specks of dust. Today a haze hung over the City. If you fell from the balcony, perhaps that haze would catch you and buoy you up before you reached the ground. I sat on my customary bench, planted my elbows on my knees, and stared at the far russet glow of the sea. The railing cut a band of black through my perfect vision. This was the day I met Glane.

A boy stepped into my frame. His dark hair whipped around his face like a mop. His skin was the color of coconut, far too pale. He looked sixteen. He wore a pouch at his waist. He fumbled with the cinch, poking the burlap and muttering as if it could hear him. He leaned his hip against the railing and peered over the edge. For me, this was half the enjoyment of watching the view — watching people and hoping they did not watch back. Some days it was so crowded on the balcony, I forgot which feet were mine. Clear days were often like that. Today there were only me, the boy, and perhaps five other loiterers, standing away out of sight. The boy took a worm from his pocket and put it in the pouch.

I leaned forward on my elbows. "Er," I said, "what are you doing?"

"Looking at the view," said the boy. "My father often comes to the Tower. Sometimes I come with him. I'm not allowed to follow him around, so I come up here."

"What are you doing with the pouch?"

"Feeding them."

"Feeding the pouch?"

"No, my cobras."

I shambled over. Sweat slicked the insides of my sandals. I did not want to fall. The boy held out his pouch and I peered inside.

"They're cobras," he said.

I stared. "They are," I said. "They are definitely cobras."

"I made them small on purpose," said the boy. "My father's an alchemist. Some of the chemicals can make snakes small."

"They are definitely small," I agreed. They were no longer than my finger. Twenty cobras at least writhed inside the bag, all coiled and knotted like Leque's employment record.

"Do you want to hold one?" said the boy.

"No thanks."

"They don't usually bite. Even when they do, it's just like a bee sting. They don't have enough venom to kill you."

"Still, no thanks."

The boy reached into the pouch. He bit his lip in concentration and came out with a snake coiled around his thumb. "This is one of the older ones," he said. "The scales on its nose are fading, see? Here." He pulled the serpent off his thumb and dropped it into my hands. "You hold him."

The snake bent around like a scaled finger. It lay still and looked up at me with eyes like polished glass. It flicked its tongue.

"They retract their fangs," said the boy, "if they don't feel threatened. If you can see the teeth it means it's thinking of biting you."

"Oh, here then, you hold it."

The cobra bit. It felt like a sliver of onion pricking into my palm: that hungry, burning sensation. I jerked my hand. The cobra arched into the air. It sailed over the railing. It hovered for an instant, midair, before it fell. It twisted, end over end, to the dust below.

"No!" The boy jumped to the parapet. His eyes protruded from his head. "It fell!" He swung a leg over the
railing.

"Stop!" I lunged toward him.

"I'm going after him!"

Across the balcony, the mutter of conversation stopped.
Men turned and stared.

The boy swung his other leg over the railing, so that
now he clung only with his hands, his feet on a ledge no
wider than my palm.

I dropped to my stomach and thrust my arm under the
railing. "I've got it!" I shouted.

"Got it?" said the boy.

"Your cobra." I waved my fist. "I caught him by the tail
but he's really thrashing."

"You caught him?"

"He wasn't falling very fast."

The boy's eyes glittered turquoise-weird. "I guess not,"
he said. He climbed back over the railing. On the other side
of the balcony, some of the spectators clapped. The boy held
out his pouch. The remaining cobras writhed away from
the light. I inserted my fist. For all he could see I may have
released a snake.

"Glane," said the boy.

"What?" I examined the red dots at the base of my
thumb. "Look where he bit me. You're sure I won't die?"

"You won't," said the boy. "I mean, my name's Glane."

"I'm Ksar." I forgot to hold out my hand.

"Do you play crystal wars?" said Glane.

"Sometimes."

"Right now?"

"Am I playing right now? As we speak? No." The boy
still stood too close to the railing. I wanted him to sit on
the bench. "I don't usually play with pebbles on the tops
of buildings," I said. "If a crystal went over the edge, it
could kill someone walking below."

"Want to come to my house?" said Glane.

"Your house?"

"Okay, my father's house." He pouted. "We can go and
play crystal wars. Please?"

"Ksar?" said Glane.

We sat on the floor on either side of a table. One leg was missing. We pretended to play crystal wars. Really I watched Glane's father. He stood on the far side of the room, half hidden behind a netted curtain. Purple light danced out from around his fingers across the ceiling. Our crystals seemed to jump on the tabletop.

"Ksar?" Glane said again. I had not responded the first time.

"Yes?"

"Say there was a little person who looked exactly like me..."

"Yes?"

"I mean very little. As tall as my hand." He thrust his hand in my face.

"Yes, very little."

"And say I killed it," said Glane.

"You killed it?"

"Well, say I killed it — the little person — would my intestines fall out?"

I tried to return his stare, long and blue-green. I turned away. "I don't know," I said. "You could always try and find out."

"I've already tried."

"Oh. And did your intestines fall out?"

"No, but my stomach hurts."

"I don't think you should have killed it," I said.

"I was afraid you'd say that." He picked up the white stone, the playing stone, and prepared his move.

I said, "What's your father doing?"

"Making gold," said Glane. "He's an alchemist. That's what he does. I should be able to do it too, but I can't. I've tried. Even my brother Sfin can turn things to copper, and he's only six. But I can't do anything."

"What kinds of things?"

"Sand. One of his fingers once."

"He turned his finger to copper?"

"No." Glane chewed on the sleeve of his toga, re-thinking. "No. Actually *Father* turned his finger to copper."

"His finger, or Sfin's finger?"

"Sfin's."

"But why?"

Glane's jaw froze in mid-chew. The sleeve of his toga hung from his mouth like a rancid tongue, brown in the purple light. "Sfin was a baby," he said. "One of his hands had six fingers, which Father thought was a waste, so he turned one finger to copper so Sfin wouldn't be able to feel it. Then he cut it off, and used it to stop up the nick in the wall over there." Glane pointed. He pointed in the direction of the purple light. I squinted but saw no nick.

"Did Sfin mind?" I asked. I did not remember which crystals were mine and which were Glane's.

"Mind what?"

"Losing his finger," I said.

"He was only a baby."

I was not sure I believed Glane's stories. He was not lying, as far as he knew. But the truth according to Glane and the truth according to the rest of the world were not necessarily the same. After one afternoon of acquaintance, that much was already clear. I wondered what time it was, and what time Leque would finish work. I could not remember his job. It was something to do with building, or knocking things down, or selling fruit. He often sold fruit.

I stood up. Glane did not seem to notice. He would make his move, stare at the place I'd been sitting, then move again. Perhaps he would lose to himself.

I walked across the room. I ducked under the netting, into the purple light. Glane's father smiled. A spark jumped up from the work table. It burrowed down into his arm and he grimaced. He didn't say anything. He held a torch in one hand, from which the purple light danced. He held a hammer in the other. Sand heaped the table. With the help of the hammer, he pounded the sand into dust. I leaned against the wall and felt the vibrations run through my shoulder. Glane's father looked the same as his son: the same pale skin, the frazzled hair, the small, geometric nose.

His ears jutted out like Glane's. At least he wore a beard, concealing much of his face. If not for the beard they would look the same.

Glane's father snuffed the torch against the wall, reached into his pocket, and produced a flask the size of his hand. He unfastened the stopper and sprinkled red powder out into his palm.

"What's that?" I asked.

"Feathers of the scarlet roc."

"They're tiny," I said. "I thought rocs were huge."

His eyes were jade, viscous-soft as glue. "These feathers are pulverized," he said. "They've been made into powder, but they came from the roc originally."

"Oh."

He poured the powder over the sand, relit the torch, and resumed pounding. I did not know what to make of this family. Glane's younger brothers had swarmed him when we opened the door. They tackled his legs and clung to his sleeves, but scurried away when they caught sight of me. I could not count how many there were — twenty maybe, or possibly more. Probably less. I could not judge age, but it looked as though most of them could hardly walk. They scurried to the back room and disappeared within. I heard them squealing from time to time.

Glane's father glanced over his shoulder. Glane still sat at the table. He'd finished the game by himself and now fed his cobras. His lips moved, though whether he was talking to me, or the snakes, or himself, I don't know.

Glane's father said: "You're hard to look in the eye."

"Sorry." I sat down on a stool.

He pulled up a second stool. He glanced at Glane sideways, but Glane was still occupied with his snakes. "What happened at the Tower?" He kneaded his hands in his lap.

"One of his cobras fell," I said. "He wanted to jump after it, but I wouldn't let him."

His father scratched his beard. "Thank you." He coughed. "For saving my son's life." He stood, relit the torch, and that was the end of that. "You should come again," he said.

19

In the dry season of the
Year of the Mandarin Turtle

The sesame cakes were stale. Jarb and Yaryk sat on either side of the fire pit and ate. Bry sat a short distance away, sharpening a dagger. The front door rattled. Yaryk jumped to his feet. What fool left his door unlocked through the night and into the morning?

Liop appeared in the kitchen doorway. "Hah! Food!" He pushed the burlap away from his face. Pockmarks dented his skin. His lip curled up, exposing his teeth. He bounded down the steps and sat beside Yaryk.

"Is it not possible for you to knock before entering?" said Jarb.

Liop dribbled sesame crumbs into his beard. He said: "You'll be interested to hear what I've done."

Jarb drank from an earthenware mug. "What have you done?"

"Last night," said Liop, "I killed Y'az Gyrt."

Jarb choked.

"Indeed," said Yaryk. He watched the bones in the old man's fingers. They jutted through his skin like the staves of a tent. Veins wreathed his temple like knotted snakes. Did he suffer from leprosy? Did Yaryk inhale the same air as a leper? He cleared his throat. "You had help, I assume."

"Possibly, possibly."

Bry crawled across the floor. "How did you do it?"

Liop drew a knife from beneath his burlap. From another recess, he pulled a strip of gauze. It shimmered with golden tracery, beads, and blood. "Gyrt's bed curtain," he said.

"Where did you stab him?" said Bry. "Did you stab him in the heart?"

Jarb's face flushed red. "Be quiet," he hissed.

"I slit his throat," said Liop. "You should have listened to me on the shore, little Yaryk. I said I would kill the Y'az."

"This is insanity!" Jarb spluttered on the crumbs of his cake. "We are already feared and mistrusted. You have validated that fear in the most effective way I can imagine. The nobles will arrest us all. We'll be lucky if our punishment is as lenient as Tallos'. They won't care that *you* did it, Liop, and not the rest of us. They see us as one body. Thank you." He threw up his hands. "You have killed us."

"They won't hate us for this," said Liop. "I only killed Gyrt. None of the nobles trusted Gyrt." Liop leaned back on his elbows. White hairs grew like worms from his wrist. He lazed in accomplishment. "I wasn't alone," said Liop. "Morren fashioned the key that let us in. Gwall took the prisoner."

"Prisoner?" Yaryk restrained the disgust in his voice. He fought the urge to spit. Why had he not been consulted? Did Liop not see the danger?

"One of the watchmen tried to stop us. We have taken him away. We shall frame him and the nobles will not even know "

"Why didn't you kill him?" said Bry. "You should have killed him."

"A human body is heavy to carry," said Liop. "It is easier if it can carry its own weight."

Yaryk stood. He rubbed his hands over the fire. Liop had made this game far more dangerous. "I want to see the prisoner," said Yaryk.

"You're not going to congratulate me on my work?"

"No," said Yaryk. "Did you find any evidence of Blade? Did you even look?" He stepped for the door. "Tell me where you put the prisoner. I want to speak with him."

"In the Guild Hall," said Liop.

❖ ❖ ❖

Yaryk slipped down the tunnel. Once in the Hall, he held the torch high over his head. Alcoves cut the wall's perimeter. Rusted grates blocked some of the niches, or boards and slabs of stone. The Guild had never kept prisoners here. They stored supplies in the hall, or offered the alcoves to destitute travelers, protection against the mold of the rainy season. Where had Liop placed his prisoner? Surely he had not dropped the man down the ladder and left him? Yaryk swept the cavern with the light of his torch. There, behind a far grate, something stirred.

Yaryk strode across the floor and squatted down outside the cage. A man lay curled behind the bars, his back to the hall. His side jerked in and out as he breathed. He wore the leather jacket of a guard.

"Wake up," said Yaryk.

The man's side twitched faster. He raised his head and turned his face toward the bars.

"Leque!" Yaryk sat back on his heels.

Leque rolled onto his back. He squinted at the torch. He lay with his arms folded tight across his chest, hands concealed. "Who are you?"

"Son of a drunkard, Leque — I'm Yaryk." He leaned the torch against the wall so the light would not glare so blindingly.

"Why are you always involved?" Leque scowled, though it may have been the swelling around his eyes.

"Involved in what?" said Yaryk.

"This!" Leque lolled his head. He glared at the bars between them. Ah, yes. This was why he had never liked Leque. Leque was always impatient; he did not weigh his words.

"I swear to the Stars," said Yaryk, "I had nothing to do with your capture. I did not even know it had taken place until this morning."

Leque continued to glare. His hair fell into his eyes.

"What did they do to you?" said Yaryk. "Show me your hands."

Leque unfolded his arms. He closed his eyes. "I don't want to see them."

His hands had been flattened, cut like raw meat, clotted in black and red.

"What happened?" said Yaryk.

"Trampled." Leque wetted his lips with his tongue. He trembled. "Two men held me down. They raked my hands with their knives. They ground them into the sand and stepped on my fingers." He glared at Yaryk. "Their faces were covered; you could have been one of them."

"I wasn't," said Yaryk.

"What are you doing?" said Leque. "Why did you kill Y'az Gyrt?"

"We are taking back the Citadel," said Yaryk.

"Why?"

"I want to find Blade. The nobles have taken him."

"Why does that matter?" said Leque.

"He's a prisoner the same as you." Yaryk clenched his jaw. "Isn't that reason enough to participate in an uprising? And you call yourself devoted to Blade."

Leque pulled himself up against the wall. He sat the same height as Yaryk. "Blade's not a prisoner."

"Why do you say that? Have you seen him?"

"Yes," said Leque. He tried to smile but the bruises twisted his mouth. "He seemed happy enough to be away from you."

"You're lying," said Yaryk. "Who was he with? Which nobles?"

"It doesn't matter," said Leque. "He was happy."

"You're lying."

Leque closed his eyes and leaned his head against the wall. "Yaryk," he said, "please let me out. I know you can. You knew I was here."

"Why should I let you out?" said Yaryk. "You've lied about Blade and insulted my people. Blade chose me as his guide outside the City. I will not prove remiss. If you will not tell me where he is, I will find him myself."

"He ran away from you," said Leque. The muscles twitched in his neck. "He never chose you as a guide. He wanted me."

Yaryk carried a satchel slung over his shoulder. He reached inside and drew out a disc of bread. He threw the loaf between the bars, into Leque's lap. "Why do I feed you, when you insult me so blatantly?"

Leque opened his eyes and looked down at the bread. "I can't eat that," he said. "I can't pick it up."

"'*In dire times, the mind must divine solutions.*'" Yaryk closed the satchel. "I suspect that such quotations are above your intellect, Leque son of Qual. In smaller words: if you find yourself unable to eat, it is of no concern to me." He picked up the torch and stood. "I don't know what will become of you," he said. "You may or may not face execution. I may or may not intercede on your behalf."

Yaryk crossed the hall. He climbed the ladder and slammed the panel door behind him.

20

The next Sfin message I found said, "I wish my father would tell him."

I sat on the floor with the black basket on one side and the white on the other, and a mountain of wish papers spread before me. There were two fundamental drawbacks to this task: first, it brought me no nearer the Radiance; second, I had too much time to myself. My mind wandered, and no one was there to help me bring it back.

I didn't want to think about how I'd met Glane, because here in these endless hours I wished I never had. I was twenty-six when Glane and I met, and he was sixteen. We had nothing in common from the very beginning, and never understood each other's comments. We did not try to understand and so we got along.

Leque did not mind Glane. He even remembered Glane's name, a great mental feat for my brother. He could now change jobs, live halfway across the City for a couple of weeks (until he got bored and moved back), without the guilt of abandoning me. I sometimes came home to find a scrap of paper on my pillow with directions to move in with Glane; he had found a better job, my brother; he did not think he'd be coming back. I would pack a few togas — all I had back then, no Clebean carpets or llama blankets — and knock on the door with the purple light, where Glane's father allowed me to sleep as many nights as I cared.

Glane's house had been better back then, before the table lost its legs, and the floor lost its cushions, back when the cupboard shelves still contained enough dishes. I used to sleep underneath the table then, before Glane's father came upon hard times. I don't know what happened to thwart his alchemy. If you could execute the impossible once, why couldn't you do it forever? Whatever the reason, I slept on the floor in those days. Glane and I stared at the ceiling. We could spend whole nights saying nothing. Sometimes we talked about cayenne pepper, shoes for camels and bread that could make you fly. We talked of whatever we pleased.

Within a few days, Leque's face would appear at the window, peering and doubtful — he never remembered which door was Glane's. We let him in. He would sit at the table and drink the warm milk, or the watered juice, or whatever Glane's father gave him. I was free to come home, Leque said, whenever I wished. He never mentioned his job across the City again. I never asked if he had chosen to leave, or if the decision had been made for him. Generally if someone else had decided, Leque would go to the tavern before coming home, and then you could hear him from the end of the alleyway, singing and colliding with walls. Glane and I would sit in the shadow of the back room. We argued over crystal wars and waited for my brother to fall asleep outside. Sfin would run and check through the window.

By the time I started wearing earrings, it was too late for Glane and I to be separated. We may as well have been attached at the spleen. We started the earrings because we were bored. Many things started that way. We were playing at crystal wars, Glane and I.

"Whoever loses," I said, "should be punished."

"Why?" said Glane.

"It would make it more interesting."

"We don't have to kill each other, do we?"

"No," I said.

"Good. I don't like killing people."

Whoever lost, we said, would have to go behind the work table — the alchemy table — and emerge wearing only what he could find there to wear. This rule provided hours of entertainment. There was enough garbage behind the table to clothe a herd of dromedaries: rugs that had once patched the roof, pieces of metal that had failed to turn into gold, saucepans, bells, and a million other trinkets I could not even name.

The enormous quantity of pseudo-earrings bore a special fascination. The next day Glane and I went to the piercing parlor and had ourselves shot with holes. Leque was away that week. We used his money. I had the idea, vague though it was, that we must accomplish as much as possible before Leque's return. We set to work on the discarded chemicals behind the table. Glane's father had discarded them because they were mislabeled. We found a bottle that could alter the color of one's skin. Another made our skin fall off. We tested each vial and pouch. Those that could color we kept for ourselves, while the others we fed to Glane's cobras.

When Leque returned he found Glane's and my treasures in a box at the foot of my bed.

"What are you doing?" he said. "I'm not happy with this." My brother has always been loquacious beyond all reason. He was drunk that night. He tipped over our chest and iron-clad tongue rings spilled across the floor. "You look like vagabonds!" he shouted. "Crazy, crazy vagabonds!"

Glane cowered in the corner.

"What do you have to say?" shouted Leque.

I did not have anything. Glane crawled out from his hiding. He clasped his hands and spread himself flat on the floor. He always feared Leque. He promised not to dress like a trash-yard peddler, if only someone would help him get the earrings out, because this one was stuck, and that one had snagged so badly he did not want to touch it.

I kept everything I'd taken from the back of Glane's house. I was not afraid of my brother. I'd spent too many hours sorting through trash to discard it now. Besides, Leque did not really care what I wore. He only cared that I had spent his money. It was too late to change that now. If the holes in my ears grew over, Leque's money would still be gone.

Glane's father gave up on the hope I would stabilize Glane. But by then I had entrenched myself in the family and there was no getting rid of me.

"Glane often goes to the Tower," his father conceded. "You never know when another cobra will fall."

I said this was true, very true, and nodded my head in solemn agreement. The hematite charm in my nostril rattled.

I didn't want to think about how I'd met Glane — how I'd saved his life from the very beginning. I sorted papers all day. What did Sfin wish his father would tell? Time, I could not guess.

The door opened and a brother looked in. "There's a man in the reception room to see you."

"'I wish my father would tell him'?" Kem unfolded the next wish paper and read it aloud also: "'I want Glane to come home.'" He frowned and rubbed his chin. "When did you find these?"

"The one about Glane coming home was yesterday. The other one was today."

Kem said: "To wish for Glane's return is self-explanatory enough. But the other note — what would Sfin want his father to tell? And tell to whom? Tell the hospital to release Glane? He's already telling us that."

"Then why don't you release him?"

"Glane is still half bird," said Kem. "The daily dosage of medication, administered by myself or Maelin, is the only thing that prevents him from finalizing that transformation."

"Maybe you should let him transform." I had all the simple solutions.

"No," said Kem. "He's terrified. He doesn't want to become a bird. His father seems a good man — soft-spoken. He visits daily. But we cannot release an intensive-care patient."

I shrugged.

"He hasn't spoken for days now," said Kem. "I'm sure that *you* could shake him from his depression. Would you not consider writing him a letter?"

"No."

"Well then." Kem rubbed his chin again. Stubble made his face look gray. I had never seen Kem with stubble before.

"I'm tired of the Tower," I said.

"I'm sorry," said Kem. "You can't leave until we've restored the Radiance." He turned and pushed open the glass doors. "Goodbye, Ksar," he called, and the City's dust swallowed him whole.

The dust consumed everything, thick in the air like fog. The spires of the nobles' palaces drifted from the haze like teeth out of gray-white gums. The rainy season had to be coming. It could not be long now. Once the rain came, it would be three years exactly since the defacement of the Radiance. Three years ago exactly that Skiy and Kem, Gyanin, Blade, and Yaryk had scratched their way into my life.

I turned away from the doors. I crossed the marble floor and headed up the stairs. The Father Paramount swept around a landing and I collided straight into his chest.

"Apology," I muttered.

He seized my elbows and smiled. "Ksar! My son! The very brother of wisdom I was looking for."

I scratched my neck.

"Though perhaps," said the Paramount, and I followed his gaze toward the crowded reception room, "this is not the ideal place for a discussion." He led me through a door behind the reception desk. I let him navigate. Wherever we were going, I did not know the way.

He led me to the Radiance room.

We entered at the bottom of its high cylinder, not at the top where the railing and the platform stood. At first I didn't recognize the space; it was just a circular room. The walls drew together as they rose, so the ceiling looked a fraction the size of the floor. The railinged platform appeared so small, constricting, bending over to watch us. It looked like a grate on the mouth of a sewer.

The Paramount pointed up. We stood beneath the Radiance. It cast a circle of light on the floor. It hovered there, high in the dome of the ceiling, high as the dome of the sky. The third sun. It shone beacon-bright in the gloom. What did Skiy say the plume represented? The path of destruction? Perhaps we had not defaced the Radiance at all. We returned the sun to its natural domain, serene and secure. The Radiance from here appeared round, not tapered, no longer falling. We had saved the sun. We should open the Tower wall and let it climb back into the sky.

The Father Paramount did not see it that way. "The damage is shocking, is it not?"

I shrugged.

"From here, the plume once appeared as a scarlet aura, or the petals of a white-centered flower."

I could not picture the Radiance a flower. I did not say so. I waited for the Father to continue. I scanned the floor for a heap of bones where the monk had landed, or a black smear, but there was nothing but stone.

The Father Paramount sat down and crossed his legs. He nodded to the floor and I folded myself down beside him. "We must now discuss the fabric of dreams," he said.

I'll have one of cotton, I thought. That would be the most comfortable. I imitated the Paramount and closed my eyes.

"Before I became a monk," he said, "I dreamed of men in a forest, felling trees and dragging them for leagues and leagues uncounted to the nearest civilization, there to be traded for food and supplies. I knew nothing of forestry, so I came to the Tower for an explanation. Such was the vision of wisdom and insight that won me a place in the order. However, my son, because my vision did not relate to any of the routines necessary to maintaining this brotherhood, I was made a common monk, as are most in the Tower, who perform any task their betters lay before them. For many years I served in such a way.

"But then, my son, a second vision appeared to me. Its exact details I will not relate, but in short I saw myself in a position of great responsibility which singled me out as the Paramount's successor." He paused.

"Yes?" I said.

"Such a vision have you been granted."

My eyes jerked open. "I have to be the Paramount?" Why not jump into an acid vat right now?

"No, no, my son. Peace. I mean that your vision guides you down a destined path. It is vital," said the Father, "that we discover the identity of the vandals who damaged the Radiance, that they may be brought to justice."

"What would you do to them?"

"I am not decided. It may depend on the state of the plume when returned, or on my good nature, or upon a score of other variables."

"Oh."

"The punishment need not concern you, my son. Your task is to meditate."

I waited for him to go on.

"You shall sit here," he said, "every day, and meditate on the identities of the criminals. Is this clear to you, my son?"

"What about food?" I gazed around at the marble walls.

The Father Paramount laughed. "I knew you were trustworthy, my son. Even in light of such responsibility, you do not allow practical matters to slip from your mind. Indeed, meals shall be brought to you twice a day. In the evenings you may join your brethren in the dining hall. Only during the day will you seclude yourself here."

21

"Last night," said Y'az Tyfel, and pulled on his pipe, "the houses of five nobles were ransacked. Five!" He rocked on his cushion. "Murdered in their beds!"

"Y'az Zelain was found on the stairs." Nobles filled the room, like the business meetings Blade's grandfather held in the City, with so many swollen stomachs and the smell of sassafras thick in the air. But here the men were frightened. Blade hugged his knees where he sat.

"He must have been bidding for freedom," said another man.

"He was stabbed in the back seven times." Y'az Tyfel shuddered. "The blood ran down the stairs to the door. Three of his servants were found on the lawns, stabbed in their faces and slashed like venison." He drew on his pipe, deeply, cheeks like caves. "Can you imagine such cruelty?"

"Eight of Hev's servants were killed," said another. They did not look at Blade. He sat with his back pressed against the wall. He clutched a pillow to his knees, as if the silk padding could act as a shield. The red tassels brushed his arms.

"Tyfel?" he whispered. "Can we go back to the City now? Please?"

"This is unbelievable. Unbelievable!" Tyfel paid him no attention. "No provocation. No possible warning. Nothing. Do you think the Bedouin are responsible?"

"It could not have been the Bedouin," said another of the nobles. His hair, thick with beads, hung over his face like a waterfall. "The Bedouin population is small," he said.

"How could they have simultaneously entered five houses?"

"Perhaps their numbers have grown," said Tyfel.

"We monitor the Bedouin." The waterfall man wore a robe of green silk. "They could not have grown." He shook his head. "There are not enough Bedouin to replace us. The people would never tolerate their rule again."

"Do you think this has been perpetrated by the common people?"

"More than likely, yes." The beadwork rattled as he nodded his head.

"In the City," said Tyfel, "the guards at the gate would apprehend such a danger as this long before it reached a head."

"This is not the City," the waterfall snapped. "The City has been under noble rule for centuries, while here we have held our seats for less than a decade. You must appreciate the difference, Tyfel."

Y'az Tyfel leaned forward. His eyes swam small in the sea of his face. "As leader of the City Guard, I—"

"As leader of the Guard, you strive to banish all criminals from the City I am sure," said the waterfall. "Is that not true? Jails are a needless expense. It is easier to exile your murderers, madmen, and thieves. By Stone, they have come to the Citadel!"

"If you suffer a surplus of criminals," said Tyfel, "I assure you it is through some fault of your own; you cannot blame us."

"Y'az Gyrt's guard was from the City," said the waterfall man, "the guard who left the note of confession. Or didn't you know that?"

Tyfel turned to Blade. "Xavier, you may leave."

"I'm fine," said Blade. Guards ringed the room. Here he was protected. If he returned to his own apartment, none would protect him except the one servant that Tyfel had given him. He hated this talk of assassination, but he hated still more the thought of being alone, here in this strange palace of wood and windows. "I want to stay," he told Tyfel.

"I spoke with Gyrt's servants this morning," said Drens, the man of the waterfall hair. "Do you know who Gyrt's murderer was?" He leaned toward Blade. "Do you remember a man named 'Leque'?"

Blade clutched the pillow. He tried to swallow.

"Am I correct," said the Y'az, "that Leque once worked for your father?"

"Leave," said Tyfel. "Xavier, ignore that question and leave. Go up to your room." He snapped his fingers for a servant. "Escort Master Xavier to his suite," he said, "and provide him with a bowl of spiced milk and a platter of peacock filet. Thank you."

"But..." said Blade. He thought of Leque, standing in the grass of the Glebe, a stepladder in his hands, smashing it down, down... "That was years ago," he whispered. "How—"

"How did I know?" said Drens. "It was in his credentials. He had bragged to the other guards since the day he was hired. Everyone knows the name of Ven."

"Why does it matter?" whispered Blade. "Why does it matter if Leque used to work for my father?"

"It matters that you know each other," said Drens, "and it matters that you arrived in the Citadel later than Tyfel. I know that. Surely you did not come alone. You would not know how. You had no real escort — I can tell by the burns on your face, like a common traveler. You may have come with a former servant, a man you trusted?"

Blade touched his nose. The skin still curled underneath his finger.

"What better guide than a man who once worked for your father?" said waterfall-Drens. "A servant who, I believe, bore you special affection? And who also, I believe, terminated his service to your family with no explanation. Few jobs pay higher than employment by a Y'az. Assassin may be one of the few."

"Come." A servant touched Blade's sleeve. "Let me take you to your rooms."

Blade woke to the sound of rain on a wooden roof. Today the meeting would be held at Kem's house, wouldn't it? Yes, and even better, it was his and Yaryk's turn at the

Marble Tower. Yaryk always came early on days like these, so they could be the first to climb the stairs of the Tower. Stealth and secrecy. Blade followed Yaryk's example. He followed him close, so he would not lose himself in the pulsing walls.

Yaryk planned everything. He brought blank wish papers for Blade to hang. "The monks must think we come to make wishes," he said. He brought a stub of graphite also, so that if Blade wanted he could write a real wish on the paper. Those days were best: when Blade could think of a wish to make, and a way to word the wish so it sounded eloquent. He wished for a new cloak once. He often wished for a stomach like his grandfather's. On days when he remembered, he wished for other people as well. Those were the best days of all. "Please can my father get better," he wrote last year. "Please can Kem raise enough money for whatever it is he is funding." Sometimes he added detail: "...I tried to give Kem twenty gold coins for whatever it was he was raising money for, but he only accepted eight."

Today, Blade decided, he would wish for Glane. He had pondered the words all night. Something like this: "Please can Glane's shoulder get better." Maybe that wasn't enough and he ought to explain: "He was stung by a bee and he says it hurts."

Some days Yaryk placed a wish as well. He laughed if Blade asked what it said. "My true desires I only entrust to the Stars," said Yaryk. He showed the blank paper to Blade. "Dormant Stone may answer *you*, Blade, but for me only the open elements listen."

Blade dreamed of the day when Yaryk would have a real wish, and read it aloud before hanging it over a pool. He imagined Yaryk explaining as they climbed the stairs. He imagined Yaryk's hands as he wrote the note. Blade had never seen Yaryk write, but of course he knew how. Yaryk had a flowing script, he decided, riddled with characters Blade did not know. Yaryk would teach him that script someday, the script of the Bedouin, used to pen legend as they sat around their fires at night.

He could not imagine what Yaryk would wish for. He stayed awake at night wondering.

Now Blade rolled over. He listened to the rain on the wood overhead, not the glass roof he had known in the City. He remembered where he lay. The blankets were clotted and sweaty. Yaryk had abandoned him. What was this talk of assassination? Yaryk and the other Bedouin had spoken of murder, hadn't they? Blade rolled again, trying to escape the memory. Why would Yaryk assassinate anyone? Why hadn't he come and found Blade? Did Blade even want to be found?

The blankets wrapped tighter as he rolled. And then there was Leque. Would he rather Leque found him? Leque had only accompanied him to the Marble Tower a few times — only once or twice before he stopped working for the house of Ven. It had not been the same without Yaryk. Leque crept like an alley rat up the stairways, lost his way, grinned and bowed and twitched when a monk went by. Why was Leque so frightened when Yaryk appeared so calm?

When Leque had stopped working for his father, it provided an excuse to go with Yaryk alone. Leque stopped coming to the palace; he no longer came to Blade's room. He still took Blade out to eating houses, different ones every time so he could try them all, and introduced him to the cooks, and the owners, but Leque never came to the palace.

But Yaryk also took him to eat, so what did it matter? With Yaryk he was Blade, whereas to Leque he was only Xavier. He was not a wanderer or a wild adventurer. Only Xavier Ven. That had changed at some point, and everyone now called him Blade, but Leque had been slow to make the change.

Today, Leque would not kill a noble, would he? Of course not. He would never kill. Not Leque. Would he? Five nobles? He wouldn't kill five. Where was the incentive? Where was the logic? Blade struggled out from under his blankets. Shivering, he scurried to the adjoining room to relieve himself. A guard in dark leather nodded as he passed.

Blade steadied his hands. Upon his return, he straightened the sheets before crawling beneath them. He tried to count the raindrops as they struck the roof. They fell too fast and he could not keep track. He tried not to look at the guard. He did not want the man to look back. He did not want to be seen; he did not want to be watched. If even Leque could kill, then couldn't this man as well? He could kill Blade easily, lying exposed in his bed.

He listened to the rain. This was only the beginning. There were days and days of rain to come.

Back in the City Blade loved this season. His bed had been twice this size, hemmed in gauze and mounded in pillows. The ceiling was glass. He lay on his back and watched the white gulls circle, the rain pour down, and the streams of water course the glass. The walls of his room were also glass. He could order a servant to draw back the hundred-fold curtains, and there was the City below, spread out like a tile mosaic, the spires of the palaces jutting like inset jewels, the arms of the hospital diadem-bright, and everywhere the maze of streets. His friends lived there: Leque, Yaryk and the rest of them. Blade used to sit and gaze over the view, and imagine what each was doing.

Now Ksar was dead. Leque and Yaryk were killers. The rest were too distant to guess.

If only his grandfather had not sent him away, he would one day have become the most powerful man in the City. He would have held control over all of them then. He would not have allowed them to kill. He would not have let anyone kill, or steal, or suffer. Blade wanted to cry.

But maybe as the head of the Ven family, he would only have singled himself out as a target for murder. Maybe everyone in the world wanted to kill everyone else in the world, and he, Blade, was the only one who did not want death. He looked at the guard. The man was watching him, but looked away and their eyes did not meet.

"Get out," said Blade.

"Pardon, Master?"

Blade pulled the blankets up to his chin. "Get out of my room!" he said. "Leave!"

The man shuffled out. He gave Blade one final, quizzical look and closed the door behind him.

Blade sank into the pillows. Should he have stayed in the City? He could have kept out of his grandfather's way, hidden in Leque and Ksar's house. He could have been stung by bees, turned into a bird ... but what did he know about being a bird? Maybe it would have been better than this. He could stay in the hospital with Glane, where none but his friends could find him.

Who were his friends? Could he trust anyone anymore? Did they all want to kill him?

He could stay in the stables. He could enter the palace at night for clean bedding and changes of clothes, candies and delicacies and soaps to keep the lice from his hair. That would not be so bad. No one in the City would know he was there. If he turned to a bird he could live in the rafters.

Blade had lulled himself almost to sleep when the door swung open.

"Xavier?" Feet waddled through the carpet, followed by the glow of an oil lamp, viscous as melted honey on the walls and ceiling. "Xavier, are you here?" Y'az Tyfel's voice. His face appeared upside-down over Blade. He smiled. He reeked of burnt tea, and the smile was watery. "Are you ill, Xavier?"

Blade shook his head. Let people think he was ill and they would kill him all the sooner.

"Tired?" said the Y'az. He motioned to a servant behind him. The eunuch pulled a velvet armchair from the corner of the room. Tyfel sank into its cushions. "Sit up," he told Blade. "We must talk."

If Blade was to die regardless, it may as well happen seated. He obeyed the Y'az.

"Xavier... My boy... I know you have been unhappy, what with the death of your father and then your disownment. Yes, unhappy..." He trailed off, rallied: "You need to understand what's happening here."

Blade nodded.

"I return to the City at first light tomorrow," said Tyfel. "I'm afraid you cannot come with me. The nobles here — Y'az Drens — want us separated."

"Why?" Blade's voice sounded stony-hard. "Why do I have to stay?"

"Because of the assassinations." Y'az Tyfel sighed. "They think we are involved. They are frightened and confused, the nobles here. Yes, confused. They fear you, Xavier, believing you came with Leque. We came to the Citadel at the wrong time, that's all. The wrong time." He lowered his voice, as if he too feared the guard outside. "Some," he said, "Y'az Drens in particular, believe that you are still in contact with Leque, and involved in masterminding these crimes." He changed his mind. "Atrocities," he said.

"I'm not," said Blade.

"Of course you're not. If they knew you, they'd realize how ludicrous these accusation are." Another benign smile. "You'll just have to show them your character, Xavier. Once they see how innocent..."

He believes me stupid, thought Blade. Maybe I am. Is this truly an attempt to help, or is he planning something new to make me suffer?

"Y'az Drens' men are escorting me back to the City," said Tyfel. "You will stay with Y'az Drens himself. I don't know how long you will stay. I'm sorry. I will tell your grandfather what's happened. I'm sure he will understand. He will send an envoy to collect you as soon as he can, I promise. Just a few weeks. You see," he hurried on, "it is unknown if the common people, or the Bedouin are responsible for these ... atrocities. Interrogations are underway. You're not the only precautionary hostage, Xavier." He gave another tealeaf smile and patted Blade's shoulder. "You should be able to spend the night here. You'll be moved in the morning. You're a political hostage, not a prisoner. Remember that."

The bedroom door slammed open. Y'az Drens frowned in through his curtain of beads. "That's enough," he said. "You've said all you need, Tyfel. You're gibbering now."

Another watered smile, another pat. Tyfel gestured to the eunuch to pull him from the chair. The eunuch helped him from the room.

Another servant remained, hovering over Blade. "Anything to drink?" he said. "Dinner? Musical entertainment?"

"Dinner," said Blade.

The man hurried away before Blade remembered that anything served may be poisoned. When the servant returned with his dinner, steaming on platters, he decided that poison was better than hunger.

Three of Drens' servants shook Blade from bed. They gave him no time to wake up. The drum of the rain had stopped. They rolled him in his blankets like a sausage in batter and carried him out down the stairs of the palace, to the litter that waited in the street below. Moisture greased the streets. The sky was so low he could reach and touch the clouds. The suns would not appear today.

The servants lifted Blade's litter. They walked through the wet-dimmed streets of the Citadel. The servants swam through the fog. It settled and dripped on their faces. The smell of acid — sharp and mineral — hung in the air. Blade closed his eyes. He buried his face in his blankets. The streets appeared deserted, but one man could be enough to kill him. A sense of calm spilled into his chest; he could be killed any moment, assassinated; there was nothing he could do to speed or delay his death. It was all inevitable.

Cold air licked his face. He wrapped the covers more tightly around himself. His head lolled against the wall with each step of the bearers. Their feet splashed in the damp. Their voices drifted in to meet his ears.

"Three more," said one man. He grunted, really, as he slogged along. "I overheard the Y'az saying that four palaces were targeted, but Kli'elm, the sly old..." — he slipped into jargon that Blade did not know — "...he wouldn't let that happen to him. He was ready with a knife in his teeth, all his guards the same, and the Stone-bloody killers didn't make it past the kitchens."

"Who were they?"

"The assassins?" said the bearer. "I don't know. Kli'elm's guards did them in without questions."

"I'd do the same," said another. "Who cares who they were, provided they're gone?"

The litter stopped at the side of a street. Arms reached in. They carried Blade across a courtyard — everything pallid in the late dawn — up a flight of steps, through a labyrinth of hallways and into a room with wood-slatted walls, almost identical to the one he had occupied in the palace with Tyfel. Maybe that had been no more than a pleasure ride, he thought. They had taken him back where he started. But this room was colder than the one he had left, and the floors had no carpet, and no cushioned chair sat waiting in the corner. This room was also smaller than the last. It was no more than a servant's closet.

"He sleeps like a slaughtered ox," said the man who had carried him in. "Y'az Drens has no need to worry about this one slipping away."

22

The Year of the Mandarin Turtle entered into its rainy season. I did not know this until my second day with the Radiance. At dinner that night, Brother Iander told me.

"We have entered the rains," he said.

A monk in a deep green robe interrupted us. "Brother Ksar?" He held a quill in his hand.

"Yes?" I said.

"Someone has come to see you. He is waiting in the reception room. He says it's very important."

I escaped the table and Brother Iander's company. I wound my way through the maze of back passageways, and came out behind the reception desk, still chewing some kind of fruit I had taken from the table. Kem leaned against the far wall. An oilskin cloak dripped over one arm. He pretended to read a scroll.

"What are you reading?"

He looked up. "Thank you."

"Why 'thank you'?"

"I've been trying to see you for two days now, but whenever I come they tell me you are engaged with important matters."

"Maybe you should stop coming, then."

"What have you been doing?"

"Meditating. I'm only free in the evenings."

"Couldn't you have told me, Ksar? I've missed hours of work because of this — trekking across the City to talk to you, only to find it's for nothing. Because of my absence from the last meeting, the Fellowship of the White Horse," — he flourished his scroll — "is now in financial straits."

"Sorry," I said.

"Well," said Kem, "why do you meditate?"

"The Father Paramount wants me to find out who damaged the Radiance."

Kem squinted. "You meditate," he said, "about the Radiance? I have, at times, prescribed meditation for stress-relief. It can be very soothing." He rubbed his chin. He smelled of soap. "But meditation as a means of exposing information? I have never heard of that before. Has it proved effective for the monks in the past?"

"It's effective now," I said. "I'm being punished for all the crimes I've ever committed. I spend more time crawling around the floor than I do thinking about the Radiance." I paused. "I still haven't found the bloodstains."

"What do you mean?"

I looked over my shoulder. I made sure the tally-monk wasn't listening. "There are no bloodstains from the monk Gyanin pushed. I've looked all over the floor, but they must have been cleaned."

"You mean you are *in* the Radiance room?"

I nodded.

"By Stone, Ksar!" He grinned. "You want to stop living here, don't you? That's not going to happen until we restore the plume to the Radiance, yes? Now you're in the Radiance room every day. Don't you think you should have told me immediately? It's almost over. Ksar, the victory is so close I can smell it. Can't you?"

"Er, yes." I wondered what Kem-victory smelled like. Soap and water, probably, or disinfectant. "What do you want me to do?" I said.

"We must restore the plume."

"But I can't actually *reach* the Radiance," I protested. "It hangs at the top of the room and I sit at the bottom. There aren't any stairs. The door to the top is always locked. It has a different key or something. I've never been up there."

"No, no, wait." Kem closed his scroll with a thoughtful air. "What time in the evening does public access to the Tower end?"

"Suns' down, I think." I jutted a thumb at the tally-monk. "You could ask him."

"No, no." Kem shook his head. "You're probably right.
I'm still thinking." He excluded me from his thoughts for
a while, then asked: "If the plume were returned to the
Radiance, do you think your secluded meditation would
end? Would the monks allow you to forget it all and say it
doesn't matter who the culprits were?"

"I don't know."

"It is worth a try." He looked at me, his grin painfully
wide. "Restored at last! Will you not feel liberated, Ksar?"

"Good," I said.

Kem rubbed his chin. "I will come five nights from now.
No..." he paused, as if counting something out in his head.
"Six nights from now. There are many details to plan. We
have to give ourselves time."

"I don't know any details," I said.

"I'll tell you the plan," said Kem, "listen. Six days from
now, I will come to the Tower as if to make a wish. I will
wear a Bedouin robe, large enough to conceal the Radiance's
crest underneath. After public access to the Tower has ended,
I will go to the upper door of the Radiance room and knock."

"You won't gain anything from that. I only meditate
during the days, and besides, I can't get up to that door."
Why did no one listen to Ksar?

"Next time I visit," said Kem, "I'll bring you a rope. With
the rope you can climb to the platform and let me in."

"I can't," I said. "I told you, I only meditate during the
day. I won't be there in the evening."

"You have to be," said Kem.

"I hate that room."

"It will be your last night as a monk. After this, you'll
never need to see the room again. Once we put the crest back,
I'll help you run away or whatever you want. But just for
this once, Ksar, you have to stay in the Radiance room into
the evening. Tell the Father Paramount you're on the brink
of revelation and you only need a few more hours."

"And of course it won't seem suspicious when the crest
reappears in the morning," I muttered.

"You will have to explain it as a miracle of enlightenment," said Kem. "Skiy and I discussed this earlier. The
Tower Brotherhood is an ancient denomination, and in many

ways removed from the logic of the rest of the world. If the crest's reappearance is attributed to mental prowess, I am sure it will be accepted as a legitimate resurrection."

"If it *isn't* accepted," I said, "and they catch me and string me up by my toenails, I will blame you completely." Kem knew more about the Brotherhood than I did. I hated him for it. "I'll tell them about you and Skiy," I muttered.

"Yes, you may expose us," said Kem, "if we fail."

I hated how self-sacrificing everyone could be, and eager to turn themselves in. I was doing more than Kem though, wasn't I? You didn't see Kem in here, in a green robe and an egg-shaved head. If he really wanted to martyr himself, he too should become a monk.

"It still won't work," I said. "See the tally-monk there? He keeps track of the people in the Marble Tower. If you hide in the Tower, the numbers won't match and they'll know you're here."

"What would they do?"

"I don't know." I scowled. "Something awful, I'm sure." The more Kem smiled, the more I was sure this would never work. He was making it sound too easy. We would both end up imprisoned, or exiled, or having our fingernails extracted one at a time.

Kem patted my arm. "You think the situation is so dire. The worst that could happen is they find me and force me to leave. In which case I'll return on another night. Really, Ksar, nothing can be lost by trying."

"But what if you're searched and they find the plume? Or what if a monk comes in, in the middle of repairing the Radiance? I bet they'll do more than ask you to leave. We'll have to push the monk off the railing like Gyanin did, and hide the plume again, and—"

"Ksar, please!" Kem tucked his scroll in his belt. He shook the worst of the wet from his cloak and draped it around his shoulders.

"I'm going to find out what happens to people who stay in the Tower after public access," I said. "If it's something horrible, I don't think you should try it."

"We'll see." He patted my arm again, smiled, and left.

23

Morren's elbow caught Yaryk in the side. "The Glebe!" he shouted. The whole crowd shouted around them. "We will take back the Glebe!"

The central ring of the meeting hall was never designed for fifty men, all shouting and brandishing fists in the air. Yaryk folded his arms. He watched the chaos increase around him. It was easier to watch than to turn to the darkness and ask it for silence. He did not look at the grate behind which Leque sat.

"Tonight, an hour past sundown," cried Liop, "we will meet at the gates. Bring only what belongings you can carry. But bring your knives, and bring your bows if you have them. Yaryk," said Liop. The torches painted his face a crazy orange. "Where's my little Yaryk?" he shouted. "Where are you?"

Yaryk elbowed his way through the crush. "What?"

"You've been on the roads recently," said Liop.

"I have," said Yaryk. He sat on the bench beside Liop. He folded his arms and spoke quietly so that none of the crowd could hear. "Why do you comment on it?" he said. "Liop, your plans are like suicide."

"What conditions are the roads?"

"I traveled in the dry season. Now the rains have begun, everything will change."

"Do you believe it would be safe to travel with this many men after nightfall?"

"I didn't come along the road from the Glebe." Yaryk scowled. "Perhaps you should have ascertained road conditions before inflaming this rabble." He jerked his head at the mob around them.

"Glebe!" they murmured, whispered, shouted between them. "We'll take back the Glebe! Liop will win the whole Citadel!"

"Be conditions as they may," said Liop, "I would be honored if you would walk with me, at the head of the procession."

Yaryk nodded. "I will do that." He stepped from the bench, back into the sea of elbows.

The rain throbbed in Yaryk's ears. Liop squatted on his right, Jarb on the left, here beneath the eaves of a barbershop window. The other Bedouin hulked in the darkness. Some held lanterns, unlit, beneath their cloaks. The Citadel gates loomed ahead, locked for the night. In the lee of the wall, the guards huddled featureless. Only their spears caught the lamplight. The rain flowed down and down.

Liop waved his arm. Four men stepped out from the eaves and slid like salamanders up to the gates. The rain drowned out all sound; they could have shouted and the guards would not have heard. They would not have had time to stop the knives. Yaryk watched the knives flash out, drive down, and wondered what Blade would do if he could see this now.

The Bedouin flowed from the shadows. Yaryk stepped out with them. Mud weighed down his feet. He stepped around the body of a guard.

Jarb cursed beside him. "This cane," he muttered. "Stars curse this cane."

Morren the blacksmith fumbled through a ring of keys. The sound came wet and heavy. He found the right key and inserted it into the gate. They pushed open one side of the barrier, slow on its hinges, wide enough for all to pass through.

Fifty Bedouin and one prisoner left the Citadel. Yaryk knew that Leque hobbled at the rear of the procession, dragged, perhaps, by a rope around the mangle of his wrists. Yaryk would not consider his suffering. Leque, he decided, was no longer a concern of his. If the man wished to act as a fool, then a fool let him be. Let him hold delusions about the nobles and their great benevolence. Yaryk would not. Benevolence was a feature of old stories and lore, not a trait of the real world. Only the young or naïve believed such things.

They skirted the outer wall of the Citadel, along the gravel shore. It was here they had gathered before, where Yaryk the fool had called them together. He had needed Blade as a catalyst — a catalyst for change, he had hoped, and revenge, but not this full-fledged slaughter. The Bedouin had forgotten Blade. They followed Liop like rabid sheep.

Once out of sight of the gates, the men produced lanterns from under their cloaks. They held the oil lights up in the darkness. Where was the path to the Glebe? Yaryk remembered how it used to look, groping away across the acid like a dislocated arm. The path was wider now, when at last they found it — wide enough for several men to walk abreast. They kept to single-file. In the rain and night, the path's verges could not be seen. If a man were to fall, he would disappear. Stars only knew how far he would fall to the acid — the breadth of a hand or the height of a tower. It did not matter; either way, he would die once he reached the sea.

The Citadel disappeared behind them. They walked an endless road, a trail of firefly lights. The first man's lantern chiseled the path, while the last man plunged it again into night. Yaryk walked beside Liop. Flowering trees wept beside the road. Colored flagstones flickered underneath their feet. The last time Yaryk had come here, the ground had been loose sand and shards of glass, narrow with crumbling embankments. Camels and nomads had shaped this road, not waddling nobles and their retinues.

They stopped at the wall of the Glebe. Smooth white marble rose before them. There had never been a wall before. The rain ran down in a solid film. There could be no scaling this wall. Vertical bars sealed them out. Morren stepped forward again. He fished the keys from his belt. With his back to the Bedouin, he stood a while, hunched as if petrified, as if he could not move the gates at all. Then there came the deep register of metal over metal. The golden bars pulled apart with a groan.

An arrow whistled down. It struck Morren in the mouth. He bubbled blood, keeled over and twitched on the ground.

Yaryk dove for the trees. He caught Liop's arm — sinew and burlap — and dragged him down. "Stay here," he spat. "They can see you on the path."

Around them, the other Bedouin splashed for cover. They cursed as the twigs caught their robes. Oilcloth slapped the mud. Dishes and weaponry clattered.

Silence followed.

A light flared up beyond the gate. Arrows spiraled down. Across the path, a scream rang out. A second scream, followed by a splash, broke the night. The stink of acid and burning skin filled the air. Thank Stone Blade was not here. Thank the Stars. More arrows. They came in bursts, wide and wild.

Yaryk clenched his jaw. They must attack now, while the gate was still open. Now, in this lull in the archery. If he waved his arm for the Bedouin to see, the guards inside would see also, and he would be shot. He lay on his stomach in the peat and mud, afraid to stretch his legs in case they touched the acid. He swore beneath his breath. What an imbecile he was, ever to return to the Citadel, ever to seek out Liop.

From the other side of the path, a hand waved into the lamplight. "Now!" It was Jarb.

The shadows erupted and charged. Arrows arced down from the wall. One Bedouin stopped. He pulled a shaft from his thigh, fell to his knees and lay still. The crowd swept Yaryk along, into the soaking wet grass and the light of the Glebe. Lanterns the size of shields glared from the arch of the gate. Yaryk stared at the light. The guards came. There were only twenty. They leveled their spears and shields. One of them wielded what looked, in the garish light, like a pair of pruning shears. They halted before the throng of Bedouin, then turned and ran.

Bry threw a knife. It struck one guard in the neck, up to its hilt. The man staggered sideways and rolled. He buried both hands in his blood.

"Let them go!" Yaryk shouted. "Close the gates. Barricade them closed."

Jarb crawled through the archway last. His cane had broken in the mad stampede. He used the wall as a crutch and stood. "Bring in Morren's body," he shouted. "There are other bodies as well, and wounded. Bring them in!"

"What good?" hissed Yaryk.

"We'll Release them tomorrow." Jarb panted but stood his ground.

"What about him?" Bry nudged the guard with his toe. The man had stopped moving.

"Recover your knife," said Yaryk, "and take him outside. We have enough with our own dead."

The Bedouin shed their packs of possessions, smothered in oilcloth, and stacked them against the wall.

"How do we block the gate?" said a man with a slash on his arm.

Could none of these men think for themselves? And where was Liop? Yaryk waved to the kiwi vines, dancing on the edge of the light. "Wood," he said. "Cut down as much as you need."

Jarb hurried after Yaryk. He clung to Bry's arm for support. "Yaryk!" His face was white in the rain. "Liop is dead."

24

The rain lulled by morning. The Bedouin stood outside the gates of the Glebe. Five bodies, Liop's among them, lay on the flagstones. Cloaks had been pulled across their faces. Yaryk stepped forward; Bry bounded to stand beside him. Together they knelt. They rolled the corpses, one by one, into the acid. Hardly a splash, and the gray sea devoured them. A handful of bubbles broke the surface, a wisp of steam, and then they were gone.

Yaryk turned to face the Bedouin, his eyes weighted and thick with exhaustion. All night they had pursued the guards — a blur of torchlight, leaves and rain. When had these trees been planted? How had they grown so fast and rampant?

Yaryk spread his arms. "Liop is dead. I don't know what he planned next. It is not too late to return to the Citadel. No one knows we are here."

"No." Gwall, the blacksmith, shook his head. His bald crown reflective in the damp. "I want to take back the Citadel."

"How?" said Yaryk.

"Liop promised us."

"Fifty men." Yaryk pointed to the cloaks that still lay on the ground. "Less than fifty now. That's not enough to take the Citadel by force. If we had ten times our number, it would still be insufficient."

"We'll make more come," said Gwall. He clenched his fists. "If we wait here long enough, other Bedouin will hear of us. They'll come and help."

Yaryk laughed. "I doubt that. *Few are the heroes of old, who sought out the needy and upheld them.*' No, if we want help, we must beg for it. We will dispatch messengers. Without more aid, this cause is foolhardy." It was foolhardy regardless, he thought, but he did not say so. As a leader you had to know when to lie, and when to omit certain truths.

"I'll go," said Gwall.

"Who else will go?" said Yaryk. "We need messengers."

"I will." Another man stepped forward. A fine representative of the Guild he made, in his yellow toga and his shaven head. "My name is Mehrzh."

Yaryk nodded.

Bry had been squatting by the acid, watching the last of the bubbles break the surface. He swelled up his chest. "I'll go."

"No you won't," said Jarb.

"I'm not a cripple." The boy stood up. "I can walk for days."

"You've never traveled alone," said Jarb. "This won't be how you begin."

Yaryk sat cross-legged on the top of the wall. Beside him, an incense stick wisped into the sky. The sea was cat-pawed, gray-pink and lackluster. One ridge of stone jutted up from the surface and ran away to the distance. Hours ago, the four messengers had passed from sight.

The first time Yaryk had come to the Glebe had been years ago, when he was only a boy. He had followed that path with his father's tribe: older brothers, uncles, cousins. They were wanderers then, the only life Yaryk knew. They walked every day, pitched their tents at night, or slept in the open under the stars. If the night was cold and they had the fuel, they would build a fire. Always they told each other stories; it passed the long hours of dark.

An old man in the tribe — of what relation Yaryk did not remember — told of the Highlands, far away, where the sea itself rose in climbing steps, each as broad as a civilization. In the rainy season, water filled the upper troughs of the Highlands and flowed in great torrents to the lower. Cascades of thunder, the old man said, diluted the acid and washed away the year's crustacean. At the top of the Highlands a crater opened in the stone. It filled with pure, black water. The bottom could never be seen, and the sides dropped away sheer without a shore, only a precipice that roiled and churned with the year's first rain. Fish thrived in the lake's black water. They were not glass fish, like the fish in the sea, but fish with scales of calcium and carbon, that darted in lithe, symmetrical schools. Some were huge, with rose-red meat like an animal's. Standing on the rim of the crater, men snared the fish in grass-fiber nets.

"Some day," said the old man, "all the world will be water again. The Lake" — that was what it was called, the Lake — "flows over with the rain each year. The upper troughs of the Highlands dilute. They are so diluted now that it is safe to swim in them. Yes, before the acid, men once swam like fish." Yaryk had thought that funny when he was young — the idea of waving your arms and moving through water. But he was always quiet when the old man spoke; he never laughed or voiced his humor.

He could not remember what the old man looked like, or what he did for the tribe when not telling stories. Did he ride atop the baggage camel, where children rode when they were too young to walk? Had he sorted through the trading goods — sunflower oil, olive oil, scented oils and salted fruits — that they gave in exchange for water and news? Yaryk remembered the old man's voice, how slow it had been, like the drip of sweat down a sun-browned arm.

The old man spoke often when only Yaryk was present to hear. "One could call it ironic," he said, "that the falling of the third sun turned the sea to acid, and that now it is the carcass of the sun itself that brings about a restoration."

Yaryk nodded. By the time he understood the man's words, years later, the old man was gone. These Highlands, did they truly exist? Were they truly the remains of the third sun? How many other legends had been created around the death of the sun? How many had he himself, Yaryk, fabricated within the last year? The last two years? Every storyteller drew from the third sun's fall. The Highlands were likely a lie. The old man told many stories that could not be believed.

"There's a civilization around the rim of the Lake," he said, "where the houses stand on stilts of pearl and fish-bone. When the people are hungry, they lower baited threads down into the Lake and snare the fish. They use machines like carts and litters to float on the water. In the dry season, when it is safe, they lower these contraptions to the surface of the Lake. A man may propel himself shore to shore without wetting a hand." Yaryk wished the stories were true.

Here in the Glebe, they had barricaded themselves in like prisoners; only this pathway below could offer help. If only the sea lapped water, not acid, they could make these "carts," and send out messengers in every direction, rally a fleet of Bedouin and storm the Citadel. They would resurrect the Guild. How many of this rabble had ever been a part of the Guild before? How many would understand what they were doing if it was reestablished? But Yaryk would understand. He had been there before. He would offer to lead them, and they would accept.

Yaryk had not believed the old man. He listened because the stories fascinated him. Stories were meant to enthrall and entertain. They were not meant to convince. When the old man left the tribe, Yaryk listened to no one. He invented his own stories, as he fed the camels with his brothers, or set up tents, or prepared what meals he could. His mind transported him to areas less mundane.

"See that star?" He would point, for anyone who would listen. "Yes, the one with the sheen of blue. It rose first of all the stars tonight, and I swear to Time it was pulled to heaven by a horde of winged creatures." He became the tribe's storyteller by the age of fourteen. How old was Blade now? Was he not fourteen? Yaryk sneered. What had Blade accomplished?

They had visited the Glebe again, when Yaryk was a young man. He broke company. He did not need them anymore, his father's tribe. They had taught him the secrets of the highroads, the different winds and their various dangers. You could not fear losing your way; as a wanderer you were always lost. You could not put your faith in the stars; the course of the stars always changed. Many travelers looked down on the Bedouin. They saw the Bedouin as homeless. Yaryk had begun to agree. He was good at agreeing if it benefited himself to do so, and sometimes he convinced himself, as well as his listeners, of the way his mind was set.

Enough wandering. He said his farewells, took his stories with him, and left. The Glebe had been a field then, not an orchard. He left his family and walked to the Citadel. They said they would visit. He never saw them again. Perhaps they had come, and they had looked for him, and he had passed them in the street without notice.

Yaryk had joined the Guild. The Guild was for Bedouin who had tired of travel. For the first five years, he stared at everyone he passed on the street, afraid of missing a brother or cousin. He never saw them. How could he look for them? The world was endless. He had not explored it all. Perhaps he should leave, and wander the highroads again, but most likely he would lead himself in circles and see nothing new at all.

While it lasted, Yaryk had loved the Bedouin Guild. All they did was talk, and Yaryk had the patience to converse on any subject. Later, maybe, he had become arrogant in his skill. Maybe. Now, certainly, no one listened to his reasoning. Use the Glebe to conquer the Citadel? Hadn't it failed two years ago, the first time Liop tried it? Why try it again, now, when the number of Bedouin had dwindled still further? Liop was dead, and still they would not listen to reason. Yaryk fanned the incense smoke into his face. He was not listening to reason himself. He should leave these men to their suicide-madness. He knew this but did not leave. He should take Leque with him and return to wandering, find some new pocket of civilization where neither of them would be criminals. He should go back to the Citadel for Blade.

Perhaps they did listen to Yaryk. When Liop died, hadn't they all turned to him? Yaryk could not refuse such bait:

open ears to his council. He would lead them as long as he could, until things were ruined and then he would leave.

"Yaryk!"

Yaryk turned. He looked down to the foot of the wall. Bry stood in the grass below. "The workers are coming!" He waved his knife. "We're shooting them! Come and see!"

"Shooting?" Yaryk ground the incense stick into his palm. He felt the point of heat, like the sting of a wasp, and the smoke trail died.

The ladder he had climbed still leaned against the wall. Yaryk swung his legs over the lip of white marble. Hand over hand, he climbed down into the swamp of grass. The murk and water almost reached his knees. Bry ran and Yaryk hurried after, past the flowering shrubs and the berry bushes, some of them drowned by the rain, the trees bent double under fruit and moisture, past the sitting area where the guards sat tied in a circle, their backs together, one rope for all their wrists. The water sloshed up to their waists. Leque sat off to the side, tied to a bench. He'd been given that luxury at least — a bench, and a tether long enough to allow him to pace. He lay on his back with his hands on his chest, swollen as fetid meat. He did not look at Yaryk.

The Bedouin crowded beneath the shelter of the gate's arch, peering between the branches and hewn trunks of the barricade. The ground here rose. The grass was saturated but not yet submerged. Above and to either side of the gate, shooting platforms jutted out from the wall. Chinks had been cut in the marble to allow the barbed shafts their exit. Bedouin clustered on the platforms, bows and arrows in their hands.

"Move." Yaryk pushed past Jarb. He climbed the narrow steps to a platform. "Let me see. Move."

Screams could be heard from the roadway below. Yaryk shuffled to the nearest view slit. Along the walkway, between the lines of trees, mayhem raged below. A score of bodies lay before the walls. Some were dead; others twitched with arrows in their sides. They bled in the puddles, moaned and writhed. One man, an arrow through his thigh, sprawled at the side of the road, his foot in the acid. He screamed as the gray smoke rose.

"I'm trying to get him." Bry pointed. He carried a satchel of rocks slung over his shoulder.

"Stop!" Yaryk turned from the view slit. He shouted loud for all the Bedouin to hear. Only the man beside him seemed to notice. "Stop!" he shouted. "Where are the other workers? Surely there were more than this."

"They ran away. We couldn't get them all."

"You fools!" Yaryk swore. "Why kill these? This is useless slaughter! Now that the others have fled, they will tell the Citadel we are here. If you hadn't killed their comrades, perhaps their report would not be so dire, but now? Everyone in the Citadel will want revenge. You fools!"

Most of the Bedouin had stopped now, watching him.

"Once you've finished your slaughter," said Yaryk, "go out and Release the bodies. Pray for the rain again, to wash this blood away."

The rain resumed. The water in the Glebe approached mid-thigh. Yaryk had changed from his tunic, back into his robes. He now cursed the decision, his clothes so heavy around him as he fought his way. He fought through the water in the direction of the sitting area.

Jarb appeared through the trees. "We're flooding," he panted. In place of his cane, he now used the branch of a fig tree. The bark blistered his hands.

Yaryk pushed his turban away from his eyes. "And without your cane, you'll be the first to drown."

"Yaryk, we'll *all* drown. It's waist deep in places. Men are seeking refuge in the trees."

"This is stupidity." Yaryk buried his hands in the sleeves of his robe and continued on.

Half wading, half crawling, the water splashing into his face, Jarb hurried after. "Yaryk, we must do something. The Glebe is a basin. It's filling up."

"I *am* doing something," said Yaryk.

In the sitting area the guards had managed to stand, still roped in a circle, backs together. They glowered at Yaryk as he passed. Farther on, Leque's bench was all but submerged. He could no longer lie, but sat now, hunched over, with his legs dangling into the froth, his hands folded in his lap. The rain had darkened his hair to the color of dung and plastered it over his face. Yaryk sat down beside him.

Leque did not look up. "Hello, old friend."

"Why the bitterness?" said Yaryk.

"You've betrayed everyone."

"What are you talking about?"

"First Blade," said Leque. "You dragged him away from the City and abandoned him."

"Leque, you're over-tired. You're not thinking clearly." Yaryk cursed himself. Why hadn't he visited Leque sooner? He needed the man's help now, and at this rate it would not be easily obtained.

"I *am* over-tired," said Leque. "Do you know *why* I'm over-tired? I have no shelter, and I haven't eaten in days."

"No shelter?" said Yaryk. "There *is* no shelter here. Your plight is no worse than ours."

"'Ours?'" Leque kicked his feet in the water, like a child in a rain barrel. "You're not one of us anymore, are you?"

"What are you talking about?"

"Burning incense in Skiy's shop? Telling stories? The Tower. That was us. *Us.* Ksar, Kem, Gyanin, Blade, all of us! Now you're one of *them*." He twitched a shoulder to the kiwi vines. "The Bedouin. You've always been one of them, haven't you?"

"Leque, you're not speaking sense."

"*You* sent the bees, didn't you?" His voice rose. "You sent them as a distraction to get away from the Radiance. But why did you take Blade with you? Why?"

Yaryk said nothing.

"You were never ashamed of the Radiance, were you?" said Leque. "You never cared about what we had done."

"Of course I cared. But I wasn't ashamed. Why be ashamed of an accident?" Yaryk reached to touch Leque's shoulder. Leque flinched away. "I've always been one of the Bedouin," he said. "If you're born a Bedouin, you'll always be Bedouin. I was still one of you — Skiy and the rest of you — as well. I swear to the Stars I was, and I still am, Leque. I'm trying to protect you." He smiled.

Leque did not smile. "I don't believe you," he said. "I hear you ordering them around. You tell them to stop shooting. You tell them to get rid of the bodies!" He spat the phrase. "Get rid of the bodies? I *worked* with those men!"

"I'm sorry," said Yaryk. The rain drummed the leaves in a deafening torrent. "Leque," he said, "I need your help, or we're going to drown."

"I don't care if you drown."

"You would die as well. Do you see how high the water has risen?"

"Of course I see."

"There must be a way to drain it. You worked here. Do you know?"

"I want you to drown."

Jarb hobbled up through the rain. He crawled onto the other end of the bench, like a stray dog up from the sewers. "Leque?" He wheezed with a hand to his chest. He caught his breath. "Look at the guards. Your name is Leque, isn't it? The guards will die too if we let the Glebe flood."

Leque was silent.

"They'll drown unless you help," said Jarb. He glanced at Yaryk. "Perhaps he doesn't know how to drain it."

"I know." Leque spat. He stood. "I'll show you."

Jarb unlocked the chain from around his ankle. Leque walked with a stoop, breathing loud, his hands still clasped between his legs. He walked as if a rib was broken, maybe more than one. He led them to the wall. "There." He nodded to the surface of the water.

"What?" said Jarb.

"The panels. You open the Time-cursed panels. They're all around the wall. They have clasps to keep them closed. Flick back the clasps—" he started to move his hands in demonstration, but grunted and returned them to between his legs. "Flick back the clasps and they open. Then the Glebe can drain."

Yaryk squatted in the swamp. He groped down to the base of the wall, his fingers throbbing in the cold. Feel, he told himself. Don't go numb now. You must be able to feel.

And there, there in the mire he felt the shiver of metal. The panel was tiny. He fingered the clasp at the top and pushed it up. It required a great wrench to pry the panel open. The water suctioned through, almost pulling Yaryk's hands along with it. He drew them back with a start.

Yaryk straightened and squinted at Leque through the rain. "How many are there?"

No reply.

Jarb said: "How many panels are there, Leque?"

"Hundreds?" Leque shrugged one shoulder and winced. "I don't know. Thousands?"

They led Leque back to his bench. Jarb locked him down without meeting his eyes. "I'm sorry," he muttered.

"Rally the men," said Yaryk. "We must have this drained by nightfall."

25

"Iander?"

He looked up from his bowl of wine. "Yes?" The monks were allowed one bowl a day, no more.

"What happens when people try to stay in the Tower after public access?"

"They're fined."

I took a bite of fried fish and considered the thought. "How much are they fined?"

"Ten, twenty gold pieces?" said Brother Iander. "I'm not sure. Nor am I sure why this interests you, Brother Ksar." According to Iander, very little was my business. Reminding me of this fact terminated many a conversation. He was good at termination and seemed to enjoy it. I wondered why we ate dinner together every night. Iander twitched throughout the meal; I could not stand him.

"If the tallied numbers didn't match," I said, "would we search the Tower? I mean, would we look for the loiterers?"

"Yes," said Brother Iander. He set his wine down on the table. He leaned forward and dipped his beard in the bowl. "They have to be found before the Tower can be opened again, because otherwise they could blend in with the crowds in the morning, and get away without punishment."

"What if we couldn't find them all night? Would we keep the Tower closed until we found them?"

"Yes."

"Even if it took through the next day?"

"I don't know." He sipped his wine.

"Does that taste like your hair?" I asked.

I suppose that the taste of his wine was none of my business either; he did not answer. After a while he asked a question of his own: "What did you do before becoming a monk, Brother Ksar?"

"I didn't do anything," I said. Poor Leque. "My brother had a job. I worked to spend his money."

"Ahh." He leaned back. "For my part, I was in the glyptic trade." I waited for the explanation. "I thought you might find it interesting," he said, "the art of gem-carving."

"I don't know anything about it."

"I'll teach you if you're interested."

I tried to look as uninterested as possible, but Brother Iander continued regardless. "It is expensive to establish yourself as a practicing glyptic," he said. "You must import gems from distant quarries. Transport costs increase every year. I had my own shop, before becoming a monk. I worked very hard to maintain it." He nodded. "Very hard. One of the secrets of retail success," and here he shook a finger at me, "is to select an appropriate location for your outlet. I had the perfect location: Merchant's Alley, where all the newcomers to the City pass by." He shook his head. "I loved my shop."

"Merchant's Alley? Was it close to Skiy's shop?"

"Skiy the cobbler?" Iander smiled. He ate a turnip from his plate. "Yes, close to there. I believe we had some customers in common, Skiy and I." He looked at the walls and the other monks at the other tables, then leaned toward me. "Brother Eln's body was found in Skiy's shop," he said. "I would not want to be associated with that man anymore." He sat back in his chair. "Nevertheless, Brother Ksar, I often think I would like to leave the Marble Tower some day to return to my work."

That evening Kem visited, and I went down to the reception room to meet him.

"Good evening, Ksar." He wrung a bucketful of water from his hood. "Could we repair the Radiance tomorrow night, do you think?"

That was a nice greeting. I gaped in his face. "Why tomorrow?"

"I know it's sooner than originally planned," said Kem, "but nothing will be gained through procrastination. Could you do it tomorrow night?"

I shrugged. "I don't think it will work, no matter when we do it. It might as well be soon."

"Very good. Tomorrow night then." He glanced around the room: crowded, wet. On the other side of the floor, people jostled into a line to pass the reception desk, one by one, for tallying. No one watched us. Kem reached beneath his cloak and pulled out a coil of rope. A fishing hook the length of my arm hung from one end. He pushed the rope into my arms. "Remember," he said, "stay in the Radiance room into the evening. My knock will come once the public has gone. And Ksar? Tell the Father Paramount you are meditating. Tell him that in order for your aim to be accomplished, you must have privacy. We must not be interrupted."

"Kem?" I said.

"Yes, Ksar?"

"There are two reasons at least why this plan won't work." I paused for emphasis. Kem only raised an eyebrow for me to go on. "I can't climb a rope," I said, "and you're not allowed to spend the night in the Tower. The monks will search for you and throw you out. The fine is more than you can pay."

"Ah yes, well," said Kem, "if you tie a series of knots in the rope, you can use them as hand-holds. It won't be any worse than climbing a ladder."

"I hate ladders."

"It will not be a problem."

"And loiterers are fined a lot," I muttered. "The tally numbers will show that you're here. The monks will look all night if they have to, and into the next day."

Kem patted my arm. "We will restore the Radiance's crest as quickly as possible," he said. "I can leave before your brothers find me. The incongruency in numbers can be left a mystery."

I scowled. "And then the Tower will never be opened again. They'll keep on looking until they find you."

"I doubt it," said Kem. "Surely tally-monks have made mistakes before." He shrugged. "After a day, I'm sure they'll forget it." Kem pulled his hood on over his eyes. He edged for the door.

I tucked the rope under my arm. I hoped no one would comment. I watched him creep his way through the press, too polite to elbow. When Glane and I used to come together, we had not needed to elbow. People saw me coming and moved aside. Stone, but I missed my face paints, my rings and my earrings.

"Kem!" I jostled after him. "Kem!"

He turned.

I bent close. "I've thought of a way to get the numbers to correlate."

"Wonderful!" He patted my arm again, as if I were a loyal dog. No, more like a camel. "If my presence in the Tower remains unknown, we have as long as we need to put back the crest. Excellent. It should be safe, then, for me to spend the night in the Radiance room? I think that would be more advisable than attempting departure during the night." He began shuffling again.

"But Kem, don't you want to know what... Kem?"

The press swept him away, through the glass doors. Or maybe he was walking away and he didn't care what I had to say. I saw his hand go up in a vague salute, and then he was gone. The rope weighed under my arm. It would be so easy to throw it away, into the rain. If this plan did not work, I would not have Leque to go back to.

I did not discard the rope. I did, however, keep to the public stairs to lessen the chances of one of my brethren seeing me. The stairway was broad and steep, like all the stairs here. I wanted to drop to my knees and crawl, or uncurl the claws on my wings, as I had in the dream, and dig them into the bark to pull myself up.

I climbed with my head down, watching the yellow veins pulse through the marble. I almost ran into the boy. He stood on the corner of a step, blocking the flow of the traffic. Pistachio twigs and wish papers waved in his face, but he did not brush them away. He stared down at the pool at his feet. The boy's hair was dark brown, unkempt. I stopped on the step below him. He looked like Glane.

"Hello, Father," said the boy. It wasn't Glane, of course. It was Sfin.

"Hello," I said, and prompted by some inner voice, I added: "A beautiful shade of chartreuse, is it not, my son?"

"The pool?" said Sfin. He still hadn't looked at me. "Yes, it's nice." If he did look at me, I wondered, would he recognize me? Did he recognize my voice? He did not seem to. Perhaps, apart from that one discussion, we hadn't spoken much over the years.

I buried my hands in the sleeves of my habit and rocked — heel to toe, heel to toe — wondering what to say. Should I ask him about his wishes, or was it best to preserve his illusion of privacy? "You seem troubled, my son," I said. "Is it an illness? A misfortune?"

"My brother's been sick," said Sfin. He shook his head. "Never mind." His tunic had a gold and tasseled border. It didn't make sense, but I did not ask; the family was supposed to be poor.

"Perhaps you wish to tell me your troubles," I said, "but you are not yet comfortable in my presence." Why didn't he recognize my voice? Maybe the Ksar he knew would never have spoken like this.

"Maybe," said Sfin.

"To increase the trust between us," I said, "I will tell you, my son, of the birth of the Marble Tower." He made no objection, and so I went on. "The Tower rose in the Year of the Goldfinch, which, as you may know, was the same year that the third sun fell." He still raised no objection. "This was no coincidence, my son."

"No?" said Sfin, staring at the acid. Was that sarcasm?

"There was once a marble walkway in the ocean," I said, "with peach trees, and pistachio trees, and almond trees growing along it. An enormous yellow tree also grew there, called the Tree of Power."

"With golden fruit," said Sfin.

"Have you had a vision?" I said.

He almost looked at me, but not quite. He twitched the hair from his eyes. "No," he said, "I read about it."

"In a book?"

"Yes."

"Did it mention the skeletons?"

"No," he said. "Should it have?"

How old was Sfin? I'd never really talked to him before. Not for this long. I'd thought he was twelve, or maybe a few days older. He sounded more like twenty.

"Should I know about the skeletons?" said Sfin.

"I don't know," I said, "I've never read the book. But there *were* skeletons in the tree. They were men who climbed up to pick the fruit and couldn't find their way down. The skeletons hung in the upper branches, with root fibers holding them in place."

"What does this have to do with the Marble Tower?" said Sfin. He sounded impatient.

"The skeletons?" I said. "Nothing, but they were there. Then the sun fell and turned the sea into acid. At the moment the sun struck the ocean floor, the marble walkway rose up and swallowed the tree."

"How can stone swallow a tree?"

"I don't know," I said, "but it did. That's where all the stairs come from. The tree's branches used to climb like stairs. And you see the yellow veins in the walls? That's the sap from the tree."

Sfin said nothing. The hair hung in his face. He might have been laughing, or he might have fallen asleep.

"It wasn't a normal tree," I insisted. "It was the Tree of Power. When you hang your wishes here, you're wishing to the tree." All the wishes should come true then, I thought, because everyone found their way down from the Tower. Except Gyanin's monk.

"What about the skeletons?" said Sfin. "If the marble absorbed the stairways, wouldn't it also absorb skeletons? Shouldn't there be skeletons around here somewhere, buried in the walls?"

"I hope not, my son."

Sfin looked at me sideways. His eyes glistened, white as red pearls. Not white at all. "I'm angry at you, Ksar," he said. "Glane was sick and you never visited."

"Everyone's angry at me."

"You make a horrible monk." He pushed past me down the stairs and was gone.

26

The intruders halted in front of the gates, on the same square of flagstones where the workers had been shot the day before. The roof of the litter, plated in gold, sang in the rain. The bearers eased their burden to the ground and stood fidgeting, staring at the wall. A detachment of guards formed a ring around them. The guards' faces were hidden in their helmets.

The Bedouin stood along the platform. Yaryk waved for them to put down their bows.

"This time," he said, "we will speak with them. We will not shoot outright." He put his mouth to the view slit. "Have you come to parley?"

The guards looked around; they could not see him.

"Who am I parleying with?" called a voice from the litter.

"The Bedouin Guild."

"Show yourself."

"No," said Yaryk. "What assurance do I have you will not shoot me? I want to remain living to reach this compromise."

"A compromise, Y'az Bedouin? After you have killed the laborers and the night guards?"

"The night guards, I assure you," said Yaryk, "are unharmed."

"Return them to the Citadel."

Bry jumped to the height of the slit. "What will you give us?" he shouted.

The litter sat and thought.

Yaryk seized Bry by the oilcloth collar. "Silence," he hissed. "I don't need your help in this bargain. Go find your brother."

"If we give up the prisoners we have to get something," said Bry. "Isn't that what they're for?" He grinned. "Or can we eat them?"

"We should never have taken prisoners," said Yaryk.

"We should shoot them," said Bry. "We should shoot all the nobles as well."

"No," said Yaryk.

"Why not?" said the Bedouin beside him.

Yaryk ignored them. He pressed his face to the view slit. "What will you give us in return for the guards?"

"If you do not release them, Tallos will be executed."

"Fine!" shouted Bry.

Yaryk pushed him away, but the boy dodged back. "Fine, kill Tallos! When we take over the Citadel, we'll kill you all!"

"Bry, silence!"

"Yes, kill you!" the other men on the platform shouted. "We'll kill you now, if you don't leave!"

Yaryk shuffled to the end of the platform and down the steps, narrow and slippery. All the Bedouin shouted above. He ignored them. He strode through the kiwi orchard. The shouts died behind him.

In the middle of the orchard, the Bedouin had constructed the Bivouac, a patchwork canopy of oilcloth over the vines. The canopy provided protection from the rain, but the ground beneath was still saturated. The longer you stood or sat, the farther you sank in the grass. There was nowhere dry to sleep in the Glebe.

In the middle of the shelter sat Gwall, hunched over a bowl of red currants. Jarb sat beside him. Neither one spoke.

Yaryk squatted and folded his hands in his sleeves. "You're back," he said. "What news?"

Gwall looked up, his cheeks inflated. He swallowed, spat, and said: "They won't come."

"Whom did you speak with?"

"Dayl."

"Dayl, Yalden's son," said Jarb. "Member of the High Council. You should remember him, Yaryk. He was there the same time as you."

"I remember him," said Yaryk. "Did I ask who he was? No, I did not. Why won't he come, Gwall?"

"He's content to wander." Gwall forced another handful of berries into his mouth. He spoke through the juice: "He says it's a foolish cause."

Since his move to Y'az Drens' palace, Blade had not left his chamber. Only to relieve himself had he left his bed. He had eaten in bed. Smears of meat and fruit now soiled the quilts and clung to his skin with sweat. He had not once changed his garments. No servants had appeared to offer their assistance. Earlier in the morning he had vomited. It was only now, hours later, that a eunuch answered his call. The eunuch wiped his clothes with a damp cloth. He sprinkled fragrance, sharper than chamomile, over the floor. The smell reminded Blade of his grandfather and made his throat burn.

"The Y'az wants to speak with you," said the eunuch, his head bent over his task.

Blade's mouth tasted only of phlegm, too thick to speak. This is how you begin to die, he thought. They all want to kill me. Now Y'az Drens has begun. He'll kill me slowly and watch every step.

"Are you well enough to be taken to the Y'az?" The eunuch ducked into invisibility at the side of the bed. He scrubbed the floor with the sound of a threatening snake. Only the top of his head could be seen, shaved and bobbing as he worked.

Blade shuffled deeper under the blankets.

"I'll tell him." The eunuch stood and left the room. He did not bow as he left. The bottle of fragrance remained on the floor.

Blade lay and tried not to think. All he could feel was the taste in his mouth — vomit, phlegm, a day of breathing, the cabbage stew he had sampled for breakfast.

Y'az Drens came in. Condensation misted the beads across his face. He fingered the train of his turban and scowled. "You're sick, are you?"

Blade feared to ignore Y'az Drens. He nodded.

"Has the damp brought it on? You don't have rain in the City? Why don't you answer me, Xavier? I know that's your name. Raw throat, is it? You look the same as ever. All very easy to fake. Very easy indeed to make a mimicry of such an ailment." He leaned forward. "Are you mocking me, Xavier?" He buried a hand in his beard and his frown deepened. "So you and your crazed servant are not the only ones plotting our demise. It seems all the Bedouin are involved. All the Bedouin, hmm?" Drens turned to his servant, the eunuch who had brought the perfume. "Is the boy truly sick?" He jabbed a finger at Blade. "Is he play-acting?"

"No, Y'az. He soiled the floor. Perhaps we should take him to the hospital."

"Hmm. There's somewhere else I want to take him first." Drens stepped closer to the bed. "Do you want to see something, Xavier? Can he stand?" he asked the eunuch. "Can he walk?"

Blade shook his head.

"Carry him then," said the Y'az. "Follow me."

The eunuch would not meet Blade's eyes. He bent and wrapped the blankets around Blade's sides, gathered him and slung him over his shoulder like a roll of carpet. The fabric fell over Blade's eyes and he could not see. Whatever the Y'az wanted to show him, he would not be able to see it. The eunuch carried him jolting down a flight of stairs. A door opened. Blade felt himself deposited in a litter, he felt it sway, heard the curtain squeal along its rail, and the rain pelting down on the roof. He smelled the wet of the streets outside. The blankets still covered his face. The litter groaned into motion. Blade prayed he would suffocate. What would it matter? He was only baggage. Yaryk had carried him, and now the nobles. Maybe they would carry him to the sea to be Released.

The sound of rain became muffled. They had passed inside, beneath a roof. The litter stopped. The bearers set it down. They pulled back the curtains, and pushed the blankets away from Blade's face. The eunuch lifted him out and set him on his feet. A scar like a red constellation speckled the serving man's arm.

An archway was cut into the wall before them, the stone stained green with algae. The haze of the outside world could be seen through the arch. Buildings stood across the street. Men huddled under the eaves. A hand clamped Blade's shoulder and turned him around. He faced an oblong room. A grated door sealed off one end. The floor rose up in steps on the other, to a set of manacles embedded in the wall. Nobles stood around the perimeter, or sat on collapsible chairs. They ignored each other. Everyone focused on the manacles.

"Shouldn't this be done in the streets?" said one, turning to Drens, "where the people can see?"

"It doesn't matter if the people see." Drens' hand still clamped Blade's shoulder, pinned him where he stood. "This is a sacrifice for the Bedouin. They have brought it upon themselves. If they are so vain as to neglect their kinsman, then so be it. And I remind you," he said, raising his voice to address the whole assembly, "that *you* were not forced here either. If you hold any complaint regarding my decision, or do not want to watch, you may leave. Now where is the prisoner?"

"The guards are bringing him," said a man with a ruby necklace.

"I saw the poor craven last week," said another, a noble with golden-red streaks in his beard. "He was so weak he could not sit up. Perhaps the Bedouin have rebelled ex-pressly to end his suffering."

"You think they care about suffering," said Drens, "after what they have done to the workers at the Glebe?"

The grate at the end of the room screamed open. Two guards ducked through. Between them they carried a man like a bundle of sticks. Arms, legs and head protruded at odd angles. The bundle coughed and its limbs twitched in time with the coughing. The nobles stood back and let the guards pass. They carried the prisoner up the steps and set him down with his back to the wall, his legs twisted out before him. He keeled to his side and lay still. An odor of burnt-out candles and excrement hung in the air. The guards pulled the prisoner up. They lifted his arms above his head and manacled his wrists to the wall. Each guard wore a horsehair band around his arm. Black flecks floated behind Blade's eyes. He blinked them away. Mold and stale breath mixed in with the excrement. Perhaps he only smelled himself. One guard lifted the prisoner's head. He pulled his hair, tufted over flaking skin. The other guard drew his sword. Neither looked at the prisoner, the nobles, or each other. Everyone stared at the blade of the sword.

"Now?" said one guard.

"Yes," said Drens. "Now."

The first guard put a hand to the prisoner's forehead. It looked like a blessing. Blade trembled. He envied the prisoner. He wanted to die that fast — one quick cut and be done. The second guard held his sword against the chained man's throat. Blood. He cut a red trench. The man's neck twitched and quivered. The layers of skin split apart and sagged like the layers of a boiled onion. Red streamed down to his clavicles. Veins and arteries glistened. There was so much blood. The head tipped back, then forward again. The eyes stared red. They could not focus.

Blade cried. He wanted to die. He did not want to see. He did not want to see who killed him. If Drens' hand had not held his shoulder he would have fallen. A nobleman passed through his line of vision — blurred to a tiny window. The other nobles were leaving. It was over already. Why did Blade have to linger?

"Did you enjoy yourself, Xavier?" came the voice of Y'az Drens.

Blade retched. He vomited stomach acid onto the floor.

The eunuch spoke; Blade could not catch the words. Drens lifted his hand from Blade's shoulder. Blade stumbled on his blankets. He tried to run. He tried to run to the manacles. Half way to the steps, the blankets caught him and he fell. He crawled. The noises of the world swam away from him, distant. His knees thudded the floor, the rain clattered, the nobles milled for the exit, talking maybe, maybe shouting for him to stop, maybe egging him on. He saw two men pick up a body. One of them held a sword. Horsehair circled their wrists.

Blade collided. He embraced the guard's legs, the man with the sword. "Mercy!" He grabbed for the weapon.

The guard cringed back. He dropped his sword and dug at Blade's hands. "I'm sorry," he muttered, "he's already dead."

"Give!" Blade released the man's legs. He scrabbled across the floor to the sword. The sword was heavy. He remembered again he was sick. He had never used a sword in his life. How did you lift a blade longer than your arm? Turn it around and drive it through your own neck? How could you drive it fast enough, before someone stole it from your hands? How could he drive it that hard? How could he be sure he would die?

A red-speckled arm ripped the sword away. Blade fell on his face.

"Hospital?" said the voice of the eunuch.

"Yes," said the Y'az. "Hospital. Now."

Mehrzh was the second messenger to return to the Glebe. He came in the late morning, during a lull in the rain and fog, when the road could be seen far into the distance. Yaryk watched the Bedouin haul the ladder up to the top of the wall. They lowered it down the far side and Mehrzh climbed over. The damp had darkened his toga from yellow to stagnant brown. Mold striped his back.

"What news?" said Yaryk.

Mehrzh had lost his sandals. He picked his way between the worst of the puddles, back toward the Bivouac. "I found Hyarmen and his tribe at the Aeolian Wall."

"Will they come?" said Yaryk.

"No." Mehrzh stopped to blow his nose on the edge of his cloak. He picked a nectarine and grimaced. "Is this all the food we have? Fruit?"

"Yes."

On a patch of ground beside the Bivouac, a fire spluttered in a ring of stones. Jarb sat beside the mess. He fed it lichen off the end of a stick.

"Your fire's dying," said Yaryk. He tore a sprig of leaves from a nearby vine and tossed them at the flames.

Smoke billowed up. Jarb leaned away and coughed. He waved a hand in front of his face. He smiled at Mehrzh with a chip-toothed, exhausted smile. "They're not coming, are they?" he said.

Mehrzh shook his head.

Yaryk squatted by the fire. "How did you know that?"

"Keiv returned by the front gate while you were away," said Jarb. "He talked to some tribe, I don't remember which, and they won't come. We might as well leave and join our wandering brothers, Yaryk, or go back and grovel for the nobles' forgiveness."

"Not grovel," said Yaryk. "We've done enough groveling here. Simply to live here, in this mud, is groveling." He stood and hugged his robes, soaked and heavy, tighter around his chest. "Jarb, I'm leaving."

"Where? Where is there to go?"

"Where do you think?" said Yaryk. He wanted to speak quietly, so that only Jarb would hear, but he could not control his voice. He spoke out loud and angry. "I'm going back to the Citadel. I'm going to take Leque, before he dies of infection. I'm going to find Blade. If I'm still alive by that point I am going to leave, and never return to civilization."

Jarb pulled himself up. "How will you do this? Walk up to the main gates and offer your apologies for leading a rebellion?" Jarb's voice was calm. Yaryk hated his calm.

"I never led it," said Yaryk. "Liop was the fool who did that."

"You're the fool who's led it now that Liop is dead."

"Why do you insult me?" Yaryk spat. "This morning, when the Y'az came, wasn't it me, Yaryk, who wanted to parley rather than kill? Wasn't it me, yesterday, who stopped the shooting of the workers? And what did *you* do all that time? Nothing. That's what you've done, Jarb son of Jareth."

"So you parleyed?" Jarb folded his arms. "For all the difference it made. Bry told me the men chanted death. After you left, they shot the guards. You call that a parley?"

"I parleyed as long as I could," said Yaryk. He dug through his mind for a quote, any quote of relevance, but nothing came. "If you don't like my leadership," he said, "you should not protest my departure. You can govern this rabble however you wish."

"You're leaving at the end of hope," said Jarb. "I would call you a deserter."

"I *never* believed we could conquer the Citadel!" Yaryk could not conceal his anger. Yes, all hope was gone. He had seen it coming. He decided days ago that when the end came he would leave. Now he was leaving. "How many times have I told you," he spat, "the futility of this masquerade? Fools!"

"Yes, you often call people fools," said Jarb. "I've noticed that."

"They *are* fools," said Yaryk. "And you also and all your family." Why did he hate this man, so suddenly and so blindly? How could Jarb hold himself so calm when he, Yaryk, had forgotten the wisdom of silence, or patience, or self-restraint? "You're a cripple," he sneered. "Bry kills for pleasure. Neath lives in jail. What would he do if he were here? Would he steal the robes off our backs? He would find some crime to commit, even here where everything has already been perpetrated. That is why I insult your family."

"Neath has nothing to do with this," said Jarb. He sat down again and poked a stick in the fire. He watched it smoke. It would not catch. "Take Leque and be arrested. Go."

Yaryk nodded. He wheeled and headed for the sitting area.

Leque sat on his bench, head bowed, arms across his chest.

Yaryk stood in front of him. "Can you walk?"

Still unmoving, "Are you taking me away?" said Leque.

"Yes. If you can walk."

"Probably."

Yaryk unlocked his chains. He moved to help him to his feet. Leque stood unaided. He shuffled around the bench, then across the sitting area. The night guards watched with apathy. They sat in their circle with rain in their hair. Leque favored one side as he walked, and he kept his hands hidden, folded tight against his chest. At least he could walk.

"Are your ribs broken, Leque?"

"Probably."

Yaryk led the way to the Bivouac. He made Leque stand beneath the drip of the kiwis while he ducked under cover and changed back into tunic and trousers. He emerged again, one of the people.

Bry followed Leque and Yaryk to the gate. "Jarb says you're deserting." His grin stretched as wide as a broken melon. "He says you're going to rescue Blade and then not come back."

"I am."

Bry danced from foot to foot. "You have to greet him for me. I'm sure he misses me."

Yaryk nodded. He turned to Leque and helped him up the steps to the platform, up onto the top of the wall and down the ladder on the other side. Leque slipped on the flagstones. They glittered like opals and hematite-glass. Yaryk helped him up.

"Go away," said Leque.

They walked slowly; Leque could manage no more. The road glared, slick as mercury, onyx and black obsidian. The suns' light turned the wet to fire.

"Yaryk?" said Leque.

"Yes?"

"Did you see Ksar die?"

"Yes."

"What happened? Bees?"

"Yes. Bees."

"Did he mention me before he died?"

Yaryk shielded his eyes against the glare. "He called your name."

"And?"

"He asked for you. He wanted to see you."

They plodded on. The clouds gathered gray overhead and the glare off the road diminished. They would reach the Citadel by night, Yaryk judged, at this spider's pace. They would find a side entrance somewhere. There must be an entrance beyond the main gates.

"Yaryk?"

"Yes?" said the Bedouin.

"That story you used to tell . . ? The one about the beggar and the purple camels . . ?"

"Yes?" said Yaryk.

"Will you tell it?" said Leque. "It would pass the time."

Blade lay in a bed in the hospital. From beyond the door came a doctor's voice, followed by the voice of Y'az Drens.

"What did you say his name is, Y'az?"

"Xavier."

"And his family?"

"Ven. They live in the City."

After a pause the doctor's voice spoke again. "And to him you are what relation?"

"A guardian." Pause. "Can you tell me his ailment?"

The room smelled of nothing. It smelled of fresh rain over glass, nothing more. The curtain walls were white. Here I am, thought Blade, inside a pearl. Beyond the curtains, everything dwindled to insignificance. He watched the play of light — amber and gold — across the hanging fabric.

"Can he be left here overnight?" came the voice of Drens.

"Yes, leave him here." The doctor cleared his throat. "We shall reach a prognosis this evening. The hospital charges according to the patient's term of residence, as I'm sure you are aware. By all means, leave him here."

"I will leave an attendant," said Drens, "to administer to his needs."

The voices dropped. Footsteps faded down the hall, one set heavy, the other light.

Blade lay on his back. When he blinked, the curtains shimmered out of focus. There must be a window behind him, over his bed. The suns must be gold and bronze, dancing in the curtains like northern birds. Moans drifted in through the cotton wall. It was only cotton, not silk or gauze. Why was he here in a public hospital, treated by the same doctors who tended to butchers and tradesmen? Why could it not be the City, where a private physician slept by his bed all night? Here the doctors did nothing. They prodded, whispered, and pronounced that yes, some ailment afflicted him, but Stone only knew what it was.

The curtain parted. "Blade?"

The pearl illusion vanished. Blade recoiled beneath the covers, huddled with his head to his knees. No one knew his name was Blade. He wasn't here. He wasn't here.

The voice repeated, "Blade, are you awake?" It was Leque. An elbow nudged him in the back, then harder in the side. "Get up," said Leque. "Hurry, before a doctor comes. Blade, it's me. It's Leque. You're not dying, are you?"

Blade trembled. He could not stop himself. Leque had murdered Y'az Gyrt. A murderer was sitting on the bed beside him, touching his arm. He was holding a knife, a club, something. Blade could not see but he knew. If he showed himself Leque would pounce. He would gut him to ribbons on the sun-dance sheets.

"Blade, come on. I can't carry you. We have to go." He prodded Blade again in the back. "The people here — they think I killed Y'az Gyrt. They have wanted posters everywhere. We have to leave now, before they recognize me." Leque's elbow dug in again.

"Stop," said Blade.

"Blade?" Leque's voice became soft.

"Please don't stab me." He sniffled.

"Stab you? Why would I stab you?"

Blade could not speak through his fear.

Leque leaned in and pulled the blankets away. Something that felt like a foot — Blade's eyes were still closed — pressed into his back and turned him over. He blinked. Leque smiled down at him, his hair like a mane around the stubble of his face. Black-currant circles ringed his eyes.

"By Stone, Blade, I'm not going to stab you. Why in—"

"Everyone wants to kill me. And you... you killed Y'az Gyrt... I don't know... Everyone says so. Are you helping Yaryk, Leque?"

"No. I don't know what Yaryk's doing." Leque's forehead creased. Under his tan, his skin blanched orchid-white. Sweat stood out in beads. "I don't think Yaryk knows himself what he's doing. One minute he's helping the Bedouin, the next he's leading them, and then he goes against them and calls them all fools. I don't know if he means to kill me or not. He's smoked too much incense, Blade. He's gone insane."

Blade trembled. "How do you know, if you're not helping him?"

"They captured me." Leque glanced over his shoulder, then back to Blade. "Listen, you've always been curious. You want to know all the answers, don't you? There isn't time. Yaryk brought me here, into the hospital. I don't know what he's thinking. I ran away. I was trying to leave the hospital. I can never find my way around hospitals, and then I heard the doctor and the nobleman talking." He leaned still closer. He smelled of wet fruit and grass, so heavy it was almost wine. "Now I've found you," he whispered. "And now that I've found you, I won't leave without you. Understand? Now please get up."

"I'm sick."

"Blade, we have to leave before someone finds me."

Leque's words stumbled, one over another. Blade could not hear what he said, not everything, but he heard the desperation. He fell out of bed. Leque held out his arm and Blade pulled himself back to his feet. From elbows down, bandaging smothered Leque's arms.

"What happened to you, Leque?"

"Happened?" Leque stood a moment, listening, before he parted the curtain. "Trampled," he said. "Never mind that now."

Blood drummed in Blade's ears like rain. He staggered and caught himself against the foot of the bed. "Where are my clothes, Leque?"

"I don't know. Take a blanket."

"The sheet, or the quilt?"

"Blade, it doesn't matter. The rain will drench you either way."

"But—"

"It doesn't matter, Blade. Come on, or I'll leave without you."

"Earlier you said—"

"Blade, please!"

Blade gathered the sheet from the bed. It weighed in his arms. He swaddled it around his shoulders. He pulled it around his waist like a mis-worn toga. He had never wrapped a toga for himself in his life. He did not know how.

Outside the curtain, they found themselves in a room full of beds. The beds were narrow, no more than shelves jutting out from the walls. From each cot, a pair of eyes watched them cross the room.

"Open the door," said Leque.

"But—"

"I can't do it. My hands, remember?"

Blade opened the door. A narrow stone hall ran away before them, the walls bulwarked in wooden slats.

"You, wait!" Three men in embroidered tunics appeared from a room beside them.

Drens' eunuch with the red-speckled arm stood among them. "Master Xavier!" he shouted. "Come back!" He grabbed Blade's arm.

Another servant lunged for Leque. Leque kicked at his knees and the man stumbled back. Blade's captor loosened his hold. Blade pulled away. The sheet tripped his legs.

Another man charged. Leque kicked. "Run!" he shouted. "Blade!"

The servants balked at the sight of Leque's face. "Gyrt's killer." They drew away.

Blade ran. Leque ran after him. The servants shouted behind him. He could not hear. There was too much blood in his ears. He found a flight of stairs and fell. At the bottom, blue tile slammed into his knees. Blade pulled himself up and ran again. With every step the sheet wound tighter around his legs. He stumbled. Leque's breath wheezed behind him.

A man with a tray of scalpels veered out of a doorway. Blade skidded into his side. The tray clattered. He dodged the spinning knives and ran on. The man cursed. Blade ran down another hall. Stretchers lined the walls. He did not look. His breath came too fast to see.

"Hey!" A man in orange robes appeared from nowhere. "Don't run in here! You, boy, stop!"

The passageway turned and turned again, like the halls of the Marble Tower. Blade paused for Leque to catch up. Leque's face was gray and he bent almost double as he ran.

"What is it, Leque?"

"Broken ribs."

Drens' servants swerved into sight behind them.

"Do you want to rest, Leque?"

"No," said Leque. "Run. Keep running."

Blade broke into a shamble, past the moaning stretchers and the silent stretchers in rows. A ramp led steeply down. Blade charged its length, then along another hallway, this one short and straight. He careered through an arched doorway, and into a sea of humanity. They had reached the reception hall.

Behind them, doctors erupted through the door. "Stop!" The man in orange shouted and waved his arms. "Thieves! Stop them!"

Someone leapt in front of Blade and he stumbled. A hand grabbed his arm. It caught a fold of his sheet. He pulled and the sheet fell away. He ran in his loincloth, blind and stumbling for the door. The rain beat on muddy streets. Blade could see himself in his mind. He wanted to laugh through the fear in his mouth. It tasted of salt. A naked boy, charging madly through the rain.

Another cry went up: "That man killed the nobles! Stop him! Murderer! He killed Y'az Gyrt!"

Blade charged past the desks against the walls, the patients, the hospital attendants, the populace spilling from nowhere. Leque ran close behind. His breath sawed. No one tried to stop them now. The people shrank back, out of their path. For one dizzy second Yaryk's face appeared, and then swirled away and was gone.

Outside it poured. Leque led the way and stumbled on, down a thousand alleys of wood and shacks. At last he stopped. Blade ran into his back and fell sideways in the mud. Blade laughed. He spat the slime from his mouth. He tilted back his head and drank the air. Leque leaned against a wall. Tears streamed down his cheeks. He hugged his chest. He coughed. He tried to wipe the blood from his chin before Blade could see.

"Aren't you cold?" said Leque, "Blade?"

"No." Blade kept on laughing. "What are we going to do?"

"Here, take out my earring," said Leque.

"Your earring?"

Leque tilted his head to one side, letting the rain push the hair away. A golden bar glittered in the wet, like a dragon's tooth poking out from the top of his ear. "Take it out," he said. "We're going to find a tailor's shop and get you something to wear. You need a cloak at the least."

Blade stood. Black mud stained his hands and the backs of his legs. He fumbled with the tooth. The rain washed the mud from his fingers and smeared it like pitch down Leque's neck.

"This alley dead ends," said Leque. He pointed in the opposite direction. "This way. We'll hope to find a shop. It doesn't look good to walk around in a loincloth. I need to cover my face. People recognize me."

"Leque?" said Blade.

"Yes?"

"I am cold."

Leque draped an arm around Blade's shoulder. "Me too," he said, and they walked.

27

I knotted Kem's rope all day; there was no way I could climb it unknotted. Even as it was, I had my doubts. What was Kem thinking? When he knocked on the door above, I would still be at the bottom of the room, whimpering and licking my fingers like a blistered cat.

I rested from the rope. I had to make the numbers correlate.

Brother Iander sat at an alcoved table, embedded in the wall of the dining room. He ate a plate of vegetables. I sat down on the other side of the table. I reached across and selected a carrot. He looked up and scowled.

"Excuse me, Brother Ksar? The meaning of your behavior?"

"I'm hungry."

"You're always hungry. Get your own food."

I crossed the hall to the serving table and smuggled a bottle of wine back underneath my robe. It chilled my stomach. I hoped it would not be noticed. I wrestled the bottle out from under my clothes and tipped a generous share into Iander's bowl.

"Thank you," he said without looking up.

My hands sweated; I hid them between my knees. I was no good at lying, not about anything important. I could tell Leque I didn't have a tattoo, or lie to Kem about breakfast, but half of my lies were born from the fact that I did not remember the truth.

"So," I said, "you used to be a glyptic?"

"I did." He looked up, but his beard concealed his expression. "I then had my vision, and—"

"You miss being a glyptic, don't you?"

"At times. Yes, at times I consider retiring from the Brotherhood and—"

"How about after dinner?"

He choked on his wine, spluttered and sipped more slowly. "My, my." He wiped his lips. "I wonder what vintage this is? By the flavor, I would judge it to be the Year of the Undulating Pendant. Perhaps the Tangerine Sphere."

"What if you went back to your glyptic shop after dinner tonight?"

"I think," he said in a voice I'd never heard before, like a real person, rather than the puppet he usually played, "that, considering Brother Eln's recent murder, we are not permitted to leave the Tower. And I think you are aware of this restriction."

"If you return my old wardrobe," I said, "I could give you a carpet to wear."

He stared at me long and hard. He looked like a llama, struck by lightning.

"It would cover your robe," I explained.

"That would be less than effective," he said. "The tally numbers would show I had left."

"The tally-monks switch at first sun's' down," I lied. "Leave while they're switching. I'll cause a distraction and they'll never notice."

Iander squinted at me. "Are you trying to rid yourself of my company?"

"That's only a side benefit."

Brother Iander led me to a room I had never seen before, where my old possessions lay folded in a pile on the floor.

"We keep the past belongings of every brother here," he said. Shelves lined the walls, packed to overflowing with crates and parcels. A bag of crystals spilled across the floor in one corner. A stringed instrument twice the length of my torso lounged against the wall.

"What did you bring?" I asked.

"Nothing."

We found my pillowcase. Iander tucked it under his robe and we scuttled our way back to the sleeping chamber. He glanced around as we turned each corner.

"Close the door," he said, and I pulled the door closed behind us.

He gave me my bag. I turned it upside-down and spilled the contents on the floor. My copper-green earrings rolled in a circle. I disentangled the carpet — tie-dyed, unraveling like hair at the edges — and held it out to him. Iander seized the rug from my hands. He did not even wrinkle his nose.

"I wear it around my waist," I explained.

Iander held it up to his hips. The tassels dragged on the ground. "I don't think," he said, "that will work."

Points of sweat pricked my back. "Try your shoulders." The perspiration felt like sand flies licking my spine.

Iander obeyed, taking on a remarkable resemblance to a spool of thread.

I pulled the sheet from a nearby cot and wrapped it around Iander's head. He leaned against the door of the chamber — "No sudden disturbances," he explained — while I struggled to secure the knot. Iander was quieter and more illogical than I had ever seen him. He did not even comment on the golden threads tied around my thumbs, or my nails chewed down to the blood. I had to do something for entertainment.

"Brother Ksar, why are you helping me?"

"You're my friend?" I suggested.

"How did you know of my desire to leave the Brotherhood?"

I shrugged.

"Were my thoughts so obvious? Do you think the Father Paramount knows of my disloyalty?"

I tied the final link in his makeshift disguise. "I doubt it," I said.

"If he discovers my flight, will he blight me with eternal ignorance?"

"I don't see why."

Iander's eyelids twitched. "Was that an insult?"

"No."

"When do the suns go down? Are we late?"

"No," I said again. I could not see the world outside; how could I know when the suns went down? Not that it mattered. All I had to do was tell Iander when to walk, at a time when I said the tally-monk wasn't looking, when in fact I knew he *was* looking, because he was always looking. Then we would both win, wouldn't we? The numbers would match tomorrow, Iander would come back from his escapades and Kem would leave. I was so intelligent my head expanded like yeast in water. I almost wished Glane were there, to see me in my moment of glory.

Brother Iander fingered his beard. "What about this?"

"I call it a beard."

"You don't have a knife with you, do you?"

"If you cut it off..." I faltered. "You *are* coming back tomorrow, aren't you?"

"Oh. Of course."

I did not have a knife. We looked under every sleeping cot in the room, and every pillow. None of the monks had a knife.

"Do you think it's first sun down yet?" said Iander.

I shrugged. "Let's see."

We reached the bottom of the Tower without incident. The reception room steamed with moisture and crowds. Visitors shuffled past the desk in single-file. The tally-monk marked each one's leaving.

Iander stopped in the middle of the crush. "Has it already happened?"

"Has what?"

"First sun down."

I had no idea. "I think it's already happened," I told him. "We must have taken too long getting ready."

"I know the Brother on tally duty." Iander did not even whisper; in the chaos, he had to shout to make himself heard. "He'll recognize me, Ksar!"

"What's his name?" I shouted back.

Iander stared at me like an armadillo. "I don't know."

"Never mind." I was getting impatient. I still needed to find the Father Paramount. "Join the line to leave the Tower. As you pass the desk, I'll do something. I'll distract him and ruin his counting. He won't see you leave."

"Do you think it will work?"

"I hope so." I pushed him in the back. I said, "Go."

Iander smiled. "Yes, we'll try it." He patted my arm. He turned and pushed his way for the doors. Why did everyone pat my arm?

Iander was shorter than the rest of the crowd. I watched his depression in the sea of heads. He never looked back. He kept his eyes on the doors at the end of the room. I did not wait for him to pass the desk. I hoped the Brother would see him in the crowd. If he wasn't seen, and the numbers didn't match, what could I do about it now? I turned and pushed my way up the Tower stairs. I darted through the first doorway and lost myself in the realm of the Brotherhood.

I regained my bearings and headed for the dining hall. The Father Paramount was not there. I tapped a monk on the shoulder. "Have you seen the Father?"

"He retired," said the monk, "to his private chamber."

"Where's that?"

"Do you need to speak with him?"

"It's urgent," I said.

The monk sighed. He stood and led me. His shoulders were as broad as Leque's, but one shoulder sat higher than the other, so that he walked like an ambling ape. We stopped in front of a set of metal doors, tarnished to a yellow sheen. My guide pointed at the doors, nodded, and hurried away, back to his food.

I knocked.

"Come in, my son."

The Father Paramount sat cross-legged in the middle of the floor. The room was circular, one wall made entirely of glass. He burned a black silhouette against the silver behind. The suns dipped low through the clouds. Brother Iander and I had been early.

I bowed.

The Father Paramount did not open his eyes. "Ksar, is it?"

"Yes, Paramount."

"What has brought you here, my son? Have you garnered rewards from your meditation?"

"I've come about the meditation." I chewed on my lip as if it were the rind of a melon. "I am no more than a hair's breadth from discovering the identity of the vandals," I said. "With your permission, Father, I would like to continue my work through the night." Those did not sound like Ksar words at all. I waited.

"Indeed, my son." The Father Paramount smiled. I could hardly see against the suns. "It pleases me to see a brother so attentive to his duties. You may retire to the chamber as long as you wish. I will inform the Brotherhood of your need for solitude."

"Thank you."

He handed me a key. I accepted it, small and cold in the palm of my hand. It felt like the petrified leaf of a flower. The yellow pulsed in the walls. I ran.

The door of the Radiance room opened into a black hole. I groped along the wall until I came to a sconce, then fumbled in my sleeve for matches. I lit the torch. I closed the door behind me and circled the room, lighting every torch. The ceiling still loomed in shadow. The Radiance watched me, changing its color with each new flame.

I lifted the rope. I had left the rope in the middle of the floor. Kem, he was such an incredible imbecile to trust me with this. The rope was more than half knotted now. It must be. It had taken all day. What if the knots had made the rope too short? What if I threw it, hooked it on the railing, and then the end was too high to reach? Or what if it took me too long to tie the knots, and Kem's knock came and went before I finished?

I sat down against the wall. The yellow veins beat like blood against my back. I began tying knots. It felt as if I was tying them for hours. Blisters ate through the skin on my palms. With each knot, I pulled length after length of rope through the loop. With every pull, I clobbered myself with the fishhook end. Curses, I didn't know what I was doing.

I tied twenty knots. My hands twitched. I could do no more. It was time to move on.

I could think of two methods to hook the railing, both of which seemed likely to break my skull. My first idea was to swing the hook in circles around my head, as fast and as hard as I could. When it blurred invisible with speed I would let it go, pray, and plaster myself against the floor. Time only knew from which direction it would ricochet back.

When I tried the first cast, I could not come close to the height of the railing. I hit a wall sconce. The torch skittered out across the floor and went black. The veins in the walls pulsed, as loud as lightning.

Method two: I swung the hook underhand. It sailed high, hovered at the zenith, black, then plummeted down like the claw of a bird of prey. I leapt aside as it came lancing down. I hated this method. Each time I tried it, I thought, What if I hit the Radiance? What if I chipped it? I doubted even Skiy could fix it then. What if the hook snapped the cord and the Radiance fell? I dreaded that weight; it would pulverize me. Even if I stepped out of the way, the whole Tower would hear the crash. What would they do if I shattered the Radiance?

The second method succeeded at last. The hook caught. Its impact rang on the railing, deep as a lead-stringed zither. I covered my ears. I chewed my beard and tried to think what to do. The walls pulsed. I pulled the rope taut. I tied the end to a wall sconce and started to climb.

It was not like climbing a ladder. My arms began to scream. I looked down. I was still so low, a monk could have run across the floor and pulled off my sandals. The railing above looked as distant as a star. I climbed. I longed to close my eyes so I would not have to see how slowly the wall crept past. But if I closed my eyes, I would not be able to find my next handhold and that would be the end.

My sandals slipped. I kicked them off. They fell a long time before hitting the floor. The Radiance loomed beside me.

A fist knocked on the door above.

"Who's there?" I shouted.

"Kem." His voice sounded far away.

The rope snapped. Not at the top. Not where it held me to the railing. It snapped at the bottom where I had tied it to the sconce. I twirled like a pinwheel, crazily, into the middle of the room. I struck the wall and ricocheted back. I hit the Radiance. I hit the Radiance itself! It was cold and I wanted to cry. The Radiance moaned on its cord.

"Kem!" I shouted. "Kem, I'm coming! Wait!"

By the time I had stabilized enough to climb, vomit bubbled in the back of my throat. I forced it down. I did not want to glaze the rope in used vegetables.

I grabbed the bottom of the railing and reached for the top. I pulled myself over with the blood vessels bursting in my eyes. I lay on my stomach and tried to breathe in the floor. Dust swirled into my lungs. I sneezed. This done, I crawled to the door. There was no sound from the other side. I knocked, my knuckles leaving four sweaty marks.

"Are you still there, Kem?"

"Yes," said a voice. I wasn't sure about that voice. Maybe I had made him angry. I had made him wait.

"I'm going to figure out this door," I said. "It's gloomy in here. All the torches are down at the bottom."

I found a doorknob. I squinted at the knob, then grabbed it with both hands and turned. Nothing happened. The door shuddered but it did not open. I had missed a bolt; it grinned at me from higher on the door. I drew back the bolt. The knob turned. Every hinge yowled. They had not been used in years.

The hallway outside was black.

"Kem?"

A shape unfolded from the floor. It stepped through the doorway, onto the platform. I wondered how long he'd been waiting, crouching, how long I'd spent swinging in the void below.

He walked along the platform to the far side. Three years ago Blade had stood there beside my brother, leaned out over the drop, extended a twelve-year-old hand, and that was how it all began.

Kem opened the front of his robe. He pulled out the plume. He pulled it out slowly from the dark of his robe, one scarlet feather at a time, unfurling like the flowers of a succulent. Yellow tendrils, the tongues of lance-sharks, whipped the floor.

"You're taller." He held it out to me. "You put it on."

I hardly heard him. I saw the red feathers pushed into my arms. I fumbled for the ring at the base of the plume. I found it at last and lifted the succulent blossom into my own arms. It was lighter than a dream; I didn't know what to do with it.

"Kem," I said, "I don't—"

"You just reach out," he said, "and put it on the top. That's what Kem told me."

"What?"

"Kem told me it clasps on the top."

"*You're* not Kem?"

He pushed back his hood. The thing pushed back its hood. It stared at me with turquoise eyes, bright under rags of hair.

"Glane?"

28

The last time I'd heard Glane's voice and known it was his was in my dream, crushed in the sand between the sapling aisles. I had not seen him since that night in the hospital. Where were his feathers now?

"Where's Kem?" The question sounded cold. I shivered. I hugged the plume. It smelled like the back of Skiy's shop.

"Kem's at home." Glane chewed his lip. "No, maybe he's working tonight."

"Why did *you* come?" I stared at him. If I looked away, the feathers would start to grow on his arms.

"Kem thought you'd like to see me," said Glane.

"I wouldn't." I shook the plume. "I want to put this back. Then I want you to leave, and I don't want to see you again."

Glane pouted. He sounded like a sulking child. "Why don't you want to see me, Ksar?" Golden thread hemmed his tunic. I would not comment.

"You almost strangled me," I said. "You told your father about the Radiance."

Glane's lip drooped past his chin. "I didn't mean to strangle you," he said. "I didn't mean to, Ksar. Why didn't you visit me?"

"I din't want to die."

"I wouldn't have done it."

I said nothing. A yellow-whip tendril tickled my chin.

"That room was a prison," said Glane. "I watched the pigeons outside the window. I watched them flying over the City, on the other side of the bars. That window had bars, Ksar. I could see the pigeons but I couldn't reach them."

I tried not to picture it, Glane sitting alone on the crumbling bed, the perch above like an endless gallows.

"The pigeons," said Glane, "used to nest in the eaves outside the window. I could watch them gather feathers and straw for their nests. They brought up a sandal once. Two of them carried it together. I tried to open the window. I wanted to give them my feathers, but they flew away when they saw me."

"I would have done the same," I said.

"But I was giving them feathers!" He waved his arms, still swathed in Kem's brown cloak. It looked as if he was trying to fly. "I wanted to help them. They could have used my feathers, really used them. My feathers were bigger and stronger and more colorful than theirs. You should have seen the colors! They would have made the nests so beautiful." He peered at me with glimmering eyes. "Don't you notice anything different, Ksar?"

"You're not a bird anymore?"

"I never was a bird. I was getting there, but I never *was* one. I wasn't supposed to be a bird. I was just supposed to grow feathers."

"Of course you weren't *supposed* to be a bird," I said. "No one's *supposed* to be a bird, but you *were* turning into one."

"Not anymore."

"No," I said, "not anymore." I didn't know what to say after that.

Glane pointed to the crest in my arms. "You should put that back," he said.

"I might fall, you know. I might die."

Glane lolled his head so he would not look at me.

"It's dangerous," I said. "Hang onto me. I'm going to lean out, and I don't want to fall."

Glane wrapped his arms — real arms — around my waist. I leaned over the railing, far, far over, over the drop to the floor a million leagues below. It was difficult to find the Radiance through the mess of feathers, find the top where the plume should rest. Glane's arms squeezed tight as pliers. His skin smelled of antiseptic. I thought he might break me in two, he squeezed so hard.

If I tossed the plume — gentle, no more than the length of my hand — the ring would catch on the Radiance. I tossed.

I overshot. The feathers leapt away from my hand. They hovered. The crest of the Radiance fell.

Glane let go of my waist. We leaned over the railing together and stared. The plume fell, soft as a flower, spiraling down. What if it hit a torch and ignited? All these years for nothing.

It landed on the floor and toppled to its side. The pearls caught the light and winked like a thousand glow-worms, a thousand eyes laughing up at my face.

"I'll get it," said Glane.

"You know you can't fly anymore."

"I never could fly. I'm going to climb." He slithered out of Kem's cloak. Underneath he wore trousers and tunic, loose-fitted and golden-hemmed. I had never seen him in clean clothes before. Nothing was right. His brown-black hair spilled into his eyes.

"Do you know how to climb a rope?" I said.

"No, but I doubt you do either."

"You're not going to kill yourself, are you?"

"No, sorry." He scrambled over the railing. I thought for a moment he was going to jump. He wrapped himself around the top of the rope and stepped off the platform. I watched him descend. He twirled around and around, jolting over each of my knots. I winced and my knees buckled. Smaller and smaller he became. His hands screeched along the fiber. At the bottom he rolled on his back, then stood and staggered in a circle. I could hear him laughing. He waved up at me. His face was a smear of white, framed in the dark of his hair and the floor behind.

"That hurt!" he shouted. "That hurt my hands!" He poked one palm to prove it. "Ouch!" he hollered. The words echoed around the room's cylinder, sounding like a hundred Glanes all jabbing and screaming in unison.

Glane picked up the plume. He lifted it high, then lowered it down over his head. It sat on his shoulders like a jester's collar. I could not see his head at all.

"Ksar!" he shouted. "How do you climb a rope?"

"It's easier if you can see," I called back. It looked as if his head had erupted, a fountain of red bursting up from his shoulders. I tried to stop laughing. "Tie the rope to a wall sconce," I called. "Use the one that's already blown out."

Glane staggered in a circle on the floor. "I can't find the rope. Where is it?"

"Walk to your left."

"I still can't find it."

"Other left."

He found the rope at last. I steered him to the wall and the burned-out torch, where he tangled the rope around the bracket.

"Will it hold?" I asked.

"I hope so," he shouted back. He was ready to climb. I didn't want him to climb. Far away I did not mind Glane. The closer he came, the more I imagined his golden eyes, and mucus over dye-blue feathers. My skin crawled.

Glane ascended faster than I had done. Perhaps it only seemed that way because I was not climbing. I leaned over the railing. I grabbed his hand and hauled him onto the platform. His hand was sticky with sweat and burst blisters.

Glane lifted the plume off his head and handed it to me. "Don't drop it," he advised.

"I wasn't going to. Now hang on to me and I'll put it back."

He wrapped his arms around my waist once more. I leaned out toward the Radiance. If Kem had been here, it would have worked on the first try, because everything worked better when Kem was around. As it was, it worked on the second. I stepped back. There. The Radiance shone like a perfect ornament, as it had before Blade ever came to disturb it.

Glane released me. "That's beautiful." He smiled. "What do we do now?"

"Until morning, we don't do anything," I said. "We sleep."

"Up here?"

"Not up here. We're not supposed to be up here." I climbed over the railing and slid down the rope. Blisters formed, burst, and ripped raw before I reached the bottom.

Glane tossed Kem's cloak down the shaft of the room. He followed more slowly. He climbed off the rope, cross-eyed beside me. "That was fun," he said. "Let's climb and slide again, Ksar."

"No." I patted my hands against my robe; it did not ease the sting of the blisters.

"What are you doing?" said Glane.

"It hurt my hands."

"Yes," he said, "me too. But wasn't it fun? It felt like flying."

I shook the rope until the hook came free, crashing down from the height of the railing. It struck the floor with a ring like a crematorium bell. I tried to decipher Glane's knot around the wall sconce. I gave up and left it tied.

"You're going to sleep now, Ksar?"

"I am." I sat down against the wall and folded my arms. Glane sat down beside me. "Will you leave tomorrow?"

"No," I said. "I love being a monk."

"Oh."

"That was a lie, you know."

"So you *are* going to leave tomorrow?"

"I don't know," I said. "I don't know how to leave." I stood and walked to the other side of the room. I folded my arms and sat down. Glane did not follow.

I woke up, and the first thing I saw was red feathers, far overhead. The Radiance. I rolled over. Glane stood by the door with his back to me. He rattled the handle. He carried the rope coiled under his arm.

"What are you doing?" I rubbed my eyes.

"I'm leaving."

He looked pathetic. I wanted to help him; I was too ashamed, and what could I do? If I spoke to him now, he would think we were friends again. Better he left before I hurt him further.

"Why aren't you gone yet?" I said.

"The door won't open."

"You have to turn the handle, not shake it."

He turned the handle, opened the door, and left. I stared at the place where he had stood. He was no longer there.

I was hungry. Some things in life did not change. I went to the dining room and found it deserted. I had no idea of the time. Was it night? Was it afternoon already? While I climbed ropes and blistered my hands, had a cataclysm seized the City? A tidal wave of camel blood? Swarms of flying worms?

"Excuse me." I stuck my head into the cave behind the buffet tables. A bevy of cooks stood around a counter, clustered together over an earthenware bowl. "Excuse me," I said again, "what time is it?"

"Breakfast is over," said one of the cooks, not looking up. "Lunch is in a few hours." He wore a green habit like the others, with a full-length apron overtop.

"Can I have something to eat?" I said.

He handed me a platter of mangled zucchini and hurried back to his work. I looked at the zucchini and thought of Brother Iander and his vegetables. He'd said he'd be back sometime this morning, hadn't he? He had probably returned already. I wondered how his night had been. I hoped he had not enjoyed it. I had not enjoyed mine. If I did not enjoy myself, no one else should enjoy themselves either. I hated the Tower.

The zucchini stared up at me, brown and limp. The slices crushed between my fingers before they could reach my mouth. I left the dish on the table and wandered the Tower. I walked up and down between the trees. Glane used to come every day to make wishes. I never asked him what his wishes were for. Perhaps I could sit here and wait. Eventually he would come and wish that last night had never happened. Maybe Sfin would come and I could tell him about the falling of the sun again, and it would make me feel important. I sat down on the edge of a step.

What would I do if Glane came? Would I apologize for sending him away? Would I be able to apologize? I could not force myself before. It was my fault as much as Glane's we had stopped being friends. There, I had said it. I wanted him back. I started to wish Glane had never existed. I changed my mind and wished I had never existed instead.

I wandered again — to the balcony, empty, on top of the Tower. Why was there no one here? Fog hung thick but it did not rain. Condensation soaked the benches. I did not sit down. I went back inside. I would find Iander and help him sort wishes. Was that his only job here? No wonder he wanted to leave. I had nothing better to do. I had completed my purpose. According to Kem, I was free to go. I didn't want to go. I didn't know what I would do if I left. I could hide in my old house — the one Leque and I used to share — and ignore every knock on the door. Kem would knock. Maybe Glane would too. I would lie in the dark, as Blade had done when his grandfather turned him away, with no idea what I was hiding from, or where I would go once the danger had passed. I did not want to stay in the Tower either.

I found the sorting room. I knocked on the door and went in before anyone answered.

A monk who was not Iander looked up at me. "Yes?"

"Where's Brother Iander?"

"He's gone," the monk squeaked. "I'm looking for clues to his disappearance."

"Gone?"

"He disappeared last night."

"Brother Ksar?" said a voice from the doorway.

I turned. The Father Paramount stood with his hands in his sleeves. Braids like corduroy fabric embroidered his beard.

"You have emerged from your seclusion, I see."

I nodded.

"And your revelation?"

"It's back," I said.

"'Back,' my son?"

I should have told him immediately. "The Radiance's crest," I said, "it's back."

"Indeed?" He raised one eyebrow and one side of his mouth. "May I have the honor of seeing this miracle?"

I led him to the bottom of the Radiance room. A few torches still burned on the wall, the floor beneath them dusted with ash. The Paramount knelt in the dust. I thought he was sweeping at first, until he straightened and turned to me. His mouth curved up in a smile. He held a piece of knotted rope in his hand. The rest of the rope chafed against my stomach, under my robe. It made me look pot-bellied and weighed me down like indigestion.

"Does this aid you in meditation?" said the Paramount.

"Er, yes..." I pointed up. "See? The crest is back."

"Well done."

"Does it matter who damaged it?" I asked.

The Paramount studied the knot in his hand. He looked at me and continued smiling. "No, my son," he said, "it does not matter. Tell me, Brother Ksar: do you think it is wise to exhibit the Radiance for public viewing? Do you think it will suffer vandalism again?"

I shook my head. "I'm sure it's safe."

"Good." The Paramount nodded. "What task of enlightenment do you wish to turn your attention to now, my son?"

I stared at the walls. "I'll sort the wishes again."

"You've heard of the disappearance of Brother Iander?"

"Yes," I said.

"Seek for news of his whereabouts."

I nodded. "Thank you." I did not meet his eyes. I could not have met anyone's eyes at the moment.

29

Yaryk's world swam in a bloodshot fog. He had not slept. He had spent all night in the alleys. He searched every doorway, and the back room of every shop and eating house, but Leque and Blade were gone. They had run past him in the hospital and now they were gone.

Yaryk leaned against a wall, beside a poster burned into a sheet of leather. Leque's face stared out from the hide. "Wanted: the murderer of Y'az Gyrt. Substantial reward." The leather reeked of mold in the rain. Carts churned past along the road. They sprayed Yaryk's shirt in mud. Rain water dripped off his nose.

So Leque had now run from him also. First Blade, and now Leque. Yaryk had thought Leque was lost — wandered from his room in the hospital and lost his way. He had gone to the reception hall to search. Had anyone there seen Leque? No? And then came Leque himself, Blade in his wake, running for their lives across the white-stone floor.

What had he, Yaryk, ever done to incur their hate? What under the Stars had he done that they found so terrible? In the City had they not been friends? Associates in crime? Associates in stupidity at least? Hadn't they all admired Yaryk and trusted him? He had trusted them, had trusted the stupidity of their actions at least.

Why run away? Yaryk dug his fingers in his beard. "I saved you from the bees, Blade," he muttered, "when your grandfather turned you out. Don't you remember that? When did I ever mistreat you on the road, or when we arrived in the Citadel? Never. And you, Leque. I never imprisoned you, or framed you as Gyrt's assassin. Liop did these things. I saved you. I brought you here, away

from the wet, to treat your wounds. And what do you do?"
He pulled his hair. "You run from me, Leque."

Yaryk watched the carts swim past. Where did they go,
all these invisible men and their oilskin tents? Somewhere
else, beyond these liquid walls, a man with broken ribs
and a boy in a loincloth followed a road without direction.
Where did Leque think he would go? Where did he plan
to lead Blade? They would not make it alive — a cripple
and a child. Yaryk cursed them. He could have led them
if they had let him. He knew safe places in the world, where
people accepted the Bedouin and would not know Blade
for a noble, where no one had heard of the Radiance, or
poisoned bees. Leque did not know of these places. He and
Blade would die on the roads. Yaryk shivered. Why had
they run? He pressed his hands to the wall. He would have
broken his fingers if he had had the strength.

Yaryk wandered. He arrived at the Gaol. It hulked in
the rain, its stone soaked gray, the mortar like blood at the
cracks. Most likely he had come too late. Yaryk ducked into
the dimness, where the lines of cages ran stinking away
to the wall.

"What do you want?" A spear pressed into his chest.

"I have come to see Tallos."

"Tallos is dead."

"Did you execute him?" Yaryk clenched his teeth to
repress his shivering.

"Why are you interested in Tallos?"

"I am strongly opposed to the Bedouin regime," said
Yaryk. "'*I would be gratified to see my fallen foe.*'" He wondered
what fable he had quoted there, and he wondered how
much of what he said was true, and how much was lies.
Now or ever.

The guard nodded down the lines of cages, to a grated
door at the end. "He's there."

Yaryk walked between the kennels. He did not look at
them, nor at the men behind the bars. He pushed the grate
aside and stepped into human decay. A tangible stench

filled the air. Yaryk pulled the collar of his tunic up over his nose. A shape lay under a cloth at the end of the room. Yaryk climbed the steps to where the body lay. He retched.

"Tallos." He prodded the cloth with his foot. He pulled the covering back. It ripped in places, where the blood had cemented it to the floor.

Tallos was dead. Veins and arteries, twisted like wire, emerged from his neck. Blood caked his eyes. It clotted his nose and mouth. Yaryk squatted beside the corpse.

"Why don't they Release you?" he whispered. He reached to close the eyes, but the lids were fixed. "Why don't they set you free at the acid?" he said. "We did as much for their workers." He covered Tallos' face. He wanted to form an apology, but he did not know the words.

"Turn around," said a voice.

Yaryk clasped his hands behind his head before he was told. He turned. Men with spears filled the doorway. Horsehair bracelets encircled their wrists.

"Is this the man?" said one of the guards.

"I can't see," said a voice, buried in the back of the crush. The guards stepped aside. They dragged a man in shackles out into the open.

"Is this Yaryk?" said the captain of the guards.

The prisoner raised his head. He squinted at Yaryk. "Yes, that's one of their leaders."

"Thank you."

"Neath," said Yaryk.

Two guards stepped forward. They tied Yaryk's hands at the back of his neck.

"Neath," he whispered. "Why, Neath? How did you know I was here?"

"Jarb told me you were back."

"Enough." The guards pushed Yaryk through the doorway, toward the cages of the Gaol. The door of one cage stood open.

Yaryk shuffled in on his knees. The guards unlocked his wrists. He sat in the filth with his feet beneath him. They led Neath away, back to his cell. No reward, not even for his treachery. Yaryk considered calling the guards. He could tell them he was not the instigator; Liop had started it all, and now he was dead. He could tell them he considered the movement madness from the outset, that he had opposed it all along. They wouldn't believe him; he knew they would not. He sat with head bowed and said nothing.

Blade laughed and stepped around a puddle. "One time," he said, "Grandfather's butler, Rael — did you ever meet him, Leque?"

"I think so. The man with the obsession for polished sandal straps?"

"Yes, him." Through chattering teeth, Blade laughed again. "One time at dinner we were eating at the low table, the one with the gold cloth that fastens around the rim, you know? I think we had it when you worked for us. Anyway, we were eating. My grandfather dropped his spoon and it rolled under the table.

"'Allow me,' said Rael. He got down on his stomach and reached under the table to get the spoon, only then he didn't get up again.

"'What is it?' said Grandfather.

"'There,' said Rael, 'what is that?'

"Of course to see what he was pointing at we all had to lay down as well, and only I was willing to do that. Grandfather and his guests were too lazy. I was still young then; I didn't mind lying down on the floor. Do you know what Rael was pointing at?"

"What?" said Leque.

"Y'az Rubel's feet."

"I don't understand," said Leque. "He must have seen feet before."

"Rubel had gout," said Blade. "He was too embarrassed to show his feet, so he wore llama-wool socks. At least I think it was llama wool. He wore big socks. Rael kept his own feet so immaculate he'd never seen llama socks before. He thought Rubel's feet had grown fur."

Leque laughed. He held his side and his face was gray.

The first sun rose. White-gold light snaked out through the clouds, through the raindrops misting the air, over the roofs of the Citadel.

Blade's eyes watered. "How far do you think we are from the gate?" Leque had bought him a donkey-hide cloak. From within its folds, the outside world was difficult to see. "Do you think we're almost there?"

"I hope so."

The tunic he wore was too large; it reached his knees and eclipsed his trousers.

They wandered the streets, quiet this close to dawn. Leque said he knew the way. Blade pretended to believe him. He pretended he was not hungry, was not cold, that his skin did not prune in the wet. He pretended his legs did not ache. Leque's skin bore a sickly green pallor around his bandages.

The gates loomed up before them. Leque draped his arm around Blade's shoulders. "If they ask where we're going," he said, "tell them we're fishermen, going out to check our nets. Say you're my son if they ask."

"Your son?"

"So they don't think I'm holding you hostage."

"I'll say you're my uncle," said Blade. He had already played Yaryk's son through these gates.

The guards yawned as they approached. One waved his spear in Leque's face. "You're not a Bedouin, are you?"

"Certainly not," said Leque. "We're fishermen. We—"

"And him?" The guard flicked his spear at Blade. "Push back your hood; I want to see your face."

One of the other guards laughed. "They're straw-heads, both of them. What Bedouin has hair that pale, you fool? Go on." He nodded. "Good luck with the squid."

They walked a few hundred paces, out of the hearing of the guards. "Squid?" said Blade.

"Fishermen have to fish for something," said Leque. "Squid are common around the Citadel."

"I'm cold," said Blade.

Leque nodded.

They walked slowly; Leque could walk no faster. The day wore on. Traffic increased; a never-ending stream of carts, caravans and litters plodded past. They walked at the edge of the road where the earth slipped away, liquid as soup, threatening to draw them away to the acid below. The traffic left the Citadel. Men trudged on foot, or trudged away on the backs of camels. Others sheltered in wagons, loaded with packs and baggage.

"Why are they leaving?" Blade had to shout in Leque's ear to be heard.

Leque said something about the Glebe and the Bedouin. He spoke softly and Blade could not hear what he said.

The crowds thinned as they walked, dispersing down side paths here, an intersecting causeway there. Leque plodded down the main road. He watched his feet and said nothing. Blade looked back. The stone ridge upon which they walked stretched away like a backbone, the spine of a beached leviathan. The Citadel's walls faded out of sight. The excitement of departure, flight, safety with Leque, all ebbed away. Where would they go? They had escaped Yaryk, and now they had nothing to eat, no shelter, no clothes but the rags they wore. Leque would die. Blade could tell by his stoop, and the scrape of his breath as he walked. Blade's stomach throbbed. His skin itched in the cold and wet. He did not ask where they would sleep, or how they would warm themselves. Things had turned out so differently — so much colder and stranger than the way he had ever imagined in the City. He would never contemplate the future again, he decided; it was always too harsh to guess.

Leque stopped. The suns dripped low.

Blade's teeth chattered. "Why are we stopping?"

"I'm tired," said Leque. Boulders lined the road. Leque chose a boulder the color of cinnabar. He sat and pressed his eyes closed. His face was white.

He's going to die, thought Blade. He'll die right now. I've spent so many days thinking someone will kill *me*, and really it's Leque who's about to die. Blade swallowed. He sat down at Leque's feet. His cloak weighed him down like a corpse. Maybe Leque didn't know he was dying. Blade did not want to tell him.

"Where are we going?" said Blade.

"To the City. You can live with me. It might be safe."

"Leque..." Blade trembled. He swallowed again. "Why did you leave without telling anyone? When you left the City, I mean."

"I was afraid."

"Of the feathers?" said Blade

Leque nodded, head still bowed, eyes still closed. The rain plastered his hair to the back of his neck. Green spread out from his bandages, up his arms. Twilight made everything green. Blade hoped it was only the light.

"They'll be glad to see you again," said Blade, "back at the City. Kem and..." he faltered. "Kem and Skiy..." That was all that was left. Yaryk was gone. Everyone was dead.

Blade crawled to the foot of the boulder. He unfastened his cloak and draped it over them both. He pulled the hood over both their heads. Only a tiny window remained, through which they could watch the rain. Blade pressed himself against Leque's legs, into the warmth.

"Are you going to die, Leque?"

"No."

He was going to die. Blade wrapped his arms around Leque's waist, and Leque held Blade with one bandaged arm. They had nothing to say.

A line of camels dragged past on the road, each animal's muzzle tied to the tail of the one ahead. A noble's litter and its escort followed. Blade curled deeper into the camouflage. Hours passed. A huge domed cart churned a path through the rain. A man in fur robes drove the cart.

Blade stared. "Wait!" He untangled from the cloak and dashed onto the road. "Wait!" he shouted. "Wait!"

The smuggler pulled up his camels and looked around. Yes, the same squinted eyes, the hide robe, the bites of lice around his collar. "You." The smuggler grinned. The cyanide hexagon glowed on his tongue. "You went to the Citadel, yes? With Yaryk?"

Blade nodded.

"What do you want now?" He thrust a hand down the front of his robe and came out with a cockroach. He dropped it between his teeth and chewed. "There—" he pointed to Leque. "Is that your father?"

"No," said Blade. "Neither was Yaryk."

"No?" The smuggler laughed. "How surprising."

"Can you take us to the City?"

"Why would we take you? We traded in the City less than a season ago."

"Please?" Blade clung to the edge of the platform. "We're going to die unless you help us."

"Everyone dies," said the smuggler. He spat the roach's shell out onto the ground.

"No, I don't want to die!" Blade stamped. "I don't want Leque to die either!"

"Get in."

"What?"

"Get into the cart. Or don't you want to anymore?" It was difficult to understand the smuggler's words; he spoke through a mouth full of insect legs. He leaned back and rapped the side of the cart. Two men emerged. They yawned. Their leader pointed at Leque and they squelched across the road to the boulders. The smugglers wrapped Leque in the cloak, smothered like a dying child, and carried him over to the cart.

"You too." The smuggler nodded at Blade. "Get in," he said. "Are you hungry?"

30

No one had wished for anything interesting today.

The door opened behind me. "Brother Ksar?"

"What?"

The monk frowned. "Such a perfunctory greeting." When I made no sign of apology, he said: "Someone in the reception room wishes to speak with you."

"Any feathers?"

"What do you mean?"

"Skinny man?" I asked. "Brown hair? Greenish eyes? Eating his collar?"

"I don't think so," said the Brother.

It didn't sound like Glane. "Thank you," I told him. I wound my way through the Tower, down and down, out through the door behind the reception desk. I did not see Glane. I did not recognize anyone in the room. The monk behind the reception desk nodded as I passed.

"Ksar!"

I whirled. Still I saw no one I knew.

"Ksar! Here!" Beside the doors to the outside world, there bobbed a short man with no hair. He waved. I squinted down at him. Razor nicks covered his face. A leather toga swaddled his torso.

"Hello?" I said. "Do I know you?"

"Do you *know* me?" He burst out laughing and would not stop. "Brother Ksar," he said, "Iander!"

"What happened to your beard?"

"I shaved it off."

"You're uglier than I imagined." I scratched my neck. "Why didn't you come back yesterday? They think you've been murdered like Brother Eln. They think someone's out to kill monks."

"Do I look like a monk?"

"No, but I mean..."

"I've left. You got me out." He grabbed my hand. "I want to thank you for saving me. I really want to thank you. You knew I wouldn't return, didn't you? Someone as intelligent as yourself? Yes, yes, of course you knew." He lowered his voice. In the crowded hall, no one could have cared what he said. "My old shop has passed on to new owners," he said. He still held my hand. I pulled it away. "I have found another shop available in Merchant's Alley," said Brother Iander. "I am going to establish myself there."

"Oh," I said, "good."

"But do you know, Ksar?" said Iander. "Would you believe it is the very same shop where Brother Eln's body was found? The previous owner simply left. Skiy left. I believe you knew him? Yes, he is gone. He disappeared after the crime. You should see all the cobbling supplies he left behind!"

"What are you going to do with them?"

"I may be able to use them," he said. "I will sell the rest to the craftsmen around me."

"Fine." I nodded.

Iander grinned like a fractured melon. "You must leave the Tower, Ksar!" He tried to retake my hand. I clasped it behind my back. "The joy of freedom," he said. "Imagine it, Ksar, to have the run of the entire City, free from the orders of the Paramount. Imagine it, Ksar!"

"I haven't been a monk very long," I said. "I remember what it's like not to be one."

"Don't you want to be free? Consider it, Ksar, no limit to the wine you can drink in a day!"

I smiled. I did not try to make the smile convincing.

"You can live with me until you find a house of your own," said Iander. "It's hard to find your way to the shop from here. I'll wait if you want to go up and get your things. We can leave right now."

I laughed at the thought of directions to reach Skiy's shop. "I have my own house," I said, "provided no one else has moved in while I've been gone. I told you — I've only been a monk a few weeks." I turned to go back up the Tower.

Iander grabbed my arm. "So you're coming with me? You're leaving the Brotherhood?"

I nodded. "I'll go with you," I said, "and then I'll see about my old house. But Iander?"

"Yes?" He bounced where he stood.

"You don't think I should talk to the Father Paramount before I leave?"

"Did *I* talk to him?"

"No, but maybe you should have. Maybe there's a correct way to leave so that people don't think you're dead."

"There's no 'correct way,'" said Iander. "The correct thing to do is to never join, because once you join, the Father Paramount expects you to stay forever."

"Fine," I said. "Wait for me."

I ran up the stairs, along the gold-pulsing corridors. In the sleeping room I lay down on my stomach and reached under the bed. I dragged out a bundle of wish papers and the bag Iander had returned to me, which held all my earrings and other accessories. Little use, now that my piercings had grown over. At the bottom of the bag lay one copper-tipped feather. I could not remember putting it there, but apparently I had.

I could not leave the Tower looking so much like a monk. I stole a sheet from the nearest bed and wrapped it around myself like a toga. I tucked up my robe out of sight beneath it.

I opened the door and ran into the Father Paramount.

"Good morning, Brother Ksar." He held me at arm's length. "Have you noticed how often we meet by chance, my son?"

"Um, often?"

"Yes, quite often. And where are you going?"

"Nowhere," I muttered.

"Do you consider yourself so enlightened you no longer need the help of the Brotherhood?"

"Er, no Father."

"You don't?" He smiled, benign as a turnip. "If you are not yet enlightened, why are you leaving?"

"I'm not," I tried.

"On the contrary, my son, you are free to leave whenever you wish."

"I am?"

"You've earned all the wisdoms but one available to you here."

"I have?" I was feeling stupid. "All but one?"

"Yes," he said, "there were two tasks I was going to give you: that of the Radiance, and then another. As you have now completed the task of the Radiance, my son, that leaves but one. However if you wish to go now, without attempting a second task, I cannot stop you. Restoring the crest to the Radiance accomplished everything you came here to do. Permission to leave is granted by both myself and your friend who works at the hospital."

I gaped.

The Father Paramount tucked his hands into the sleeves of his habit. "Most men enter the Brotherhood to escape from something," he said. "You escaped from your guilt. When I questioned you on your first night here — you remember, do you not, my son? When I asked you about your older brother? — I sought to discover your goal, so that once you had achieved it I could anticipate your departure."

I willed myself to transform into an insect. He could step on me then and have done.

"I divined your guilt in the Radiance's defacement beyond all doubt," he continued, beaming, "and so allowed you full freedom to return the crest, as I hoped would be your aim. I did not mention my discovery to the rest of the Brotherhood for fear they should mistrust you. But now that the crest has been recovered, all misdemeanors of the past may be forgotten."

My mouth had the taste of a camel's bladder. "Can I go now?" I said.

"You may," said the Father, "after I show you one thing." He stood back from the doorway. I shuffled through. "Come with me." I felt like an ox with a ring through its nose. I would have made a weak and useless ox.

He led me down a hallway that dead-ended in stone. "The Marble Tower constantly expands," he said. I stared at the stone, waiting for growth. "In your vision," he said, "you sat in the Tree of Power. You remember its winding branches, do you not, my son?"

I nodded.

"Others have had similar dreams," said the Paramount, "and have told us of the branches of the tree forming stairs. The yellow blood of the tree still runs through the stone." He tapped his knuckles on the wall, where a vein slowly pulsed. The sound of his knuckles echoed hollow on the marble. "We are always delving," said the Father Paramount, "in search of further rooms and chambers." He pushed on the wall. It opened inwards, into blackness. The Father stepped in. His voice echoed. "You are the first to have mentioned the skeletons, my son."

I stood in the light of the corridor. I did not want to go inside.

An oil lamp flared in the black. Its amber-white light spilled over the walls. "Come in, my son," said the Paramount's voice. "I only wish to show you one thing, and then you may leave. You may leave forever, if that is your wish."

I stepped through the door. The room was large and circular, dim on the far side where the oil lamp's glow could not reach. The Paramount stood with his back to me. He bowed his head. I stepped beside him and followed his gaze. A pelvic bone grinned up from the floor. A rib cage lay half cemented in the marble beside it. The skull lay turned on its side, as if eyeing my feet for consumption. I squatted and peered in its mouth. No golden fruit shone back. I stood up quickly and looked away.

"Even the fruit of wisdom rots with time," said the Paramount. "The smell of it filled this room when first we opened it."

"How long ago?" My eyes slid back to the skeleton.

"Many years," he said, "when I was no more than a brother here. The room has been kept closed since then.

The discovery of such a chamber may be viewed with misgivings by the public."

I nodded.

"And," he said, "it was not until you told me your vision, my son, that I was sure of the skeletons' connection to the Tower's birth. If you wish to remain in the Brotherhood, you may meditate on the stories of these men." He swept the oil lamp around the walls. Other faces grinned up from the floor, embedded as if in quicksand.

I closed my eyes. I could not imagine spending days here alone. Would I have to kneel beside each skull and ask each one in turn, "So why did *you* want to be the father of kings and warlords? What made you think you would be able to find your way back to earth?"

"I want to go," I said.

"Give my regards to Brother Iander."

Iander, Brother no longer, waited outside in the mud. He held a metal sheet over his head to ward off the rain.

"Ah, Ksar!" He clobbered me with his roof. "Sorry, sorry. I thought you'd never make it out!" Was this man truly the same who, only a few days earlier, had harbored such a fixation on vegetables and logic? "My shop is this way." He pointed down a road I had walked a thousand times before. "The Father Paramount didn't catch you, did he?"

"No," I said.

We passed the sewer grate, where Glane had sprawled on the road and looked down. That was the last day before he went to the hospital.

I wondered what the Paramount thought of *Iander's* state of enlightenment. And where was the purpose in wish paper clues, when the Paramount knew Iander had left of his own volition? Perhaps he thought Brother Eln had left freely as well. And when it came down to it, if I killed a tiny person who was not real, who happened to look like me, *would* my intestines fall out? The world swam futilely around me.

"Here we are," said Iander.

"I don't think intestines fall out that easily," I said.

"Do you want me to say something dampening? I will if you drive me."

"Sorry."

"Most things will change now that we're out of the Tower. But only *most* things. For instance..." He led me past the display tables on the street, and into the front room. "Look at how spacious it is! No more sleeping like jewels in a sack!"

"Jewels in a sack?" I guffawed in my beard. Iander stared at me like an armadillo. "Sorry," I said. "It sounds like... never mind."

I sat down on a table. Something cried deep down inside me. Maybe something to do with my meeting with Glane, or the things the Father Paramount had said — that he'd known about the Radiance all along — or the fact that my makeshift toga chafed my neck. I did not want to think about unhappiness. Iander bubbled. He overflowed with self-satisfaction. Every other sentence thanked me for saving him, or told me of his plans for the shop. I nodded to all his proposals. I needed to escape before my unhappiness overflowed. It felt like vomit inside my chest.

Tables still cluttered the front room. Shoes were strewn across the floor. Brother Iander led me upstairs to the room where Skiy had once slept. A painting of Skiy's extended family hung on one wall. Each man wore a matching earring bloody red as wine. I looked for Kem. In another corner of the room, a pile of sandals lay heaped. A stack of blankets dominated another. Bookshelves covered the walls.

"Fascinating, isn't it?" said Brother Iander. "He ran away and left everything behind."

I nodded.

"I hadn't known Skiy was a collector," he said, waving an arm at the books.

"No," I said, "he reads them all." We paused to gaze around the room. "I should go," I said. "I want to see if anyone's stolen my house."

"I'll come with you."

"I know my way."

"I want to see where you live," he said, "so I can visit."

We descended the stairs. The stairwell smelled of leather and candle wax. Iander held the front door open for me, and locked it behind us. "We will maintain correspondence, won't we?"

"Of course." This was not the Iander of the Marble Tower. Until he transformed back into the old Iander, I might as well be his friend. Stone knew I didn't have any others.

"How long were you a monk?" I asked.

"Eight years."

"That's stupid," I said.

We turned down the dead-end road where Leque and I had lived. The road was deserted. Only the rain barrels stood out to greet us, singing as the silver drops flowed down. The door of every house was closed, the curtains pulled over the windows, the cobbles slicked in mud. At the end of the street our house sat closed as an oyster. The entrance rug had disappeared from the doorstep, probably stolen. Curtains covered the windows. I could not smell Leque's wine. He normally stored it just inside the door.

I tried the handle. It opened with a sound like gravel. Since when had we stored gravel inside our house? Stale air wafted out, thick and dark. I coughed. I shuffled to the window and opened the curtains. They were stuck at the bottom, held down between the wall and the back of a chair. It made no sense, until I remembered Blade. He had barricaded himself in against the bees. I struggled through the sea of toppled furniture, back to the door. The gravel was not gravel. Hundreds of insect bodies curled like dust in the doorway. They crunched when I stepped on them. I bent, blew, and they rustled like dry leaves. The crystalloid wings seemed to dance and flutter.

"What are you doing?"

I looked up. "Blowing on them," I said. "See how it looks like they're flying?"

"Why are they here?" Iander stood in the slush of the street and did not come in.

"They attacked me," I said. "Perhaps the taste killed them."

"Bees don't bite," said Iander. "When they sting, their stingers rip out, taking many of their vital organs with them. They committed suicide to sting you; that's what killed them."

"Oh." I stood and brushed the wings off my toga. "So I'm home," I said. "Are you going to stay and help me clean up bees, or are you leaving?"

"I think I'm leaving." He swallowed.

"Goodbye," I said. Brother Iander was my only friend; I may as well be civil.

"Goodbye." He waved.

I watched through the window as he walked away, hopping over and around the puddles. He waved his hand as if in conversation. He was not the same Iander I had known in the Tower.

I lay down on my stomach and squandered all the air in my lungs. I blew every bee out the door and into the wet. The water beat them down. It broke them apart and washed them away. I did not want to think about bees any more. I trembled. I pretended the cold was to blame, and I closed the door.

Blade had shoved the welcome rug into the crack beneath the door. Now it lay to the side, folded and torn. He had pushed my clothes chest up against the door as well. Kem, or someone, had rifled through it and removed a few odds and ends. I dragged the chest into the middle of the room. A wig with braided tassels lay on the top. I took it out and raised it to my nose. I inhaled its musty reek and laid it on the floor beside me. Next to the wig lay my extra sandals. They were all single shoes I wore in any combination I chose. I did not sniff them, but tossed them over my shoulder, one by one.

A strip of carpet came next. I used to wear it as a shirt. I unearthed a hat made of leather, a hoard of bracelets, a tunic dyed green, and another tunic upon the front of which I had attempted to paint an aardvark. It looked like a haunch of meat with legs. Tunics upon tunics lay crumpled in the bottom of the chest. I shook them out and spread them on the floor around me. I stood and surveyed the chaos. What a mass of garbage. I shook the chest upside-down. The remaining scrap metal cascaded. The holes in my ears were growing over, and the holes in my nose, and all the holes on my body. Why did I need earrings now?

I made my way to the back room where Leque and I had slept. Neither bed had been occupied for weeks. Where had Leque gone? I stood in the doorway and stared at his cot. I missed my brother so much it hurt. I missed everyone. Maybe I hated them; maybe I loved them. It didn't matter; now they were gone. I had saved Glane's life and now he was gone.

I was sorry. Stone, I was sorry for everything. I had dragged on Leque's wallet for years. I'd abandoned Glane. I was always such a child, and now I had lost Kem and Skiy as well. How could I tell them about the Father Paramount? He had watched me all the time, laughed at my attempted secrecy. Not even the Father cared about the Radiance. No one cared about the Radiance. We should have thrown the crest in the acid the day it was broken. We should have left it in the room. I could not face Kem and tell him.

Time only knew who had sent the bees. Time and Stone were the only ones who knew anything. And maybe the Stars, but maybe the Stars only cared about Yaryk. Maybe none of them cared about anything.

I was hungry; that was all I knew.

Leque kept a casket of money underneath his pillow. I'd always thought that must be uncomfortable — to sleep with a block of metal underneath your head. Leque never complained. I had a key to the casket. Leque had given it to me when he was drunk. I opened the chest. Ten coins stared up at me. Ten.

I left the house. I paused at the door to look back at the clothes strewn over the stone. Once I'd spent the ten coins, I decided, I could sell my wardrobe. That would earn another penny. After that I didn't know.

I had no idea; Leque had always been there in the past.

31

"I haven't played crystal wars in almost nine years," said Iander.

We sat cross-legged on the sleeping shelf that had once been Leque's, the blankets relocated to the floor. Some nights, if it was cold enough, I laid his blankets overtop of my own. We opened our crystal bags — Iander and I — and poured our opposing armies out onto the mattress. His stones shone russet, flecked in yellow. Mine glowed a solid green. Leque and I used to fight over the orange as children. Together, the green and the russet looked like vomit. I leaned my elbow on the wall and put my head on my hand. In the five days since leaving the Tower, how many times had we played this game?

Iander surrounded the battlefield with a piece of string, then produced from his pocket the definitive white pebble. It was time for another loss.

"You first." Iander handed me the pebble.

I dropped it at random. The crystals ricocheted in every direction. One of my own spiraled out of the ring.

"You'll find it more effective," said Brother Iander, "if you aim at an angle." He bent over sideways and squinted. "Target a group of your opponent's men. See? See how I judge the distance between my hand and your pieces? See that? You must take the force and velocity into account. See how I practice my swing before releasing the pebble?"

It looked as if his wrist was broken; I didn't say so. He let the white pebble fly. It massacred five of my men. I stifled a yawn.

"Like that, Ksar." He bounced up and down, hugging his ankles. "Did you see that? Yes, yes, just like that!"

I snapped my fingers; I could not be bothered to clap.

"I sold the last of Skiy's tools this morning," said Iander, as if such news would bring me joy. "Those that I had no use for, that is. I sold the shoe horn for instance." He slapped his knees and laughed. "I mean, what use is a shoe horn for carving gems?"

"Did you sell the books?"

"The day before yesterday a hospital worker came in and bought them all." He handed me the white pebble.

I repeated my maneuvers of the previous turn.

Iander shook his head. "Angle, Ksar, angle!" He hugged his knees. "Oh, did I tell you of the herkimer order I placed? Apparently a herkimer vein has been discovered in a village south of here." He waved his arm northwest. "Herkimer's not an expensive gem in itself, but the mine shafts must run so deep that extraction prices are often high. Yesterday evening, though, the head of the Miners' Guild came to my shop. He was so impressed by my work he commissioned a herkimer necklace. He will give me a deal on herkimer shipments for the rest of the season. Of course, I—"

Someone knocked on the door.

"Who's there?" I shouted.

"Ksar?" said a voice.

"Who is it?" I shouted again.

"Kem," he said. "Let me in."

By Stone, why me? "Come in," I said.

"The door's locked."

"No it isn't. The wet makes it stick. Push harder."

"It won't open!"

I rolled off Leque's bed. The boundary string snagged my toe. Crystals cascaded to the floor.

"Ksar! Look what—"

I wrenched the front door open. Skiy coughed in my face. "Sorry," he said. He wrung the water from his hood and stepped into the house. The smell of burnt dung radiated out from his skin. Kem followed his cousin. He stopped at the sight of clothes strewn over the floor, and the mud-encrusted sandal prints tracking from wall to wall. He eyed the flock of wine bottles huddled in the corner.

"How much money did Leque leave you?" said Kem.

"Not enough."

"How did you buy that alcohol?"

"Iander." I pointed to the back room. Iander peered around the door frame. He tossed the white pebble from hand to hand. "I didn't drink any of this wine," I said. "Iander drank it. I took the bottles so they wouldn't be thrown away."

"That's what you do with bottles," said Kem. "You return them to the Glass Guild. Why haven't you done that?"

I shrugged. "Iander owns your shop now, Skiy."

"I know," said Skiy. "I had to pay him for my own books."

Iander squinted at Skiy. "Why did you leave without taking them with you?" He narrowed his eyes to the width of a thread. "What happened to Brother Eln?"

Skiy said nothing.

Iander disappeared into the back room. He reappeared a moment later, tying the cinch on his bag of crystals. "Goodbye, Ksar," he said. "I'll see you tomorrow, if you haven't been stabbed in the eye by then." He squinted, glared and left.

Kem led the way to the couch beneath the window. Cloth and twisted metal — my previous wardrobe — littered the seat. He pushed the rubble aside and the three of us sat, me in the middle where I couldn't escape.

"I've missed a lot of work at the hospital," said Kem, "searching for you at the Tower, Ksar. You could have told me you were leaving."

"Sorry," I said. I knew what they would ask me next.

"Why won't you visit Glane?" said Kem.

"I don't want to see him."

"Why not?"

"He tried to strangle me."

"He was in the hospital," said Kem, "under medication and close to death. He is as stable as you or I now."

"Good," I said, "not stable at all."

Skiy coughed. He thumped his chest, dislodging a cloud of dust. "Ksar," he said, "are you familiar with the fable of the beggar and the kumquat tree?"

"No."

"It bears great relevance to the situation at hand. Would you like to hear it?"

"Not especially."

"There was once a beggar," said Skiy, "whose chief source of food was the kumquats he picked from a certain tree."

"What are kumquats?"

"A fruit similar to an orange," said Skiy, "but smaller — half the size of your thumb. The name 'kumquat' derives from the original Clebean 'kulque,' meaning 'gold.'"

"So the beggar ate oranges," I said. "Then what?" It reminded me of Yaryk and his stories of the stars. Only Blade ever cared for his stories. We never interrupted him. I don't know why. I would not be so passive now; I would interrupt Skiy as I chose.

"One day the tree began to sicken." Skiy brushed the loose dust off his chest. "The beggar tended it with care, but when he ate a kumquat from the ailing tree, he himself fell victim to the illness. Believing that the tree had betrayed him, the beggar packed up all his meager belongings and moved to the other side of the City, where he soon became emaciated with hunger. He realized the tree was his source of life. By the time he returned, the tree had already withered."

"I'm not a beggar," I said.

"You will be soon if you do not find employment," said Kem. "Or if you do not stop drinking. How much money, do you think, have you wasted on alcohol since returning from the Marble Tower?"

"It's not *my* money," I insisted. "The money's Iander's. I already told you. He bought the wine. I've never been a drunk. That was Leque. I only took the bottles because—"

"Why did Iander leave the Marble Tower?" asked Skiy. "Did he leave with you?"

"No," I said. "He left before me. He left for the same reason all the monks leave — because everything is stupid and none of it makes any sense. All they talk about is wisdom and enlightenment, but none of them know anything about it, or care about it either. The Father Paramount cares least of all. He doesn't know anything about enlightenment. He knows we broke the Radiance."

"What?" said Skiy.

"Oh, don't worry." I sneered. "He's known a long time. We came to the Tower every week. We rattled the handle and left. We made ourselves obvious."

Kem and Skiy stared; I ploughed ahead.

"And the wanted posters?" I said. "You know the posters that covered the City?"

"That you and Glane urinated on?" muttered Skiy.

"*I* urinated on them!" I shouted. "It was *my* idea. Glane only copied me. He always copied me." I tried another sneer; it did not work. "The wanted posters were bogus," I said. "If someone exposed us, maybe the monks would have given them money, maybe they wouldn't. I don't know. They could have, though, with all the money they have. People donate gold to the Tower. They fine you if you stay after dark. The monks have plenty of money. You should see what they eat. But that's not what I'm talking about!" My fist hit the couch. Skiy jumped. "There's no point to anything the Tower Monks do," I said. "Nothing. Why do they shave their heads? What does it mean? It doesn't mean anything!"

"When the Brotherhood formed—" Skiy began.

"I don't care!" I shouted. "Maybe it served some purpose two thousand years ago, but not anymore. Think of the wishes. We're told the monks pray and whatever we wish will come true. Do you believe that? No, they burn the papers. Did I ever, in all my time at the Tower, see a single monk emit a single prayer? No. I'm telling you, the Father Paramount gives out these duties to keep the monks occupied, so they don't get bored and realize none of it has any purpose. None of it!" Neither Skiy nor Kem said anything. I turned on Skiy. "You stink like camel dung," I said.

"It's incense."

"It smells horrible," I said. "Why do you burn it?"

Kem stood and brushed off his toga. "I have to work this evening. I must attend to other matters first. Are you ready to go, Skiy?"

Skiy stood and walked to the door. He chewed a fingernail and turned back to me. "It reminds me of Gyanin," he said, "the incense. That's why I burn it."

"Come on," said Kem.

Someone knocked on the door. Skiy and Kem looked at each other. Kem opened the door. He opened *my* door. I sat on the couch unmoving.

Sfin's head peered around the doorframe. "Hello?" He looked at me, eyes as green as jasper. "Can I come in?"

"Of course," said Kem.

Sfin stepped into the room. He dripped on my carpet. Glane followed in a cloak of oilcloth.

32

Blade blinked at the leader of the smugglers. They sat together on the driver's platform as the world crept past. The cart groaned with every turn of the wheels, every step of the camels. "How long to the City?" said Blade.

"A few hours." The smuggler did not turn as he spoke. "We left the Citadel six days ago, yes? It takes six days from Citadel to City. In the dry season, not so long, but now the roads are wet."

"Why does that make a difference?"

"They could flood." The smuggler spat. "Provisions could rot. We may lose ourselves, or the men may mutiny. Robbers could attack."

"Do you think any of that will happen?" said Blade.

"Today?" The smuggler laughed. "We'll reach the City today. There are few robbers this close to civilization."

The rain-washed world spread out around them, the acid sea white and dappled. The road ran straight and deserted, swallowed by the mist before it met the horizon.

"And you will pay me when we reach the City, yes?" The smuggler did not have a name. In the last few days, he had asked this question more times than Blade could count.

"Yes," said Blade, "I'll pay you."

From around the side of the cart, the conversation of the other smugglers rose in a constant drone. Clicks and gargles punctuated all their words.

Blade swallowed. "Will Leque die?"

"Hah. You never know, do you?"

"No, I don't know."

"Probably not," said the smuggler. "He has broken ribs and his hands are crushed."

"Yes," said Blade, "I think so."

"On the Fortress Meadows," said the smuggler, "I once pinned down a gazelle and crushed his side with stones until I could no longer feel his ribs. I let him up and he ran away."

Blade was silent for a minute. "Why did you do that?"

"I did not want to damage the hide." He pulled a millipede — black and yellow — from his collar and ate it. "Shoot a gazelle, it tears a hole in the hide. We can't have damaged skins for sale."

Blade chewed a strip of salted meat. It was llama, the smugglers told him. Last night had been ostrich. Salt coated all of the smugglers' meat so thickly he could not tell the difference. Blade watched the millipede disappear between the man's teeth. He wondered how much longer he would have to ride this cart before he too would cultivate his own menagerie. He burrowed deeper into the protection of his donkey-hide robe, so heavy with wet he could hardly lift it.

He asked another question to distract from his chattering teeth: "Why are you called smugglers?"

"Because we smuggle. Hah! What manner of question is that?"

"But... you trade furs. There are spice traders and fabric traders, aren't there? Why can't you be fur traders?"

"Many people do not like how we work." He looked at Blade. "There *are* fur traders in the world. Yes there are. They have bought themselves licenses to hunt the deer and the wild cats. We hunt the same cats, but we do it on no one's authority."

"Why don't you get licenses?" said Blade.

"They come from the nobles. Any noble in any palace will do. But when they find that we are from the Errata, they won't license us."

"Why? What is the Errata?"

"You ask a lot of questions." The smuggler licked his lips. "Yaryk said you did. I could ask you what happened to Yaryk, but I can guess for myself. You want to know

about the Errata? No, you don't. You only think you do."
Before Blade could ask what the difference was, the smuggler went on. "The Errata is home to criminals," he said,
"except that most of us are criminals only because we live
there. The Citadel and the Metropolis" — he waved his
hand to the west — "used to send their convicts to the
Errata. They hoped the convicts would lose themselves in
the web of caves and never come back." He spat.

"How long ago was that?" said Blade.

"Two hundred years?" said the smuggler. "The criminals
found each other inside the stone. They wandered in the
dark, banded together, multiplied, and took over the
Metropolis."

"Oh," said Blade. "That was a long time ago."

The smuggler laughed. "It was," he said. "Of course
people returned to the Metropolis. Eventually they did.
The nobles led them back. There wasn't enough room in
the Citadel for all the people. They had to go somewhere.
The Metropolis is now much the same as before. The nobles
there hate the Errata."

"Could the people in the Metropolis move to the Errata?"

"They could," said the smuggler. "They wouldn't want
to, though. We still have a monarchy. No one wants to live
under a king anymore."

"What do you mean?" said Blade. "King?"

"One ruler."

"Like the nobles?" He talked of them now as 'the' nobles,
as if he were no longer one of them.

"No, not the nobles. There are hundreds of nobles. In
a monarchy there is only one ruler, one king, who makes
all the laws."

"How do you decide who he is?"

"He's born the king. The son of the previous king becomes king."

"Like an heir?"

"He is an heir."

"I was an heir," said Blade, "before I left."

"An heir of what?"

"I'm not sure," said Blade.

"You're a curious boy." The smuggler laughed. "I thought you simple the first time I met you."

The hours dragged on. The dampness plastered Blade's robe to his skin. He dozed. He tried to plan what he would do when he reached the City. Would he go back to the palace, insist that his grandfather take him in and shelter him? He could stay there quiet, secret; no one would know he was there. No one could send bees. Blade shook his head. He didn't even know who he was avoiding, who the man was who had come to his grandfather. What did it matter if everyone knew of the Radiance? What did it matter if the Ven family fell into shame? Blade was no longer part of it. And what harm — what bodily harm — could it do his grandfather? He had enough riches for the rest of his life.

Blade would not go to the palace. What did he care about the jewels of the Vens? Nothing at all. What did he care about life as a noble? Servants? Did he enjoy being dressed every morning? Bathed? All those hands on his body? Was that what he missed? He thought of Bry and the laughing white teeth, all the dust and blood in the alleyway. No hands. Please no hands. It was only the food he would miss.

No. Leque had taken him to hundreds of eateries around the City, open to any and all. He could thrive on those. He only wanted to see them again — Kem and Skiy. He wanted everyone, but only Kem and Skiy were left. Kem could save Leque. Yes — find Kem and save Leque.

"Look." The smuggler nodded into the fog ahead. "The City." The rain drizzled down. The mist swallowed everything. Out of the mist reared the nobles' spires, off-white like finger bones groping the sky.

"I'm getting Leque." Blade kicked free of his robe. He pushed aside the hide curtain to the cart's interior and scrambled over heaps of furs and bedrolls. "Leque!" he called. "Leque, wake up! We're almost at the City!"

Leque yawned and rolled over.

"Wake up. You have to come and see!"

Leque yawned again. He sat up slowly, and followed Blade through the swaying darkness to the front of the cart. Blade held the curtain back and pointed out, past the back of the smuggler on the driver's seat, and into the gray of the world. The spires drew closer already. The Marble Tower, brighter than hematite, glittered like polished glass. To either side of the cart, smaller paths crossed and merged, bloating the road to a highway.

They passed into the cloudbank. Blade could drink the air, sour with acid. The City disappeared above them. Other travelers materialized: men on mules, on foot, leading great birds on tethers. They cursed at the sight of the cart and swam away again into the fog.

One of the smugglers ran up beside the platform. He grabbed the platform's lip and swung himself onto it. He gibbered at the leader.

The leader of the smugglers pulled the cart to a halt. "You can walk from here," he told Blade.

"You won't take us all the way?"

"We visited the City last season. We don't want to return yet. We will make a spectacle of ourselves if we do." He grimaced.

Blade pulled the donkey hide over his head. The weight of it crushed his neck. He shuffled to the edge of the platform. The smuggler lowered him down to the road below. The cobblestones slid beneath Blade's feet. One step sideways would tumble him down the embankment. The sea glowed red, muted to rust in the fog.

Leque was helped down beside him. The leader of the smugglers followed unaided. He picked a moving speck from the collar of his robe and grinned at Blade. "You don't say much about my payment."

"But you have to come to the City," said Blade. "I don't have money with me."

The smuggler gestured to the driver. The cart groaned into motion again. "We're turning around," he said. "It is difficult to turn the cart." The bright blue hexagon glowed on his tongue. "If I don't come to the City, you can't pay me, yes?"

Blade nodded.

"I have no complaints."

"But—" said Blade.

"Thank you." Leque nodded in place of a bow. "Thank you very much. Come on, Blade, let's go." He strode into the fog. If his ribs still hurt him, he did not show it.

Blade stared after the retreating cart: huge, black, the furs swinging from its body like rags of skin. The gray wall devoured it. Blade hurried after Leque, afraid to lose him.

"You realize," said Leque. He wheezed now. "You realize that if your grandfather does not allow you to return, you don't have any money at all. You wouldn't have been able to pay him."

"I don't want to go back to the palace," said Blade.

"Why not?"

"I don't. I don't want to be a noble anymore."

"You wouldn't have been able to pay," said Leque. "What would you have done if he had insisted on pay?"

"I don't know."

They walked in silence. Leque slowed and leaned to one side. He continued on and said nothing. The sandstone arch of the gates appeared, looming ahead like a giant key-hole. They had only a few hundred steps to go.

Leque held out an arm and Blade stopped. "There may still be bees," he said.

"I know," said Blade.

A handful of guards stood at either side of the gates. They questioned each traveler as he passed through the arch. Gyanin was not among them.

"What brings you to the City?" said a guard with a red-black beard.

"We live here," said Leque, "on Armadillo Street at the end of the row."

The guard nodded. He waved them through. The square beyond the gates milled with people.

"It looks the same," said Leque.

"Does it?" Blade shivered.

Leque nodded. "But you've only been to the gates once before, haven't you?" He leaned toward Blade. "Maybe the rain will keep the bees away."

"Maybe they're gone," said Blade.

"Kem and Skiy also," said Leque. "Keep your eyes open for large blue birds."

Blade wished it was a joke, but he knew it was not. A cart of vegetables swerved to avoid them. The wheels sprayed mud, and the driver cursed. Leque herded Blade to the side of the square.

"Let's go to Gyanin's rooms," he said. "I doubt we'll find anyone there, but they're the closest to the gates."

"All right," said Blade. He could not stop shivering, however he tried.

Leque led them down a side road until it ran up against the City wall, a dripping bulwark of sandstone. To the left stretched line after line of shacks. Heaps of debris — doors, torn curtains, saddles, cart shafts — balanced one on top of another in imitation of shelter.

"Do people live here?"

"Yes," said Leque.

"Does Gyanin?"

"No." Leque nodded to the other side of the road, the right, where a block of sandstone jutted out from the wall. The sandstone block loomed up to the sky. A door had been carved at street-level. Leque led the way. Inside was a narrow stairwell, the steps uneven. They climbed. At intervals, other doorways had been hollowed out from the walls.

Leque counted the steps as they climbed. "Fifty-eight, fifty-nine. Here," he said. "This door." He knocked. "Gyanin?" No answer. Sacking muffled the window.

The door on the other side of the stairwell opened, and a man with a large nose and no shirt looked out. "Noise!" He shook a finger. "Stop the noise! I don't know you. Are you moving in? That room's vacant. Don't move in! I don't like the noise. Go away. Go away!" The door slammed.

"Let's go," said Leque.

Blade pounded on the shirtless man's door. "What happened to Gyanin?" he shouted. "Is Gyanin dead?"

"No noise!" shrieked the man inside. "No noise! Some of us have eardrums, you know! Go away!"

"We'll try Skiy's house," said Leque. He pulled Blade away.

They slogged along the muddy trench of Merchant's Alley. Blade paused at every step to shield his eyes, turn and look up and behind, where the Marble Tower leaned into the sky.

"It's not straight," said Blade. "The Marble Tower. It kind of bends. There, and there. Had you ever noticed that, Leque?"

"Look at this," said Leque. He pointed with a green and bandaged arm. "I don't think it's Skiy's shop anymore."

Gone were the display tables in the street, with their piles of shoes and sandals. The canopy that had once protected the tables now hung useless over bare cobbles. Spider webs, dust and smoke no longer coated the windows. The glass had been polished invisibly clean. Beside the door a sign read "Glyptic."

"What's that?" said Blade.

"Gem engraving."

Blade pushed open the door. Inside, turquoise-blue carpet muffled the floor. Pedestals stood around the room. Gems and crystals gleamed beneath glass.

A little man with no hair sat behind Skiy's workbench, a plate of vegetables before him. He ate as he worked. He glanced up, saw Blade, and bounced to his feet. "Can I help you?"

"No." Blade left. His eyes stung with tears. He rubbed them away with his hand and leaned back through the door. "Thank you anyway," he said, and closed it behind him.

Outside, Leque squatted underneath the canopy, reading the smaller writing on the sign. He stood up with a grunt.

"Skiy's not there," said Blade. "Where should we go now?"

"Kem's?" said Leque. "I don't think it matters."

The suns were fading low. The aroma of food drifted from every direction. Lights winked on in the public eating houses and private homes. A man walked past with a cauldron of garlic stew steaming over his shoulder.

Leque led the way deeper into the maze of the City, down the side road where the hospital workers lived. They stopped in front of Kem's house. The curtains were pulled closed, no light through the window. No one answered their knocks.

"Maybe he's working," said Blade. "He often works at night."

"Maybe he's dead," said Leque.

"We could write him a note and push it under the door."

"And what if the sender of the bees is still watching the house? What if he comes back every day to see if there are any clues about where we are — the other criminals who haven't been found?"

"We could ask for Kem at the hospital."

Leque shivered. "I don't want to go there."

"Glane's house, then?" said Blade. "It's close, isn't it?"

"Yes, fine. We'll ask his father. I doubt he will know. Glane's father may be dead by now."

"Why?"

"The whole family is poor. They may have starved."

Twilight hung thickly by the time they reached Glane's alley. They stumbled through the gloom and the puddled archipelago, past the closed doors and the windows with firelight behind the glass, the sounds of voices over a meal. Many of the window frames could not afford glass. One door was open: the door to Glane's house. They did not even have curtains.

Leque ducked through the doorway. Blade hung back in the mud of the alleyway. Leque's footsteps echoed over stone.

"There's nothing here!" he called. "All the furniture and everything — it's gone." He came out and sat on the doorstep. "At least it's dry. Do you want to sleep here tonight?"

Blade looked at the doorway, like a mouth or the entrance to an acid vault, a place to Release the bodies. "No," he said. "Where do you think they went?"

"I don't know." Leque stood. He stood stooped over, crunched to avoid the strain on his ribs. "You want to find a different doorstep to sleep on?"

"What about your house?"

"I don't want to go there," said Leque. It was too dark now to see his expression, to tell what Leque's face was doing. "We could go," he said at last. "I suppose we could go. I don't think we'll find anything there."

33

I looked at Glane. "Why are you here?"

"Ksar, he's your guest," said Kem. "Show some respect."

"He's not my guest. You're the one who invited him in."

"We're moving," said Glane. "My father decided. We've already left our old house."

"So?" I wanted to know where he was going. I wanted to ask him, but not with Kem standing there smiling, as if we were children and it was his duty to supervise. I had had enough supervision in my life; I didn't want any more.

Glane rocked on his heels. His clothes dripped a puddle on my carpet. "I just wanted to tell you," he muttered. "If you want to visit, you'll need to know where I live — I don't live where I used to."

Kem cleared a patch of my floor and sat down. He beckoned for Sfin and Glane to sit with him. Skiy returned to the couch and sat down beside me. He did not look at me. I wanted him to go away. I wanted them all to leave, except maybe Glane. I wanted to kick Glane in the ribs, really hard so it hurt, and then we could call it even.

"Where *are* you living now?" said Kem.

"Somewhere on the other side of the City."

"Close to the Library," said Sfin. "Do you know the area where the sandstone is russet-red, not white? That's where we live."

Skiy leaned forward. "How does your father afford it?"

Sfin fought free of his oilskin cloak. Underneath, his toga was olive green and woven with golden threads. They shimmered like running stallions when he moved. He took a pouch from a cord around his neck, undid the clasp, and poured a mound of coins on the floor.

Everyone stared. Glane said, "You promised you wouldn't bring that."

"Where did you get it?" said Skiy.

"My father has a lot of it."

"Sfin!" Glane raked the coins off the carpet. "Put them back in the bag. You said you wouldn't bring them."

"Why else did I come?" said Sfin. They glared at each other — Glane and his brother. They looked so similar it was uncanny. It looked as though Glane were arguing with himself, or a smaller version of himself, a few years younger. "Glane," said Sfin, "we have to explain it to them. Ksar would like you better if he knew what was going on."

The silence pooled.

"I don't care what's going on," I said, to fill the void. That was not what I had meant to say.

"No, no," said Kem. "Please tell us, Sfin. Here, your cloaks are wet; let me take them for you. You must be cold. Would you like a blanket?"

Glane tangled himself in his oilskin. He wrestled it off at last. His tunic was pale blue with a silver collar. Kem took the dripping cloaks — Glane's and Sfin's — and laid them by the door to dry. He invaded my bedroom and returned with blankets, one for Sfin and one for Glane. He then sat down. "Please tell us, Sfin. Is this about your father and his money?"

"Yes," said Sfin. "He's an alchemist. He makes gold."

"I thought he wasn't doing well," I said.

"Be quiet," said Skiy.

"He's doing well now," said Sfin. He glanced at his older brother and swallowed. "Glane's made him successful. No, no, I'll explain." The boy rocked where he sat. He bit his lip. "I don't know how to explain."

"Do your best," said Kem. "Would you like some tea while you think?"

"No he wouldn't," I said. "I don't have any." Maybe if I was rude enough, Kem would leave.

"No thank you," said Sfin. He bit his lip until it bled. "One time my father made himself grow feathers."

"What?" said Kem.

"About three years ago." Sfin studied the ceiling. "I must have been little then. I was only eight. No, maybe nine. The day before he grew feathers, he'd been stung by a bee on the back of his hand. Then, when he was working at his forge the next day, he spilled some chemicals on his hand and where the bee sting was, he grew white feathers." Sfin thought for another moment. "It was pretty funny," he said. "He spent all day staring at his hand. In the evening he pulled out his feathers. He only grew one or two a day. After a week they stopped. I thought they were beautiful."

"No they weren't," said Glane. "They hurt."

"I mean Father's feathers," said Sfin.

"But then Glane grew them," Skiy pointed out. "Are you saying Glane's feathers were an accident? He just poured chemicals on himself, and because he'd been stung by the bee... What about Gyanin?"

"Oh, it wasn't an accident." Sfin shook his head. "My father meant to do it."

Glane covered his face with his arm. "Sfin, you promised you wouldn't..."

"Your father made Glane grow feathers?" Kem stared intently at the brothers. "Why? I cannot imagine why a man would inflict such suffering on his own son."

"He needs the feathers for his alchemy." Sfin rubbed his lip. The blood smeared off on his finger. He bent close to Kem and whispered. We all heard his words. "He used to use the feathers from the crest of the Radiance. He would take just a strand at a time. He was afraid the monks would notice if he took too much. Scarlet roc feathers are magic if you know what to do. You only need a tiny strand." He looked around at us, eyes wide. "Please don't tell the monks what my father did."

"They wouldn't care," I said.

"When the crest went missing," said Sfin, "my father needed more feathers. His alchemy wouldn't work without them. He couldn't make any gold. We almost starved. He had to make Glane grow feathers so we wouldn't die."

The rain dripped like falling beads outside the house. "How did he know Glane's feathers would work?"

"He tested on himself," said Sfin. "He let me watch when he did it. It took twenty of his feathers to make three gold coins. With scarlet roc feathers, you could use a tiny strand — so tiny you could hardly see it — to make ten coins. Human feathers weren't as good, but we had no other way to make money, so Father decided it was worth it."

"He should have inflicted it upon himself," said Kem. "As a father—"

"It hurts a lot," said Sfin.

"It does," said Glane.

"He couldn't concentrate on alchemy when he was in that much pain," said Sfin. "Also, you lose your hands."

The rain dripped down still harder. Kem swiveled toward Glane. "Did you know what was going on?"

"No." Glane shook his head.

"It sounds like Sfin knew well enough," I said. "Did you help your father plan it all?"

"Of course not," said Kem. "Don't you remember his wishes? 'I hope my brother stops growing feathers'? 'I wish my father would stop'? He wouldn't wish such a thing if he had been the cause of the dilemma. Isn't that right, Sfin?"

Sfin stared at us. "You read my wishes?"

"I'm a monk, remember?" I spread my arms. "Or I was."

"I didn't know what Father was doing." Sfin looked at Glane, who hid his face behind his arm. "I didn't know at first, at least. I figured it out."

"Yes." Kem smiled. It was almost condescending. No doubt he meant it as encouragement. "How did you figure it out?"

"I wanted to visit Glane at the hospital. I'd found his cobras and I wanted to give them back. But the people at the hospital wouldn't let me see him. I was angry because I didn't know why they wouldn't." Sfin dared a look at Kem, but Kem wasn't angry, and so he went on, "Whenever my father came back from the hospital, his pockets bulged with feathers."

"Revolting!" said Kem. "He plucked his own son like a chicken?"

"We were all so hungry," said Sfin. "I asked and he kind of told me."

"Who?"

"My father. He kind of explained what he was doing to Glane. He said it wasn't natural for people to grow feathers. Of course, it would wear off soon. He hoped it would wear off, at least. The chemicals he'd given Glane were stronger than the ones he had spilled on himself though, and so now he was worried."

"Me too," said Glane. He stared at the floor.

"Why did he use bees?" said Skiy. A strange thing was happening with Skiy's face. It looked as if it was going to burst. Maybe he was going to cry. "Why be stung by a live bee? If bee venom is needed, why not mix it with the rest of the poison?"

"He didn't want Glane to know," said Sfin. "He hoped Glane would blame the bee and not look for anyone else. He injected the bees with Glane's smell." Sfin followed Glane's gaze to the floor. He dropped his voice to a whisper. "They were only supposed to sting Glane."

Skiy stood. He hurled a length of chain across the room. It had once been a necklace. "What about Gyanin! Gyanin is dead. Have we forgotten him? Have we forgotten he had feathers when he died?"

"Some of the bees escaped." Sfin edged across the floor, closer to his brother. "The night my father first made gold from Glane's feathers, I think he got drunk. He kept the beehive in a net, just inside the door. He was drunk and he didn't seal the netting properly. We hid in the back room and stuffed every crack with blankets. We stayed there for more than a day. So the bees went outside instead." He swallowed and held Glane's knee. "I guess they found your friend."

"But Glane's smell?" shouted Skiy. "Gyanin didn't smell like Glane!"

"Please, Skiy," said Kem, "sit down."

Or you could leave, I thought. Why don't both of you leave.

"Gyanin took Glane's pouch," said Kem. "Maybe the pouch smelled like Glane. He wore it against his chest, you remember."

"Your father killed Gyanin." Skiy's face flushed red as garnet. "I hope he doesn't enjoy his gold for long."

I'd been stung by a hundred bees. I didn't say anything. If no one cared about Ksar and his suffering, I wouldn't bother them with the recollection. I sulked instead, too stunned to say anything. I folded my arms. I willed them all to leave my house. I needed to think without people there.

"What about Ksar?" said Kem. "He didn't grow feathers."

"The poison burned off as they flew," said Sfin. "The bees burned it off in energy." He looked at Glane. "Father said that. It passed through their bloodstreams or something. Maybe he hadn't injected them all."

"Did Father tell you that?" Glane bit his collar.

"He didn't want to," said Sfin, but he nodded. "Yes, he told me."

"You're sure you weren't helping him?" said Skiy. "You seem to know everything your father did."

"I didn't help him!" Sfin planted his face in Glane's shoulder. The pale blue of Glane's tunic smeared dark with tears. Sfin cried without making a sound. "Why would I want Glane to grow feathers?" He hugged his brother's arm. "I was afraid you were going to die. I missed you. I really missed you, Glane. I asked Father. I finally made him tell me. I *made* him. I swear I never wanted you to grow any feathers!"

Glane patted Sfin's head. He puckered his face like a sour orange.

Kem shrugged a carrying bag from one shoulder. He snapped the clasp and rifled through its contents, came out with a metal tin and laid it on the floor between Sfin and himself. "Have a sweetened sesame cake," he said. "No more questions until you've eaten."

Glane opened the tin. Sfin took a cake. We passed the tin around. I took three cakes. I would have taken more, but Kem glared. Skiy refused them. He took a scroll from his belt, hid his face behind it, and read. Kem produced a bag of dried papaya from the same mysterious recess.

There were not enough slices to be passed around, so they stopped at Glane.

Sfin relinquished his hold on Glane's arm and sat up. "You're going to ask about Blade now, aren't you?" he said. Papaya filled his mouth. His voice was unnaturally calm.

"Yes," said Kem, "I was. Do you know what happened?" Sfin nodded.

"Are you ready to tell us?" Kem replaced the tin to his bag.

"My father went to the Ven palace," said Sfin. "He told Y'az Xzaven that Blade had to leave the City. He didn't mean to be cruel. Honestly he didn't. This was after the bees had escaped. My father knew who all of you were. All of Glane's friends, I mean. He wanted Blade to leave so the bees wouldn't find him. It would be all over the City if a noble turned into a bird. So really it was for Blade's own good that he left."

"Except that Blade came to my house," I said, "which was exactly where the bees were headed."

"I used to spend a lot of time at your house," said Glane.

I caught the past tense but I didn't say anything, not with Kem and Skiy listening in. I was sure they had caught it also.

"If Blade grew feathers," said Sfin, "I'm sure his grandfather would have investigated. It was good my father made him leave."

"How did he persuade the Y'az?" said Kem. "Surely if all he did was threaten, he would have been arrested."

Sfin bit his lip.

"He told the Y'az about the Radiance," I said.

"You don't know that's true!" said Glane.

"Blade told me," I said. Spat, more like. I would rather strike Glane, hard in the face, not fight him with words. Neither of us understood words. I wanted to hurt him in a way he would understand. I said, "And I wonder, Glane, how your father knew about the Radiance? Hmm, I wonder. Wait — could it have been because you told him?"

"Please, Ksar." Kem held up his hand. "I'm sure—"

"I was dying!" Glane pounced to his feet. "That's why I told him." He stood over me with his fists working, like a mongrel puppy at its first fight. "Maybe if you were turning into a bird and dying, you would have told your father the truth as well!"

"My father was a drunken idiot," I said. "As far as I'm concerned, all fathers are idiots. Yours certainly seems to be."

"How many successful alchemists do you know?" said Glane. "There aren't many, and my father is one of them."

"Because he steals feathers. If he had to do the spells by himself, he would fail like everyone else."

"He has nine children!" shouted Glane. "If you had nine children—"

"I'd be stupid," I said.

"You'd try to feed them."

"No, he was stupid to have so many," I said. "Look how they're all turning out."

"That insults Sfin!" Glane jumped. He jumped on top of me. "No one insults Sfin!" He crushed me into the couch. My head hit the wall. His hands found my throat and ate into it. Blue feathers swam in front of my eyes, and the rail around the bed in the hospital, and the pigeons breaking their wings against the glass.

"Glane!" squealed Sfin. "Glane!"

"Get off!" shouted Kem. He pulled Glane away and held him, wriggling.

I struck Glane's stomach as hard as I could. He grunted and folded in half. Kem stepped back suddenly. Glane fell and his shoulder struck the floor with a sound like snapping wood. I shook my hand. It throbbed. I stared at my knuckles, as if I hadn't intended to hit anyone. Skiy, on the couch beside me, still read his scroll. Kem knelt beside Glane. Glane lay on the floor with his face in the rug. He breathed like a swarm of bees. The skirt of his tunic was ripped. He sat up at last, his face an amazing shade of white.

"I came to tell you I'm moving." He pouted, still clutching his stomach. "I won't live close to you anymore. You don't need to worry about me. Maybe you won't see me any more. Maybe never again."

"Sorry," I said. My neck hurt where he'd grabbed me. I was so humiliated I could have eaten my shoe.

"Surely you won't go back to your father?" said Kem. "Please, come and stay with me for a while until you find other lodgings."

There he went again, Kem the martyr. It wasn't enough to make *me* the villain; he had to be the savior atoning for my sins. It wouldn't work this time.

"They can stay with me," I said.

Someone knocked on the door.

I stood before Kem could move. "Who's there?"

The knock came again.

I stepped to the door and jerked the handle. It was dark outside now, night. The rain drizzled down. A shape loomed out of the dark — a hulk of wet fur, twice as broad as a man.

"Ksar!" It leapt on me. I jumped back, too slow. Half of it leapt on me. The fur fell away, and there was Leque, grinning through the dirtiest beard I had ever seen. His cheekbones jutted like spoons. He dug his elbows into my shoulders. "Ksar! I thought you were dead. Blade told me you were dead! Blade, you buffoon, what were you talking about?"

The other half of the creature sneezed. "I *thought* he was dead," said Blade. "I saw him stung." Blade's hair stood up in a frazzled mass of yellow-white. Donkey hair covered his tunic, camel hair, and hair of other animals I did not recognize. If I had seen him lying in an alleyway, I would have mistaken him for the corpse of a dog.

Blade extended a hand and I shook it. "I'm glad you're alive," he said.

He tried to do the same for Kem — shake his hand — but Kem swept him up in an open embrace. "We were talking about you," said Kem, "weren't we, Ksar?"

"Maybe." I didn't remember.

"What did you say about me?"

"We said what an awful nuisance you were and how nice it's been to have you gone. No, of course not." Kem crushed him again. Blade's fur rubbed off on Kem's arms.

"Where's Yaryk?" he said. "Has Yaryk come back with you?"

"No." Leque shook his head. "We should all be glad."

Skiy grunted his welcome from the couch.

I extricated myself from Leque. I was not like Sfin; I did not like being plastered to my brother for more than a second, possibly two. "We put the crest back on the Radiance," I said, "and the bees are gone; we haven't seen them in weeks."

"Did you hear that?" Leque shouted. "Everyone! The bees are gone!"

Glane crawled to the door. Sfin followed. Sfin fished his sandals from the pile and put them on. He extricated Glane's and handed them over.

"Where are you going?" I demanded.

"Glane!" Leque jumped at the sight. "What happened to your feathers?"

"No," said Kem. "Leque, what happened to your arms?" Bandages swaddled him up to the elbows. Through tears in the wrapping, my brother's skin showed green. "Come, sit on the couch," said Kem. "I must see this immediately. How did this happen?"

"Sfin and I are leaving," said Glane. "We have to unpack."

"You moved?" said Blade.

"Most of our brothers are too small to help," said Sfin.

The room felt full to bursting. After so many days alone, and so many days with the Radiance, this sudden crowd made me claustrophobic. "I'll come and help you," I said. I found a pair of sandals, hoped they were mine, and slipped them on. No one noticed as we left; Leque's arms had distracted them all.

"Did you ever get your cobras back, Glane?"

"He gave them to me," said Sfin. "Do you want to see them? I brought them with me."

"No, that's all right," I said quickly.

"I got tired of cobras," said Glane. "I have miniature llamas now." It was too dark to see his face. I could not tell if he was lying or not. It did not matter with Glane.

"You're crazy," I said.

"You're worse."

"No, actually..." And so we debated, on the long wet
walk through the dark.

34

Someone prodded Yaryk's spine. He looked up. The guard stood back from the cage and fumbled through a ring of keys. He selected one, inserted it into the lock and turned.

"Stand up," he said. "Clasp your hands behind your back. Face the wall."

Yaryk obeyed. The guard tied his wrists together. He was led from the cage. Moans and jeers washed around him from the lines of prisoners. Yaryk's feet weighed like stone, tingling after so many days without use. But he kept pace with his captor; he would not be dragged.

Rain hit his face.

"Who ordered my release?" said Yaryk.

"Y'az Drens."

"Why?"

"I don't know," said the guard. He led Yaryk on through the Citadel streets, around corners and through black puddles. "You should be grateful," said the guard.

"I grovel in gratitude."

They reached the gates. The gate wardens nodded salutations. They continued down the highway. At last they stopped. The guard from the Gaol pulled the keys from his belt. He unlocked Yaryk's manacles.

"Go." He waved a hand at the open road. "Don't return to the Citadel. You'll be shot if you return. Now go."

Yaryk folded his arms. He tapped one foot. He watched the guard walk away. The man walked with one hand at his belt to hold his sword from chafing his leg. Yaryk turned to the roadway. The acid stank. Sea level had risen since he had last passed here, though that might be no more than his perception. He willed it to rise still higher and drown the road.

The first traveler to pass him was a man on a donkey. Yaryk hailed the man, and he steered his beast over and stopped.

"Tell me," said Yaryk, "how do affairs stand in the Citadel?"

The man snuffled into a handkerchief. "What kind of affairs?"

"The conflict between the nobles and the Bedouin." Yaryk smiled. "The Bedouin's capture of the Glebe, the workers slaughtered before its gates. How stands the situation now? Has the Glebe been surrounded?"

"Shouldn't think so." The man puckered his face. "Haven't heard of any trouble with the Bedouin. If there was trouble, I suppose it's been stamped out by now." He kicked his donkey in the belly, the blow producing a wet slap. The two of them waddled away.

Yaryk watched them go. No trouble with the Bedouin? Stamped out? So this is what becomes of all your work and bloodshed, Liop. The people — they don't even know it happened. Nobles assassinated in their beds? That wasn't enough for the people to notice? No, but they must have noticed; Leque's picture had been all over the Citadel for killing Gyrt. Perhaps not everyone had seen it. Not the idiot man on the donkey. If you wanted to travel, you should walk on your own legs. You should not trust your journey to a common beast. Perhaps everyone in the Citadel, with the sole exception of that man and his animal, had heard of the rebellion. Why had Yaryk even asked the fool, when his words were no proof of anything? He would wait for another, more competent traveler. But no other travelers came. So he would not ask. Perhaps, if he did, they would only answer the same.

Yaryk gazed down the endless road. It was time to wander and never return. Instead, Yaryk's feet were drawn back down the road, back the way he had come, toward the menace of sepia stone. He turned to the right before he reached the gates, down the path that hugged to the wall, then branched away, over the expanse of the sea: the tree-lined corridor to the Glebe. Once he'd left the main highway, he passed no one, neither going nor coming. The road was deserted. The rain sang like feathers on the face of the sea, a gentle, silken slap.

Yaryk stopped. The gates of the Glebe stood open. Inside, the kiwi vines bowed in the wet. The roar of water on leaves was deafening. He crossed the entrance square where the workers had died, the bald and rutted earth where the Bedouin had wrenched the young vines from their beds. He ducked under the foliage. He fought his way to the old site of the Bivouac. The oilskins thrashed. Yaryk watched them writhe with the beat of the rain. There was no wind. A man appeared from behind the Bivouac, his arms loaded down in cloths.

"What are you doing?" said Yaryk.

The man jumped. He pushed the hair from his face. "Taking these Stone-accursed skins off the vines before they suffocate." He waved an arm at the mess of ropes and pelts. "You've been sent to help? Why didn't you bring a cloak? You've never seen the rainy season before?"

Yaryk stared at the remains of the Bivouac. "This is all that's left?"

"Oh, there was a lot more this morning, but some of us have been working for our pay."

"What happened to the Bedouin?"

"They left yesterday." The man glared. He glared a long time. "I don't remember you being hired." Yaryk said nothing, and so he went on, "You're not a restoration worker, are you?"

"No, I'm not."

"Who are you then? You just wandered in here to see what's going on? Well now you've seen it, you rag-tag. If you want to be useful, you can find the overseer and ask for a job. Otherwise leave."

Yaryk's jaw twitched. It made it hard to speak. "Did all the Bedouin leave?"

"All but one."

"They left of their own accord?"

"Drens parleyed with the leader. If they didn't leave, the nobles would surround the Glebe and force them out.

Frankly, it's a good thing they left." The man laughed. "A
siege of the Glebe could have lasted seasons." He waved
an arm. "Now go find the overseer."

Yaryk pushed his way through the trees. Leader? When
had they ever had a capable leader? Who had taken the
puppet-posting after Yaryk left? Was it Mehrzh, Gwall?
More likely Jarb. Jarb the hypocrite. He had criticized Yaryk
for abandoning the cause, and then he threw up his own
hands and walked away. So much for Bedouin pride.

Yaryk passed handfuls of workers as he walked, gathering the fruit into baskets, piling fresh soil around the roots
of trees. None of them turned as he passed. The last line
of peach trees ended, giving way to beds of strawberries.
Yaryk squatted between the rows. He kneaded his hands
in the mud. Why in the Stars had he returned to the Citadel?
He had sparked an uprising, but the uprising accomplished
nothing. Nothing but the deaths of nobles, and the ruination of a handful of Bedouin lives. He had driven Blade
and Leque away. Had Yaryk done all that? Had he truly
destroyed so much?

No, stop. He must stop thinking. He stood and pushed
his way through the bushes again, all the way to the sitting
area, with the open grass where the guards had been tied.
A black cloth plastered down in the rain, draped the bench
where Leque had been tied. A body lay beneath the cloth.
He recognized the shape of a body. He had seen enough
of them in the last few days. The sitting area was empty:
only him and the unknown dead. He crossed to the bench
and pulled back the cloth. A boy lay cold on his back, arms
folded. His chest was a clotted gore. The rain had pushed
back his hair, glittering damp from his face. The boy was
Bry.

Yaryk stared at the body. He stared a long time, while
the water ran down and dripped from the end of his nose.
It fell and pooled across Bry's eyes, ran down his temples
and into the marsh of his hair. Why had Bry remained,
when everyone else had gone?

"You idiot boy," he muttered. "You know you're insane.
You thought we could take the Citadel? Us? A handful of
men? Uncoordinated? Unsupported? You thought that

stabbing guards with your knife was enough to win back
the Guild? You fool." Yaryk spat. "Did you think you could
hold the Glebe by yourself? Look where it has brought you.
Death. You couldn't do it. It couldn't be done." Yaryk pulled
the cloth back over the corpse. "'*Find a better home in the
Stars,*'" he quoted. "I hope they Release you."

Yaryk left the sitting area and ducked beneath the cover
of trees. He took the first ladder he found, leaning up
against an orange tree. "I only need it a moment," he told
the worker. He carried the ladder through the strawberries. He set it against the marble wall, climbed to the top
wrung, onto the flat of the wall, then reached and dragged
the ladder up beside him. He climbed down the other side.
Behind the wall, the churn of rain on leaves died away.

Ahead was the path, lapped close by the acid. Yaryk had
not walked this path in decades. He did not remember
where it led. He pushed the ladder into the sea. It hissed
and dissolved.

Time to walk.

Epilogue

In the dry season of the Year of the Sentient Onion

At ground level, Glane and I were tallied by the green-robed monk at the reception desk. They liked to keep track of numbers at the Marble Tower, one sheet for arriving and another for departing visitors. Someone told them it was important, this constant tabulation.

The Marble Tower is the tallest structure in the City. We climbed a million stairs, up through the labyrinth of rooms where pools of acid, multi-colored, bubbled beside the steps. Over the pools grew the trees: almond, peach and pistachio, their branches decked in wish papers, scribbled and hanging on golden threads. We passed other early risers as we climbed, here to make their prayers. I wondered if the man with the squid in his teeth had received salvation.

Halfway up the Tower we turned off the main stairwell, down a twisting corridor, all gray marble and yellow veins through the walls. We climbed more stairs, ramps, along another passageway, and arrived at last at a door that was open. A drop of crystal, huge as a casket, hung from the ceiling. A railinged platform ringed the wall. No one stood in the room.

"He'll never be here," said Glane.

"Eventually he will."

"You're only going to find him if you go to the tally desk," said Glane, "and ask. Come on. They're probably waiting for us."

We ran down the almond-lined stairs, through the marble reception room, back through the doors and out into the street. Glane crossed the road, between the camel carts that passed no more than a breath away from spurning him into the dust. He squinted down into a grate, half-hidden in the lee of the curb. "Just sewage, do you think?"

"I think so."

"Ksar?" He adjusted the satchel on his back. He blinked at me through the dark rags of his hair. I must have been a silhouette against the light of the suns behind. "Ksar, if I killed a little person who looked exactly like me, do you think my intestines would fall out?"

"No," I said. "Intestines don't fall out that easily."

"I didn't think so." He looked over my shoulder to the Marble Tower, its pinnacle devoured in the haze. "Come on," he said.

Merchant's Alley stirred into life as we reached Iander's shop. Turquoise-blue awnings waved above the street, matching the carpet that covered the floor. Pedestals and gem cases ringed the room. A table spread out with tools sat in the corner. A short, plump man stood behind the table. He held a candle against a piece of rock, and glared at the stone. He glanced up, saw Glane and I, and set down his candle.

"You're early," he said.

"Sorry," said Glane. "We tried to be on time."

"The key to punctuality," said Iander, "is to look at clocks."

"There aren't any clocks in the Marble Tower."

He thrust the rock he'd been examining under my nose. "Look at this!" he cried. "A crack! They sold me a fractured amethyst!"

I was saved by the door. It opened to admit Kem, timely as always. He held the door open and Skiy and Sfin followed in his wake. Sfin carried a clipboard of medical statistics under his arm. He had cut his hair short like Kem's. He donated more money to the hospital than the rest of us combined. Kem thought it important that there be eight of us, though our meetings now held no purpose.

Skiy crossed the carpet to Glane. "Did you bring the fleece?"

Glane shrugged off his satchel. He upended a bundle of llama wool, amber-brown and softer than cloud, into the cobbler's arms. We were all entitled to the use of Glane's merchandise.

"You really must sell this City-wide," said Skiy. "Do you have any idea, the profits you would make?"

Glane shook his head. "I told you — it's too much for the llamas." Glane's llamas were the height of his hand. "Their coats grow slowly," he said. "Maybe next year when the herd expands." For now he and Skiy were partners. Glane provided the wool and Skiy made the clothes. I should no longer call him a cobbler. He was now a tailor — it was easier on the lungs. He only occasionally coughed up black tar.

"Ksar," said Kem, "did you find the Paramount?"

"No," I said. "I'll never find him."

The door opened again, this time to admit a young man in a stone mason's tunic. "Good morning!" He pushed the flaxen-blonde hair from his eyes and smiled at us all. "Is Leque here yet?"

"Not yet," said Iander.

"Did he tell you if he'd be late, Ksar?"

I shook my head. "I'm sure he will be."

Blade always assumed. He assumed that I, Leque's brother, always knew Leque's whereabouts. I never did. Now that Leque had moved away and really did live on the other side of the City, Blade knew twice as much about his doings as I ever did.

"I overheard the most amusing conversation on the way here," said Blade. He turned the sign that hung in the window from 'OPEN' to 'CLOSED.' "I was in the confectionary's shop. Two customers were arguing about the cost of sugared dates, each mistaking the other for the shop-keeper. After that, I simply had to buy some." He produced a parcel from his pocket. "Who wants a sugared date?"

We all held out our hands.

The door opened for the last time and Leque came in. He extended his hand — his one and only hand, with its three fingers — along with the rest of us.

"We've begun another housing complex beyond the palaces," he said, by way of greeting. Sugared date filled his mouth. "Again, more workers to hire. I wish they could all be as respectful as you, Blade. But no, the same questions: How did you lose your arm? Was it when you were a mason? Is this work dangerous?"

"You assure them of their safety, I hope," said Kem.

"Of course. Even if I *had* lost my arm in construction, I wouldn't tell them so. That would reflect badly on the Guild."

"You do warn them of their risks though, don't you?" said Kem.

"Of course, of course." Leque waved his arm. He looked around. "We're all here now," he said. "Shall we begin?"

We filed into Iander's back storeroom. The space was dim. It smelled of polish and grinding stones. We sat down on our cushions, Glane and I with our backs to the curtain, so as to be able to escape as quickly as possible when the opportunity came. An incense stick lay before each cushion. We left them unlit. They were only there because no one had taken them away.

"To begin," said Kem, "I act as financial manager for a number of charities." He rustled papers in the gloom. How could he read in this light? "The Fellowship of the White Horse, for one, is in desperate need of donations."

"What do they spend their money on?" said Glane.

"We rescue horses," said Kem, "that would otherwise be given up to the slaughterhouses because of age or injury."

"What do you do with them?" said Blade.

"Once they have recovered, we sell them at low prices. If there are no buyers, they remain in our care until the end of their days."

"I need to buy a horse next year," said Blade, "for when I go traveling."

As if he had ever been out of the City more than once in his life. As if he hadn't been miserable all that time, and wanted nothing more than to return to his home.

Sometimes I wanted to kill them all, I really did. Sometimes I wanted to close my eyes and listen to their voices forever. Blade promised to write from his travels. I hoped he would.

Skiy's voice: "Have any of you heard the legend of the Tree of Power?"

"I haven't," said Iander. "Tell us, please!"

I closed my eyes and listened.

Our titles are available at major book stores
and local independent resellers who support
Science Fiction and Fantasy readers like you.

EDGE Science Fiction
and Fantasy Publishing

Tesseract Books

Dragon Moon Press

www.edgewebsite.com
www.dragonmoonpress.com

Our titles are available at major book stores and local independent resellers who support Science Fiction and Fantasy readers like you.

Alien Deception by Tony Ruggiero -(tp) - ISBN-13: 978-1-896944-34-0
Alien Revelation by Tony Ruggiero (tp) - ISBN-13: 978-1-896944-34-8
Alphanauts by J. Brian Clarke (tp) - ISBN-13: 978-1-894063-14-2
Apparition Trail, The by Lisa Smedman (tp) - ISBN-13: 978-1-894063-22-7
As Fate Decrees by Denysé Bridger (tp) - ISBN-13: 978-1-894063-41-8

Billibub Baddings and The Case of the Singing Sword by Tee Morris (tp)
  - ISBN-13: 978-1-896944-18-0
Black Chalice, The by Marie Jakober (hb) - ISBN-13: 978-1-894063-00-5
Blue Apes by Phyllis Gotlieb (pb) - ISBN-13: 978-1-895836-13-4
Blue Apes by Phyllis Gotlieb (hb) - ISBN-13: 978-1-895836-14-1

Chalice of Life, The by Anne Webb (tp) - ISBN-13: 978-1-896944-33-3
Chasing The Bard by Philippa Ballantine (tp) - ISBN-13: 978-1-896944-08-1
Children of Atwar, The by Heather Spears (pb) - ISBN-13: 978-0-88878-335-6
Clan of the Dung-Sniffers by Lee Danielle Hubbard (pb) - ISBN-13: 978-1-894063-05-0
Claus Effect, The by David Nickle & Karl Schroeder (pb) - ISBN-13: 978-1-895836-34-9
Claus Effect, The by David Nickle & Karl Schroeder (hb) - ISBN-13: 978-1-895836-35-6
Complete Guide to Writing Fantasy, The - Volume 1: Alchemy with Words
  - edited by Darin Park and Tom Dullemond (tp)
  - ISBN-13: 978-1-896944-09-8
Complete Guide to Writing Fantasy, The - Volume 2: Opus Magus
  - edited by Tee Morris and Valerie Griswold-Ford (tp)
  - ISBN-13: 978-1-896944-15-9
Complete Guide to Writing Fantasy, The - Volume 3: The Author's Grimoire
  - edited by Valerie Griswold-Ford & Lai Zhao (tp)
  - ISBN-13: 978-1-896944-38-8
Complete Guide to Writing Science Fiction, The - Volume 1: First Contact
  - edited by Dave A. Law & Darin Park (tp)
  - ISBN-13: 978-1-896944-39-5
Courtesan Prince, The by Lynda Williams (tp) - ISBN-13: 978-1-894063-28-9

Dark Earth Dreams by Candas Dorsey & Roger Deegan (comes with a CD)
  - ISBN-13: 978-1-895836-05-9
Darkling Band, The by Jason Henderson (tp) - ISBN-13: 978-1-896944-36-4
Darkness of the God by Amber Hayward (tp) - ISBN-13: 978-1-894063-44-9
Darwin's Paradox by Nina Munteanu (tp) - ISBN-13: 978-1-896944-68-5
Daughter of Dragons by Kathleen Nelson - (tp) - ISBN-13: 978-1-896944-00-5
Determine Your Destiny #1: Petrified World by Piotr Brynczka (pb)
  - ISBN-13: 978-1-894063-11-1
Distant Signals by Andrew Weiner (tp) - ISBN-13: 978-0-88878-284-7
Dominion by J. Y. T. Kennedy (tp) - ISBN-13: 978-1-896944-28-9
Dragon Reborn, The by Kathleen H. Nelson - (tp) - ISBN-13: 978-1-896944-05-0
Dragon's Fire, Wizard's Flame by Michael R. Mennenga (tp)
  - ISBN-13: 978-1-896944-13-5
Dreams of an Unseen Planet by Teresa Plowright (tp) - ISBN-13: 978-0-88878-282-3

Dreams of the Sea by Élisabeth Vonarburg (tp) - ISBN-13: 978-1-895836-96-7
Dreams of the Sea by Élisabeth Vonarburg (hb) - ISBN-13: 978-1-895836-98-1

Eclipse by K. A. Bedford (tp) - ISBN-13: 978-1-894063-30-2
Even The Stones by Marie Jakober (tp) - ISBN-13: 978-1-894063-18-0

Fires of the Kindred by Robin Skelton (tp) - ISBN-13: 978-0-88878-271-7
Firestorm of Dragons edited by Michele Acker & Kirk Dougal (tp)
   - ISBN-13: 978-1-896944-80-7
Forbidden Cargo by Rebecca Rowe (tp) - ISBN-13: 978-1-894063-16-6

Game of Perfection, A by Élisabeth Vonarburg (tp)
   - ISBN-13: 978-1-894063-32-6
Green Music by Ursula Pflug (tp) - ISBN-13: 978-1-895836-75-2
Green Music by Ursula Pflug (hb) - ISBN-13: 978-1-895836-77-6
Gryphon Highlord, The by Connie Ward (tp) - ISBN-13: 978-1-896944-38-8

Healer, The by Amber Hayward (tp) - ISBN-13: 978-1-895836-89-9
Healer, The by Amber Hayward (hb) - ISBN-13: 978-1-895836-91-2
Hounds of Ash and other tales of Fool Wolf, The by Greg Keyes (pb)
   - ISBN-13: 978-1-894063-09-8
Human Thing, The by Kathleen H. Nelson - (hb) - ISBN-13: 978-1-896944-03-6
Hydrogen Steel by K. A. Bedford (tp) - ISBN-13: 978-1-894063-20-3

i-ROBOT Poetry by Jason Christie (tp) - ISBN-13: 978-1-894063-24-1

Jackal Bird by Michael Barley (pb) - ISBN-13: 978-1-895836-07-3
Jackal Bird by Michael Barley (hb) - ISBN-13: 978-1-895836-11-0
JEMMA7729 by Phoebe Wray (tp) - ISBN-13: 978-1-894063-40-1

Keaen by Till Noever (tp) - ISBN-13: 978-1-894063-08-1
Keeper's Child by Leslie Davis (tp) - ISBN-13: 978-1-894063-01-2

Lachlei by M. H. Bonham (tp) - ISBN-13: 978-1-896944-69-2
Land/Space edited by Candas Jane Dorsey and Judy McCrosky (tp)
   - ISBN-13: 978-1-895836-90-5
Land/Space edited by Candas Jane Dorsey and Judy McCrosky (hb)
   - ISBN-13: 978-1-895836-92-9
Legacy of Morevi by Tee Morris (tp) - ISBN-13: 978-1-896944-29-6
Legends of the Serai by J.C. Hall - (tp) - ISBN-13: 978-1-896944-04-3
Longevity Thesis by Jennifer Tahn (tp) - ISBN-13: 978-1-896944-37-1
Lyskarion: The Song of the Wind by J.A. Cullum (tp)
   - ISBN-13: 978-1-894063-02-9

Machine Sex and other stories by Candas Jane Dorsey (tp)
   - ISBN-13: 978-0-88878-278-6
Maërlande Chronicles, The by Élisabeth Vonarburg (pb)
   - ISBN-13: 978-0-88878-294-6
Magister's Mask, The by Deby Fredericks (tp) - ISBN-13: 978-1-896944-16-6
Moonfall by Heather Spears (pb) - ISBN-13: 978-0-88878-306-6
Morevi: The Chronicles of Rafe and Askana by Lisa Lee & Tee Morris
   - (tp) - ISBN-13: 978-1-896944-07-4

Not Your Father's Horseman by Valorie Griswold-Ford (tp)
- ISBN-13: 978-1-896944-27-2

On Spec: The First Five Years edited by On Spec (pb)
- ISBN-13: 978-1-895836-08-0
On Spec: The First Five Years edited by On Spec (hb)
- ISBN-13: 978-1-895836-12-7
Operation: Immortal Servitude by Tony Ruggerio (tp)
- ISBN-13: 978-1-896944-56-2
Operation: Save the Innocent by Tony Ruggerio (tp)
- ISBN-13: 978-1-896944-60-9
Orbital Burn by K. A. Bedford (tp) - ISBN-13: 978-1-894063-10-4
Orbital Burn by K. A. Bedford (hb) - ISBN-13: 978-1-894063-12-8

Pallahaxi Tide by Michael Coney (pb) - ISBN-13: 978-0-88878-293-9
Passion Play by Sean Stewart (pb) - ISBN-13: 978-0-88878-314-1
Plague Saint by Rita Donovan, The (tp) - ISBN-13: 978-1-895836-28-8
Plague Saint by Rita Donovan, The (hb) - ISBN-13: 978-1-895836-29-5

Reluctant Voyagers by Élisabeth Vonarburg (pb) - ISBN-13: 978-1-895836-09-7
Reluctant Voyagers by Élisabeth Vonarburg (hb) - ISBN-13: 978-1-895836-15-8
Resisting Adonis by Timothy J. Anderson (tp) - ISBN-13: 978-1-895836-84-4
Resisting Adonis by Timothy J. Anderson (hb) - ISBN-13: 978-1-895836-83-7
Righteous Anger by Lynda Williams (tp) - ISBN-13: 897-1-894063-38-8

Shadebinder's Oath by Jeanette Cottrell - (tp) - ISBN-13: 978-1-896944-31-9
Silent City, The by Élisabeth Vonarburg (tp) - ISBN-13: 978-1-894063-07-4
Slow Engines of Time, The by Élisabeth Vonarburg (tp) - ISBN-13: 978-1-895836-30-1
Slow Engines of Time, The by Élisabeth Vonarburg (hb) - ISBN-13: 978-1-895836-31-8
Small Magics by Erik Buchanan (tp) - ISBN-13: 978-1-896944-38-8
Sojourn by Jana Oliver - (pb) - ISBN-13: 978-1-896944-30-2
Stealing Magic by Tanya Huff (tp) - ISBN-13: 978-1-894063-34-0
Strange Attractors by Tom Henighan (pb) - ISBN-13: 978-0-88878-312-7
Sword Masters by Selina Rosen (tp) - ISBN-13: 978-1-896944-65-4

Taming, The by Heather Spears (pb) - ISBN-13: 978-1-895836-23-3
Taming, The by Heather Spears (hb) - ISBN-13: 978-1-895836-24-0
Teacher's Guide to Dragon's Fire, Wizard's Flame by Unwin & Mennenga - (pb)
- ISBN-13: 978-1-896944-19-7
Ten Monkeys, Ten Minutes by Peter Watts (tp) - ISBN-13: 978-1-895836-74-5
Ten Monkeys, Ten Minutes by Peter Watts (hb) - ISBN-13: 978-1-895836-76-9
Tesseracts 1 edited by Judith Merril (pb) - ISBN-13: 978-0-88878-279-3
Tesseracts 2 edited by Phyllis Gotlieb & Douglas Barbour (pb)
- ISBN-13: 978-0-88878-270-0
Tesseracts 3 edited by Candas Jane Dorsey & Gerry Truscott (pb)
- ISBN-13: 978-0-88878-290-8
Tesseracts 4 edited by Lorna Toolis & Michael Skeet (pb)
- ISBN-13: 978-0-88878-322-6
Tesseracts 5 edited by Robert Runté & Yves Maynard (pb)
- ISBN-13: 978-1-895836-25-7
Tesseracts 5 edited by Robert Runté & Yves Maynard (hb)
- ISBN-13: 978-1-895836-26-4

Tesseracts 6 edited by Robert J. Sawyer & Carolyn Clink (pb)
  - ISBN-13: 978-1-895836-32-5
Tesseracts 6 edited by Robert J. Sawyer & Carolyn Clink (hb)
  - ISBN-13: 978-1-895836-33-2
Tesseracts 7 edited by Paula Johanson & Jean-Louis Trudel (tp)
  - ISBN-13: 978-1-895836-58-5
Tesseracts 7 edited by Paula Johanson & Jean-Louis Trudel (hb)
  - ISBN-13: 978-1-895836-59-2
Tesseracts 8 edited by John Clute & Candas Jane Dorsey (tp)
  - ISBN-13: 978-1-895836-61-5
Tesseracts 8 edited by John Clute & Candas Jane Dorsey (hb)
  - ISBN-13: 978-1-895836-62-2
Tesseracts Nine edited by Nalo Hopkinson and Geoff Ryman (tp)
  - ISBN-13: 978-1-894063-26-5
Tesseracts Ten edited by Robert Charles Wilson and Edo van Belkom (tp)
  - ISBN-13: 978-1-894063-36-4
Tesseracts Eleven edited by Cory Doctorow and Holly Phillips (tp)
  - ISBN-13: 978-1-894063-03-6
Tesseracts Q edited by Élisabeth Vonarburg & Jane Brierley (pb)
  - ISBN-13: 978-1-895836-21-9
Tesseracts Q edited by Élisabeth Vonarburg & Jane Brierley (hb)
  - ISBN-13: 978-1-895836-22-6
Throne Price by Lynda Williams and Alison Sinclair (tp)
  - ISBN-13: 978-1-894063-06-7
Too Many Princes by Deby Fredricks (tp) - ISBN-13: 978-1-896944-36-4
Twilight of the Fifth Sun by David Sakmyster - (tp)
  - ISBN-13: 978-1-896944-01-02

Virtual Evil by Jana Oliver (tp) - ISBN-13: 978-1-896944-76-0

Lee Danielle Hubbard

"Well, to begin with, I could not really read until grade five. I continued on as an atrociously creative speller until well into middle-school. I always told stories in my head. I attempted my first novel in grade five, back when I spelled fire like 'fyr' half the time and could not master words like 'they'. That one didn't work so well. In grade eight I finished my first long piece. I have written one a year ever since, barring my nomad year in Australia."
— Lee Danielle Hubbard

Lee Danielle Hubbard was born in Victoria, BC, and still considers the Island her home. She lived in Victoria until the age of nineteen, before striking out for Australia, New Zealand and Hong Kong, safe with her backpack and notebook for company. After a few more adventures around Canada, she has now returned to the Island to resume her studies in art history at the University of Victoria.

Danielle's poetry has appeared in literary magazines, including Event and the Claremont Review. She has jointly compiled several chapbooks, the most recent of which is entitled "We Have Osmosed."

Clan of the Dung-Sniffers is Danielle's first novel.

She prefers to write early in the morning. After an hour's run, swim, or bicycle adventure, dawn's first light will find Danielle curled up on the couch with a pen in one hand and an apple in the other.

When Danielle is not writing, adventuring or eating she is most likely to be found at her easel, indulging in the joys of oil paints.

"I want to enthrall people. I want to capture them and whisk them away to another reality. I am bubbling with stories that need to be told — some of them funny, some of them dark, some of them random and twisted." — Lee Danielle Hubbard